The Latitude Series Book 3
Bifröst

THE LATITUDE SERIES BOOK 3
BIFRÖST

T.S. SIMONS

4 Horsemen
Publications, Inc.

Bifröst
Copyright © 2024 T.S. Simons. All rights reserved.

4 Horsemen
Publications, Inc.

Published By: 4 Horsemen Publications, Inc.

4 Horsemen Publications, Inc.
PO Box 417
Sylva, NC 28779
4horsemenpublications.com
info@4horsemenpublications.com

Cover & Typesetting by Autumn Skye
Edited by Jen Paquette

All rights to the work within are reserved to the author and publisher. No part of this publication may be reproduced, stored in a retrieval system, or transmitted in any form or by any means, electronic, mechanical, photocopying, recording, scanning, or otherwise, except as permitted under Section 107 or 108 of the 1976 International Copyright Act, without prior written permission except in brief quotations embodied in critical articles and reviews. Please contact either the Publisher or Author to gain permission.

All characters, organizations, and events portrayed in this novel are either products of the author's imagination or are used fictitiously.

All brands, quotes, and cited work respectfully belongs to the original rights holders and bear no affiliation to the authors or publisher.

Library of Congress Control Number: 2024942137

Paperback ISBN-13: 979-8-8232-0611-2
Hardcover ISBN-13: 979-8-8232-0612-9
Audiobook ISBN-13: 979-8-8232-0614-3
Ebook ISBN-13: 979-8-8232-0613-6

DEDICATION

To all the critters who have shared my life, both past
and present, you make my life richer just by being in it.
You are my everything.

The 45th Parallel (North)

- Yellowstone Lake Wyoming, USA
- Nova Scotia, Canada
- Pyrenees, France

The 45th Parallel (North)

- Piedmont, Italy
- Caspian Sea
- Hokkaido, Japan

CONTENTS

Dedication..................................v
Acknowledgements xi

Chapter 1..................................1
Chapter 2.................................17
Chapter 3.................................27
Chapter 4.................................35
Chapter 5.................................39
Chapter 6.................................62
Chapter 7.................................76
Chapter 8.................................86
Chapter 9.................................97
Chapter 10...............................106
Chapter 11...............................112
Chapter 12...............................118
Chapter 13...............................130
Chapter 14...............................137
Chapter 15...............................148
Chapter 16...............................159
Chapter 17...............................174
Chapter 18...............................178
Chapter 19...............................184

Chapter 20	192
Chapter 21	199
Chapter 22	214
Chapter 22	219
Chapter 23	226
Chapter 24	233
Chapter 25	250
Chapter 26	265
Chapter 27	276
Chapter 28	289
Chapter 29	294
Chapter 30	304
Chapter 31	312
Chapter 32	316
Chapter 33	341
Chapter 34	346
Chapter 35	359
Chapter 36	368
Chapter 37	376
Sneak Peek of TRIPLE HELIX	380
Book Club Questions	385
Author Bio	387

ACKNOWLEDGEMENTS

EVERY BOOK IS A labor of love. Authors write because we need to get our stories into the world, secretly hoping readers will enjoy them. It is the legacy we hope to leave behind. Personally, it means everything when readers contact me and tell me they enjoy a story I have spent months working on. When I sit in my cave alone, writing and drinking cold coffee, it is my deepest desire that someone loves this story and these characters as much as I do.

My heartfelt thanks to those who read my books and take the time to leave a review. To everyone in my life who supports me: family, friends and colleagues, I couldn't do this without you. Thank you! xx Tanya

CHAPTER 1

ILLY PUSHED HER CHAIR away from the table with a contented sigh and rested her hands on her perpetually flat stomach. "That was sensational. I don't remember when I last had a meal that good."

Gio rose, accidentally knocking me with his elbow. He always looked awkward, his six-foot height wedged under our tiny table. He added Illy's empty bowl to the stack he was juggling. As he moved toward the kitchen, I caught his reflection in the window, his face beaming almost as bright as the moon's reflection across the ocean outside. Aside from aiding people in his medical career, which continued to fill him with joy, cooking was his passion. Gio adored preparing meals for family and friends, experimenting with traditional Italian cuisine, the recipes adapted to the foods we grew here. While eating, he would hound us about what we liked and what needed to be improved. Fennel was his new favorite flavor, something my father had introduced him to, and he added it to everything.

"I don't think I can move," Illy groaned, her head rolling back in exaggerated discomfort and pushing her chair three inches from the table, as far as she could before the wooden backrest hit the wall.

"Well, you don't have far to stagger. Best get moving." Jealousy rose in me as I watched her pretend to be bloated, and I instantly regretted my cheeky comment. Sometimes, I spoke without thinking, but Illy knew me well enough to know I wasn't trying to be rude. Exhaustion made me cranky. As much as we loved the company and the conversation, which was always entertaining and usually ended in hysterical laughter, I didn't want them to stay all night. A hot shower and bed were what I desperately needed.

Illy didn't appear to have taken offense as she sighed again and took a dainty sip from her wineglass. I grappled with the urge to snatch it from her tiny hand and knock it back in one gulp.

"We have something we want to discuss before we leave."

"I thought you said leaving work in the office was important," I fired back, seeing my early night fly out the window.

Illy peered over her small, black-rimmed glasses, eyebrows raised at my sharp tone. Her smirk transformed into something a little more mischievous as she observed my frustration simmering. "This involves both of you, or I would have already discussed it with you."

Matching her smug expression and ignoring her parental tone, I lifted my chin and made complete eye contact, indicating that she did not intimidate me and that she should continue.

"We have a proposal for you."

CHAPTER 1

My cheeky grin morphed into a grimace as I stretched awkwardly in my chair, silently pleading for Gio to return from the kitchen. My back was killing me now that I was the size of an elephant. Well, what I imagined an elephant would look like. Like everyone born in the last thirty years, I had only ever seen pictures, although Mum had told me there was a dedicated breeding facility for animals in England to ensure no species became extinct. She had visited before I was born when she was still a veterinarian. A lifetime ago.

"Whaaaat?" I tried not to let the suspicion infuse my words, but I couldn't help it. Growing up with her, I knew Illyria better than anyone. Plotting, scheming, or simply running a million scenarios through her head to assess the best outcome, Illy got her way. Every single time.

Illy twinkled at me. "It involves all of us."

My shoulders slumped, and my head rolled forward, too heavy for my neck. *Of course it does. The master manipulator strikes again.* Glancing around the table, I evaluated the assembled party. Illy glowed, her blue eyes brilliant and sparkling, betraying her wit and intelligence. She looked like she had pulled off a monumental coup before speaking a word. Towering beside Illy's elegant birdlike form, Carmelo beamed at me, little crinkles appearing next to his warm brown eyes. But then again, he was perpetually happy. Carmelo was much like my father, always willing to help anyone, no matter how inconvenient it may be to himself. A bear of a man, he was more than twice her size, yet we all knew she was in charge. Carmelo was full of light. It was almost like his heart was so full of love that it overflowed and infected everyone in his world. They gazed at each other, and my stomach dropped further, knowing we were being set up. Clouds of suspicion darkened Gio's chiseled face as he took four strides across the room, his brow furrowed. He dropped into the chair beside me, facing Illy and Carmelo. The pile of dishes could sit in the sink for now.

"What?" Gio echoed my question as his hand slipped onto my thigh, giving me a gentle reassuring squeeze under the table. If we both objected, perhaps we had a chance not to be railroaded into another of her grand schemes, the last of which had seen us end up here. *Please, please don't relocate us now.* Gio's rigid posture beside me belied his similar concerns. Neither of us trusted Illy's grandiose plans, which she had a habit of dropping on us as a fait accompli.

Illy peered over her glasses at Carmelo, obtaining his final consent. With an infinitesimal flick of the eyelids, she turned back across the table to us. Making full use of her flair for the dramatic, she took a deep breath, pushed her glasses back onto her nose, and paused. My heart sank further.

"Promise you will let me finish. I will explain the offer and our reasoning. But let me speak first."

Gio's eyes met mine, and his fingers squeezed my thigh again. We had both endured a lifetime's experience of Illy's proposals by now. Even after all these months of working together in the shared role of Chief, occasionally Illy still surprised me with the creativity of her schemes. That woman always achieved her goal.

"Speak," I warned, a touch gruffly. Illy had a knack for grating my cheese, always knowing how to irritate me to maximum effect. Besides, it was late, and I was exhausted. Watching the three of them

CHAPTER 1

savoring a delicious-smelling wine over dinner was the final straw.

"Carmelo and I were wondering how you would feel about sharing both the role of Chief *and* the parenting of your babies."

Illy paused and watched my eyes spring wide before holding a hand up, hurrying to explain. Gio's fingertips pressed slightly more firmly into my leg, but I couldn't tell if he was annoyed or warning me to listen. Settling back into my chair, I squirmed to get comfortable, the wooden slats pressing firmly into my back, the table into my massive midriff.

"I've had twins. They are a ridiculous amount of work in the early months. The first year or two, to be honest. One gets sick—they both do. They feed off each other, so if one cries, the other does. There is an endless stream of nappy changes and feeds. One wakes in the night and wakes the other one. Frankly, you need to be an octopus. You feel like you never have enough hands. So, what we are proposing is this: Carmelo will act as your nanny, although he would like to be known as *nonno*, if you don't mind. He can help care for the babies and bring them to you, Caitlin, for feeding. He will assist when you need another set of hands, even if it is just preparing meals and helping with the laundry. Then you and I will continue to be joint Chief, just for a year or so, until you are ready to take over entirely, and I can retire. But this allows us both to work part-time and share the load. Your mother has already told you she wants you to deliver the babies on Lewis, where she and the other doctors can supervise and where we can collect the cord blood discreetly. We all agree that having them there is best. But we need to make some decisions soon. You can take time off for the birth and the months immediately after. I can do all the traveling for the first six to eight months, or at least until you are ready to leave the babies or take them with you. Carmelo would stay with you and support you. You can still chair meetings from here or wherever else you choose. Take some time to think about it, but I think it is a win-win."

Illy leaned back in her chair, observing my face.

Illy's negotiation tactics were familiar to me by now, and I noted several key elements. It was clever of her to claim Gio was supportive of where I had the babies, but I was experienced enough in the art of negotiations to know that he had no knowledge of the rest of her proposal. Squinting at her, I was immensely suspicious of this seemingly generous offer. There must be a catch. With Illy, there was always a catch. While these would be our first children, I had been around enough babies to know she was telling the truth. Babies were ridiculously hard work. Ask any parent how they felt, and "tired" was always the response. Illy had raised four children, two of them without a partner. She had done far more than her fair share, and no one would blame her for skipping off into the sunset with Carmelo, leaving all that behind. On the surface, it was a fantastic offer. Four adults to two babies would undoubtedly make life a whole lot easier. She was still watching me closely, waiting for a response.

"Are you sure?"

"We are positive. As you know, Carmelo never experienced the joy of his own children and desperately wants to be actively involved. He is your biological uncle and Gio's godfather, so he wants to be in the everyday lives of these children and more than

CHAPTER 1

just the occasional visit. Think of us as 'sparents'—spare parents. But that means us living wherever you do. After much soul-searching and discussion, I am not quite ready to stop working. I can't see myself spending my days gardening or knitting, and this arrangement allows me to bow out slowly, hand the reins to you, and you can take on more responsibility as you feel ready for it."

"Are you sure you still want me for this role? I mean, you have time to train someone else. Riccardo, nîpiy, Seraphine even. I feel like I am letting you down. You have spent all this time training me, and now I am walking away."

"No, you aren't walking away. You are pregnant; there is a difference. We all have families, so we understand. I want you and the other ambassadors do, too. Not one of your colleagues doubts you are the best choice. We will wait as long as necessary."

"But... really? Riccardo is..."

"Riccardo is not *you*. He is great at advocating for the Piedmont team, but he doesn't have your sense of collegiality and high-level strategic vision. You know how to listen to all perspectives and make tough decisions, even when it makes some people unhappy. Riccardo actively avoids conflict. He wants to keep the peace; a Chief can't always do that. He who shouts the loudest can't always win."

That phrase made me smile. Illy regularly said that when a single interest group started getting very vocal about a particular topic.

"What about..."

Illy knew where this was going and cut me off. "Caitlin! They want you. The ACC will wait until you are ready. As I have said before, you can perform this role from wherever you like. Long gone are the days when women with children can't hold down leadership roles. We will make it work; I assure you."

"What about me?" Gio interrupted. "Where do I fit into this *schema* of yours?"

Illy grinned broadly at his use of the word scheme, although I noted she hadn't really given us much opportunity to refuse.

"We thought this plan gives you as much flexibility as possible. You can take time off when the babies are born or later. Anytime you choose, knowing that Carmelo is here to support you both. Me too, of course, although I could sometimes be away. The medical team needs you, Giovanni. With additional help at home, you can also work part-time, if you wish, or take the time to pursue further training."

Gio nodded gravely. Illy had read the tea leaves well. It was no secret that Gio desperately wanted to be a hands-on parent, having lost so many years with his parents, but he also felt the pressure of contributing to the medical community. After training with my mother, aunt, sister, and Jorja, as well as with Magali and Nasir, he was one of the best generalists in any aboveground or underwater communities. People trusted him and heavily relied on his expertise, regularly consulting him on a wide variety of cases. His techniques were excellent, and he always made decisions in the patient's best interest, coming up with innovative treatment plans that many would never have considered.

Almost weekly, another community contacted us seeking medical advice, and they always sought Gio's opinion, although I noticed he diplomatically included his colleagues in discussions and proposing

CHAPTER 1

a course of treatment. He and Sorcha were renowned as the best general surgeons, but his dream was to specialize in pediatrics. Nasir was the best person to train him, and we had spoken at length about taking a placement in France when we could. While he had never stated it aloud, Nasir couldn't be too far from wanting to retire and spend time with his grandchildren. After supporting Gianni and Charlie, Gio desperately wanted to work with children and make a difference in their lives.

"We need to talk about it, so we are not making any promises tonight," I warned as I glanced at Gio, and his hand relaxed on my leg. "But on the surface, it appears to be an idea worth considering. Does that mean you would live here?"

"Assuming you choose to stay here, it does. But we would follow you anywhere. The Canadians are not ready to let you go either. We need to shuffle living arrangements so that we are next door. You need a larger place. We don't. But if we stay here, we thought we might take this apartment, and you can take the larger one next door." Illy gestured to the apartment to our right. "That one is two bedrooms. We can install an intercom. That way, you can buzz us if you need us. Even overnight."

"You have thought this through." I didn't mean to sound suspicious but was unable to disguise the tone as the words trickled from my mouth.

"Would you expect me to present you a half-baked plan?" she fired back with a grin. "Do you know me at all, Caitlin Claira Mackintosh-Accardo?"

I knew her extremely well, and that was precisely the problem. She had been in my life since the day I was born, and I had ample experience of Illyria's plotting. She had conjured up this plan, likely over weeks, bullied Carmelo to agree, worked out all the reasons we might say no, and had already counteracted them. In short, Illy was not a woman who took no for an answer. The rebel streak in me desperately wanted to say, "No. They are our children, and we can do this ourselves," but the truth was, it was a wonderful offer, and I recognized it as such. Maybe I had matured, not letting my stubbornness prevent me from taking up a potentially beneficial opportunity.

"What about Sera?" I asked softly as I stroked my burgeoning belly, one of my inhabitants flip-flopping as they often did after I had eaten. Sera had one child, little Raidon. He was already a year old, but I knew from speaking with her daily that Rai was her world. She gushed about his achievements and milestones: first steps, words, and smiles. I suspected it wouldn't be long before she wanted another. Unlike me, who felt enormous and as ungainly as a chunky baby hippo, Sera had loved being pregnant. Tall and slender, like our mother Freyja, she was willowy and graceful and hadn't even looked pregnant until she stood side-on.

"I have thought of that, and I will speak with her, explain the situation. But I wanted to raise it with you first. You know she gets a lot of help in Japan. They have a wonderful setup, and their nursery facilities are exceptional. Children are the focus of their community, highly valued, and they receive wonderful care and education. Besides, twins are more than twice the work of a single bubba. Seraphine has no desire to be Chief and actively supports you in taking the role. She will understand, Caitlin."

"Will she?" While we shared a biological mother, Illyria had been Sera's mother since the day they

CHAPTER 1

brought us to Lewis from Clava. I was the only child raised by Freyja, our biological mother. Our biological father, Luca, died many years before we were born. Friends of my parents had adopted all our siblings, but Sera and I had grown up knowing we were full sisters, just raised in adjoining households. Knowing that Illyria would be an active grandparent to my children would hurt Seraphine, especially as she and Matt were so far away, and Illy wasn't so active in Rai's life.

"Caitlin, she would never begrudge you anything. You know that. Besides, you are having twins, and you are the Chief. She will understand. She is my daughter too. I would never do anything to upset her."

That made me feel slightly better. The last thing I wanted to do was to damage my relationship with my sister. It surprised me how much I had enjoyed being Chief and working with Illy. Knowing that decisions we made together benefited people's lives. Sharing technologies and strategies. But most of all, we got along. She valued my input and didn't demean my ideas, especially when I saw things from a different perspective. Illy was an expert in managing people, motives, and soft diplomacy. I often saw things from a technical viewpoint. We discussed issues as colleagues, not the mother and child we once were. We laughed and enjoyed our time working despite the age gap and all those times she had punished me as a child. Our relationship had evolved into something new, and I looked forward to going to work each day. She was one of the few people who knew me and understood the insecurities I let no one see. Before every crucial decision, an underlying fear crippled me that I would let people down, that I wasn't making the right decisions, or I was missing a vital piece of information before enacting a resolution. She also knew what it was like to be pregnant with twins, to feel huge and unattractive. She forced me to rest, take time off, and place my relationship first. As I grew larger, she took over the long days, rescheduling meetings for the mornings and letting me attend essential meetings only. As much as I appreciated it, ultimately, it left me feeling guilty, knowing she was carrying the burden.

nîpiy, formerly my assistant, had partially and unofficially taken over the role of Canadian ambassador since I had accepted more responsibility, but despite my insistence that she accept the role and title, she refused, claiming that she couldn't fill my shoes. Her work was invaluable, doing much of the legwork, attending meetings with the teams here, and collecting opinions and feedback on proposals and plans. But she stopped short of making decisions. Repeatedly, I begged her to take it all on, but she insisted I continue to function as the ambassador in an official capacity. For many tasks, I could do both. Still, I often felt overwhelmed with the competing priorities, especially as what might be good for the collective may not be best for the Canadian community. Then there was the sheer volume of work. How was I going to get these projects finished before the babies arrived? Not having an official Canadian ambassador also meant that I wasn't able to move to France or anywhere else in a hurry. In coming here, Gio had supported me. While we had decided to relocate based on my work, I desperately wanted him to have his turn and follow his dream. I made a mental note to convince nîpiy again or try to find someone to step up. There simply weren't enough hours in the

CHAPTER 1

day, and I panicked at the thought of all the work I needed to finish before the babies came.

Illy and Carmelo insisted on helping Gio clean up, encouraging me to shower before bed. Gio was already in our room as I left the bathroom, the living room furniture faintly outlined, illuminated by the brilliant show streaming in from outside. Dad had told me once that, in the old world, it was difficult to see stars from cities, as the glow of civilization outshone the night sky. I had always found it hard to believe that people would want to outshine something so blissfully perfect. Dad loved mythology and had often told us bedtime stories of how ancient explorers and mariners navigated by the stars and how societies tracked their year by the constellations they could see at different times of the year. But by the time he had been born, people living in cities had lost touch with the spectacular, ever-changing image above.

"What are you thinking?" I asked Gio as the mattress plunged from my massive bulk and the old gray t-shirt of his I was wearing lifted, exposing the burgeoning mass as I squirmed, clumsily trying to get comfortable. I sensed his mood. He was pensive, which was unlike him.

Leaning over, he kissed my bare belly before responding. "It is a wonderful offer. I just can't help but feel—"

"What?" I tried to sit up but couldn't get past the massive watermelon-shaped bulge. Shifting my approach, I tried to face him by rolling, not entirely successfully.

"I want you and I to be these children's parents—only us. Don't you worry that if Illy and Carmelo play an active role, these children may grow up and not see us as their family? Don't misunderstand; I love Carmelo. For many years, he was the father I lost, and I want him to be their *nonno*. But not the *father* of these children."

"No, my darling, you are. You have seen where I grew up. Illy's house attached to ours. Essentially, I grew up with three parents. I called her Mum, and she parented me like one, which I admit was often. I wasn't an easy child. But I always knew who my parents were. Don't forget—I had much older siblings in Louis and Katrin. Xanthe too. Even Sera's sisters helped manage the household. They often got us ready for school, prepared meals, and made us do our homework. But you work it out pretty quickly. I was never confused about my place in the world or who I was. Look at Seraphine. She is my full sister, yet I always knew that Illy was her mother. Louis is technically no relation to me at all, but he is one-hundred-percent my brother. So no, I don't think that is a problem. These children will know they are loved and that we are their parents. Tell me—what else are you worried about?"

"There are so many things, but right now, only that. More than anything, I want to be their father, guide them, and experience all their firsts—to see them take their first breath, first step, and first laugh. It is more important to me than anything that we walk beside them as they learn about the world. I want us to be the ones who teach them. I don't want to outsource parenting."

My mother once used that expression and told us that was what her parents had done. Born into a wealthy family, Mum's parents had the money to pay for nannies and opportunities other families only

CHAPTER 1

dreamed of. Both her parents worked long hours and traveled a lot. They had engaged au pairs and other supports to fill the gaps, but Mum still knew her place. Her family. The air escaped in a deep cloud as I sank farther into the mattress.

"My darling, you are their father. You always will be. A father is not the sperm donor, although I guess that part is somewhat important. A true father is the person who is there every day of their lives, supporting them, guiding them, being their champion. My father may not be my biological father, but not for one second did I ever think that I wasn't his daughter. He loves me unconditionally. You have been around my family enough. Do you think my father treats me differently from the others? My siblings, I mean?"

Gio didn't hesitate. "No. Until I think about it, I forget he isn't your biological father. On our wedding day, I had never seen a prouder man than your dad."

"Parenting isn't just biology; it is who is physically present. You will be there for our children, no matter what. When they are sick, important milestones, when something bad happens. We will support them and love them. That is what a parent is."

"You are saying I am a fool to worry about this?"

"Not a fool. No one is freaking out about being a parent more than me. These children are a gift after all we have been through, and I don't want anyone else near them."

"Is this offer a gift?" Gio wasn't even trying to hide his suspicion.

"I recognize it for what it is—a fantastic opportunity. To have help and only next door? That would be wonderful, don't you think? Don't tell Illy, but I don't want to give up my job, and I was wondering how to make it work. Now, maybe, this means there is a way forward."

"Did she ask you about it before she announced this? You seem remarkably accepting of her barging in on our family."

"I would have told you. My loyalty is to you, our family. No, this is the first I have heard of it. Are you saying you have doubts?"

"Not exactly. But you are the one who is most affected; I know that. The question is: do you want to accept?"

"Let's talk tomorrow. But in theory, yes. I think we should consider it."

"Do you remember when I told you I would follow you anywhere?" Gio's lips caressed my neck, causing my head to roll back and my eyes to close.

"Hmmmm," I moaned, feeling lighter than I had in hours.

"I would do anything for you."

"Anything?"

CHAPTER 2

I GLANCED UP FROM MY cluttered desk, and my heart skipped a beat. I was drowning in proposals that required me to review the papers and supporting documentation, consider all the variables, and recognize that I could inadvertently set a precedent for future decisions, then generate an official response in the shortest possible timeframe. So overwhelmed with the magnitude of work and how I was going to get it all finished, I hadn't heard Illy enter my office. She moved so quietly that I often jolted when noticing her presence.

"We need to get you an alarm," I grumbled as I jerked back in my seat, realizing she was grinning at having startled me.

"Like a cat collar?"

"What do you mean?" Throughout my childhood, there had been a steady stream of cats and kittens, all descendants of Dad's first Scottish Wildcat, Jam. Illy had two cats she adored. None of them had worn a collar, though. In books, I had seen pictures of domestic cats wearing them, dogs too, but never in real life.

Illy laughed at my confusion, sounding like a tinkling stream. "Sometimes I forget you are too young. Back home, in the old world, people used to put a collar with a bell on their cats. I did it with my two back in Australia."

I grimaced, hating being reminded that I was young, and there had been an entire world *before*. A bigger one with freedom to travel, clean water and air, more choice, technology, and far more people. Besides, now she was just interrupting my work. Still, the concept intrigued me.

"Why would you do that?"

"Because cats were allowed to roam outside. Often, they caught birds and other wildlife, so if they wore a collar with bells, in theory, the noise alerted the bird to the approaching cat, giving it a chance to escape. Even though they wore them, my cats were too fat and lazy to hunt. They just wore collars so I didn't get judged. But I knew plenty of people who said bells made their cats better hunters, but at least they tried. In some towns or areas, there were curfews and laws that said cats must be inside by dark."

"Laws for cats? Seriously? Did it stop them from catching mice? Dad always said Jam was the best hunter he ever had."

"Do you know—I have no idea. My cats were so useless I don't think they caught anything that didn't come from a can."

"Well, there are no non-law-abiding cats here. Did you need something? I'm still working on my response to France's proposal to present at the Heads meeting tomorrow as well as five other time-critical

CHAPTER 2

responses. Why do people always throw work at me at the same time?"

"You can finish it later. There is something I need to show you."

"Now?" I groaned, glancing out the window. An interruption meant I would be late for dinner, and I would lose my focus. Writing didn't come as naturally to me as it did to Illy. If the words were flowing, I could write. However, if there was an interruption, I often needed to begin again. The last thing I wanted to do was read through the proposal from the start so I could address each pertinent point.

"Now."

With a sigh, I let my pen clatter on the desk and roll toward her. She stopped it and waited intentionally. I knew that tone. History had taught me the futility of arguing with Illyria. Hauling my belly from the chair and using the desk as leverage, I stood and grabbed my wool wrap. Illy turned and stepped through the doorway, beckoning me to follow her out of the office and into the hallway. I followed at a safe distance as she led me through the community and began striding across the bridge to the landside pods. A pang of guilt gripped my stomach as I waddled across the bridge, glancing out the windows scattered intermittently in the metal walls. Our footsteps clanged on the grate floor of the metal tunnel. It was late afternoon; the sun was already casting shadows across the land beyond. I grimaced. I should finish my response and move those proposals forward. Illy glanced back at me but didn't speak as she quickened her stride.

"I have been to the greenhouses before, you know," I teased, hoping that by injecting some humor, she might tell me where we were going. "I was pretty much raised in one, if you recall, and helped Dad set these up. What is so urgent that we need to visit now? The team isn't having any major engineering issues, are they? I haven't heard anything."

"No, but I need to show you something."

My hips ached terribly as they often did now that I was so freaking huge. Although, Gio said it was expected, just the ligaments loosening in preparation for labor. Lying down was my only pain-free position at the moment, and doing that just reminded me of the helplessness of being incapacitated and injured last year. Trying not to wince at the pain generated by each movement and exasperated at this little field trip, I groaned, wishing I was on my way home so I could rest.

"You couldn't just tell me?" I called out, trying not to sound whiny. Illy slowed, realizing I was struggling.

"This is best seen in person. We can talk when we get there. Come on. It isn't far."

Illy walked out the end of the bridge and directly into the greenhouses. She nodded as the workers walked the other way, leaving for the day. As they passed, I greeted each of them by name, but their departure surprised me. I had expected that we were here to attend a meeting. Illy paused, checking that we were alone.

"No one left?" she asked, but it was rhetorical. She could see as well as I could that the place was empty. The rising wind coming off Lake Huron was buffeting the shell. It reminded me of home, and a pang of homesickness for Lewis pierced my chest. I hadn't seen my parents in months, not since I had learned I was pregnant. Suddenly, an irrational fear

CHAPTER 2

gripped me. They wouldn't get to see me pregnant, and more than anything, I desperately wanted them to be here with me.

Scanning the enormous greenhouse, I confirmed, "It's just us, so we clearly aren't here for a meeting, engineering fault, or conciliation. What is so important that it couldn't wait until tomorrow? Are you impersonating my father and urgently need to show me a new variety of potato?"

Ignoring me, Illy slipped into the back room containing potting benches, seedlings, tools, and other equipment. As I watched in astonishment, she slipped a panel to the side and stepped through, indicating she expected me to follow.

Stalling, I raised my eyebrows, but she gestured that she wanted me to hurry. Far slower than Illy due to my size, I clumsily clambered through into the crisp, open night air. She and I were immune, so that wasn't my concern. It was being seen by others outside the domes. Within a nanosecond, I knew that was foolish. It was patently obvious we were alone, and in the twilight, we couldn't be seen. The landscape surrounding us was silent and still. The only sound was the wind gusting across the lake, the susurrous whoosh echoing around the rocky outcrop. Illy firmly clicked the panel back into place behind us. Quickly, I tied my hair back into a messy bun with the band I often had around my wrist to stop my hair from whipping me in the face.

The shadows of dusk were settling over the earth, and I filled my lungs with the deliciously chilly air as it struck my face like sharp fingers. There was nothing quite like fresh air, and I felt sad that most people in the domed communities would never experience the bliss. Scanning the view, the glowing orange light tinting the landscape mesmerized me, flaming over the horizon, the radiating orb lingering, casting its shadow over the brilliant blue lake. I didn't get outside often, not wanting people to know I could. Since I had last left Lewis, before my pregnancy, I had spent very little time landside. Inhaling deeply, my shoulders dropped slightly. I had missed this, the clean scent of air, dirt, and water. Petrichor, I remembered my father calling it. Closing my eyes, I inhaled deeply, the crispness of the pine forests of home filling my senses, memories of childhood flooding back in a torrent.

"Come." Illy strode purposefully off across the uneven, rocky clifftop, and I dutifully waddled along behind her like an overweight penguin. She disappeared beyond a rugged stone outcrop, and I followed, gripping the cold, slippery rocks for support as I struggled over the uneven earth, wondering where she was going. The light was dimming rapidly, the air was frosty, and we would need to be back soon before someone realized we were missing. For the life of me, I could not fathom why we were out here, alone, when the team had all left for the day. We had plans for many more greenhouses, even land-based pods in which to raise animals. But for now, we only had one, although all experiments had been highly successful, and we were already building greenhouses on land adjacent to other communities. Lack of easily accessible resources and the intensive labor required meant we were still the only one with a permanent bridge, although the design process was underway for several other underwater communities to have permanent bases on land. We had already proven that natural light through the thin breathable fabric

CHAPTER 2

encouraged plants to grow much faster than inside the underwater pods with their thick Perspex windows. If we could move our growing to land, then we would have more living space. My mind whirred with the possibilities.

I was yanked from my mental planning as I rounded the rocky cliff, and a clear geodesic dome came into view about thirty feet away. The size of a tiny studio apartment, it was completely transparent, hidden from the greenhouses and bridge by the rocks but with uninterrupted views over Lake Huron. Inside, the pod was lit with strings of fairy lights, illuminating a double bed, perfectly made, with crisp white sheets, pillows propped up ready for use, and woodland green blankets draped over the end. I stopped and gaped. Illy waited for words to return to me.

"What is this?" I gasped, unable to take it in.

"This is your babymoon." Illy stood slightly to the side, giving me an unobstructed view of the tiny pod.

"Baby ... moon?"

"Before the babies arrive, and you learn no parent gets a full night's sleep for years, Carmelo and I wanted to give you and Giovanni a few nights of peace. Or not. Your choice." She dimpled wickedly at my rapidly reddening face.

Illy slid back the access hatch, and I stepped through as she waited outside.

"You did this?" The room was warm, and tiny lights hung on multiple strands crisscrossing the domed roof. A selection of books, a bottle of wine, and two glasses lay on the bedside tables. Behind the solid timber headboard was a small kitchenette and bathroom, and two white towels were folded and neatly hanging over the shower. Oxygen-producing plants filled the spaces, the greenery stark against the bleak backdrop of the outside world. It was perfect and just big enough for the two of us.

"The kitchen is stocked," Illy continued, ignoring my silent bewilderment. "I have ordered no work in the outside greenhouses for four days, so you are free to do whatever you like. If you think you can last out here that long?"

"I can't drink wine," I muttered stupidly, mesmerized by this fairytale.

"You can have a little. I checked with your *personal* physician. A small glass won't hurt. You are past the key developmental stages, and the bubbas are just gaining weight now. It isn't like they will be born drunk."

"Wow," I breathed, ignoring her taunt. "I can't believe you did this. Who built this? Who knows about it?"

"We planned it together, but Carmelo has been working evenings and nights for the past few months. He needed to take it slow, so he didn't faint from lack of oxygen. Haven't you wondered where he disappeared to after dinner each night? He isn't so old that he needs a nanna-nap that early. So, do you like it?"

"I am in awe," I admitted, still dazed. "When can we stay?"

Illy reached outside the door, extracted a bag from the darkness, and handed it to me. "Now. Your lovely husband is on his way."

"He knows?"

"No, it is a surprise for him as well."

On cue, the low rumble of two men talking broke through the sound of the wind echoing off the water and striking the dome. Giovanni's face went blank as

CHAPTER 2

he rounded the corner and took in the sight of the fairy-lit small igloo made of breathable, transparent fabric. Carmelo gestured toward the opening with a flourish, and Gio stepped through. He was taller than me, and the roof scraped the top of his head in places.

"What is this?" he breathed, turning to Illy and Carmelo, who stood beaming outside the doorway.

"A gift."

"Why?"

"We want to thank you for giving us grandchildren," Carmelo explained, the beaming smile not leaving his face.

"We thought you might like a few nights alone before the babies come," Illy explained, looking like a child as she curled into Carmelo's enormous side, the silver highlights around her face the only giveaway to her age. "We wanted to give you something private and a little special. And as the family is immune now..." She broke off, realizing Gio wasn't listening as he stared past them to take in the spectacular view of the sun dropping behind the lake, the oranges and pink hues of dusk reflecting off the surface. It was simply breathtaking.

I regained control of my speech first. "Thank you. This is magical."

"*Grazie. Grazie mille.*" Gio reverted to his native tongue, as he often did when surprised or overcome. Most evenings, when he was tired, he spoke in a hybrid of Italian and English. He reached through the opening and shook Carmelo's hand fervently before turning to hug Illy.

Illy lowered Gio's bag containing his personal items inside the door beside mine and closed the hatch firmly, her brilliant grin showing through the transparent fabric of the tiny dome. She turned to Carmelo, who wrapped his arm around her as they turned. The loyalty and unfailing sense of respect they held for each other radiated as they moved into the distance, holding each other close, and disappeared into the night.

Gio turned to me. "Wow."

"I know. Are you hungry?" I asked, feeling suddenly shy.

"Only if hungry for you counts." His dark eyes glinted mischievously.

"This place is completely transparent!" I hissed as he tore at my clothes, exposing my breasts to the outside world.

"But no one is here to see us. We are alone. Hidden but at one with nature. This is like the forest on Lewis, only more comfortable."

"You'd never get me against a tree at this size," I groaned, feeling as enormous as I looked.

"Where there is a will..." he teased, tossing me on the bed.

"You don't think you should wait a bit? What if they come back?"

"They won't. Didn't you hear what Illy said? We have three nights and four days. I, for one, intend to use every precious minute."

CHAPTER 3

"**ARE YOU READY FOR** this? Being parents, I mean," Gio called from the tiny kitchenette, raising his voice to be heard above the howling wind as he put away the last dishes from dinner. The gusting wind hadn't ceased since we arrived, waves roaring in the distance. Letting my eyes adjust to the dark, I could see them creating a spectacular backdrop to the moon shining over the water.

Resting the book on my chest, I thought about that. "I guess, in some ways. I mean, I have been growing them for months, so logically, I know they are coming. But in other ways, I feel horribly unprepared. Like I will never be ready to be a mother. Sometimes I feel like this is all a dream. Who turned me from being a girl into a parent? It isn't like I can hand them back if I fail. We can't just walk away and say, 'Oops, realized we are a bit shit at parenting. Another time, maybe.'"

"You won't fail," Gio said with complete conviction, wiping his hands on a cloth and sitting on the bed beside me.

"How do you know? I have never been a parent. You neither, as far as I know. What if we suck at it?"

Gio knew my colloquialisms by now, but I still recall the first time I had used that expression, and he had turned purple trying to work out what I meant.

"*Amore mio,* you have never failed at anything in your life. In the space of three years, you have gone from a strange woman who crashed into my life to the youngest ambassador in the ACC and now Chief. You were raised by two parents who adore you and are fantastic role models. What makes you think you will fail?"

"Sera is also an ambassador," I pointed out feebly. "We are the same age."

"She is not Chief."

"Maybe she should be. How do I manage it all? I know I joke about wanting it all, but what if I start dropping balls? Maybe it isn't possible to do everything well. I don't want to be a shitty parent."

"Why would you be shitty? Were your parents so terrible? They both worked. Your mother even worked away."

Grinning at Gio's accented pronunciation of "shitty," I replied, "Of course not! They were all wonderful. Illy too. Supportive, firm, loved us unconditionally."

"So why would you think you won't be equally wonderful?"

Frustration rose in my chest, a bubble I couldn't push up or choke down. I couldn't put my feelings into words. That deep-rooted fear that I would fail these children like I had Stella. Heaving myself up with a groan, I moved to the dome edge and gazed across the night sky.

CHAPTER 3

"You are thinking of Stella," he whispered from behind me as I stared out into space.

"I failed her."

"How did you fail her?"

"If I had accepted their offer to be one of their team, maybe she would be alive," I whispered. "Sometimes I regret that decision, knowing it resulted in her death."

Gio's larger body engulfed mine. His arms barely reached around my belly now, and I looked down at his slightly darker skin, the brown hair on his arms contrasting my paler stomach. Gio's large hands caressed my belly, feeling the constant movement within as my inhabitants bounced off my bladder, as they did with increasing frequency.

"I wonder what she would have looked like. Like you? Me? A mix?"

Gio ignored the last comment and deftly pinpointed the cause of my distress. "If you had agreed, you would still be there. Stella may or may not be alive. She may not be with you. We will never know. But what I know is that by doing what you did, you returned to me. These blessings are because of the decision you made that day. Life is not linear, Caitlin. We make choices, and we take different paths. We overcome some obstacles; we avoid others. Sometimes, we even backtrack and try again. There is rarely right or wrong, just what we feel in our heart is the right decision to make in the moment. Every decision has consequences, even if we do not know them at the time."

I leaned back into him, enjoying the sensation of my bare back on his warm chest. "What decisions do you think led you here?"

"So many, when you think about it. Had I not chosen to take Matt down to the lake that day, it would not have been us who found you. We may never have met. I was not rostered to work, so another doctor may have been called to treat your head wound. If I had not taken a chance and kissed you. Going back even further, had I decided, as many people do, that being partnered and unhappy was preferable to being alone, I could have met you but been committed to someone else. Every tiny decision we make leads us to where we end up—our life path. There is no time for regrets, Caitlin. Just celebrate the joys."

"Celebrate the joys," I repeated slowly, thinking of all the joys I had to be grateful for. Him, my family and friends, these children. Even though my wounds still occasionally caused me pain, especially now that I was so heavy, I didn't regret refusing. I could never have lived with myself had I accepted. My only regret was losing our child as a direct result of that choice.

"You know, that was why Matt broke up with his girlfriend. Before he met Seraphine."

Leaning back into him, I asked, "What happened? You told me he was in a dark place. But I don't think I know the story."

"Lauretta desperately wanted to have children."

"And he didn't?"

"Matt did, too, at some point, but he wasn't ready. She put pressure on him, so he ended it, thinking she would move on, meet someone else, and have the children she so desperately wanted. Only she didn't. Lauretta took the ultimate step without telling anyone, and Matt blamed himself."

I gasped. "Poor Matt! He couldn't have known she would do that. Besides, that wouldn't have been the only reason."

CHAPTER 3

"Maybe. We will never know. But he became a shadow of himself. Stopped eating. Wouldn't go out. He was in a dark place, and I knew he wasn't far from taking the ultimate step when he started encouraging me to reconcile with Francesca."

"Why?" I asked cautiously. Francesca and I had a complicated history, and I didn't feel entirely comfortable hearing her name.

"He knew I would be alone if he passed."

Memories of her betrayal threatened my sense of peace, and I tried to move the subject away from Francesca. "But he and Sera had Rai quite quickly, so he must have been over it."

"They did. Perhaps that was just as well. Matt was older than me when our father died. He lived through more of the trauma, seeing how it affected our mother."

I flinched, remembering my mother's role in that. But he ignored my involuntary jolt and continued.

"Matt had to step up and help Mum. Although he wasn't much older than me, he needed to help more and take on more responsibility. He had to assume the role of father, I guess."

"That happens to lots of children. Illy's older girls, Summer and Ally, certainly needed to help her with Alasdair, Seraphine, and me." A feeling of unease made my blood chill. "Is that the only reason he broke up with Lauretta?"

Gio nodded. "I think so. Matt's deepest fear was that something would happen to him, and his child would be raised either fatherless or by another man. Or worse, that his child would die before him. It kept him up at night; I could hear him having nightmares, screaming, and when I asked, it was always the same thing."

31

All my childhood, I had heard my mother wake screaming after what happened to her on Clava, so I could empathize.

"Is he over it now?"

"Honestly, I don't know. I don't want to ask. But that kind of deep-rooted fear doesn't go away."

That feeling I knew, especially after my childhood trauma and the events of the past year. But I tried to be logical.

"Honey, the odds of them losing Raidon in a protected community are minuscule. As for Matt dying, why would that happen? We are all going to die one day, but many years in the future. Surely, he knows that. These communities are safe and Japan in particular. Yes, Piedmont was invaded—once—but that will never happen again. We are in the safest position we have been for many years."

"Fear isn't always rational. I kept telling him our father dying... It was a... How do you say, *colpo di fortuna*, ahh... Floo?"

"Fluke," I corrected gently. "Random. Just bad luck."

"Fluke." Gio nodded, his Italian accent making the word sound deep and guttural. "Our father was in the wrong place at the wrong time. We know that now. But Matteo still holds a deep-rooted fear that his child will end up like him. Fatherless and adrift. He does not want this."

"Bit late for that. He and Seraphine have a child." My stomach churned, wondering if I should check in on Seraphine. We hadn't spoken in a few weeks between me trying to finish up projects and the time zone differences. But the way she gushed about Raidon, I suspected they may not be too far from having another.

"Have you spoken with your brother?"

CHAPTER 3

"Matt and I have been trying to call for weeks but keep missing each other. It is becoming a joke. Now we just leave messages with the communications team—in code, you know."

"Well, they are coming to Lewis for the birth. Maybe they are avoiding us deliberately and will share some news then?"

"Not unless it is about his new project. It is all he talks about lately."

"The bathymetry one?" I questioned.

"Yes, I know. You are also intrigued by mapping underwater topography," Gio teased. "Now all he talks about are landforms and the world under the sea, mountains, and valleys. I am well aware it was you who set him the task."

"He loves it," I replied coyly. "He gets to play with all sorts of cool toys."

One of the babies pushed off my stomach as Gio held me, and he laughed softly in my ear, a low rumbling sound like water flowing over the rocks of a mountain stream at home.

"They are very active tonight." His hands pressed into my belly as the foot pushed again.

"They are always active at night. I am worried they will learn bad habits and sleep all day when they are born."

"We will teach them everything they need to know."

"What will you teach them?" I asked, curious.

Gio beamed. "That they are loved. They need to know nothing more than they are loved and wanted. We will always nurture them and support them. My mother used to call it 'holding space.'"

"Holding space?"

Gio thought for a moment. "Let me try to explain in English, because she used to explain it in Italian. It means you are willing to walk beside someone and support them on their life journey. Make no judgments. Never make them feel inadequate or try to change their path. Mama described it as opening your heart for another, walking beside them, and them knowing that no matter what, you would catch them if they stumbled or fell."

"I like that," I murmured.

"No matter what life throws at us, we are a family, Caitlin. We are forever bonded through these children. Generations of children will exist because of us, because of our love."

"Do you know I have never really thought of it like that? But you are right. These children may have children and grandchildren. They will all be linked back to you and me."

"All of our children will be because we love each other. For generations to come, they will remember us."

"All of them?" I groaned. "How many are you planning? Are two not enough? I'm sick of feeling like a suitcase. My hips hurt all the time, and even walking is a struggle. I just want my body back."

"Ah, you forget, *angelo mio*. It is my body. Always and forever."

CHAPTER 4

THE DAYS FLEW. I had never felt so relaxed, spending our time taking short walks, reading, talking about everything and nothing. Telling snippets from our childhood, describing memories of our parents, and expressing our goals and dreams for these children. Contemplating how their lives would differ from our own. We savored our meals, eating slowly, which was rare for me, and enjoyed taking naps during the day. Gazing at the stars and over the crystal blue lake, spending hours intertwined with each other, both inside the pod and overlooking the water. The air was thin, and we couldn't stay outside for longer than a few hours, but the chilled air on our skin was exhilarating. When it rained on the second morning, I insisted Gio come outside and dance with me. He protested but quickly relented, and the look of immense joy that spread across his face as he felt the raindrops hit his face proved I had made the right choice. As he laughed and splashed like a child, raindrops hanging from his eyelashes and face upturned, I realized what a simple pleasure rain was, a luxury we had lost. Aside from the morning drip of the condensation from the dome on Lewis, Gio had never felt true rain. Sera and I had sometimes slipped outside the Lewis dome as teenagers, dancing in the rain, being careful to dry off before we returned so no one knew our secret.

"Do you ever think it will be safe to live out here again?" I queried as we lay on a rug a few hours later, enjoying the sunshine break through the clouds and watching the wind blow the lake into waves with almost as much surf as the North Sea. I couldn't believe Huron was actually a lake with waves rising that high.

"Why not? Now that we know how, we can slowly inoculate people. We can build out here. Your father has trained the team to propagate the moss, and it grows well here."

"The climate is much like Scotland," I admitted. "Cold and wet for much of the year. We can grow the moss physically and rehabilitate the earth. But do the people want to live landside again? For many, life in the pods is all they have ever known."

"Some will be scared. I know many of the older people here and in Italy will likely not want to leave the safety of the unhabs. But some may surprise us. Many more will relish the chance to be out here, free, breathing the fresh air, feeling the sunshine on their skin. I will never forget the sensation of heat on my skin the first time you took me outside. It was quite different from anything I expected. The feel of the icy wind blowing my hair, the smell of the salt water. It made me feel alive in a way I never had before."

"I am so glad to be the person who showed you so many new things." I rolled over on the rug to snuggle my back up against him.

CHAPTER 4

"So many things you taught me." His voice dropped an octave, making my stomach lurch as it always did. Even after several years together, he still made me turn to jelly.

"Like what?" I forced the words out, my breath coming quicker as his hands lifted my top and found my enlarged breasts, cupping them, weighing them expertly.

"I had never walked on grass, lain on it, walked through a forest, or gone swimming in a lake."

Unable to control the mirth, I taunted, "You are only talking about all the places you have had me."

"My love, I am only just beginning. Those wonderful ancient stones. Clifftops with views to other worlds. Stars. The northern lights."

"I stand by my original statement." I sighed as his hands slipped lower, pulling my skirt up and panties to the side. "You are only listing all the places we have been together."

"You don't think they are not the most wonderful experiences of my life?"

I rolled to face him, meeting his gaze. "Is that why you insist on making love in every one of those places? So you will remember?"

He chuckled, his chest reverberating under my chin. "Oh, I would have remembered them anyway. But this way, they were memorable. Do you remember the night in the forest when you agreed to marry me? Against the stones in the middle of the day? In the freezing loch? Although, how we managed that one is a minor miracle."

At the time, I was not impressed. I remembered how frigidly cold he was and knew he was being foolish by insisting on wading in up to his chest. Not being raised outside, the temperature fluctuations had affected him far more than I would have thought.

"Seeing you on our wedding night, in boots and so beautiful, I couldn't restrain myself. All of these memories are etched into my brain. It was all I could see when I thought I had lost you. All those wonderful memories would be all I had left."

Just as I thought I would get choked up, one of the babies kicked, making me gasp and clutch my stomach.

"Well, all of our practice paid off. You got what you wanted." I grimaced as the foot rammed into my ribs again.

"That was not practice. That was love. Come on. It is time to get inside."

CHAPTER 5

THE HALF-GLASS PANE RATTLED and threatened to shatter as I slammed my office door behind me. Staff quickly ducked their heads below their screens as I stormed past on my way home to pack, steam billowing from my ears. There was no doubt in my mind how this had played out. Gio had betrayed me by contacting my mother and informing her of my increasing blood pressure and crippling hip pain, making it difficult for me to walk without being in constant agony. The part that pissed me off was that they had blindsided me. Gio had led me to believe it was a harmless obstetric consult, and stupid me believed it. Instead, Mum and Sorcha were on video link, waiting for me to enter the room, and had taken turns to grill me, making me stand and demonstrate my degree of movement. Finally, they delivered the punchline, ordering that I see out my last weeks of pregnancy on Lewis. Mum firmly announced before disconnecting the video link that, as my pregnancy had now reached thirty-two weeks, she had already dispatched Summer and Ally. No excuses or attempts to delay would be tolerated.

Feeling much like a recalcitrant child, I stormed back to my office and packed up my desk, trying not to be too cranky at nîpiy and Illy. It wasn't their fault, but I knew they had already been consulted. Everyone was talking *about* me and not *to* me.

Once I arrived home, the fury overflowed as I hurled clothes into a bag, reserving the worst of my wrath for my betrayer. Gio lurked in the shadows of our apartment, slipping past me to pack his bag when I was safely in the bathroom, refusing to engage as I let fly with the insults.

"Anger is not good for the babies," he said quietly as I stormed past him for the thirteenth time.

"Betraying your wife is not good for your marriage!" I bellowed back. He lapsed into silence until I got into bed and turned out the light, silently slipping in beside me. *You had better not even think about touching me, buddy.* I seethed. He knew better than to lay a hand on me when I was fuming.

By the time my sisters arrived the following morning, my temper had cooled significantly, and I allowed Gio to accompany me to the helipad that sat just outside the central pod. Their faces shone, and mouths dropped with excitement as they watched me haul my immense bulk onto the helipad. Seeing their joy at my enormous state made it difficult to stay angry. Rarely did the twins get hyped and squeal about anything, but their joy was blatant. Unlike most people, where I was overly protective of my onboard load, I willingly let them touch my stomach and ask a million questions while they felt the babies kick.

CHAPTER 5

Half the community turned out to see us off, making me even more self-conscious.

"Can they stop making such a fuss?" I muttered to Illy with my back turned.

"They care about you both," she remarked a little sharply.

"They want the entertainment of watching me waddle around," I grumbled.

"Turn and wave," she growled in a tone I knew well.

Dutifully, I did as ordered, remembering that the last time I left here, it had been traumatic for everyone and not just for me. I just hated being the center of attention.

"All aboard," Summer called, and Gio turned to me, offering his hand. It looked so elegant until I needed help being hoisted aboard amid the final cargo loading.

Making short hops through airports and other communities where we could refuel, we made the slow trek back to Lewis. Despite my frustration at being made to leave on someone else's timeframe, secretly, I was thrilled to be heading home. I missed my family immensely and knew I was in the best place possible. Sorcha had a great deal of experience in complicated births, including multiples, and Nasir was nearby in France and could be with us in a matter of hours if there were complications with the babies. Mum would take no risks with me or her grandchildren. But each scan had revealed that they were fine and growing well. It was just me who wasn't coping.

"Chosen names yet?" Ally asked excitedly as she sat with me on one leg of the journey.

While I suspected Gio knew the gender, he hadn't told me, so we had spent many hours shortlisting male and female names that encompassed both our cultures and families. "Not yet," I admitted. "Tell me all the news."

France was our last stop as the community had a helipad, and nearby, they maintained an old commercial airport where Summer could refuel. Nasir was in surgery when we arrived, but Magali was overjoyed to see me, cooing and babbling in lyrical French at my enormous belly. Seeing her happiness, I relented and let her touch me.

"I blame you," I sniped as she sang a lullaby to my belly in French. I was still cranky after being stuck in an uncomfortable seat for hours and unable to move.

She looked confused. "*Moi? Pourquoi?*"

"Because you removed my contraception," I griped as one of my invaders somersaulted in my stomach, using my spine to push off like a springboard.

Magali giggled as she felt the head push into her hand and flashed her brilliant teeth. "That was a long time ago, *mon cheri*. You know, I thought Nasir and I would never be blessed with children. It took many years. You are most fortunate."

"I don't feel fortunate right now," I grumbled.

"I cannot imagine you do. Sit, *s'il vous plait*. You look most uncomfortable."

"I can't sit," I admitted. "My hips and back hurt all the time. Being confined in the helicopter with no room to move was hell."

"*Mon cheri*, it's not too long now," she soothed in her lilting French accent, which hadn't waned despite

CHAPTER 5

all the years she had lived in predominantly English-speaking communities. "Every woman finds the last few weeks difficult. You will forget all the pain when you have these miracles in your arms, I promise. I tell all my girls this."

"How are they all?" I asked, keen to shift the focus of the conversation.

"Ahh..." Magali launched into a monologue about their three children, one of whom, Mariette, was my half-sister and immune. All of Magali's children had partnered and had children of their own, and she and Nasir regularly traveled between the French unhab, the French above-ground community, and their home of the past twenty years, Newgrange.

Magali and Nasir, along with Illy, Bridget, and Jorja, were some of the few original scientific team members who defected to the communities in the early years when they learned of the experiments being conducted on the population. When Illy had taken over, a few migrated, but most remained in their communities at Clava and Auckland Island. While communications were civil with the Association of Collective Communities, our original community designers mostly kept to themselves. It was just as well. My parents' generation would never forget some of the horrifying practices they had followed, my existence being the result of one of them when they had kidnapped my mother and forcibly subjected her to the type of appalling medical procedures no woman should endure.

The low whirr of medical machinery in the background, combined with exhaustion, made me zone out as Magali regaled me with stories of what her children were up to, their milestones, and their achievements.

Truthfully, while I had met each grandchild, I couldn't differentiate them. Magali was a doting grandmother, besotted with each of them, and spoke warmly about each child. As I half-listened to her chat in a hybrid of French and English, I wondered how my mother would react to my babies. Mum loved us but was blunt to a fault. Mum spoke her mind; she was always honest. You always knew where you stood. So very different from my gentle father, who would do anything to avoid conflict. But they were active grandparents to Louis's three children and Xanthe's son, who all lived near their small farm on Lewis. Envy pricked my skin, making the warmth surge through me. Those children all had two sets of grandparents. My children only had my parents, although Illy and Carmelo too, by choice.

"Please send my regards to your parents," Magali finished, pulling me from my daze.

"I will. And when you next speak with your family, please pass on my best."

"*Oui*. You know, they still speak about how beautiful you looked in your wedding dress."

Like most family and friends not living in the Lewis community, Magali and her family hadn't seen me in over two years. Even many people who lived in the main settlement of Garynahine hadn't seen me when I returned a year ago, broken. Mum had taken great pains to shelter me, so while people knew I was there and what had happened, they hadn't seen me. What a different person I was when they last saw me at my best. Newly married. Before moving to Canada, being kidnapped and assaulted. Before Stella. For a moment, I wondered if that would forever be my yardstick. Before and after.

CHAPTER 5

Gio and I left a few days later, Jake escorting us on the last leg from France. Summer was traveling in the opposite direction to collect Seraphine, Matteo, and Rai. The smaller craft she preferred piloting was more economical for longer trips but far slower. I could barely contain my excitement at seeing Jake as he waited for us on the floating helipad. Seeing me approach, he taunted me mercilessly about my size.

"Catie! My gorgeous girl. Look at you! Waddling like a seal. You said you never wanted children," he teased as he hoisted me into the passenger seat beside him, Gio far more gracefully slipping into the smaller seat in the back. "Just hadn't met the right man?"

"Something like that," I mumbled, accepting the good-humored teasing. Although he had helped Summer build the bridge from my home in Canada, I hadn't spent much time with him at that time, still healing mentally and physically. Heading home now under far better circumstances, I had the overwhelming urge to thank him. My last memory of Jake was when he and Tadhg had collected Illy and me, both near death, from Kazakhstan. Even as broken as I was, I was so grateful for his reaction, treating me like he always had despite my horrific injuries and appearance.

"Jake," I started to say, but he cut me off with a wave of his hand as the helicopter lifted from the helipad, and he turned us toward home.

"No."

"You don't even know what I was going to say."

"Well, let me guess. Since the last time I saw you properly was over a year ago, the last time I brought you back home, I am guessing you want to say thank you for coming to get you. But Catie, I would always have done it. Luca was one of my best friends, and he would kick my ass from beyond the grave if he knew I didn't help his girl. The love of his life, too. That man changed when he met Illyria. Did you know he asked your father and me to stand with him at their wedding? Never has a man loved a woman as much as he adored her."

"I was going to thank you for not treating me like a victim," I said quietly so Jake could still hear me over the rotor noise, but so Gio couldn't hear from behind us. "I saw Tadhg's face as I lay there. Even with the single eye that functioned, I saw how he reacted. When he blanched and gulped, I thought he was going to vomit across the floor. That was when I knew for certain how bad it was. How I looked. But you … you just treated me like you always had. So that is what I need to say. Thank you for that. It made an enormous difference. Sometimes, I think I chose to survive because you treated me like you always have."

"How is that?" Jake asked without lifting his eyes from the windscreen and shifting direction toward Scotland.

"As a father."

His gaze warmed my cheek as I tried to focus on the horizon, gulping back emotion.

"I feel that way, you know. Your mother and I have been close since before you were born. Your father too. Both of them, I consider part of my family. I would always have done anything for you, Catie. Still would."

I laid a hand on his arm as he moved the controls. "I know. And it means the world to me."

"I need to ask. What do you mean by you 'chose to survive'?"

CHAPTER 5

Looking out the window across the ocean, I choked back the emotion. Jake was ex-military, hard and rugged but dependable. Would he understand? But I had said it, and now I needed to explain.

"They killed my baby. My husband too, or so I thought. I didn't want to join them, the Caspians, and honestly, I had nothing to live for. Until you came. Told me he was alive. But even then, I thought I had nothing to live for. No one would want me or ever look at me the same way again. Truly, I thought I was better off dead."

"I know what you did for Illyria."

Unable to respond, I inhaled deeply, but he knew I had heard.

"You are a hell of a woman, Caitlin. Just like your father."

"Do you think Dad would have liked Gio?"

"Let's be clear: no man would be good enough for his girls. Ever. But yes, I think he would have liked him a great deal. He is a good man. I hear you put him through the wringer before you accepted him again." Jake cast his eyes back to ensure Gio couldn't hear, but there was little chance of that in the noisy craft. "Can I ask why?"

I didn't know how to answer that and hoped Jake would see my discomfort and ask me something else. But he held the controls and looked over at me, his eyes filled with sympathy.

"You saw me," I finally whispered, not caring if he could hear me. "They broke me, and not just physically. I didn't think he would want me."

Jake placed his large, calloused hand on my belly, and I looked down at his masculine hands, broad fingers with closely clipped fingernails, nothing like

Gio's long, tapered, almost elegant fingers. Ordinarily, I found it invasive when people touched my stomach like I was suddenly public property. But this was reassuring. He was preparing himself; I sensed the tension in his arm.

"I don't know if you believe in an afterlife, Caitlin. Likely, you don't, being raised here. But I was raised in a Christian family, and those teachings never leave you. Without a shadow of a doubt, I can tell you that if your father is up there looking down, he will move heaven and earth to keep you safe. You and your children. You put everyone else ahead of yourself that day, and while not many people know it, he does. Illyria and his girls were his world, and that includes you. He would have been so proud of you, his daughter, standing up for what was right for your people. I know it sounds strange, but I still feel him sometimes. Just for a second, just letting me know he is there."

"What do you mean?"

Jake paused, choosing his words. "It could be that a picture has moved ever so slightly, an item of his appearing somewhere I didn't leave it. Or just flashbacks of memories of places we visited together or conversations we had. Sometimes, I just feel him there. He is still with me. I know he is watching over you, too. That entire trip to repatriate you, I could sense him, anxiously looking over my shoulder and urging me to hurry."

"I wish I could have met him."

"You don't need to, Catie. I see him every time I see you or your sisters. Not just the physical resemblance but your strength, tenacity, unwavering sense of loyalty, and leadership style. You *are* him."

"Thank you. That means everything."

CHAPTER 5

"You are a survivor, Catie, not a victim. Your mindset saw you through. Always will, no matter what challenges you face."

We arrived early afternoon, and Dad met us at the airport, the ecstatic glow not leaving his face as he watched me haul my bulk from the passenger seat, waiting for the rotor blades to slow.

"Catie!"

Dad could barely keep his footing as I hurled myself into his arms, nearly knocking him flying, forgetting I was far heavier these days. After clutching me to his chest, he pulled back and looked at me.

"What?" I teased. "Are you going to tell me what a whale I am, too?"

"No. I was so worried about you when you left. Then, when we saw you in Canada, you were still in so much pain. I am so happy for you, Caitlin." He pulled me in for another hug as Gio clambered to stand beside us.

"Giovanni." Dad smiled at him awkwardly before extending a hand.

"Where is Mum?" I asked, desperate to see her.

"She is debriefing with Illy and will meet us at home. They have organized a surprise for you."

"Please, not a party?" I asked, suddenly feeling sick. Now that I was fat and unwieldy, and especially after a flight, I felt sweaty and uncomfortable. Unlike Dad, who hated crowds and large social events, I had no issue with gatherings. It was being the center of attention when I felt at my most unattractive that I had an issue with.

Dad smiled awkwardly. "Everyone is desperate to see you well and happy. We agreed it was best to get the reunion over and done within one day. Otherwise, you will spend weeks catching up with people who want to see you and not spend these last few weeks resting. Your mother is adamant that you need some quiet time."

"It is a lovely idea," Gio interjected, knowing I wasn't happy about being thrown into a social event when tired and grumpy but diplomatic enough to know there was little choice when a party had already been arranged and likely everyone was already there. "Will there be a chance to clean up first? We are weary from travel."

"Of course."

Dad chattered away about all the events of life on Lewis. Who had married, had new children and grandchildren. Illnesses, injuries, and even the occasional death. His projects with the greenhouses and his success in propagating the Mousa moss. As the car descended into Roseglen, I sucked in my breath as the crowds of people lingering around the common grassed area between the houses came into view.

"Bloody hell, Dad," I muttered, trying to smile as I was in full sight of the guests. "Did you invite everyone from Newgrange and Orkney, too?"

As usual, Dad missed the sarcasm. "Just from here. I told Di it was too much. But she insisted. I am sorry, my darling." Dad shrugged, and I knew he was. But Di adored a party. Any opportunity to entertain, and she was there. Mum often teased her that she would attend the opening of an envelope.

The crowd surrounded the small car, and even while seated, Dad tried hard to shoo them away, feeling me

CHAPTER 5

tense beside him. Gio took the lead, jumping out and greeting everyone warmly, singling out my aunt Di for a long hug and loudly thanking her for arranging the gathering.

"We will be back in just a moment," Gio said to the waiting crowd. "Caitlin just needs to freshen up, and we will be out and can't wait to see you all," he announced as he opened my door, blocking me from view. I silently blessed him as everyone moved back toward the food tables. He helped me stand, his powerful arms around my ribs. Dad would never have been forceful enough to clear them so quickly.

"Caitlin?" Illy called as we entered the house, closing the door on the chatter of the crowd milling around outside.

"Were you expecting someone else?" I called back.

"Back off, Illyria!" Mum sniped good-naturedly as the footsteps clattered down the hallway. "You get to see my daughter every day. I don't." Her blonde head entered the kitchen and her mouth fell open seeing me.

"Look at you!" Her arms barely reached around my back, but I felt her joy radiating through her arms.

"Yes, I am the size of a house," I grumbled. "I can't believe I still have weeks of this to endure."

"Darling, you look wonderful. Doesn't she?" She turned to Dad, who had slipped in behind her, never one to make a scene or be the center of attention.

"She does."

"I keep telling her this," Gio said from behind me. "She doesn't listen."

Mum stepped forward to embrace him. "Thank you for taking care of our daughter. She looks amazing, glowing. Truthfully, I never thought I would see this day."

Mum returned her attention to me and started firing off medical questions about my blood pressure, my weight gain. To my surprise, it was Dad who intervened.

"Not now, Frey," he warned in his gentle tone. "Giovanni has taken excellent care of her to this point. There is nothing so urgent that it can't wait until tomorrow."

My parents' house was empty of children, so Illy and Carmelo had moved into my old room temporarily, leaving Gio and me to take up residence in Illy's half of the house. Technically, Ally and Summer still lived there, but they were frequently away and were so now. Sera and I were the youngest and hadn't lived here in years. Alasdair was partnered and lived on a croft nearby. Xanthe had also moved out, so Jake was staying in my parents' side of the house. Knowing he was around made me feel better.

Seraphine and Matteo were still in Japan with their child, although she had sent a message to Illy, promising to be here for the birth. Summer and Ally had already departed from France, so they should make it in plenty of time. Soon, the house would be overflowing with people I loved, so why did I feel so uncomfortable?

Closing the door to change, it felt strange being in Illy's room, even though I had been in here a million times. It was a large room, and someone had already

CHAPTER 5

set up two cots under the window. I lifted the natural-colored crocheted blanket and held it to my chest, smelling the lanolin from the new wool, wondering who had made this for us.

Dad and Gio carried our bags in, and Dad smiled, watching me. "Isla made that for you."

"Please thank her. It is lovely."

"Thank her yourself. She is outside with the others."

Accepting my fate, I changed into fresh clothes, and after a quick hairbrush and wash, Gio and I descended into the madness.

Throughout the course of the afternoon, Gio constantly had a child in his arms, one of Louis's three, Xanthe's new son, Hayden, or one of the many other children I didn't recognize. Children gravitated to him, and he toward them. I held no fears for his parenting skills; it was mine I worried about. Apart from Louis, my siblings hadn't started having children until I had left to live in Newgrange, and I was the youngest. My experience with babies was severely limited, and I was secretly terrified I would hurt them. For a moment, I desperately wished Sera were here. She would help me. Teach me. But Illy had advised us on our way out the door that they would be a few days late. Rai was unwell, and Sera didn't want to travel with him until he was better.

"Where are Kendra and Mei?" I asked Di when people finally trickled away after swarming us, showering us with their best wishes. Gio was beside himself with so many people wishing us well. He loved being part of a community and hadn't seen many of these people since our wedding.

"On August Island," she said, a strange look crossing her lovely face, her almond eyes opening a touch wider.

"August? Why?" No one traveled between Lewis and August anymore. Cargo was sent and received on solstices and equinoxes but rarely people. Everyone lived their own lives now, settled and established.

"They both wanted to train in natural medicine. After our time with the Punan people, they wanted to help heal but in a natural form."

"I still don't see why August. Can't they learn medicine here, from Sorcha and Mum?" Neither Kendra nor Mei got along with Katrin, prickly as she was. They were both gentle, quiet girls, while Kat was confrontational and forthright. Much like Illy regularly declared Mum had been before she softened. Mum was still a hard-ass as far as I was concerned, but Illy insisted that Mum had mellowed a great deal since having children.

"Well, there is a lady on August, Jacinda. She lived here when you were a child," Di said, and I caught the cautious undertone.

"Jacinda? You mean Aroha's mother?"

Di pursed her lip and exhaled. "I do."

"The one who tried to kill us?" The question was rhetorical. When questioned, Aroha had admitted to being one of the players, the group of radio teenagers who made it their mission to hunt us. They had murdered three of my sisters, two of them aged only six. While Aroha herself hadn't killed anyone, she had tried.

Di nodded, watching for my reaction.

CHAPTER 5

"Why would you let them go there? Wasn't it Mei she tried to poison?"

Di took a moment to respond to my loaded question. "She was a child too, Cait. We are all better than the worst thing we have ever done. She made a mistake, and she has paid for it. Made amends. It was also a long time ago, more than fifteen years. Mei is an adult. Letting them go was an act of trust on our part. They are fine. They check in every day. We aren't stupid, and neither are they. Sorcha and I told them everything, and they still chose to go."

"You are a better person than me," I admitted. "I will never forgive the men on Caspian for what they did."

"That is a little different. Aroha didn't hurt anyone." Di was clearly uncomfortable with the situation.

"But she tried," I pushed. "I can't believe Mei wanted to go."

"Mei especially wanted to go. She is quite forgiving, you know."

I believed that. Mei was a thoroughly decent human being.

"Jacinda is a good person," Di continued. "She and Jamie didn't know. Your parents have known them since they were first settled on August Island in their early twenties. I did too. Your dad, Jamie, and I all worked together and relied on each other heavily in those early years, ripped away from everything we knew. They are good people. That was why we never suspected her. But Aroha has grown up and matured. Married and has kids of her own. She has owned her past, told her husband, and he supports her. Kendra says she has apologized so many times it is embarrassing."

"So, are they enjoying it?" I asked in an effort to not dwell on memories of that time. It was not long after when her own nephew had attempted to drown me. That was the first beating I had sustained, triggering a lifetime of trauma and nightmares.

"They have found their purpose in natural healing," Di admitted. "They have been there nearly six months and will return on the next solstice, which is in a little over a week. Zane, of course, and little Henry accompanied Mei. Zane checks in with me and lets me know they are safe. The four of them are living in my old house. I kind of feel bad that Jacinda kicked someone out, but August is a tiny place."

"You must be so excited with them coming home soon." Raised in a traditional Chinese family herself, Di was so close to her children, both of them. After leaving Sorcha's son, Sam, behind in Australia, she barely left their side.

"I have missed them so much," she admitted. "I was scared that Kendra would meet someone and stay there. But it looks like they are all returning on schedule."

Not like me, I thought with a pang of guilt. I left to go to Newgrange at seventeen, and aside from a few short trips, I hadn't lived here since. To cover my discomfort, I asked, "What did they learn?"

"Jacinda is what we used to call a naturopath, although she also qualified as a compounding pharmacist. Basically, that means she uses herbal treatments to treat medical conditions. Lots of people here used to see her for things that didn't require a doctor or surgery."

"Aunt Sorcha allowed that?"

CHAPTER 5

Di giggled at my incredulous reaction. No matter how old she got, Di still giggled like a small child. The infectious sound made you want to laugh along with her.

"Sorcha didn't have a lot of choice. They were lovely people. They lived just down the hill, on the way to the school. You would often see Jacinda with a basket, picking wildflowers or sitting on her step, making something in a mortar and pestle."

"Oh! I remember her!" I had a sudden vision of who Di was speaking about. While I knew the names, I had only been six when they left. "She had long, dark hair past her waist and a band of art around her upper arm?"

"That was her. She was part Māori, a native New Zealander. That was a tribal tattoo. I asked her about it once, what it symbolized. She said that, in Māori culture, the tattoo reflects the individual's *whakapapa*, their ancestry, and their personal history. Jacinda had deliberately had hers finished before she was mobilized to August so that she had a living memory of her ancestors."

"She was gone when we came home from Australia," I said, trying to remember that time so long ago. I had been so traumatized when I returned home, nightmares plaguing me. "I don't remember much. But I do remember Illy not coming back with us."

"You were so young, and we didn't want to overwhelm you. That was when they asked her to be Chief."

I nodded, trying to piece things together in my memory. "Well," I said, standing up and arching my back, trying to shift the pain in my hips. "It will be wonderful to see them. I hope they get to meet my babies."

"Oh, they will. The solstice is soon. You will stay for a while after they are born, won't you?"

"Mum says I will probably need a cesarean, so at least six weeks. I am not quite thirty-three weeks now, so I will be here a few months this time. It is the longest I have been here in years."

Di squealed with joy. "I am so happy! I missed you, Catie. Seraphine too. I can't wait to meet your bubbaloos! We need more babies!"

Her enthusiasm made me smile. The thing was, I believed her. Aunt Di was one of those people who saw the good in everyone and loved being around people. She brought out the best in people, including her partner, Dad's sister Sorcha. Sorcha was much like Katrin, cool and assessing, and she let you know precisely what she was thinking the moment she thought it. They were so different, yet so in love. Di softened her, made her edges less sharp.

"Will you come and visit me in Canada?" I asked, suddenly desperate to show her everything we had done there. Di had done it all. Horticulturalist, then teacher, and now back to horticulture with a side hustle as a party planner. She had arranged my wedding.

Her eyes sparkled with joy. "I would love that! I have never been to Canada."

"Perhaps you could organize a blessing for the babies when they arrive?"

Di's mouth sprung open, and another squeal of joy escaped. "Oh my goodness, yes! Here or in Canada? Both maybe?" She prattled on, and I hastily glanced around for someone to rescue me as she began quizzing me about what cultures I would like represented in the ceremony. Scottish first footings? Chinese

CHAPTER 5

traditions? What did they do to celebrate a new arrival in Canada?

Neighbors and friends drifted home as the sun began to drop below the horizon and the cool night air rose. I felt a soft wool wrap slip around my shoulders, and I snuggled into the gray warmth.

"Thanks, Mum."

"We don't need you getting cold. Although, I recall growing babies was much like having a small furnace inside you."

"Clearly, I have been in Canada for too long. The temperature in the underwater communities barely fluctuates a degree or so. I am really noticing how much the temperature varies here this time. I hope I'm not sick."

"I am sure you are fine. We will give you a thorough examination tomorrow. But in the afternoon. Illyria wants you in the morning. Planning meetings, she said."

My shoulders slumped. Mum gave me her cool ice-queen stare as I grimaced at the thought of work so soon after returning home. She leaned in and whispered, "Whatever you do, don't tell her I told you, but she loves working with you. She thinks you do the job better than she does."

I studied Mum's face. "Oh, come on. That isn't true."

"Actually, it is. The team respects you a great deal. She is worried the other ambassadors won't want to deal with her. She is fearful that they will wait for you to make key decisions, wanting your input, especially on the many landside construction projects underway at the moment. If that happens, nothing will progress for months."

"Me? They listen to me?"

"You. It was you who reactivated the portals and who keeps coming up with new projects and monumental ones that will change the lives of all inhabitants. She said they all want to expand landside, and you conceptualized, designed, and oversaw the bridge project. Plus a lot of other schemes she keeps rabbiting on about, all of your design. She is concerned everything will come to a screeching halt when you have these babies. Give her something to do, will you? And for goodness' sake, don't let on I told you."

Illy was standing across the clearing, talking to Bridget and Jorja in front of one of Dad's greenhouses. Despite her being engrossed in conversation, I knew Illy well enough to know that she was still scanning the crowd, taking it all in.

"She is watching us. Touch my stomach." I turned my head slightly, trying to hide my moving mouth. Mum obliged and made a show of pressing in various locations.

Mum, ever the doctor, instantly forgot what we were discussing. "Are you sure your scans are accurate? They seem awfully big for thirty-three weeks."

"Have you seen the size of my husband?"

"True enough. Your father, Luca, I mean, was also a large man. Perhaps you are having twin boys."

"What was easier? Boys or girls?"

"Neither!" Mum shot back, but then rethought that. "Actually, Xanthe and Thorsten were my easy ones. Louis too. You and Katrin were bloody hard work. Alasdair was a dream, and Illy's girls drove me to the

CHAPTER 5

point of murder. So perhaps boys are easier," she considered. "But then again, we had more girls. Anyway, we will find out in a few weeks. Off to bed. You have a big day tomorrow."

CHAPTER 6

BEFORE I WENT TO bed, Illy had requested I attend final handover meetings over the next two days before officially taking leave. Conflicting feelings had me in turmoil: relief that I could finally catch up on rest for a few weeks but also guilt that she was shouldering the load, especially after what Mum said last night. After arriving in the afternoon and greeting my entire extended family, plus everyone else from Roseglen and many from farther afield, I hadn't slept well. Despite leaving the party early, pleading exhaustion from travel, I knew the party had gone until the small hours, the chatter outside the window keeping me awake, and as a result, I had overslept.

Gio was gone when I woke. As I peered out the window at the familiar scene, I was startled to realize it was mid-morning. Hauling my enormous bulk out of bed and pulling on the only semi-professional clothes I owned that now fit me, I staggered into the kitchen, wishing I could return to bed. Gulping a coffee to stave off the exhaustion, and guilt-ridden that Gio would likely tell me off for consuming caffeine, I quickly

CHAPTER 6

brewed a second to take with me along with a bottle of water so I could wash out the travel cup before he saw it. I hadn't driven in over a year and swore at myself for stalling the car, making me even later. Likely the meetings were well over, and Illy would have needed to make excuses for me. As I rounded the crest and headed into Garynahine, I grimaced. The sun was at its zenith indicating it was close to midday. *Fuck*!

"Where is everyone?" I asked, taking in the conference room on Lewis as I burst through the door, the sun illuminating the room through the wall of windows opposite. Illy was sitting alone, her back to me, staring at a blank screen. "I'm so sorry I am..."

"Sit," Illy ordered. Her tone was flat, making my stomach drop. *Fabulous. Now she is pissed at me. Just what I need. Maybe I missed something important?*

"I'm so sorry," I pleaded. "Can we reschedule? I was just so tired, and..."

"Sit down."

"You know if I sit, I won't be able to get out of the chair again?" I said, only partly teasing. The tension in the room was thick, and I was desperate to disperse it. "You know I can't fit in a standard chair."

"For fuck's sake, stop apologizing and sit down," Illy barked, and I dropped. Rarely did she use that imperious tone with me anymore.

"I'm so sorry..." I began, only to be cut off by a dismissive wave. "What happened?" I asked, my heart dropping watching her stony face. *Shit, I am about to cop a barrage from her about my unprofessionalism.*

"Goodness knows how, but Caspian heard you are the new Chief. It clearly surprised them that you and I are still alive."

"How did they find out?" I gasped.

"We don't know that yet. Tadhg is working on it. Sera too. Not really important at the moment, but they know."

"Okay, so what? We survived. What are they planning to do? Have another go?"

While I had known her my entire life, Illy's demeanor was unlike anything I had seen before. She was cold, stilted. But not toward me. She was grappling with something. Finally, I realized what it was. She was mentally balancing the odds of telling me something unpleasant.

"Just tell me. Are they planning to try again?"

Illy's shoulders slumped. "They sent the footage as a warning of what they do to people who defy them."

"Footage?" I stumbled over the word. "What footage?"

Illy studied my face before continuing. "The Caspian community released detailed video footage of Viktor beating you. Not what led to it, which I thought was a notable omission. So, not you refusing to join them, just the consequences of the refusal."

My heart burst out of my chest, followed by my heart rate accelerating. Stiffening my spine, I steeled myself to remain calm, images flashing into my mind. "I was there. I doubt it is anything new."

Illy swallowed hard, and her voice dropped to a thickened rumble, even though we were alone. "I saw it, Catie. It was awful. Worse than you think."

"What?" I croaked, my stomach plummeting. "What did they do? They kicked and punched me. I should know. It was me on the receiving end."

Illy exhaled shakily, steeling her tone. "It showed them bellowing at you, and you defiantly refusing to submit. I was so proud of you, the way you gritted your

CHAPTER 6

teeth and stood up to them. Then it showed Viktor and his colleagues holding your arms back as he struck you the first time. That made me sick, watching the blood fly from your mouth."

"That wasn't the worst of it," I admitted.

"No, it wasn't. They transmitted the full video. It went on forever."

"What did you see?" I whimpered.

"It showed them beating you, crumpled into a ball on the floor. The four of them taking turns. There was no sound, which was probably a blessing, but your face was clear. The pain of each blow as they struck you. You, lying in a pool of blood. Your blood. At one point, they dragged you to a new place on the floor so they wouldn't need to stand in it. They paused to wipe their shoes on you. Then, they kept going like it was a regular day. Anyone watching who knew you could see you were protecting your child. But they just kept going."

Seeing her pain, I tried to reassure her. "It is over. I survived. Did it show them dropping me through the moon pool hatch?" That was the part I didn't recall, and the moment before. Probably just as well. By that point, I was a mess. I still hadn't recovered if I was to be truthful about it. Physically or mentally.

"No. Just what happened in that room. It was clearly a single fixed surveillance camera."

I nodded, inhaling sharply but trying to maintain my composure. That was enough to make their point.

"Their leader, Viktor, was the one who transmitted the video. He proudly announced that he wanted to show the world that the ACC's Chief was no leader, and this was what happened to people who crossed them. We could all see him clearly on the tape. It was

Viktor who halted them when it was obvious you were unconscious or dead. Not soon enough after you stopped moving, but he did finally call a stop to it. But not before one more humiliating act that he made sure we all saw."

Illy paused, letting that sink in. My throat closed over as I croaked, "What did he do?"

"Do you really want to know?"

"Tell me." The words were barely audible.

"In the military, we used to call it turkey slapping. Do you know what that means?"

I shook my head. I could see the discomfort as the color drained from Illy's face. Clearly, it was something derogatory.

"Just tell me. I will see it eventually."

There was a long pause before she answered. "Viktor got his comrades to hold you upright. You were unconscious. Your head flopped forward, but your hair was tied back, allowing your face to be visible. Then, he took out his penis and slapped you across the face with it. Viktor rubbed it over your face, in your hair and put it in your mouth. He and his colleagues laughed as they held you there, unconscious, and he kept rubbing himself on you."

I gagged instinctively and turned away. "Anything else?" I muttered.

"Grabbing your breasts and other inappropriate stuff, but that was the worst of it."

"No, the worst of it was losing my child," I whispered.

"Agreed. But when Carmelo and Gio saw it, Gio's face went purple. I am certain I could see steam pour from his ears. Even the hairs on his arms were bristling. Then he stormed out, Carmelo following. I thought I would give them time to calm down.

CHAPTER 6

Carmelo is logical and balanced. I could hear them talking outside, but I couldn't hear what they were saying. Regardless, it was a horrendous thing to see, especially for your husband."

The words registered in my haze. "How did they see it? You were supposed to be meeting me here for meetings. How did Gio see it?"

"Just bad timing. They were heading up to the whisky still and came in to tell me you wouldn't make the morning meetings; you were exhausted and still asleep. They walked in just as Viktor cut into our satellite feed. They clearly knew we had a full meeting scheduled this morning, which is something else we are investigating. The large screen was on, and I had just finished greeting the other delegates as they came online. As you know, that can take a few minutes to iron out the access issues. But everyone was connected. Gio and Carmelo entered the room, and I went to turn the screen off. Those meetings are confidential, but it was too late. Viktor hacked it. Gio saw it was one of the Caspians; he recognized the uniform, although he had never met Viktor. He demanded I let him see it, and honestly, I didn't think. If I had known, Catie, I would never have let him watch. I genuinely thought it would be a few seconds of Viktor boasting about how great they were, honestly. Just to prove that they could hack our transmissions, that they were powerful, and our communications weren't safe. Never did I think it would be that. By the time the footage started, Gio wouldn't let me turn it off."

"And Carmelo?"

"Carmelo saw it. He watched silently, taking it all in. After their invasion of Piedmont, he knew who they were."

Illy was more distressed than I had ever seen her, so I tried to put on a brave face. "It doesn't matter. It happened. I can't change it."

"It does matter, especially when you hear how they reacted."

"Why? What did Gio say? Threw a few things?"

"I didn't have time to speak to him. As soon as the transmission ended, he stormed off, Carmelo in his wake. They were outside, speaking rapidly in Italian, and while I couldn't make out all the words, I could hear the volume escalate, so I thought I should give them time to calm down. Maybe an hour later, I heard the helicopter taking off from Stornoway."

"Is Summer home already? I thought she was on her way to Japan."

"Jake."

"Jake?"

"He was planning to hang around for a few days after he dropped you off. He was at the party last night, remember? Officially, he was waiting to catch up with Summer, although secretly, I think he wants to meet the babies. Jake saw you. He has been seething about it quietly, feeling guilty that he couldn't help you. Don't forget that Jake was one of Luca's closest friends. He couldn't save Luca, so he is likely avenging your abduction as Luca's daughter."

"Oh, for fuck's sake. I thanked him yesterday on the way over. It is ancient history."

"Well, it was clearly on his mind, plaguing him. It was plain on his face yesterday at the party. The way he watched over you. He has appointed himself your guardian."

"Did he say that?"

CHAPTER 6

"No. But I can tell." She could. Illy could always tell what someone was thinking.

"What is this? Three grown men engaging in an exercise of testosterone-fueled chest beating?"

"Something like that. They want revenge for what the Caspians did to you."

"Awesome, so now they are getting us neck-deep in another cross-community fucktastrophy. Bloody fucking men. Can't they leave it in their pants? Why does it need to be a pissing competition? Where are they now? Can we get them back?"

"Tadhg says the three of them are on their way to Caspian."

"Oh, fucking brilliant. To do what?"

"I don't know, but it can't be good."

"Look," I tried to reason, "Gio is likely going to blow off some steam. What can he do? I am here about to drop twins. He wouldn't do anything stupid. Jake wouldn't let him engage in an all-out war. Carmelo is calm. He will be the voice of reason."

"Caitlin," Illy's tone dropped, warning, "Carmelo loves you like a daughter. He also knows they took me and is likely now fearful of what they did to me whilst I was there. But Giovanni will take this the hardest. Your husband just witnessed what those animals did to you. There is no more imagining. He *saw*. He already felt helpless that he couldn't stop them from abducting you, quite literally tearing you from his arms. He didn't see you when we first rescued you. It was ten days before he arrived. You were held captive for five days. He is a doctor; he had some idea of the severity of the blows to cause those kinds of injuries. But that footage was nothing short of horrific. Your face was clearly visible, and that was deliberate. You could see them turning you, so the camera caught it all. The agony etched on your face. Watching them kick you in the stomach, in the head, watching the blood fly."

"What did I look like?" I asked softly.

Illy took a deep breath.

"Tell me. If they have seen it, I have a right to know."

"You put up a good fight at first. But you were outnumbered, and they were bigger. You could never have stopped it. But as each blow landed, the torment on your face was crystal clear. The blood flying and your head being snapped back. Not one of us who has seen it has come away unscathed."

Air escaped my lungs as I took in those words. "How many people have seen it? Who?"

"The Caspians accessed our satellite. They were clearly monitoring it as they waited until all communities were online. I had just welcomed all the delegates. That was when they cut in; Viktor laughed at us and transmitted the video. So, whilst only senior officials from each community have seen it, all of your colleagues were online."

Bile rose up the back of my throat. Everyone. All of my peers, colleagues, and workmates had seen me being abused.

"How can they respect me now?" I forced the words out as my face flushed with humiliation.

Illy's eyes narrowed as she gripped my shoulders and gave me a slight shake as she hissed at me. "Don't you dare be embarrassed! Be *angry,* Caitlin. Furious. You did nothing to be ashamed of. You saved people, and they did this to humiliate you. They heard that you survived, and we promoted you to Chief. This was a deliberate attempt to force you to hide. They are

CHAPTER 6

cowards, and I will not allow you to do that. You will never let them win. Promise me."

"So what do I do?"

"You hold your head up high. I will stand beside you. Tomorrow there is another meeting, and we will script a speech for you to give at the meeting tomorrow. You take the moral high ground. You march in there, and you let them know you will not cower from these animals. Caitlin, you are the Chief. Remember it. Act like it. If you slink away and hide, they win. Then they will forever have power over you. It will haunt you. If you don't act now, you will regret it. You need to react decisively and quickly. You condemn them for what they did, and you ask for support. Trust me when I say you are one of us. You will have the full support of your colleagues."

"Are you sure?" I whispered, the bile continuing to rise, making me desperately want to spit.

"Let's take those people one at a time, shall we? Me. My loyalty goes without saying. You saved my life and I owe you everything. Tadhg sees you as a daughter. Your mother is the Ambassador here. Seraphine is your sister. Nasir has known you since birth and will support you to the ends of the earth. Riccardo, you saved his people. This happened because you protected *them*. So we remind him of that. nîpiy is acting Ambassador in Canada, and she is loyal to you like no other. She was there the day they took you, wasn't she? The other communities may not know you yet, but they know me. I have been to them all, even the recently connected ones in China, Mongolia, and Croatia. You are my daughter, Caitlin. Maybe not by birth or genetics, but by choice. We will stand shoulder to shoulder, and we will condemn any community that treats any person in this way. This goes against our charter, our moral code. The women will sympathize, and the men will empathize. They all have wives, sisters, or daughters. No one would ever consider treating a citizen this way. But Catie, I think you need to tell them all of it."

"All of it? Didn't you say they had seen the full tape?"

"About Stella."

"How did you know what we named her?" I whispered at the sound of her name.

"Giovanni said something to Carmelo about Stella. He needs someone to talk to as well. Did you know it was a girl?"

"It was never confirmed," I admitted. "But I just know."

Illy nodded. "Making this personal will help people to join us in the fight against them. Name her. Make her real. You are the survivor here, but she didn't make it. We don't make threats—we explain. We remind them of what the Caspians did to the people in Italy, what you did to save those people. You protected them, a community that was not your own."

"I am so tired of fighting. Why can't they just leave us alone?"

"I don't know. Jealousy. Anger. Revenge. They are all powerful motivators."

"Tell me why I need to be the public relations exercise?"

"You don't. But the longer we let this go unaddressed, the more people gossip. They will talk anyway, so we are best to lead the way. Condemning them. Don't let them win. But I will be there. Your mother, too."

CHAPTER 6

"Mum saw it?" My stomach dropped even further, and I needed to close my eyes to quell the rising nausea. Of course she did. Since Illy had moved to Canada to be with me, Mum had been appointed ambassador for Lewis.

"She did. Thank goodness your father didn't. It would have killed him."

"Is Mum okay?"

"Your mother is one of the strongest women I have ever known. She was sitting beside me. She stiffened when Viktor came on, and I could feel the chill emanating from her as she watched it. Then she stood and left the room. I heard her vomiting in the bathroom. But like you, Caitlin, she will rise, and she will conquer, every time. You are powerful women, both of you, forces of nature. Do not let this pull you down. Do not let them hold this power over you. If you do, then you will be a victim forever."

I nodded in agreement. "When?"

"Tomorrow."

"So soon?"

"We need to. We act quickly and decisively. There can be no time for gossip."

"Did Gio leave a message?"

"No. They have switched off all communication devices, thinking they can't be tracked, no doubt. But Tadhg can track them via satellite. He can see which way they are headed. Truth be told, I am surprised Tadhg didn't ask to join them."

"Why? Carmelo and Jake are ex-military and have never backed down from a threat. Gio is my husband. Why would Tadhg want to go? He is a pacifist."

"Do you not recall the look on his face when he saw you in Kazakhstan? I was there. I might have been delirious, but I saw. You are as much a daughter to him and Callie as Fairlie and the others. Callie met your father in Melbourne on the day they were assessed, by me, incidentally, all those years ago. They have been like family ever since. It gutted him to see you like that, both of them. Tadhg would have gone, happily, had he been here. So many people love you, Catie, so many more than you realize."

One of the babies lurched suddenly, making me double up in pain.

"Are you alright?" Illy's eyes sprang wide.

"Fine. They are just getting comfortable at my expense."

A weak smile crossed her face. "It has been so many years, but I remember distinctly. I may have been smaller than you in height, but I was huge. Luca used to tease me that my belly entered the room a full minute before the rest of me."

"That sounds like something I would say."

"But I can honestly tell you, despite all the dramas with my pregnancy in the later stages, those girls were still easier in than out."

Laughter rippled through my chest. Summer and Allison had been daredevil troublemakers since they were children. They were eight when Seraphine and I were born, or arrived, technically, as we hadn't been born here. But they had always treated us like sisters. I owed them so much. On top of getting Illy and me out of Kazakhstan, Ally and her basic medical training likely saved both of our lives.

"If one of them is a girl, as a middle name, Gio and I want to use the name Sally," I told her gently. "Summer and Ally. It means a lot to us to recognize that without them, I wouldn't be here, and these

CHAPTER 6

babies wouldn't be born. Well, about to be born. A middle name means it is special for us. Only people close to us will know their middle names, the special ones."

Illy's hand flew to her chest as her mouth dropped. "That is so lovely. Thank you. That will mean a great deal to them both. So, do you think one is a girl?"

"I have no idea," I confessed. "But the odds are fifty-fifty, aren't they?"

"Surely Giovanni knows?"

"We agreed not to find out. He didn't even do the latter scans. We allowed one of his colleagues to do it. If he does know, he hasn't let on. He was the one who wanted a surprise, not me. But part of me thinks he knows."

"Come on. Let's get you home. Tomorrow will be a long day. You need rest."

"Mum wanted me to drop by the med center for a checkup."

"Tomorrow. She was in no fit state to do anything, so I sent her home. Let's plan this meeting first. My advice is that you don't wait."

CHAPTER 7

ILLY DROVE ME HOME in silence, both of us pondering the situation at hand. Mum greeted me at the door, her face white and streaked. She had clearly been crying but would never let me know that. She held me to her chest, then steered me toward the bedroom, the pain etched into the fine lines of her face.

"Sleep," she whispered, trying to keep her voice light, but the words choked in her distress.

Despite my exhaustion, I couldn't sleep. Images of what Illy had described floated through my mind, haunting me. She refused to let me watch the footage and issued an order that every community delete it, which they all reported they had done. It would traumatize me, she advised. I didn't need to see it. I remembered some of it, the bellowing and the blows raining down on me. But my memory had gaps, where it skipped, and part of me wanted to view the tape, to see what everyone else had. To learn why Gio, Carmelo, and Jake took off the way they did. Sighing, I padded down the hall to find Mum and Illy in the living room, discussing the best course of attack.

CHAPTER 7

Looking up as I entered, I saw the shadows of concern darken Mum's eyes.

"Let's get this done," I announced with more confidence than I felt.

The three of us carefully scripted some notes for me to deliver the following morning. Describing the sequence of events. How I had protected the people of Piedmont. How this was retribution, payback. Losing my child. I read the script over and over, memorizing it so I could read the words without emotion choking me. Mum went to make tea, and Illy coached me on how to deliver it with enough emotion that people felt for me, but not so much that emotion was all they saw and didn't hear the words.

"But I *am* emotional," I griped as she made me run through it again. "I am here, about to burst, and my husband is off gallivanting around the globe with his mates. You are asking me to recall the most awful time of my life, alone."

"It is important, Caitlin. I wouldn't ask you to do it otherwise. You are not alone. I'm here. Your mother, too. We will stand with you. One more time, please."

Seeing Mum's face as she acted as my audience made me feel ashamed all over again. My face flushed as I felt the heat rise, and she pulled me to her unexpectedly.

"I will be here with you every step of the way," she hissed, choking back emotion from her usual ice-queen façade. "If Gio hadn't gone after them, I would have. I would happily tear their throats out with my bare hands and paint your name with their blood, dancing on their dead fucking bodies."

"Freyja." Illyria's tone was low, warning.

"Oh, get off your high horse, Illyria," Mum snapped over my shoulder, pulling me closer and speaking over my head. "You and I have done far worse. She is my daughter. Yours, too. If that had been Seraphine..."

"I am not disagreeing with you, Frey," Illy said in a low, soothing tone. "I am just saying making threats right now is not helpful."

Mum scowled and ignored her, pulling me out slightly so we stood face to face. "Anything you need, say the word."

I nodded, forcing myself to remain calm. "I'll be fine."

Giving my impassioned speech, I read the faces and body language on the large screen. Illy had set the view so I could see them all, people I knew. Some in real life, others I had only spoken to via videoconference. But I knew them, and they knew me. The faces staring back at me as I spoke were shocked and horrified, and I watched as the wave turned to indignation and anger. There were no questions. No comments. The hardest part was when I spoke about my baby and tried not to sniff back the tears. Despite my best efforts to maintain my composure, I needed to pause and wipe my eyes at one point, and I saw Seraphine and nîpiy tear up themselves. As the feed disconnected, I slumped down into my seat, exhausted. It was as if someone had drained the energy from me, and it was barely 10 a.m. The room lapsed into darkness when the feed cut. Mum turned in her chair and gripped my hands, squeezing reassuringly, but I knew it was as much for

CHAPTER 7

her as it was for me. One of the administration officers came to the door, tapped gently, and indicated he wanted to speak with Illy. After checking that I wasn't about to collapse, Illy slipped out, leaving Mum and me to process in silence.

"What is it?" Mum asked, looking up from me as Illy returned, closing the door firmly. Suddenly, I felt shattered, and I wanted nothing more than to sleep for a month.

Illy watched us both for a moment. "I've just had a report of Jake and his band of merry marauders."

"What did they do?" I asked, looking up from Mum's reassuring face.

"Jake flew the helicopter as close as he dared, landing at night on the mainland, near the medical center. But far enough away that the Caspian community couldn't see or hear them. Jake is immune now, you know. Jake and Makayla's daughter, your sister Lulu, had a baby a few weeks ago, and we used the stem cells to inoculate the rest of their family. It seemed fair. To keep it in the family, I mean."

I nodded, not really caring about Lulu and her baby right now.

"Gio and Carmelo are already immune, so the three of them swam to the outer concrete wall, the outer ring containing their water supply."

"What did they do?"

"Jake rigged an explosive device."

"They didn't! Please tell me they didn't blow them up. Despite everything they have done, there are likely innocent people in that community, too."

"No, they didn't. But would you believe it was Gio who was the voice of reason in the end?"

"You are kidding me?"

"I'm not. Jake and Carmelo would happily have blown the facility sky high. Something you said once to Giovanni stopped him. But he wouldn't say, fearful of being tracked, I guess, especially as we still don't know how they hacked our comms. Jake and Tadhg know each other well enough to speak in Gaelic, which very few other people speak. But they left it there, rigged, ready to be detonated remotely."

"Where did Jake access explosives?"

Illy smirked. "Here. We still have a stash, you know. After Clava's actions all those years ago, we took precautions. On Newgrange, too. Jake and your father were part of that planning."

"How were they not seen if they swam right up to it?"

"They did it at night."

"They will know it was us."

"It is on the outer wall. Likely, the Caspians don't know. None of the underwater communities that we know have sensors or surveillance outside. They have access to satellites and communications. We know that. Tadhg is watching for any sign that they are on alert. But there is no indication they were seen."

"Fair enough." The overwhelming urge to lie down dragged at me. Illy saw me wilting.

"Take her home, Freyja. She needs to rest."

"Who is the doctor here?" Mum's eyes sparked daringly. "And the ambassador?"

"You, but I am the Chief. This time, I pull rank."

Mum threw her head back and roared with laughter. "You can pull rank with your husband, Illyria. With your minions. Not with me."

"But that doesn't mean I will ever give up trying."

CHAPTER 7

"Mum!" I croaked down the hallway as I staggered out of Illy's bathroom, clutching the wall for support. After taking off my work clothes, showering, and pulling on some old clothes, I hadn't even made it as far as the bed.

"Whaa... Are you in labor?"

"How ... would ... I ... know?" I gasped. "Never ... been ... labor."

"Tell me what is going on." She snapped into doctor mode; I had seen it often enough.

"Think ... waters ... broke," I gasped as the tight band squeezed around my stomach, sucking all the air from my lungs.

"Shit, Caitlin, you are barely thirty-three weeks. It is too early. I wanted to get you to thirty-five."

"Can't help that," I groaned, hanging off her shoulders as the cramping weighed me down. "Coming. Now."

"Shit," I heard Mum mutter as she pushed me back onto the bed and laid a hand on my stomach, feeling the contraction. "Shit. Fuck. Wait here."

"Not ... going ... anywhere." I grimaced through the vice-like grip.

Mum opened the front door and bellowed, "Campbell!"

As I lay on the edge of the bed, curled over in pain, I could see out the large window pointing toward the common area. Dad's messy, dark head popped out of the greenhouse closest to the house.

"Cam, she is in labor," Mum called across the garden, sounding cool and in control. "I need Kat and Sorcha. Jorja will need to take over all the other patients. Take care of it, please."

"Who first?" Dad's voice was calm, although I detected a slight undertone of panic.

"Your sister."

Mum strolled back into the room, her shoulders back. "Right. No time to do anything. Let's go."

"Go ... where?" The pain had passed, but it left me feeling drained.

"I need to get you to the clinic. Multiples are tricky, and these babies are premature. Besides, we always planned a cesarean for you after your pelvic injuries."

"Where is Gio?" I huffed as she shuffled me slowly up the hall toward the kitchen.

Mum nodded. "I'll check with Illy. She is in her room, I think. Can you sit here for a minute? I won't be long."

I nodded unconvincingly as she steered me into the chair in Illy's kitchen, one I had eaten in hundreds of times. It was strange seeing it now, having been away for so long. So many times, Sera and I had eaten here, done our homework, or cooked up plans that had ultimately seen us get into trouble in this lovely, yellow, light-filled room.

The light patter of Mum's feet echoed down the hallway into her own house. She banged on the bedroom door and barged in without waiting for a response. I heard the lilting sound of women's voices and the sound of two sets of footsteps coming up the hall.

"Couldn't wait?" Illy teased gently. "Is this your way of telling me you don't want to attend any more meetings?"

CHAPTER 7

Breathless from the pain, I couldn't respond immediately. When it passed, I looked up from the chair and begged, "Please. Get him here."

"I'm on it." Illy looked up at Mum. "Does she have long?"

"Hours at a guess," Mum said, looking at me. "Until we check, I can't be sure. But her waters have broken, so unless something changes, it is happening today."

"Can you check?"

"Yes, but I would rather just get her to the clinic. In case."

In case. In case of what? I wondered.

"Fuck," I heard Illy mutter as she dashed up the hallway.

"Can you walk?"

Now that the tightening had passed, I was okay. I felt like they had put me into a human-sized vice and squeezed me, much like the grape crusher I had assisted Antonio with back on Piedmont. But I could walk.

"Do you want to change first?" Mum asked, looking down at the rolled-up cuffs of my track pants and oversized t-shirt over bare feet. Gio's clothes, technically, but he rarely wore them. Since we had met, the agreement had been we wore nothing to bed. But now that I was enormous and unwieldy and didn't want him near me, I had worn his old gym clothes to bed. He had moaned and grizzled about not being able to get near me, but I had stood my ground. While initially pregnancy had been a joy, glowing hair and skin, and I had loved caressing the new lives growing inside me, now that I felt like an enormous barrel had been strapped permanently to my stomach, I had reached the end of my patience. My breasts were enormous and hurt all the time, and I just felt gross.

"Change into what, Mum?" I snapped, feeling judged. "Nothing fits. I look like one of Josh's pregnant cows."

Instead of berating me, Mum smiled. "I remember what that feels like, and I only had singles. It won't be long, sweetheart, and you will hold these little miracles in your arms and marvel at them. I promise."

"Mum, what if he doesn't make it in time?"

Mum was uncharacteristically diplomatic in her reply. "Well, two things. We can slow down labor, naturally." Seeing the look of concern on my face, she added, "It is safe. I promise. And Illy will do everything she can to get them here as quickly as possible. You know she will. If anyone understands, it is her."

Mum checked my pulse and rested her hands on my belly as it constricted again, and I moaned as the pain gripped me.

"Change of plan. We aren't waiting to get you changed. We go. Now."

Sorcha came flying up the valley in her electric car as we exited our house. Coming to a screeching halt behind ours, she bolted out before it had even come to a complete stop, dropping under my other shoulder and helping Mum escort me to the car.

"Kat is on duty and will meet us there. How close?" She spoke to Mum over my head without even greeting me.

"Too close," I heard Mum whisper over my bent head. Some days, I regretted my exceptional hearing.

"Damn girl, you never make anything easy, do you?" Sorcha teased, but I barely heard her.

CHAPTER 7

"I need him here," I begged as she half sat, half laid me across the back seat. Not that it mattered. No position was going to be comfortable.

"Illy is on it. Where did Cam go?" Sorcha spoke over my head as she strapped me in and slipped into the seat beside me, half hanging out. "He yelled at me through the door, waited for me to respond, told me to get to your place now, and then disappeared again."

"Down to see if Jorja is home."

"Good. She will know to meet us there. Let's go."

CHAPTER 8

SORCHA SAT BESIDE ME, making me lean into her so she could support me in the back seat as we bumped and jolted our way to the main clinic in Garynahine. The last time I had been here was after my assault on Caspian. Mum had barely brought the car to a halt when another shuddering cramp crippled me. Sorcha held me until the pain passed.

"They aren't too close," she muttered to Mum. "This is good. Salbutamol should do the trick."

"I don't have asthma," I wheezed through the pain, wondering if she had diagnosed me with something I didn't even know I had.

Sorcha laughed. "Good memory. While I use salbutamol for asthma, it also slows contractions of the uterus. It will buy us some time."

"For Gio to get here?" If they could slow this down and he was already on his way back, I was hopeful he would make it. How long did labor take?

She saw the hope in my eyes as she supported me to walk. "For your sake, I hope so, but mainly as these bubbas are early. We need to prep you for a cesarean.

CHAPTER 8

I am not keen on you delivering naturally, especially twins, after the injuries you sustained."

She meant it factually, but I cringed, seeing my reflection in the glassed wall in the foyer to the hospital. The first time I had seen myself properly after my abduction had been in that mirror, and I flinched involuntarily. Mum felt the shudder.

"There is nothing to be afraid of," she announced. "Your aunt has delivered hundreds of children, including some of your siblings and Illy's girls, too."

I nodded, appreciating the confidence, but my heart was in my mouth. Giving birth wasn't what was paralyzing me, although that great unknown was terrifying enough. Gio was in Caspian, or had been. Goodness knew where he was now. Suddenly, irrational anger bubbled past the ball of anxiety in my chest. He was off seeking revenge for something that happened well over a year ago, while I was here, enduring this alone. My skin grew hot, and I tried to tamp down the volcano threatening to erupt. *How fucking dare he?* Prickles of heat exploded on my skin. Enormous, in pain, and now alone. *Fucking asshole.* When would I be the priority?

"Let's get you settled." Mum and Sorcha flanked me and steered me through the foyer and past the room where I had recovered last time and into one of the slightly darker, older rooms. This one had been part of the original clinic, not the extension that was built to accommodate the new equipment and burgeoning community.

"I know these rooms are older, but they are for a single patient, have a little more space, and you will have privacy back here," Mum announced. Together, they lowered me onto the bed, and Mum disappeared to wash her hands and check that Jorja had taken over from Kat as the on-duty doctor while Sorcha hooked me up to the blood pressure cuff. There was no way either of them would leave me until the babies were born.

"Goodness, your blood pressure is high," she muttered as she released the pressure.

"Are you surprised?" I snapped, immediately remorseful. I hadn't meant to sound venomous. Sorcha didn't appear to notice.

"It isn't good, Caitlin, especially at this stage. Are you worried about giving birth?"

"Not as much as I am about being back here and alone," I admitted, a touch gentler.

She nodded, making eye contact as she unwrapped the black fabric strap from my upper arm, the ripping sound reminding me of her doing this to me a year ago.

"Caitlin, we are here. No harm will come to you or these children while I still have breath. Do you understand me?"

Aunt Sorcha was the complete opposite of my father. Allegedly, like her own mother, she was forceful and bossy. She rubbed people up the wrong way, and more than once, we had argued heatedly, but right now, I appreciated her domineering manner. She made it clear she was in control, and that was reassuring.

"And," she continued, "Illy will get your recalcitrant husband back here if she needs to drag him by his ear. Trust me. Not much gets between Illyria and a goal."

The grin broke through my concern. I knew this to be true. While tiny in stature, Illy was a force of nature. She got stuff done, either through cajoling, ordering, or harassing people into doing what she wanted.

CHAPTER 8

"Argh," I groaned as the pain struck again, and Sorcha palpated my stomach. "I need the ultrasound," she muttered. "I can't tell what is going on with the two of them. It is a jumble of limbs. Illyria will get him here. Now let's get you hooked up."

Several hours later, the intravenous drugs dripping through the clear tube into my arm had slowed the contractions until, finally, they ceased, leaving me cooling my jets, lying in a hospital bed, even more frustrated and snapping at everyone who came near.

"Can I go home, Mum?" I begged. "I have nothing to do here, and I am bored stupid. I can feel my brain rotting. Please let me do something."

"You know you can't, sweetheart," she said, lifting my hand and checking my blood pressure for the millionth time. "Your blood pressure is too high, and your membranes have ruptured, so now we need to keep you under observation, mainly for infection. You can't go home now until after they are born."

"Does that mean the babies are still coming today?" I asked, terrified. I had no idea how far away Giovanni was and desperately wanted him here, no matter how cranky I was that he had disappeared on his harebrained mission of revenge.

"Not necessarily. This is what we call a preterm, prelabor rupture of membranes. Usually this means they will be born within a week, but your babies will still be premature. That said, they are a multiple birth, so they tend to come early."

"Is there anything else you can do to give me more time? I need more time." Mum knew what I meant. Time for Gio to get home. Time for me to prepare for my life changing in a matter of minutes. There would never be enough time.

"I am going to give you a steroid injection."

"Why?"

"In this instance, steroids can help to reduce the seriousness of breathing difficulties for your babies. They can also help reduce the likelihood of other complications from being born early. But as they take about twenty-four hours to be effective, we will do everything we can to ensure that you will not meet your children today."

As much as I desperately wanted to no longer be the size of a barn, and I dreaded the thought of spending more days lying helplessly in this clinic, I also was not prepared to go through this, especially not alone. Clenching my fists so tightly my fingernails dug into my palms, I uttered the only acceptable response.

"Okay."

"We will get him here, Catie."

Over the course of the evening, Mum, Sorcha, and Katrin brought me books and snacks, but nothing held my attention. They took it in turns to stay with me and talk, asking me about Canada and other places I had been while the others slept in the small on-call room or caught up on paperwork.

"I'm not dying," I snapped at Kat as I paced around the tiny room, dragging a metal frame on wheels hooked up to my IV. "Surely one prison guard is enough."

Kat raised her eyebrows. "Prison? You don't think that the Chief is an important patient?"

"You know, I'm not really..."

"Yes, you are," Illy announced as she breezed in. "Besides, these babies are special. We need to save

CHAPTER 8

the umbilical cord for stem cells, and you need special care."

"I'm *fine*," I jumped down her throat, making her grin at my frustration. All I had done was read and walk the halls, trying to avoid people. I was so freaking bored I was ready to kill someone. "Did you bring me some work?" I asked hopefully.

"I can take over if you like," Illy advised Kat, although it wasn't presented as an option.

"If you don't mind being constantly whinged at by an ungrateful bitch of a patient," Kat grumbled, standing and assessing me as I waddled in bare feet across the gray linoleum floor.

"I don't whinge!" I fired back. Despite her being my sister and loving her dearly, I knew Katrin was a pain in the ass. Bossy, opinionated, and exactly like Mum and Sorcha. No wonder they all worked together so well. She softened but only slightly.

"I know you are scared, Catie, but you have nothing to be worried about."

Being her sister, my instinct was to needle her, to fire back and ask her to please bestow upon me her vast personal experience of giving birth. But my voice wavered as I placed my hands on the bed to rest my hips, and I responded more honestly than I usually would.

"What if I don't make it? What if the babies don't? I couldn't save my last one. What makes you think I can do it this time?"

Illy was beside me in a shot, her arm across my back, supporting me. "Nothing will happen to you or these children, do you hear? They are my grandchildren, and I forbid it!" Her tone was abrupt, and that made me laugh past the welling tears. Only Illy could think she could stave off death by commanding it.

"I need to lie down." I groaned as the laughter made my hips clench.

"What is it?" Kat asked instantly, concern rising.

"My hips are killing me," I admitted, grateful for the relief as they helped me to lie back against the pillows.

"How long has this been going on?" Kat snapped, and I looked at her fearfully, my eyebrows reaching my hairline.

"Why?"

"Just answer the bloody question!"

"A few weeks. But it has been getting worse for a few days," I mumbled, not really wanting her to hear and recoiling as I heard the sharp intake of breath. "It hurts to walk, and I can't sleep. But it is just my size," I wheezed, feeling foolish.

"Fuck, Caitlin, for an intelligent woman, you are a grade A idiot. I have never met such a fucknuckle in all my life. Why didn't you say something, you enormous buffoon? All your bloody life, you have taken unnecessary risks and engaged in pure idiocy. But this time might take the cake, even for you. Risking your babies and your own health!"

"Katrin," Illy growled as Kat's tirade continued but was slightly less heated. Kat was fuming, muttering under her breath about my childhood escapades as she flicked through my medical notes, the sister momentarily overtaking the doctor.

"Can you x-ray?" Illy asked, pulling Kat's attention away from me. Frustration had darkened her face, and she glanced at me, her lips pursed.

CHAPTER 8

"I'd rather not. The radiation exposure is comparatively small, but they are babies, and my preference would be none. An MRI is safer. We can..."

"No!" The word shot out of my mouth before I thought it. The MRI had been excruciating with all my wounds a year ago. "I can't. Not again."

Illy's hand gripped mine, and she looked up at Kat. "No MRI." Her words were quiet, almost whispered, but a command, nonetheless.

"Let me wake Mum. She is the ortho." Katrin, still cursing me under her breath, slipped out the door, but I noticed she had made no promise.

Soon, the full team had assembled in my room, arguing about the best course of action. Mum was pushing for a conservative approach. Sorcha and Kat vehemently wanted to conduct an MRI to find the source of my hip pain. I flatly refused an MRI, and Illy tried to negotiate, but five strong-willed women were challenging, even for her. Finally, confined to bed, with ongoing pain relief and salbutamol to slow the contractions, was what the team prescribed, which made me even more agitated. Basically, lie here and do nothing. Now my stress levels were sky high, worried sick about my babies, in pain, and frustrated as hell that they had trapped me in a bed again.

Illy stayed with me for the remaining daylight hours, talking to me about projects and community issues. She even pretended to take notes, but I knew she didn't need my help. I appreciated the distraction but became increasingly anxious as the day passed. Lying still was impossible, and rolling over was difficult and painful. Frustration grew, making me want to shake someone until their teeth rattled.

As much as people trying to keep me entertained all day frustrated me, I soon learned that night was worse, lying on an uncomfortable metal hospital bed with a crackly, thin mattress and trying to sleep in a chilly, sterile room. I knew Mum or one of the others were only a yell away, but I hated the thought of disturbing them from their slumber. Just because I couldn't sleep didn't mean they shouldn't. For the millionth time, I needed to piss. Fuck these fluids running through me. It was bad enough being pregnant and needing to go every half hour. Now the pressure on my bladder was incessant, and I could only release a few drops at a time.

Sighing with exasperation, I unhooked the blood pressure cuff and swung my legs, which I hadn't seen properly in weeks, off the bed and held on to the IV pole as I recovered my balance. I hated lying in bed for so long. It brought back painful memories of the weeks of the lengthy recovery I had endured, alone, mourning the loss of my child. Shaking my head to dispel the images of my fractures and bruising, I padded off to the toilet, pushing the mobile IV pole ahead of me, forcing my enormous belly past the bathroom door. "I am an elephant crossed with a whale," I grumbled as I pushed it shut, pointlessly, but still feeling the need for some privacy. Everything hurt. My feet were swollen, my hands looked like plates of meat, and my back was killing me.

As I stood to wash my hands, I looked in the mirror. Great. To top it all off, I looked like a sickly Victorian child dying of some obscure disease. Greasy, messy hair and pallid complexion. Maybe it was better that Gio didn't see me like this. He might run a mile. The explosion of pain was so sudden that I was doubled

CHAPTER 8

up and on the floor before I even processed what had happened. Lying there, I tried to catch my breath, the ripping sensation so fierce I knew I would split in two. The cries broke from my lips as I hugged my belly, willing the pain to stop. I blessed the cold tile floor against my cheek, the only salve against the torture of being dissected. Unable to form words, I lay there, panting, trying to focus my brain into formulating a plan. Another cry forced itself past my lips as more surges threatened to mutilate me from the inside.

A draft nudged my upturned cheek as the door opened, and I heard Mum gasp as she saw me on the floor. In a second, she was on her knees beside me and didn't even ask what had happened, not that I could have strung the words together.

Time passed in that peculiar way it does when you can't focus. The next thing I knew, the lights were on, and everyone was there. My brain was fogged, and I couldn't process the whir of people, equipment, and noise. I felt myself being lifted onto a bed, but not my bed, as they wheeled me into another room.

"No," I gasped. "Not yet."

"Giovanni is coming," Mum promised as she clattered around beside me, checking equipment on a metal tray. "They are at the airport in Stornoway. It was what I was coming to tell you. Illy is heading there now. He will be here soon, Catie. But we can't wait."

They stripped me of my clothes, and I was hastily thrust into a crisp, white, open-backed robe. It scratched horribly across my chest, but I had no mind for the itching or the lack of dignity in front of my mother, aunt, and sister. Sorcha stretched out my hand, and I flinched as she perforated the vein. It felt like a roofing nail being rammed in.

"Sorry," she muttered as she heard me gasp. "It is a larger gauge than I would like, but I am not taking any chances."

Mum placed the mask over my face, smiling reassuringly. "It won't be long now. When you wake, you will meet your children."

My head rolled back against the crunchy hospital pillow as I inhaled the acrid smelling gas. My eyes closed, and I felt the pull of the weighted vapor dragging me under. Just as the world began to go black at the edges, I heard the commotion in the doorway. Someone lifted the mask, and as I blinked hard to dispel the fog, I made out the shape of Gio racing toward me. I wanted to bellow at him, make him understand the trauma he had put me through, abandoning me. Making me relive the loss of Stella alone. But the words wouldn't come. Instead, tears filled my eyes as he gripped my hand, squeezing my fingers tightly.

"We can't wait," Mum told him hurriedly. "No time for an epidural. We need to use a general. Hold her hand and tell her you love her. When she wakes, she will meet your children."

"*Amore mio*," he murmured in my ear. "I am so proud of you. Soon, my love, soon we will meet our children. I am here. I won't leave you."

Mum nodded at him, and he looked up at her, affirming, as she placed the mask over my face. His stressed, unshaven face was the last thing I saw as the fog crept in from the edges, still feeling his warm, solid hand squeezing mine.

CHAPTER 9

SUNLIGHT STREAMING THROUGH THE windows woke me, and it took me a moment to recall where I was. My hands instinctively traveled to my stomach and pressed through the scratchy white gown. Puffy and fat, but soft. No longer filled with life. My eyes sprang wide, fearful. As the fog cleared, I took in the room and saw they had moved another single bed alongside mine. Gio was asleep, his dark hair spread across the white pillow in line with me. He cradled a white blanket-wrapped bundle in each arm, kept safe by the raised metal railings of the bed. He hadn't shaved. Quietly, I tried to shift positions so I didn't wake him but couldn't sit, the pain making me gasp aloud. He was awake in a shot, careful not to wake the sleeping babies.

"Two?" I whispered, barely able to believe it. "Boys or girls?"

"We have two daughters." Gio beamed at me. "Two beautiful little girls."

"Are they okay? They are a little early."

"They are small, but they are perfect, my love. Both of our daughters are healthy. You did a wonderful job."

I leaned back into the pillows. *They are well. I am alive.*

"Illy is going to think we copied her." I smiled at him.

"I think everyone is so pleased to have you all safe that they wouldn't mind if you had stolen them."

"Did they collect the stem cells?" I asked, knowing how crucial their cord was to inoculate people.

"They did. But that isn't important now."

"Can I hold one?" I whispered, not wanting to disturb the three of them but longing to hold my daughters.

Gio gingerly sat up in his bed and handed one girl over to me, then lowered the barriers on both beds with his free hand. With the other child still nestled in the crook of his arm, he reached over and held my free hand and gazed adoringly at me.

"We are parents. Can you believe it?"

"Not really," I admitted. "It all feels a little surreal, to be honest. What happened?"

"Your Mum said you collapsed."

I nodded, trying to remember. "Did they say why?"

"Nothing obvious, but your pelvic fracture was quite severe, so it was likely just pain emanating from that."

"Did it break again?" I asked quickly, fearful of another long rehabilitation process.

"No. But it hasn't been that long, all things considered. Some of the pregnancy hormones soften muscles, too. But you are fine. The girls are fine."

A shadow cast across the room, and I saw Mum standing in the doorway.

CHAPTER 9

"I need to check you over. Then your father is outside, dying to meet his granddaughters if you could tolerate a visitor." Mum gently extracted the sleeping baby from my arms and gazed at her before handing her back to her father. Gio looked so natural with children in his arms, and I couldn't help but smile at the image of his larger dark head gazing down over the smaller dark heads, two tiny versions of himself.

Mum checked my cesarean wound and assisted me to the bathroom to remove the catheter. Moving around after abdominal surgery was as painful as I recalled from last time. But I knew the sooner I got moving, the better, and I was desperate to get out of there.

"Do you mind if I let your father in?" Mum asked when we were safely alone in the bathroom as she removed all the tubes. "He has been here since dawn, and he is driving me mad."

"Could you please brush my hair and make me look semi-presentable first?"

"Of course."

As Dad walked through the door of the room, his face lit like a storm had passed and sunshine was beaming for the first time in years. I settled back onto my pillows, trying to find a comfortable position.

"Caitlin, my darling girl." His face was beaming with pride. He kissed me on the forehead, and I closed my eyes, recalling how safe that had made me feel as a child. That simple gesture, a kiss on the forehead, made everything right with the world.

"Have you met your granddaughters?" I whispered, not wanting to wake them.

Dad lifted the baby offered to him by Giovanni and sighed contentedly as he stared down into the tiny face screwed up in the blanket. Mum took the other and stood beside him, looking the picture of grandparental bliss. Now that he was freed of his burden, Gio wriggled closer to me, kissing me on the cheek, his beard scratching my skin.

"Thank you, *amore mio*," he whispered. "Thank you for this wonderful gift. More than anything, I wish my parents were here to see this."

With Gio resting his head beside mine on the pillow, immense relief swept through me. Our children were alive. Unlike my previous failure, I had done my job this time and kept them safe. Gio was glowing with pride, watching my parents like a hawk. He was tired but so proud.

Within the hour, Illy had arrived with Carmelo, Sorcha, and Katrin. It felt like my entire family was here, and I suppressed the anxiety of having so many of them here, crowded into this tiny space.

"Have you decided on names?" Kat asked, perched on the end of my bed, looking up from the niece in her arms.

Gio and I hadn't had time to finalize names, but we had discussed it at length. We had planned to make our ultimate choice in the few weeks we were here, but then he had left, and the ladies had made their arrival early.

"We were thinking," I said, then paused, looking at him for confirmation. He gave it, a smile and a tiny nod. "Please meet Aurora Sally Freyja, and Khione Stephanie Illyria."

"Beautiful," Dad murmured.

"Explain," Kat whispered, not looking up from gazing lovingly at her niece.

CHAPTER 9

"Aurora, our firstborn, is the Roman Goddess of the dawn and named after the night we saw the aurora here," Gio explained but not going into any more detail. The night where I first started to believe we might find our way back to each other after our loss. But also as a tribute to Stella and this fresh start we had been given. Stella, meaning star, handed over the reins to Aurora, the dawn, each morning.

Katrin nodded but didn't look up.

Gio continued with his explanation. "Sally is a hybrid of Summer and Ally, without whom Caitlin wouldn't be here, and to whom we are eternally grateful. Freyja, well, that is fairly obvious. We wanted to honor their grandmothers, all of them strong, intelligent women. As for that little lady you are holding, Khione is the Greek goddess of snow, and as special children, it is our deepest wish that one day, because of them, we may all get to experience snow. For us, snow is a symbol of the future, something that is unique, like every snowflake, but that no person has enjoyed for over thirty years. Stephanie is in remembrance of my mother, and Illyria as their third grandmother, but again, as without her, my darling wife would not be alive."

"Welcome to the world, Miss Khione," Katrin whispered as she softly laid a kiss on the tiny pink nose. "You and your sister will be the most loved little ladies in the world."

Two days later, thoroughly irritated at being poked and prodded post-surgery, and after spending many hours struggling to learn to feed twins, we took our ladies home. An unexpected challenge was constantly needing to pronounce Khione's name.

"Kee-ohh-nee," I patiently explained for the seventeenth time, this time to Isla and Fraser. "The Greek goddess of snow. Though we are thinking we will call her Khi, and Aurora will be Rori."

"Key?" Isla barely heard as she cooed and sighed over the baby in her arms. I couldn't even tell which one she was holding from where I sat on the sofa. Everyone wanted to meet them, and they tolerated being passed from person to person happily, barely waking up.

"Don't get too used to it," Mum warned as we watched Isla and Fraser swap. "They sleep a lot in the first few weeks, then, not so much. You need to practice sleeping when they do. You will be up and down during the night. Now I have a favor to ask. While Giovanni is here, do you mind if we spend some time using him in the clinic? I know he wants to specialize in pediatrics, and while Nasir is the best choice, your aunt Sorcha is also exceptionally good with children."

"He would love that," I admitted, pulling my attention away from my sleeping bundles as Isla and Fraser bemoaned their grandchildren getting older and no new babies on the horizon.

"Are you sure you are okay to have him away from you? You aren't exactly mobile yet. You know the rule: no lifting anything heavier than your baby. That is particularly important for you."

"I'll be fine. Dad will be around, and he knows what to do. Carmelo, too. You heard he is coming with us back to Canada? He wants to be their nanny. Though I do wonder if a few weeks caring for them here

CHAPTER 9

won't scare him off. It isn't like he ever had children of his own."

"I heard. Have you thought about when you will go? You can't leave for at least six weeks, not after your surgery. Honestly, I would suggest twelve weeks is a safer time to travel."

"Not wanting to lose them so soon?"

Mum grinned, looking away from Isla and back to me. "That obvious, is it? They grow so quickly. It could be months before I see them again. I want to spend as much time as I can with them while they are here."

"We'll see, Mum. Maybe eight or so? When I go back, I will be expected to work, even if it is part-time. We both know that part-time work really means a full-time job squashed into part-time hours. Before I leave, I want to get the hang of feeding, changing, bathing, and even dressing them. I had no idea dressing a wriggling baby was so difficult. Not to mention washing two sets of nappies a hundred times a day."

"If Carmelo can't do it alone, Illy will get you some help with that when you get back to Canada. Feeding, you alone need to do, but you can get help with the rest. You should accept any help offered to you, Caitlin. It is a lot of work raising a child, and two are more than double the work. I know how stubborn you are and how desperately you want to do it all yourself, but you can't. No one can. Accept the offers of help: meals, cleaning, watching the girls while you sleep. Don't be too proud to say thank you and accept. Even in the old world, they used to say that it takes a village to raise a child. It's true."

"Is it wrong of me to admit that I don't enjoy changing nappies?" I quipped, copping a whiff of something.

Mum laughed as Isla mournfully handed over the baby she was holding to Dad for changing. "None of us do, darling. After all, I changed yours enough times, and it never gets more pleasant."

Carmelo and Gio took lessons from Dad on how to care for babies as Mum and I stood back and watched. It fascinated me how relaxed my father was. Nothing fazed him, including being vomited on or being wet on. He knew how to burp them, hold them so their heads were supported, and I learned as much as Gio did. Carmelo took it all in, didn't stop smiling the entire time, and always seemed to have one of the girls in his arms. Having two babies meant Dad had one to demonstrate with and one we could try out our terrible nappy-changing skills on. With so many adults, the only really challenging part was feeding them concurrently. We worked out quickly that one at a time wasn't going to work. The hungry one would scream until the sound echoed around the room, forcing me to adapt.

"Luca was a natural, too," Mum whispered as we watched Dad teaching Carmelo and Gio to bathe the girls. "He just took to it like he always had children, but in fact, Lachlan—you know, Isla and Fraser's son—was the first baby he ever held. His mother was a single parent and couldn't afford college, so he went straight from high school to the army. He didn't know anyone with babies until he came here. Then Xanthe was born, so he learned about raising babies with her. By the time Summer and Allison came along, he knew exactly what to do."

"I wish he could have met his grandchildren," I whispered, feeling a little foolish. "These girls and Rai." Luca had died before I was born, yet Mum and

CHAPTER 9

Illy had kept him alive for us through stories and anecdotes.

"Goodness, he would have spoiled them." Mum chuckled. "Summer and Ally used to twist him around their tiny fingers. They manipulated him, and he didn't care. He was besotted with those girls. But he is alive in you, Caitlin, and in those girls. It is so special that Carmelo can be here for them now. The half-brother Luca never knew he had."

"How do you think he would feel about him being with Illy?" I asked and immediately regretted it. Illy's private life was none of my business. Mum took a moment to reply.

"He would have loathed her to be with any other man. Goodness, he loved her more than he loved life itself. But he also wouldn't want her to be lonely. In time, I think he would approve of Carmelo. After he put him through his paces, that is. Tortured him. You always knew where you stood with Luca."

"Much like you," I teased.

"There was a reason we were such good friends. Now the girls are ready for a nap. We can settle them. Get some rest."

CHAPTER 10

"HOW ARE YOU ADAPTING to life as a parent?" Mum asked me over breakfast. I sipped at my green tea, grimacing at the unfamiliar taste. I missed coffee but accepted that, while I was still feeding the girls, I didn't want to pass caffeine through my milk to them. They had mixed up their days and nights and regularly spent hours awake overnight and slept for hours during the day. I detected the interrogative tone.

"Why?"

"Nasir has scheduled a medical conference in France. It is for ten days with a variety of specialties. Pediatrics and oncology, and I am presenting a session on orthopedics. I want to use Charlie as a case study, so if you wouldn't mind, I would love to take your original sketches to show them the process you worked through and what you were trying to achieve. Sorcha is also attending to speak about women's health, which I know the underwater communities are really keen on as they are so limited with space and want contraceptive options. Katrin is coming as well, but more as a learner. But if you can do without

CHAPTER 10

Gio, it would be highly beneficial for his career. But Jorja will stay here. Hamish, too. We can't leave the community with no medical staff. Not that you need any medical treatment," she hurried to say.

My heart sank. Truthfully, I didn't want to be away from him for a fortnight. The girls were so small, only four and a half weeks, and needed me all the time. But equally, I would never want to do anything to impede his professional development. "He hasn't mentioned it, but he would love to go," I said.

"I'm not convinced. He won't want to leave you and the girls. He is devoted to them."

I smiled. He was. Every waking minute, he had one of them in his arms, carrying them around the garden in the slings Kendra had made, singing to them in Italian, or pointing out animals, plants, and objects, naming them in English and Italian. Regardless, he had done so much to support me in my career. I was never going to impede his.

"There is a way you can get him to go." I turned my attention back to Mum.

"How?"

"You ask him to present a case study on Gianni. Likely, none of the other communities have seen muscular dystrophy before, and they would be interested. I can give him my designs."

"That is a brilliant idea," Mum admitted, sipping her steaming coffee.

"Please, can I have a sip?" I begged. "This tastes like a cup of brewed grass."

Mum smirked and pushed the mug toward me. "Don't tell him I let you drink that. You are supposed to be on green tea for the *antioxidants*." She mimicked Sorcha's forceful voice.

The heavenly scent of freshly roasted beans reached me first, and I closed my eyes in bliss at the first taste of the rich flavor, rolling it around on my tongue before swallowing. I pushed the mug back before I was tempted to down the entire mug.

"Thank you," I breathed. "Ask him to present and explain how important it is for people to know what to look for in their children. He will go. I will make sure he accepts."

"He is one of the good ones, Catie," Mum said in a low voice, barely a whisper.

"What do you mean?"

"What he did, going to Caspian. When I saw that video, I would have done it myself without hesitation. Only I would have detonated without a second thought."

"Was it so bad?"

"Illy didn't tell you?"

"She said it was graphic, and they focused on my face. She also told me what Viktor did in the end."

A dark cloud rolled across Mum's face. "Honestly, I thought we had left such behaviors behind in the old world. It makes me sick to think that such men still exist. In the past thirty years, women and men have finally taken equal footing. Everyone who was chosen was selected for their skill. There is no role, no task, that is purely male or female. We have come a long way, and then I see something like that, and it sets us back decades."

"Illy said it made you physically sick."

Mum's cool demeanor cracked just for a second before she regained control. "You are my baby, Caitlin, always will be. If Viktor had been in front of me, I would have torn his balls off, rammed them down his

CHAPTER 10

throat, and smiled while he choked. Now that you are a mother, you will understand. The mother lioness's instinct is strong. Someone threatens your babies, no matter how old they are, you would go into battle for them. I was pleased to see Giovanni would do that for you. I always knew Jake would. He has his priorities sorted. Carmelo was a surprise, but he comes from the same blood as Luca. Luca would have been on the first flight out if he had seen what they had done to one of his own."

"Not Dad?" I asked.

"Your father is different. It would destroy him if he knew. He knows the recording exists, of course, but not the details. And I will never tell him, Caitlin. You can't either. He isn't weak, never make that mistake, but he processes so deeply. It would eat at him that he couldn't protect you. It is best if he doesn't know the extent of it. So," Mum stood, looking down at me, "we head off to France next week for a fortnight. By the time we get back, the girls will be nearly seven weeks, although being premature, they aren't as developed as a full-term baby."

"Do you want me to go, Mum? You want your home back?"

"No!" The vehemence of her reply took me by surprise, and I jumped, spilling a little of my revolting dirt tea. "I want you to stay as long as you want. You are welcome to stay permanently. Your father and I love having you here, having babies under the roof again. We missed it. Babies grow so fast, Catie. Enjoy it. I know it is hard when they don't sleep and vomit everywhere, but this time is so short. Besides, they are our granddaughters. We won't get to see you again for a while. I want to cherish this time."

"What about Illy and Carmelo? Surely, she wants her home back. Her bedroom. We sort of arrived and took over."

"She is returning with you, and I love having her so close again. Late-night chats. I have missed her. Did you hear she and Carmelo are heading off next week to visit some of the local communities: Clava, Orkney, Shetlands, Newgrange, and the isolated ones on the mainland?"

"No, I didn't know. Just as well Sera, Matt, and Rai aren't here, then. She would never want to leave," I said.

"That was one of her deciding factors. When Rai is well enough to travel, she will be back, so it made sense to move up her travels. So it will just be you and Dad, although we are still expecting Seraphine and Matt soon. Are you sure you will be okay?"

"We will be fine. Dad is so wonderful with the girls. I am surprised you didn't have more."

"We had five. That was enough. Nine if you count Illy's brood. There were always kids running around, making a mess, bickering, and needing something."

I addressed the real topic we were skirting around. "You know we need to return to Canada at some point."

"You could do your job from here," she breathed, almost inaudibly, looking out the window. "Illy did for a long time."

"I'm sorry, Mum. I took your best friend, didn't I?"

"No, you took my daughter. Now you will take my grandchildren and my best friend. You are lucky I love you so much."

Throwing my arms around her neck, I pulled her close. "Mum, you and Dad gave me such a wonderful childhood. You were always there for us. Taught us to be strong and stand up for what we believe in.

CHAPTER 10

You showed us how to help others. That is what I want to do: make a difference. It isn't forever. I will come home."

"That is the first time I have heard you refer to Lewis as home for a long time."

"I guess because it hasn't been until now. I went to Newgrange at seventeen. Then Italy, and now Canada. But in my bones, maybe because I am a mother now, I know this is my home. One day, I will return to live."

"How does Giovanni feel about that?"

"He loves it here more than I do," I admitted. "His mother, Stephanie, was English. She told him wonderful stories of green meadows and forests when he was a child. Described snow and wind. The sights and smells. Things residents in those underwater communities have never experienced. He always dreamed of it. Now he is here."

"You know he would follow you anywhere, Caitlin."

Opening the back door, Dad and Carmelo saved me from answering.

"Think about it. Staying here," she added.

"I will."

111

CHAPTER 11

"YOU'RE HOME! I MISSED you!" I flung myself into his arms.

"How are my girls?" he asked animatedly, looking around the room. I pulled back from his embrace.

"Oh, so I play second fiddle now, do I? You got the children you desperately wanted, and now I take a back seat," I teased.

"Never. You are all my girls. I have missed you all more than I thought possible."

A startled cry rose from the cot, and Gio was beside them in a shot, looking up at me in confusion.

"You sleep them together? Don't they wake each other?"

"Dad and I did some trials, and they sleep better, longer that is, when they have each other. But yes, when one wakes, she wakes her sister. But overall, I get more sleep, so we figured it was worth it."

"I didn't sleep well without you," he whispered, kissing my neck after lifting Khione and kissing her cheeks and forehead. "It was so strange to sleep alone and not have someone to hold in the night."

CHAPTER 11

I didn't have the heart to tell him that once Dad and I had worked out that Aurora and Khione slept better together, I hadn't slept this well in weeks.

"I missed you," I said sincerely, hoping he wouldn't notice that I hadn't replicated his comment, but he was too fascinated with his daughter.

"She is huge! She is doubled in weight. When did this happen?"

"You have been gone two and a half weeks," I berated him. "They can't have grown that much."

Mum slipped into the room, not waiting to be invited. I handed Aurora to her.

"She has grown so much!" Mum exclaimed. "I feel like I have missed months, not weeks."

Gio flashed me an "I told you so" look behind Mum as she lifted Aurora.

"Quick cuddle, and then they need feeding," I advised.

"How is all that going?" Mum asked, not looking up. Mum typically had a cool, assessing look, but now, she was glowing as she beamed at her granddaughter, making silly faces to get her to respond. For a moment, I wondered if she had ever looked at me like that, especially as she didn't plan me.

"Dad and I muddled through." Knowing Gio's guilt at leaving, I didn't want them to feel like they had missed out, but the truth was Dad and I had thoroughly enjoyed this time with just the two of us. Illy and Carmelo had departed the same day, chaperoned by Jake, and were due back tomorrow. Di and Sorcha were busy with Mei and Kendra, now returned from six months of professional learning on August Island. With no one else around, Dad and I had fallen into a relaxed routine. He had stayed in Alasdair's old room so he could hear us in the night if he was needed. Dad was simply wonderful. I secretly wished it was him coming to Canada with me. Dad had been attuned to the girls' needs from the day they came home, knowing when they needed to sleep, to feed. He was always there but never in our faces. He was available to us around the clock, not going to work, but pottering away in his greenhouses when they were asleep and bringing me tea and snacks, and copious bottles of water. I had no idea I would be so thirsty producing milk for two hungry little ladies. But Dad was never pushy or demanding. I knew he was only a call away, but I was finally able to spend time with these babies. I lost hours watching them, comparing them, seeing how they were alike. Their tiny differences. Finally enjoying their awake time, setting up mobiles and toys. For the first time, I felt like their mother. We had bonded somehow. My priorities had shifted. Without me being called to meetings or needing to think about meals or laundry, they had become my sole focus, and I felt more relaxed than I had in months.

"You are finally in a routine," she said, not really directed at me. "They are healthy, putting on weight. You look rested. I am pleased, Caitlin. Most mothers don't hit their stride this early. We need to ensure you get your rest and minimize disruptions to your sleep. That is critical if you are to continue to care for them both and take on work." She flashed a warning at Gio, who didn't notice, as obsessed as he was with Khione, holding her aloft and kissing the small, exposed tummy. She was beaming at him, her mouth shaped into an 'O' as he smiled at her.

"Her eyes are turning green," he noted. "Like yours."

CHAPTER 11

"They are. But Aurora's are brown, like yours."

"I told you in the hospital they are fraternal," Mum noted, moving Aurora onto her shoulder and swaying with her.

"Trust you to make it medical, Mum."

"Sorry. It was just an observation."

"How was the conference?"

"Your husband here was quite the hit."

Raising my eyebrows at Gio, I wondered if the French girls had been throwing themselves at him again. "Really."

Mum was sharp. She saw where my brain had gone and continued, "He gave his presentation on Gianni, and we co-presented the case study on Charlie. It piqued lots of interest. You may end up with a side business in making braces and orthopedic equipment if you ever decide to relinquish your role as Chief. It turns out there are a few other children with developmental and skeletal issues that we never knew about."

"With all that spare time I have," I teased.

"It won't take long before these young ladies are independent."

My eyebrows hit my hairline. "Mum! They are only seven weeks old! Putting them out to work already, are you?"

"Think about it. Between your skills and Gio's medical knowledge, you could help a lot of children and improve their quality of life."

"I tried to tell my colleagues that it was your design," Gio explained.

"It was a team effort."

115

"Speaking of teams, how about you feed these little cherubs, and then Dad and I will take them for a walk, leaving you two to catch up?" Mum asked.

"Don't you want..." I started to say before Gio's firm voice interrupted me.

"That would be wonderful. Thank you."

As we curled up on the bed, finally child-free, a ruckus outside pulled my attention away from my husband.

"What now?" I grumbled, pleased to finally have him all to myself.

Gio lifted his head to peer out the window. "It's Carmelo and Illyria," he advised, and my heart sank. It wasn't that I was unhappy that they were home, I loved them both dearly, but her return signaled that my brief holiday had come to an end. Without meaning to disturb me, Illy felt the need to keep me in the loop with work matters, what issues had arisen, and the various trade deals. She told me about her meetings and calls, so the catch-up wouldn't be so great when I returned to work. With her gone, I had two weeks of being able to focus on my children and myself. Her return meant the vacation was over.

"Do you want to go and help them?" I asked.

"No, your parents are there."

"But they have the girls."

"No." Gio strained to see out the window from the bed. "Actually, Illy and Carmelo have the girls, your father is carrying the bags and your mother ... your mother and Illyria appear to be discussing something."

"Of course they are. Me, at a guess."

"You?"

"Specifically, when we will return to Canada."

"Ahh. Why? Do you want to go soon?"

CHAPTER 11

"No," I confessed. "I am enjoying our time here."

"Well, let's enjoy this time even more," he rumbled into my ear, rolling me over to face the wall and curling up behind me. "Close your eyes. I want to hold you while we sleep."

CHAPTER 12

THE FAMILIAR SOUND STARTLED me from sleep. Already, I was used to being woken, but it didn't mean I liked it.

"Do you want some help?" Gio groaned, feeling me roll out of bed, not wanting to wake the rest of the house.

"No." I sighed, pausing at the edge of the bed, still trying to stop my head from spinning. "You haven't been home long. Get some sleep. I can manage." It didn't feel necessary to tell him that sometimes when I pushed past the bone-deep weariness and nauseousness that came with being woken rapidly, I enjoyed sitting in the large armchair in the dark. Illy regularly told me how Luca had adored that chair. Being a tall warrior of a man, he had struggled to find one large enough to accommodate him. Back when the settlers used to travel across to the mainland to source supplies, he had brought it back, struggling to transfer it from the dock at Stornoway Harbor to their home at Roseglen. Illy had used it to feed her twins, then the two babies he never met, Alasdair and Seraphine. This

CHAPTER 12

chair had sat in her bedroom since she had Alasdair. Now it was my turn. As I settled in, it was comforting to know that he was watching over me as I fed my babies in the dark. They were faster to feed now but took time to settle again. When it was just Dad and me, it didn't bother me so much. Our days had been blissfully chilled, eating when we were hungry and sleeping when the girls did. Now the pressure had returned, and I was feeling the need to conform to a standard daily routine as Gio and Mum would be going to work, and I felt guilty about disturbing them.

Juggling one in each arm, I maneuvered them as gently as I could to lie beside each other, yawning and wriggling in their wraps. As I stood over the cot, patting them rhythmically, I stared out the window, through the clear dome to the twinkling night sky. The view of the sky was different from here, and with the limited vision from the window, I felt unsettled not being able to see Stella. As their breathing changed and became more rhythmic, I slowed my patting and finally slipped away. The crying started again as soon as I laid my head on the pillow, and I bolted out of bed to avoid them waking Gio. Clutching Rori to my chest, I rocked her steadily, staring out at the night sky, sending a message to her sister to watch over these girls.

After their morning feed and a shower, I followed Mum's order and took a nap. My nocturnal pacing up and down the hallway had alerted Dad, and although I had sent him back to bed, he knew I was exhausted. No matter what I had tried, Rori hadn't settled after her early hours feed, and all night, I had fretted something was wrong. Despite my worry, I couldn't bring myself to wake Mum or Gio. They needed rest, too. The community was relying on them, and they couldn't treat patients with no sleep.

"I'll take her," Mum ordered, plucking the fussing baby from my unresisting arms. "Go. Now."

Gratefully, I handed her over and staggered back to bed. I let my head be engulfed by the cloudlike pillow, the sounds of chatter and chickens outside barely registering as I plummeted into oblivion.

The sound of voices outside woke me, and I groaned, feeling the cotton wool of waking unexpectedly making my head swim. Closing my eyes, I willed sleep to drag me down to its murky depths but bolted upright when I recognized the high, clear voice outside my window. Seraphine. Throwing back the blankets, I hastily pulled on yesterday's clothes and rushed into the hallway to meet her. She saw me coming and hurriedly handed her son to Illy before barreling into my arms.

"I missed you so much!" she squealed and sobbed into my hair as we collided with a thud.

We held each other for the longest time, finally meeting as two mothers. Her tiny frame felt even smaller against mine now that I was engorged with milk. Finally, she pulled back and held me by the upper arms, studying me. "Goodness, you look tired." She laughed. "The sign of a true mother."

"I never get a break." I wilted. "It is always one of them."

"I don't know how you do two. One was enough."

"You might get two next time," I teased. "It runs in the family."

Sera's face blanched. Perplexed by her reaction, I simultaneously noticed that everyone had entered the house behind her, carrying luggage. Summer and

CHAPTER 12

Ally were here, Illy and Carmelo, my parents, and my husband. Everyone ... except Matteo.

"Come and talk to me while I change," I said brightly, not wanting to have her tell her story in public, even though we were all family. The tenseness in her face was barely visible, but I knew her better than anyone. She was holding it in. It wouldn't take long for her to erupt, and it would be best if we were alone. Steering her down the hallway and into her Mum's room, where Gio and I now lived, I called back over my shoulder, "Could someone please make us something to eat? I am starving!"

Illy laughed merrily as she answered, "Something little or something big?"

Gio guffawed behind her, eliminating the need for me to answer. I had always had a healthy appetite, but now that I was feeding twins, I was constantly ravenous and always thirsty.

As soon as the door closed, I hugged my sister tightly to my chest. "What happened? Where is Matt? Do you want me to kill him? I am the Chief; I can do that, you know. It is within my power. Say the word. I will end him."

Despite my joking, I touched a nerve. Sera went limp in my arms and erupted into a flood of tears, and I steered her toward the bed, sitting beside her, my arm around her, apologizing profusely. She was so tiny next to me. Nearly as tall but slimmer in build. I had always felt like a heifer beside her. Now I just feel the overwhelming need to protect her from whatever evil he had inflicted. She was in pain. The red beast rose in me as I waited for her to speak, imagining everything he could possibly have done to distress her so much.

"He met someone else," she sobbed between half gasps, the air not making it to her lungs.

"He *what*?" In the thirty seconds it had taken us to walk up the hallway, I thought perhaps they had fought and he had refused to get on the helicopter. Even sitting here, I was envisioning a difference of opinion. Not that he had cheated.

"He *cheated* on you!"

"Yes! No! Not exactly." Sera's words were broken, stilted. I held her as she cried, letting her catch her breath until she could speak.

"We agreed to take a break so he could work on his mental health. He has been struggling the past few months. So many times, he couldn't get out of bed; the darkness threatened to consume him. Whenever his work needed him, I would cover for him and tell them he was sick. But he withdrew from me and was always lashing out at me."

"Did he hurt you or Rai?"

"No, nothing like that. Just bitter. It was so sudden, I thought he was jealous of Rai or of my success. So I suggested we take a break. He didn't want to. He said no. He just needed some time. I was an idiot. I really thought it was best for him to work on his mental health alone and work out what was really important without me adding pressure. Realize he loves Rai and being a father. I even offered to resign from my role so we could move back to Italy, thinking he was homesick. But then..."

"Then what?" I growled, pleased Matt wasn't here as I suppressed the urge to wrench his still-beating heart from his chest cavity with my bare hands and force-feed it to him.

"He met someone else."

CHAPTER 12

"How *could* he?" I seethed, unable to contain my fury. "You have a child! I was there when he committed to you."

Sera shrugged. "I wasn't enough, clearly."

"When?" The word hissed through my lips like a snake. "When did he do this?"

"About eight weeks ago, just before Summer arrived. I went to ask him if he was still keen to come and see you, Gio, and the babies. Schedule our departure. There was no answer, so I walked into the apartment he was staying in so I could leave him a note. That way, I could avoid confrontation, especially in public. He had moved into the tiny temporary accommodation, the place that Mum usually stays in. It was empty, or so I thought. He should have been at work. The bedroom door was ajar, and I called out, and no one answered. So, I quickly scribbled a note and left it on the table. As I turned to go, I caught sight of him in the oven door. Damn those bloody cleaners. It was like a mirror. I could see the white sheets and his hair against the pillow. And hers. Long black hair, snuggled into his neck."

"Does he know you saw him?"

"He must know. I was lost in my own thoughts and didn't expect anyone to be there in the middle of the day. I was so taken by surprise that I dropped the pen on the floor. It was loud. He would have heard me, seen me stop. Besides, I could see him, so he could see me."

"Oh, Sairs, I am so sorry." My chest physically hurt, seeing her pain. It was one thing to know your husband was with someone else. It was quite another to actually see it.

"I wasn't good enough," she sobbed as my arms wrapped tightly around her. She felt like a frail doll.

"All the things we have done, all the projects, celebrations. Marriage and a child. None of it was enough. To top it all off, she is my assistant! I have to see Izumi every day, be civil to her, while she is fucking my husband!"

"Whaaat! Can't you fire her? Move her on to another role?"

"That isn't the done thing in Japan. Trust me, I would love to relegate her to toilet cleaning duty or worse. But I can't. She has been in that office longer than me and has earned her status. Her father was the *Sōri-Daijin* before me, the leader, so she is respected. Everyone thinks she is so perfect. Porcelain skin, tiny, petite body, and a giggle that makes me want to cram my fist into her gob. She plays up her tiny stature too, acting like she is angelic, like a kitten that needs to be cared for. Beside her, I feel like an elephant."

"Do people know? About her and Matt?"

"Of course not. She is their perfect Izumi-Sama. No one would dare believe she would do such a thing. She has everyone wrapped around her perfectly manicured fingers."

"Sama?"

"It is an honorific term for a high-ranking official."

"Right. How does she treat you?"

Sera scowled, then relented, sighing deeply. "Truthfully, she is lovely. Compliant, respectful, and wonderful at her job. She speaks English and Japanese fluently, and truthfully, I couldn't do the job without her. She is the perfect assistant. Does all the background work and seeks none of the praise or accolades."

"She sounds just like nîpiy. But wow, that situation is tough."

CHAPTER 12

Tears filled Sera's eyes. "It is so hard to maintain poise and act dignified at all times. Japan is so structured, built on politeness and respect. The worst part is that I really like her. She is so good to me. But she slept with my husband!"

"How long have you been holding this in?" I whispered as she completely shattered in my arms.

"Weeks," was the only word I could decipher from the mass of tears.

Stroking her hair and murmuring to her like Dad used to do, I seethed, trying not to let it crack my exterior. *How could he?* Seraphine sobbed so hard I thought she would break in two, but as we sat there, finally, her sorrow exhausted her, her tears dried up, and eventually, she fell asleep in my arms. Safe.

"Get both sides of the story before you pass judgment, Caitlin." The low growling undertone was warning enough when I told Gio what had happened.

"Oh, come on!" I snapped, tiredness and emotion making me sound angrier than I felt, at least with him. If Matteo had been here, I would happily have broken his nose for what he had done to my sister. "He left his wife and child and is fucking someone else. Don't you dare condone his actions and take his side! She is the victim here. Not him."

"I'm just saying you don't know all the facts." The thickening of his voice should have warned me to back off, but anger at him for not siding with my sister had taken hold.

"I do know. He isn't here, is he? Not with his wife and child? Didn't bother to come and visit us, meet his nieces?"

Fury had taken hold, and I could see Gio also fighting to retain control of his temper. Despite his public pride at my success and my leadership, and while we were a team, he still considered himself the dominant partner in our relationship. Behind closed doors, at least.

"Don't pass judgment until we hear both sides. They need our support, not our condemnation," he hissed, his face only centimeters from my own.

Taking a step back, I let fly. "They needed some time apart so he could deal with his depression. Then he goes and fucks someone else. She saw it! What else is there to know? Is that what you would do? Leave me with two children? Abandon me? You tried, didn't you! You left me alone in that fucking hospital while you lived it up on the other side of the planet!" The memory of Gio deserting me to go to Caspian overwhelmed me suddenly and tears formed, breaking through the anger. *Bloody baby hormones*, I raged, fighting to stomp on the emotion before it burst into the world.

His arms folded me into his chest and held me there. "I will never leave you. Even if you want to leave me. I will never let you go."

"You have always said that. But look at me now. Flabby. Greasy hair and dull skin. I look like shit, and you know it. It is all too much. I can't do this."

"You have just had two babies and major abdominal surgery. Now you have had bad news on top. You are exhausted. I heard you up last night, walking up

CHAPTER 12

and down. This is nothing new. All new mothers look tired, Caitlin."

"But I am so gross!" I blubbered, not meaning to make this about me. This was about Sera and Matt. Not me. "Even you don't want me anymore. You want to find someone else, don't you?"

Gio's arms pulled me harder into his chest. I inhaled his scent, intermingled with the smell of fresh trees. His voice rumbled in my ear. "I will always want you. It is killing me to have you lie beside me and not have you. I know we need to wait, but I want you so much, Caitlin, that it hurts."

"I never want to be pregnant again," I sobbed. "Everything hurts. I am tired all the time, and my body isn't my own. There is always some little parasite sucking or grabbing at me."

"No, it is not your body. It is mine," he rumbled, his hands slipping up my back. I pulled away, scowling.

"How can you touch me? I'm disgusting. Bloated, saggy skin and my boobs are huge."

Gio stood and left the room, making me burst into tears again at being abandoned. I was repugnant. Disgusting. Maybe he would find someone else too? I sat on the end of the bed; my head dropped to my chest. I didn't even have the energy to lie down.

A minute later, he returned, firmly closing the door and sliding the bolt.

"Come." He stood at the end of the bed where I sat, wallowing. He held his hand out and pulled me to my feet.

"Wha..."

"No speaking."

Gio pulled me into the bathroom and, again, closed the door. As I stood there, zombified, he stripped off my stained top and pants. While I wasn't huge anymore, I still couldn't fit into my normal clothes, and there was a soft pouch of excess skin drooping around my belly, crisscrossed with stretch marks. I cringed seeing it and the crimson scar, raised and angry that ran several inches across my lower stomach. I ran a finger over it and winced as the pain pushed through, hearing the water run behind me. Silently, Gio maneuvered me into the shower cubicle and spun me around, his strong fingers lathering shampoo into my hair. My shoulders sank as I let him carry the load, and I leaned back against his solid torso, my legs suddenly unable to bear my own weight. His hands came around me, heavy on my thighs, slipping upward along the wet skin until he found his target.

"Ohh," I gasped, surprised by the sudden contact, and pushed into him, wanting more. I closed my eyes, savoring the unfamiliar sensation. Alertness took hold for a moment, and I jerked out away from his touch.

"We can't. Not yet."

"We aren't," his deep voice rumbled in my ear. "It is too soon. But I want you to know I love you, Caitlin. Now. Forever." One arm gripped me firmly around the waist, holding me against him as the other explored and pleasured. I could feel him behind me, hard, wanting me.

"I need you," I gasped. "Please."

"No," he murmured. "We can't, and I won't hurt you. I can wait. I want to pleasure you, worship you in the manner you should be. The mother of my goddesses. My girls. God, I love you, Caitlin."

It didn't take long with no willpower to object. As the pulsing started and my muscles trembled, I pushed back into him, my mind only registering that he was

CHAPTER 12

holding me upright. There was no way I could have remained standing as my knees collapsed beneath me and my weight dropped. I heard him chuckle as he rinsed my hair and switched off the shower, all one-handed. Effortlessly, he lifted me from the shower and dripped behind me as I wilted, and he toweled me off, combed my hair, and carried me to bed.

"Now sleep," he ordered. "I will take care of the girls. I will wake you before I leave for work."

CHAPTER 13

"**DO YOU EVER WONDER** what we must have been like as kids?" I said, watching Rai sleep two days after Seraphine's arrival on Lewis. His breath was shallow and rapid, his face flushed. Being surrounded by medical professionals all my life, I knew children breathed faster than adults, and their hearts beat faster, too, but I had never been close enough to a sleeping infant to realize how fast they breathed. Rai's little chest was visibly expanding with every pant as he slept on a tatami mat on the floor, Japanese-style, according to Sera. He was louder than Khi, who slept in the cot beside him as I fed Rori.

"I can't imagine how our parents survived having us."

"What do you mean?" Sera asked. "We were angels!"

We dissolved into giggles, recalling the trouble we had gotten into. Sera often came to talk to me while I was feeding the girls. Captive audience, I called it, and I loved having this time to sit and chat with someone. Although Sera had only been here a few days, they relied heavily on her for decision-making in Hokkaido.

CHAPTER 13

Since her arrival, she had constantly been in meetings. Finally, we had scheduled her lunch break during the girls' midday feed so we could spend time together each day.

"Rai is so compliant, and he sleeps a lot." I gestured with my chin at the sleeping child. "I remember you and I used to run around madly, then collapse in a heap. Your mum used to tease us that she would find us asleep in random places."

"I remember that. In sheds, haystacks, even in one of the cars once."

"Does Rai take after us? I am wondering what to expect from these two. Is Rai crazy energetic like we were?"

Sera considered. "Not really. He has always been a quiet boy."

Choosing my next words cautiously, I asked, "Does he have allergies? He seems a little wheezy?"

Sera assessed her child, sleeping only a few meters away, and shrugged. "No more than normal."

"You don't think he might have asthma?"

"No, he always sounds like that. Maybe I am used to it. I asked the med team in Japan to check him once, but they told me all children are mucusy and cough. It is just him, I guess."

"Likely," I agreed, but my intuition was tingling. Something wasn't right. "He is very thin," I pushed, not wanting to rush to my proposal.

"Yeah, but he eats well enough."

"You and Matt are both lean," I agreed. "It is likely genetics."

"Spill, Caitlin. I have known you long enough to know when you are biting your tongue."

I relented. "Have you asked Kat or Mum to check him over?"

"Why? He is perfectly healthy. Are you questioning my parenting skills?" The indignation rose in her voice along with the volume. She stood, glaring down at me.

Affecting a dismissive tone, I laughed. "New mum here! It is not like I would know. Now tell me all about this chick Matt is banging so I can hate her, too. Ooh, do you remember that book we found about voodoo dolls when we were kids? Do you think we could find it and learn about how to make one?"

Sera paused a moment before responding. "Two," she said, settling in beside me. "Do I need to source something of hers, too?"

That weekend, Aunt Di hosted an impromptu party for the residents of Roseglen, as Sera had missed my welcome home party. Everyone brought a plate of food to share, which usually meant there would be far more than anyone could eat. Long ago, I had worked out that everyone genuinely believed that they were doing their neighbors a favor by over-catering, but all that happened was leftovers being forced upon us and needing to eat them for days afterward. No one wasted food here.

"Are you sure you want to do this?" I asked Sera as we dressed. She had brought her change of clothes into my room so we could talk. I could finally fit into normal clothes, although my top half was far bigger than it had been pre-children. "Ugh," I groaned as I

CHAPTER 13

squashed my enormous breasts into a bra and hoped they wouldn't leak through my dress.

"Not really," she admitted, "but it is easier to have everyone in a group where at least I can escape. Meeting people one at a time, and I can't avoid the inevitable question."

"Stick near me. I will intervene if anyone gets too personal."

"Thank you. I suspect most people know, so it will be awkward rather than intrusive."

The girls had been bathed, fed, and dressed in clean outfits. Sera and I carried one child each as a shield. Gio had taken Rai to meet his cousins, dressed in a pair of navy pants and a pale blue shirt. He looked so much like Matt that it hurt. It must pain her too, I realized, seeing her watching him run around, Aurora on her front in a sling.

Gio waved from across the open space, already filled with neighbors, family, and friends. Dad had been cooking up a storm all afternoon, filling the long trestle tables with food. While everyone had met the girls individually, it was lovely to present them more publicly with everyone asking how they were. Sera clung to Rori, and I soon realized that the baby was a welcome distraction and gave her something to talk about that wasn't the demise of her marriage. We settled into some seats beside Gio, sighing to finally take the weight off my hips.

"Grumpy little man, isn't he!" Gio teased Sera as Rai threw a tantrum, playing with Louis's girls on the lawn as we watched. "Reminds me of..." Gio trailed off, realizing what he was about to say.

"He is just tired!" I quickly cut him off, seeing Sera's face darken.

"It's fine," Sera snapped. "He has a father. Always will. But one who has prioritized his new girlfriend over his child and meeting his new nieces."

I flashed Gio a warning. *Do not get into an argument with my sister.*

"Poor kid. He always seems tired. Is he not sleeping well?" Gio asked, watching Rai yawn.

The exhaustion was clear in Sera's voice. "He has never been a good sleeper. Matt used to get up with him, but now I have to do it all."

There was no easy way to respond to that. My loyalties would always be with her. But Matt and Gio had been through a lot together. Rai came over, crying, with grass stains smeared across his new pale blue top, shattering the uncomfortable silence. He threw himself at Sera, waking Aurora in the process. Gio took Aurora, settling her into his chest, and took her for a walk to rock her back to sleep. Sera lifted Rai into her lap, soothing him. Between the sobs, his breathing was strained, making it hard for her to calm him.

"Sairs, are you sure he doesn't have asthma? I've not heard it much, but he is congested. I don't think this is right."

"I have told you already. He is fine," she snapped, standing to leave, clutching him to her.

"Well, that went well," I muttered as her back disappeared around the house, and Gio returned to sit beside me. Aurora was now yawning and rubbing her eyes.

"What did you say?"

"Just that his breathing doesn't sound right."

"What do you mean?"

Lowering my voice, I explained what I had observed.

CHAPTER 13

Gio furrowed his brow. "It could be nothing. Or it could be something. Has your mother checked him out?"

"Mum has been with you, and she and Dad have spent the last two days either together or with us and the girls. Illy has spent time with him, but no one who might pick up something is wrong."

"I hope to be like your parents."

"Why?"

"They are both independent and have their own interests, but they are so in love. They light up when the other comes into the room. Surely you see that?"

"I guess."

"You would need to be blind to not see how devoted they are to each other."

"They are my parents; that is all I see. They have had their ups and downs, too. You know they even broke up once when I was a child?"

"You told me, not that you would notice now."

"Maybe it was because I was older, but it was when Illy met Carmelo that my heart skipped a beat. I'm not the swoony type, but watching her fall in love was magical. She has been alone my entire life, and I never thought I would see her like this."

"Swoony? What does this mean?"

I laughed. "In English, people describe it as having butterflies in your stomach. You know, that feeling when you meet someone, and they make your tummy go all buzzy? Like Dad's bees."

Gio pulled me into his lap, somewhat awkwardly with the girls in slings strapped to each of us. "I still feel like that whenever you walk in the room unexpectedly. My love. I hope I will always feel that way. Buzzy."

"I missed you so much."

"Have you had your checkup?" he whispered, making my stomach tense.

"This morning."

"And?"

"Clear."

Before the word had left my lips, I was on my feet being pulled toward our parents. My face flushed as Carmelo offered to hold one, and Illy the other, in theory, to allow us to eat in peace. Gio made a show of steering me toward the food table, then quickly veered off around the house and into the forest beyond.

"The girls!"

He ignored my protestations, hauling me up the dirt path and out of sight of the houses. He didn't pause. "If they wake, someone will respond to them. But I need you, Caitlin."

"Lying down would be easier." Being dragged was making me dizzy. "You and trees!"

"I have dreamed about having you in a forest since our wedding. There is nothing like it anywhere else."

"My hips!" I protested.

"I will hold you. Now, Caitlin. Before I need to share you with our daughters again."

CHAPTER 14

METHODICAL STEPS CAUGHT MY attention, and I popped my head through the kitchen door. Sera paced the length of the hall, resembling a blonde tiger as her hair streamed behind her and whipped around as she spun at the end. She wasn't stomping, but something was eating at her. By the time Gio and I returned to the party the night before, she had left, and we had thought it best to give her some time.

"Can you walk with me?" I asked merrily. "I really want to get out of the house but need to take the girls, and I can't carry two."

Sera's shoulders dropped, looking like she was about to object, so I lowered my standards. "Please. I need to get out of here. Everyone is in my face all the time. I can walk, but I can't do it alone. I need you."

Guilt wracked me for lying. Everyone was wonderful, giving me space and helping me. But I desperately needed to speak with her alone. The gulf between us hurt more than I would have thought. We had always been so close; we had slept together for much of our lives, as close as twins. Now we were strangers, missing the major chapters of the past few years.

"Do you have both slings?"

"I do." I flourished one. "It is such an expedition taking them out. I need to feed them, change them. It takes forever."

"It gets easier." Sera smiled for the first time since she had arrived, slipping the sling over her head and pulling her arm through.

"Oh, I hope so," I breathed. "I can't believe how much I love them already. They open their eyes, and I am in love. But taking them anywhere is so damned painful."

Sera giggled. "Come on, I will help. Rai needs a nap, too. I'll ask your dad to watch him."

"Have you noticed how Dad is the nurturing one?" I asked as we entered my room, Rai scurrying along at her feet. "Anything that needs to be done with the girls, and it is always him."

"He always was the hands-on parent." She looked at me, surprised, as she rolled out the mat on the floor for Rai. "How did you never notice?"

"After Kiewa," I paused, searching for the right words, "they were both so attentive, so I thought maybe I wasn't remembering right."

"That isn't how I recall our childhood at all." Sera stared off out my bedroom window as I lay the girls on the bed, preparing to simultaneously feed them. "I remember him being here every afternoon after school, making us snacks, helping us with our homework. If one of us was sick or injured, it was always your dad who helped. When I was in Japan and trying to envision what a good parent looked like, your dad was who I thought of."

CHAPTER 14

"That is so sweet. Why did you never tell me that?"

"I never thought I would have children. Then, when I did, I felt like I couldn't talk to you about it."

That stung, and I avoided the comment. "Truthfully, I never thought I would have children either. So much has changed, for both of us."

Sera grimaced and I let that topic go, struggling to find something neutral to talk about. We chatted about common friends, people we worked with. I had spoken with many of her colleagues on video link, often via interpreter, but never met them in real life and was intrigued to hear about their personalities and interests. Similarly, she had spoken with nîpiy, Gabriel, and a few others from Canada but hadn't met them in person. Rori's eyes drooped as she drank her fill, and with some deft maneuvering, we managed to get all three children down for a nap.

"Dad!" I called down the hall, hearing the clattering in the kitchen. "Can you listen for the kids? Sera and I are going out for a walk."

The sound of the knife on the chopping board paused for a moment. "Sure," Dad called back.

We walked in silence until we were well clear of the houses. Slipping my arm through hers, we ambled along the path, our arms linked in a way we hadn't done since we were children.

"I'm so happy for you, Cait," she finally said, her voice choked. "After everything you have been through, you deserve this."

"You deserve it, too."

"Sometimes I wonder if I haven't suffered enough to deserve happiness. Unlike you or all our parents, my life has been fairly relaxed. Uneventful. You have all overcome enormous struggles to find the loves of your life. Maybe it isn't my turn."

I stopped dead in the path and gave her a shake. "What the bloody hell are you talking about? Happiness doesn't come after trauma. What other ridiculous ideas have you got floating around in your head? Speak."

"It was something Matt said. He was angry at me, as he often was after Rai was born. He said I had lived a charmed life, and I wouldn't know what it was like to be him. To have his family wrenched away. One night after a fight, it made me think. Maybe it is true. I was special, a chosen one, raised by three loving parents with siblings. I was loved. Unlike you and Louis, my childhood was idyllic. My mum and your dad both lost a partner; your mum has been to hell and back. Then there was what you endured. I started thinking maybe it was true. Maybe Matt was right."

"Oh, for fuck's sake, Seraphine! Don't be a drama queen hosting a pity party. Xanthe is happy. Your sisters, too. Alasdair, Thorsten, Katrin. None of them had my challenges, but they are all happy. What makes you think you have been singled out and are being punished?"

Sera exhaled. "That is true, I guess. Matt just made it sound like he and Gio, you too, had lived through challenges, but I hadn't. The Ambassador position was handed to me. I didn't earn it."

"Nor did I," I pointed out. "Did your mum tell you I tried to turn it down several times? She wouldn't let me, of course."

"All Mum said when she was training me in Japan was that she went too hard on you in France. She took it easy on me. Not that it felt easy, mind you."

CHAPTER 14

"She did. I hated every second of learning about the role. I truly thought if that was the job, then I didn't want it. But after I arrived in Canada and learned I could pursue my own projects as well as be an Ambassador, I didn't hate it quite so much. It was hard learning French, being surrounded by strangers and no one to rely on—except Gio. He was my rock."

"The first months in Japan were dreadfully hard. Not speaking the language, not being able to read anything. People were polite but distant. I felt like an intruder. Everything is different, the food, the customs. I tower over most of them and always felt like the bumbling visitor, making gaffes. Like all of the underwater communities, they are based on geothermal vents for heating and power, but they also have onsens. Only they were public, not private like the ones in Italy. What I didn't know was that they are gender segregated, but women bathe naked. Men too. I was so embarrassed, being tall and blonde, and all the women were petite and dark. I could sense them staring at me, like a giraffe, as I got in and out, but I got used to it. There was nowhere private, except home."

"Is that what came between you? The different culture and lack of privacy?"

"Matt was wonderful, attentive, and concerned when I was pregnant, even when Rai was first born. The first few weeks are tough, as you know. I was exhausted and just felt like it was a blur. He took time off so I could return to work, but later, he threw that at me, too, accusing me of abandoning our child to further my career."

"Oh, Sairs, that isn't true. He was just being spiteful to hurt you."

"It still hurts."

"The words?"

"All of it."

"Do you want to stay here? Or come to Canada with us? I'd love to have you. We need an ambassador. nîpiy does an awesome job, but she doesn't really want the role. I can speak with your mum and…"

"No. As bizarre as it sounds, Japan is my home, and I finally feel like I am part of the community there. They trust me and consult me on everything. I have worked so hard. If anyone should go, it is him."

"What about Rai? Does he want to co-parent?"

"We started that conversation. How we would share custody. Plenty of people do it. But then I walked in on him and Izumi, and…"

"Do you not want to co-parent?" I couldn't quite get the vibe, and the last thing I wanted to do was to overstep the mark.

"I do. But I don't want *her* around my child. It is bad enough that I have to see her at work every day. Does that make sense?"

"Of course it does. I would rather stab myself in the eye with a stick than watch another woman raise my child. Is that why you were late? Rai wasn't actually sick, was he?"

"No." Sera's eyes cast downward as she kicked up the dirt. "I couldn't face you all. Tell you my marriage had failed. I didn't want to drag you down in your time of joy. These are your first children, and especially after what happened, you should be over the moon, not worrying about me. Matt and I married too quickly. I know that now. But he was well, stable. I never saw what Gio spoke of, the darkness. Then, when Rai came, I began to see the chinks in the armor. He started sleeping on the couch, ostensibly so that

CHAPTER 14

he could get a better night's sleep, so Rai didn't wake him, but then we weren't together at all. For a while, that was fine. I was exhausted from lack of sleep and work and appreciated the space. But it soon became clear that he didn't want me anymore."

"Oh, Sairs, I'm sure that isn't it."

The sob broke free from her chest. "Actually, it was. I was trying to … arouse him one night. Rai was asleep. We were on the couch, and I tried to kiss him. When I tried to take it further, he snapped at me that sex was all I wanted him for. He pretty much called me a whore."

My blood chilled along with my body. "Whoa. What did you say?"

"I crept back to my room and sobbed until I fell asleep. I never went near him after that. That was three months ago."

"Oh, Sera." My arms found their place around her thin frame and held her as she shattered after holding this in for so long. Recognizing that this would not be a brief conversation, I led her to a grassy bank and held her, murmuring to her as she released the pain and anguish of the past few months. Being an ambassador meant we had no close friends, no one we could confide in. It was lonely at the top.

"Why didn't you talk to me?" I muttered into her hair as my chin rested on her head, nestled into my chest. "I would have listened."

"How could I? You were finally pregnant and so blissfully happy. I couldn't burden you with my problems. And Giovanni is Matt's brother. Creating a rift was the last thing I wanted. Keeping to myself was easier."

My heart was beating in time with hers. I could feel the old synchronicity realign. "Being happy with my news and sad for you is completely valid. Did you stop being happy at your own pregnancy when I was taken?"

"I felt all the emotions," she admitted. "Joy for us but pain for you, knowing what you lost."

"So what makes you think I couldn't have done the same for you, you goose!"

Sera half sobbed, half giggled at my use of the expression Dad used with us when we were young and had done something foolish.

"As for Giovanni, yes, he is my husband. But you are my sister. I would do anything for you, you know that. We can work that out. It isn't all or nothing."

"I know. But I felt so alone."

"Why didn't you come home sooner?"

"Shame."

"You never need to feel ashamed with me."

"Mum said you were ashamed of what happened to you. I saw the tape, Catie. It was brutal."

"Your mother has a big mouth."

"She was stacking the odds. She knew she only needed to get a few ambassadors on her side, and the rest would fold and condemn what they did. She was right, of course. I felt sick watching that tape, seeing your face. Had Izumi not been there supporting me, I would have cried. I have never seen anything like it in my life, and I hope never to again. Mum called me before your speech, not that there was any doubt of my support."

"I haven't seen it and don't think I want to. I was there. That was enough. I lost my Stella that day. The last thing I need is a visual reminder."

CHAPTER 14

"I'm so sorry, Catie, for not being there. We were always a team, and they took you, and you were alone. I wish I could have been there for you."

For the first time since my loss and hers, we held each other as we had all our lives, supporting each other. Knowing that we had each other's back. As the shadows darkened the forest floor, I looked up from where we sat. "We need to get back. My boobs are about to explode."

Sera nodded, visibly drained. "I am so happy for you, Catie. You deserve this."

"What ... huge tits?" I asked deadpan, making her snort.

"Oh, you always had more than me, but now they are positively enormous. I assume Gio loves them."

"Is he that predictable?"

The mood between us was gentler on our walk home, almost like we had been before we married. I finally asked what had been on my mind for several days.

"Sairs, please don't take this the wrong way. I mean this with all good intent. But I am a little worried about Rai."

"Rai? Do you mean emotionally? Because of Matt and I? Do you think us breaking up is affecting him?"

"No. I mean physically. You remember I read all those medical texts back when I wanted to be a doctor?"

"Sure, but you aren't a doctor."

"I know that, but I am worried. Most likely, I am just a freaked-out new mum. Or aunt. Both. Whatever. But I am asking you to please let Gio take a look at him. He won't say anything to my mum or yours, I promise. It is likely nothing, and I am a worrier. I get it. Then you can tease me all you like and say, 'I told you so.' But please, there is no harm in him spending five minutes to give him a quick examination, is there?"

"I guess not. Why? What are you thinking?"

"Nothing, truthfully. But my Spidey-sense is tingling."

"Where on earth did you get that expression?"

"Dad!" I laughed. "Do you remember when we were on our way back from Australia on the yacht? I didn't sleep well. I kept having nightmares after what that guy did to me. Well, one night, Dad let me watch a movie with him. There was the disc player—remember? Well, we watched a movie called *Spiderman*."

"*Spiderman*?"

"It was about some guy that was bitten by a chemical spider. Something like that. Anyway, he had special powers, and I remember Dad telling me that I had special powers, and that was why people wanted to hurt me. He promised to always keep me safe. So, in the movie, the character gets this 'Spidey-sense,' kind of tingling when danger is about to happen. I told Dad that maybe I could have super senses, too, and he laughed and said we all have a Spidey-sense. We all can recognize something that isn't quite right. Just before danger, lots of people have a feeling, a premonition. I had forgotten about it until nîpiy said it one day, and it brought back the memory. I just kind of have a feeling that Rai's breathing isn't just age. It is likely as simple as asthma or maybe bronchitis, and we can treat that. Sorcha still uses her medication to control her asthma, so it is an easy fix. What do you have to lose?"

"He is my baby," Sera whispered. "I would do anything to protect him. Yes, Gio can check him over."

CHAPTER 14

That night, as we lay in bed, I told Gio about the conversation with Sera. Not the part about Matt but about Rai.

"I can't help but feel something isn't quite right."

"You've said that before. What do you suspect?"

"Honestly, I have no idea. But I know there is something wrong. I feel it. But now she has agreed to let you take a look."

"Sleep. I will check him over tomorrow."

"What if I don't want to sleep?" I crooned in his ear, running my tongue along the groove of his neck.

"My favorite kind of checking over," he growled before flipping me deftly atop him.

CHAPTER 15

SERA DROPPED BY OUR half of the house after breakfast. Rai was a squirmy toddler, walking and talking in accordance with his age and, like all toddlers, inquisitive and getting into mischief. But the more I observed him, the more I thought he was pale and lethargic with no bounce. Underweight and with a distinctive wheeze, he felt brittle to pick up, almost like his bones were too close to the surface. Unlike my girls, who were chubby and cuddly, he was almost uncomfortable to hold. Gio shot me a concerned look as Sera bent to pick him up and lay him on the bed. He could see immediately what I had. This was not a well child.

"I only have basic equipment," he warned her. Sera had flatly refused to let us take him to the clinic. Instead, Gio had made a pre-dawn trip to the clinic and brought his medical bag home.

"Well, what do you need to diagnose asthma? Surely a stethoscope is enough."

"One step at a time. Rai, may I lift your top? We are going to listen to your chest. I warn you, it might be a little cold."

CHAPTER 15

Rai nodded solemnly and giggled as Gio lifted his own shirt and demonstrated on his own chest. Every time I saw him interact with children, it took my breath away. Asking their consent, demonstrating on himself, often letting them do it to him first. He adored children, and they responded in kind.

Gio popped the stethoscope into his ears, and I handed Khione to Sera to distract her as Gio examined Rai. Sera sat in the armchair cooing at Khione, who put on her best adorable baby face.

"Oh, she looks like you," Sera sighed, pulling her attention away from the gurgling baby in her arms. "I never thought I would see the day that you even held a baby, and now you have two."

"I do." I sat beside her, cradling Aurora, doing my best to distract her. "Do you remember when Iona had her first, and we refused to hold her?"

"*You* refused to hold her," Sera teased. "You were scared you were going to fall pregnant by osmosis or something. Who were you seeing then? Jeremy? If I recall correctly, you wouldn't let him near you for weeks."

Gio glanced up at me, the flush rising from his chest and coloring his neck. I quickly changed the subject. My past relationships were just that: past. I shifted the conversation onto the pain of breastfeeding, and soon, we were engrossed in a conversation about how ridiculously long feeding took. I could see a worried look cross Gio's face as he held the stethoscope to Rai's chest and back. He was taking a lot longer than I would have expected for a routine examination. Sera pulled her attention from making faces at Khi and asked, "So all good, then?"

Gio nodded slightly, indicating he had heard, but the puzzled expression on his face remained, making my heart race. Finally, he removed the buds from his ears, helped Rai to dress, and chatted to him about getting morning tea. With a quick look back at us, he escorted Rai down to find my father. Gio returned alone a few minutes later. He had his doctor's face on, and my heart sank.

"Is he okay?" Sera looked confused.

Gio exhaled and sat on the bed facing us. "Seraphine, there is no easy way to say this."

"So just say it," she snapped. "We are family. Tell me."

"I am fairly certain Raidon has a congenital heart defect."

Sera's jolt and gasp startled Khione, making her cry. Gio reached for her and held her against his chest as Sera absorbed the news.

"Congenital?"

"It just means he has had it since birth."

Sera nodded, processing that. "I know what the word means."

Gio began speaking again, slowly, so she could take it in. "This is good news; we have caught it early. One in a hundred babies have it, so it isn't rare. Even I have seen it before, although I wasn't the lead surgeon. We can operate and fix the issue. But he needs to have scans first so we know what we are dealing with."

"Are you sure?" was all she could say when she could finally form words.

"Almost positive."

"Why did the team in Japan not pick it up?" she gasped. "I have taken him to the medical center several times."

CHAPTER 15

"I can't answer that, but it is fairly pronounced. I suspect he has something called a ventricular septal defect."

"What is that?" I asked, although I had a fairly good idea.

"The heart comprises four chambers, two aorta, and two ventricles. The ventricles are the lower pumping chambers. Ventricular septal defect means there is a hole in the wall between the ventricles. This hole lets oxygenated and deoxygenated blood mix. His symptoms are fairly typical."

"Will he die?" Sera gasped, all the color draining from her face.

"No. It is a fairly straightforward surgical fix. But I need to speak to your mother. Freyja, I mean. I really think he needs an ECG and an echo. There is a cardiac specialist in France, but I know Nasir has also operated on such conditions. Do I have your permission to consult your mother?"

Sera blinked, then nodded, staring blankly.

Gio left the room, and I pulled Sera to sit beside me on the bed. The girls were happily lying on the floor and were safe. All of my attention needed to be with her now. She was shell-shocked. I could feel her pulse thud rapidly beneath my arm as I held her. Within minutes, a flurry of activity was happening around us. Refusing to leave her, I left the babies with Dad. Gio, Sera, Rai, and I took two vehicles to the clinic in Garynahine. Sera clutched my hand with one of hers, the other holding Rai to her chest. She looked like a ghost, deathly pale and clammy.

"It will be okay," I soothed. "I am here. You aren't alone."

Reaching the clinic, Mum took charge immediately, reassuring Seraphine that Rai was in excellent hands. She fired questions at Gio, who responded calmly, describing what he had heard.

"Put him on the bed, please." Sorcha examined him and nodded as she listened to Rai's chest.

"Good catch." She threw the off-the-cuff remark to Gio as she removed the stethoscope before engaging in a rapid-fire conversation with my mother about diagnostics and the best course of action.

Gio knew as well as I did that this was praise from Sorcha.

"I should have come sooner," Sera gasped beside me, clutching Rai's hand and watching the flurry of activity around her son as Sorcha stuck patches on Rai's chest and back and hooked him up to the electrocardiogram. "He would have been treated before if I had come when I was meant to."

"It's okay, Seraphine," Mum reassured her as she and Sorcha pointed to the squiggly lines on the graph, speaking in low voices.

"Get the echo," Sorcha told Mum, who disappeared. She returned pushing a trolley with a monitor and the echocardiogram, preparing to ultrasound his heart. Mum glanced up at Sera's face.

"Caitlin, perhaps some fresh air would be a good idea." I knew that look. While they weren't going to hurt Rai, and Rai was quite enthralled with all the action and being the center of attention, it would distress Sera to see him being scanned. Sorcha's tense posture betrayed that we were in her way, but she knew better than to say anything. Gio was entertaining Rai by showing him the wand and the gel, explaining how lucky he was that he was going to see his heart.

CHAPTER 15

Rai puffed up with pride at being told he was special, giving me the opportunity to steer Seraphine out of the room.

"He is going to be fine," I assured her as I guided her to the gardens, unresisting.

"No thanks to me!"

"You can't blame yourself. This isn't your fault."

As we moved through the foyer, Sera looked older than I had ever seen her. I tried not to stare at her reflection in the mirrored wall. All her youthful exuberance had dissipated with the diagnosis. She looked worn, like a piece of paper that had been screwed up and flattened out. The same item fundamentally, but it would never look as it once had. Side by side, we sat on the old bench seat outside the front entrance. Many times I had waited here for Mum to finish a shift or to be picked up after I had injured myself and been stitched up. The gardens were peaceful here, full of flowers that I knew some of the older women in town maintained.

"Have you ever seen my mother not be successful? Or Sorcha? Kat, too, for that matter. As for the three of them together? They could stop an earthquake."

Sera sniffed and leaned on me, dropping her head on my shoulder. "Giovanni is hardly a pushover."

"Exactly. So now you have the Four Horsemen, all fighting to ensure Rai receives the best care. Would you take them on?"

"I wouldn't take any of them on individually, let alone collectively."

"Precisely. They will call Nasir if they need to, but a heart is a heart, regardless of age. This isn't their first cardiac surgery, and it won't be their last. Besides, they won't operate now. He will need to fast."

Sera slumped, her head rolling forward. "That is true. At least I will get to see him first. Tomorrow, maybe?"

"Let's just wait for Mum. You know her. She won't keep anything from you."

While I knew they needed to be certain of the diagnosis and the proposed course of action, I was getting frustrated at how long they were taking. What I had thought would be an hour turned into several. The babies would be awake and starving by now, and I was torn between supporting my sister and being home with my babies.

An electric car rounded the corner, Illy and Dad inside. Illy was clutching the babies to her chest, but they didn't seem to mind being bounced around.

"Hungry," Dad said by way of explanation, and I thanked him. He knew I couldn't leave, but the girls needed me, too. For a man with Asperger's, sometimes he was more intuitive than neurotypical people.

Illy sat with Seraphine as the tears returned, and Dad helped me into a comfortable chair in the clinic, latching on one baby and then the other. "Football hold" Illy had called it when she saw me once, and that was how I referred to it now. Dad was too diplomatic to ask what was going on, but I filled him in anyway. Everyone would know soon enough.

"Rai has a heart condition," I explained, not really knowing how else to put it. "Gio suspected, and Sorcha and Mum confirmed it."

Dad nodded gravely. "You suspected first."

CHAPTER 15

Wriggling slightly to get comfortable, I looked up at him. "How did you know that?"

"Watching you and your sister at the party. It was obvious you had said something that upset her, as she disappeared and didn't come back. You were right to push it. You might have saved his life, Catie."

"She was angry at me," I admitted. "But my Spidey-sense told me not to let it go."

The grin broke across Dad's face. "Do you remember when I taught you that?"

"I do. You know, I have so many fond memories of that trip as well as the negative ones. It took me a long time to see how wonderful it was to spend months with my family, my sisters, and see where you came from."

"Do you still get the nightmares?" Dad asked softly.

"I did until I met Giovanni. They became fewer and then, not at all. Until last year. But even then, they were short-lived."

"Because you feel safe." While I hadn't really thought about it, he was right. "You know your mother had horrendous nightmares for months after she and Illy returned from Clava. It was before you were born. She would be asleep, but I would feel her start to convulse. She would whimper, and then she would start screaming. Often it woke your brothers and sisters."

"What stopped it?"

"She said the same—feeling safe. It was a process, not one thing. She knew that I would never hurt her and would protect her. So being in bed became a safe place, where previously it wasn't. The nightmares lessened, and then stopped."

"Knowing I existed must have come as a terrible shock."

Dad paused. "Surprise is a probably a better word. But Caitlin, not for one day in your life did she regret you or your sisters. That was hard for her. Knowing you existed, all of you, and wanting to raise you all. We seriously considered it, you know."

"Callie told me it was your idea to contact your friends."

"Your mother was in a flat-spin. She wanted you all but knew logically we couldn't raise that many children. So I made some calls. Do you think I made the right choice?"

"That's not my decision to make," I admitted. "While I can't imagine someone else raising my children, I am struggling with two. I can't imagine having twenty-four babies at the same time. But every one of those girls was loved and had a wonderful life."

Dad was interrupted by Illy appearing in the doorway.

"They want to talk to all of us, together."

With Dad and me holding a baby each, we entered the meeting room behind Illy. I had been here before when consulting with Charlie on Orkney, as well as with other cases where Mum asked for my input. But it was the first time I was directly impacted. Sera was sitting on a chair, Rai on her lap, although he was squirming to get down. Gio pulled out the chair beside him for me, and Mum did the same for Dad. Katrin was here now, too, I noted. We sat, an extended family around a table. Sorcha took charge.

CHAPTER 15

"I'm not going to sugarcoat this, Seraphine," she began and was immediately cut off by my mother.

"For fuck's sake, after all these years. When will you develop a bedside manner?" she snapped.

"No," Seraphine said quietly, and everyone stopped to listen. "I want Sorcha to tell me. Tell me straight. No bullshit. What is going on, and what do we need to do?"

Mum flushed, and Sorcha resumed her explanation, but I noted it was softer in tone.

"As Gio suspected, Rai has a ventricular septal defect. They are not uncommon in children, although they are usually small, less than five millimeters in diameter and don't require surgery. A larger one like this is usually picked up sooner."

Sera went pale but continued to listen.

"What this means is that there is a hole in the wall between the ventricles. In many cases, especially in children, they close on their own."

"Can we do that? Monitor and wait?"

Sorcha looked at her team for support. Mum took over. "Honestly, Seraphine, all surgery comes with risk. I would never operate on a child unless I thought it was in their best interest. The best we can tell, his defect is over eight millimeters. That is big for a child of his size. If we don't operate, there is a risk that he will develop Eisenmenger syndrome. He may also sustain permanent damage to his heart and lungs, which reduces his lifespan."

Sera exhaled forcefully. "What's that Eisen ... syndrome?" Sera asked.

"Eisenmenger syndrome is irregular blood flow in the heart and lungs. It causes blood vessels to narrow and raises blood pressure, casing pulmonary arterial hypertension. Left untreated, it can damage the blood vessels in the lungs. In the old world, there were medications for this. But we don't have that now."

"So what you are telling me is that I don't have a choice?"

Gio kneeled in front of Sera's chair, forcing her to look directly at him. "You always have a choice. We will never force you to do something you don't want to do. But we are not doing our jobs if we don't give you all the facts. The best outcome for Raidon is if we operate, and soon. He is two. If we don't do this soon, the damage could become permanent."

"Do it," Sera croaked, making me desperately want to hold her. Support her. To my surprise, she stood and hugged Gio, Rai squashed between them.

"Thank you. You, too," she said, looking over at me. "When do you want to do this?" she asked, returning her attention to Gio.

"Tomorrow morning, first thing. He needs to fast for twelve hours and…"

"Can you tell me what you need later?" Seraphine interjected. "I am going to take Rai on a picnic." She stood and left the room, leaving the rest of us looking at each other uncomfortably. Dad finally broke the tension by addressing me.

"Let's get you and the ladies home, shall we? I am sure the medical team doesn't need our help."

Mum flashed Dad a look of gratitude as we closed the door.

CHAPTER 16

THE STOMPING FOOTSTEPS CAME thumping down the timber-floored hallway, increasing in volume. The door crashed against the wall as it was flung open.

"*You fucking asshole! How could you?*" Sera burst in, not waiting for us to wake. For a second, I thought she was going to launch herself across the room and tear Gio's throat out. Her knuckles were white, and her face crimson. Jerked awake, Gio pulled the blankets up to cover his nakedness. Sera took three steps into our room, bellowing at him from the end of the bed. "*What made you think you had the right...*"

Gio sat up, fighting to keep the quilt strategically placed over both of us. "What? I don't know..."

"Your fucking brother! You told him about Rai! That twatwaffle is on his way here, now. They just landed. When were you planning to tell *me*? I trusted you, you fucking asshole!"

"Ahh... what?"

"Summer picked the cheating fucknuckle up a few hours ago from France. How fucking dare you!"

Gio's face went blank. "Seraphine, I..."

"I called Matteo." Illy's low, calm voice sounded from the doorway. She didn't need to raise her voice. She pitched it perfectly to be heard by them both. Sera froze and whirled on her mother. Slinking down under the quilt, I felt exposed, naked, in what was Illy's bed with my husband. Aurora began to cry with the rude awakening.

"I was also the one who instructed your sister to collect him from France."

Sera's face rapidly turned multiple hues of purple, and I shrank back against my pillow as she let fly at her mother.

"Do you mind having your conversation in the living room so I can tend to my children?" I snapped when Seraphine took a breath. Being woken early was not my favorite activity at the best of times and certainly not when I had a late night, awaiting Gio to return home after Rai's surgery. Hearing him arrive, the girls had woken, resulting in me getting very little sleep. But I had needed to receive a full briefing after the long and grueling surgery and an assurance that our nephew would be fine before I could sleep at all.

Illy firmly escorted an open-mouthed Sera out of our room, closing the door firmly behind them.

"Good morning," I muttered, mostly to myself.

"Good morning," Gio murmured in that deep rumbling tone that made my stomach catapult, his dark hair blocking the light as he stole my oxygen.

"Mmmmm," I responded, feeling slightly less cranky as he made me melt into his arms. Aurora chose that moment to escalate her screech, and we rapidly pulled apart.

"I'll get them." Gio threw the covers back and stepped into his pants before I had even moved.

CHAPTER 16

Dashing off to the bathroom before I was immobilized for a lengthy period, I called, "Can you change one and give her to me?"

Mobilizing our family of four took a lot longer than it had a few months ago when we were two, but eventually, we were all showered and dressed, Gio bringing me breakfast as I fed the girls.

"Time to step into the Colosseum," I quipped as we finished changing them a second time. "I feel much like a sacrificial beast."

Gio's face cracked into a grin. "My mother used to tell us stories of the gladiators."

"Mine too. Well, my money is on Seraphine. She is a dirty fighter. Hair puller, too."

"Just quietly, mine, too. It was pretty easy to take Matt in a fight. I'd wager she could, too."

"I'll bet you could. Can you take Aurora? She is always more settled with you."

With Khione clutched to my chest, I opened the door and waited for the shouts to descend on us. To my astonishment, the low drone of conversation had a calm air about it. Glancing up at Gio, I saw the mood had surprised him, too. Putting on the best smile I could, I walked down the short hall into the living area.

"Matt," I said as warmly as I could, trying not to bare my teeth. It wouldn't do to tear his throat out the second I saw him. But my loyalty would be with my sister, always.

His face lit with joy at seeing us emerge, holding his nieces. He fired off something in Italian to Gio, so rapidly I only caught one word in three. Something about the girls being a blessing and how pleased their mother would be to finally have granddaughters.

Gio thanked him calmly in English, holding out Aurora. Trying not to show my discomfort, I fully expected her to scream. She was the more bonded of the two. But to my astonishment, she adjusted to the change in surroundings happily, making gurgling noises at Matteo. I glanced over at Seraphine, checking she was not distressed with this display of familiarity, but the fire had left her.

"Do you want to hold your niece?" I asked, not wanting her to be upset by Rori's reaction to Matt.

Sera smiled, and I placed Khione in her arms.

"Coffee?" Several nods, and I headed into the kitchen, Illy on my heels. "That is going better than expected. What magic did you work?"

"They have both agreed to focus on Rai for now. We will be heading up to the clinic as soon as your mother calls to say he is awake."

"Your doing?"

Illy smiled. She was the eternal diplomat and could always get people to negotiate. Getting them to focus on their common goal was clever.

"Did Mum come home?"

"Have you ever known your mother to abandon a patient? Freyja slept beside him all night. She considers him her grandson, too, you know. Your mother is kicking herself for not noticing his condition."

"She has barely seen him." I spoke in a low voice, not wanting to be overheard, but the conversation coming from the living room indicated things were amicable for the moment. "Sera arrived only two days after they got home from France. Apart from you, Sera wouldn't let anyone near him."

"You know your mother. Just like you."

CHAPTER 16

"What is that supposed to mean?" I hissed over the grinding of coffee beans.

"Both of you place the needs of others ahead of your own. You are both perfectionists. You both run yourselves until you are running on vapor."

"That's..." I stopped my disagreement mid-sentence. "Okay, maybe that is partially true."

"It takes one to know one, my darling girl. It took me years of being an overachiever, burning out every six months before I learned to pace myself. I will teach you before I retire, even if it kills me."

"You always said Sera and I would be the death of you." I smirked as I arranged the mugs for her, ready for the glorious, thick espresso.

"I haven't changed my opinion on that," she shot back, ignoring me as I turned my back and downed the shot before Gio noticed.

The mood was tense but not angry as we rode together to the clinic, leaving the girls with Dad. Gio desperately wanted to check in on Rai. Sorcha had allowed him to perform part of the surgery. While Gio had assisted with cardiac surgery in both Italy and Canada, Kat and Gio had never performed a ventricular repair, especially not on a child. Gio had been fascinated with the procedure of sewing a small fabric patch over the hole. The surgery had taken hours with the hole larger and more complex than previously thought. Guiltily, I had fallen asleep listening to him tell me the finer details of the surgery in the deep of the night.

"You saved him," I whispered as we leaned into each other in the hallway and watched Sera and Matt flank Rai, looking tiny and frail in the hospital bed. He was sporting a white chest bandage, hiding a long wound running down his torso. Gio had warned me it wasn't pretty.

"You were the first to recognize something was amiss." Gio bent down to kiss my neck. "You likely saved our nephew with your instincts."

"It was just a gut feeling. You detected it."

"It was a team effort. Your aunt took the lead. Not that I ever doubted it, but she is a powerhouse."

"She is. She and my mother are very alike."

"You should see the two of them operate together. It is like an elegant dance. They don't need to speak. They read each other, anticipate. It was the smoothest procedure I have ever seen. At one point, your mother just tapped Sorcha lightly on the shoulder, and Sorcha stepped away, holding out her instruments, letting your mother take her place."

"Why?"

"She was fatiguing and needed a break. Your mother saw it. She said nothing, just recognized that all surgeons push themselves beyond their limits, and stepped in. It was something special."

"They have worked together a long time. They are a team. When they operated on me, I never doubted I was in excellent hands."

"Speaking of together, do you think they will work it out?" he whispered, gesturing at Sera and Matt, still sitting on either side of Rai's bed.

"Unlikely. He has a new girlfriend." I tried not to sound bitter.

"He doesn't. I asked him when you and Sera walked in ahead of us. It is over."

"Regardless, he cheated. Sera won't forgive that."

"Did he?"

CHAPTER 16

My mouth dropped as I felt the red beast rise. "Yes," I hissed, barely able to believe that he was defending his brother in cheating on his wife. What kind of morals did these boys have?

Gio flicked his hand in dismissal, making the beast expand against my ribcage.

Storming outside, I sensed him close behind me but refused to turn and check. As soon as we were clear of the entrance and out of earshot, I whirled. "He cheated on her. They are married, and he fucked someone else. Don't make excuses."

"They had broken up at the time. That isn't cheating. They lived apart."

"They were taking a break. They are married."

"Exactly—a break. So they were free to see other people."

My hands slammed into his chest. "Does that mean marriage vows mean nothing? *We* took a break when I was here last time. Recovering. Did you take that time to fuck someone else?"

Shadows crossed his face, his gaze cast down to his feet. The breath escaped my lungs in a rush.

"You did!"

"No... I..."

It was too late. I couldn't hear it. His reaction had told me everything. He reached me as I climbed into the car and started the ignition. As silent as the electric cars were, my ears couldn't take the words he was saying in. All I could hear was "he cheated on me" repeated on a loop. As I pulled away, I wasn't sure where to go. Going home to Dad would invoke questions I didn't want to answer, but I knew I couldn't stay away from the girls for long. They needed to feed, and so did I. I had never realized how symbiotic breastfeeding was, how reliant we were on each other. Driving slowly, I played the conversation over in my mind. Feeling my chest, I knew I had some time. Setting a course for Callanish, I headed toward the stones. It was safe. It wasn't the solstice or equinox.

Parking the car in the old carpark, I wandered around the stones, touching them and feeling the mystical force they radiated. The air was clean and crisp, and I inhaled, staring out over the loch. The stones were cool to the touch, and I leaned against a large menhir in the main circle, wondering what I would do now. Return to Canada alone? Stay here? I nearly jumped out of my skin when the voice sounded behind me.

"Will you stop running away? I didn't cheat on you."

Spinning so rapidly, I nearly overbalanced on the uneven earth. I scowled at Gio as he stood a few meters away, watching me.

"Something happened. I can tell."

"It did, and I should have told you a long time ago."

Bile rose into my mouth as I looked over the ocean. "Who?"

"Francesca."

Of all the names I had played over in my mind on the journey here, that wasn't it. "What?" I could barely contain my incredulity. In the space of a split second, I had envisaged all the times she and he could have been together.

"She sent me a message a few days after I was stabbed. But I returned the call from here."

The ticking of my brain must have been audible. "She was still in Italy. We didn't know." Then. We hadn't known she was the one who had fed information about my movements to the Caspians. How she

CHAPTER 16

had ultimately been responsible for them kidnapping me. Torturing me. Murdering my baby.

"You saw her?"

"No, I spoke with her. Only she didn't know I was here. She thought I was still in Canada, recovering. She begged me to come home to Italy. She thought you had ... died ... and knowing I had no family, she offered to care for me."

Words formed in my mind, but with the blockage obstructing my throat, I was unable to verbalize any of them. He watched as I swallowed hard.

"She wanted you back? Days after I was tortured to an inch of my life, she wanted you back?"

"She didn't know you were alive. Illy and your mother kept that secret. No one knew what had happened other than the public pieces of information. You were kidnapped, and I was wounded. The medical teams in all communities knew I survived. The Canadians kept them informed; no one wants to lose one of their own. But you were presumed dead."

Recalling her face when I limped into the Lido deck on Piedmont, I asked, "Did you tell her I was alive?"

"At that point, you were lost to me and severely wounded. There was still a chance you wouldn't make it, and I couldn't bear to talk about it. I said nothing about you, only that I appreciated her offer but would recuperate at home."

"What did she say?" I whispered.

"That I would always have a home with her. I didn't know, then, that she was the one behind it all. I felt guilty enough for returning her call when you were lying in bed, unable to take two steps unaided. Haunted and unable to look at me. But when I called her, I thought perhaps she had information that could assist us in working out what had happened. So I never told you. It was a minute, maybe two. Then we went back to Italy, and Illy learned about her role. She was banished, and you and I were still so distant. By the time you found your way back to me, she wasn't even a fleeting thought in my mind. My entire focus was on you. Truthfully, I hadn't even thought of that conversation until today."

"That isn't cheating."

"No, but I didn't tell you either. But not because I was hiding it from you. Because it was a two-minute conversation that meant nothing."

"Except she hasn't let go. Even after knowing that they snatched me from your arms, she still wanted you back. This was always her endgame."

"She did. But again, I didn't know then that she played a part."

It was stupid, but I needed to know. My voice cracked as I spoke. "If I had died, would you have gone back? To her, I mean?"

"Never. Our relationship was over well before I met you. When you came into my life, I realized how wonderful life could be. It wouldn't have been fair to her, or me, to settle for second-best. No, I would never have done that."

Satisfied, I nodded.

Gio reached for me, pulling me toward him. "I am so sorry for leaving you when you were in labor. I was blind with rage. Although I always knew what you had been through, seeing it with my own eyes made me snap. I have never felt like that, like I was outside my own body. I wanted to kill them, all of them."

"Was it so bad?" I slipped an arm around his waist.

CHAPTER 16

"Your face. Even when I closed my eyes, I couldn't stop seeing the agony, and I was powerless to stop it. Knowing you were protecting our child until your last breath? I have never loved you more. The conflict tore me apart. I needed them to die. I swore to help people and save lives, yet I was consumed with the overwhelming urge to make them pay for what they did to you. I had to go. Carmelo and Jake knew I would have gone alone if they hadn't accompanied me."

"You could have made things so much worse."

"I know. We didn't. It was your voice I could hear in my head, telling me to walk away. The last thing we want is their wrath raining down on us again. So we set the charge and left. Jake and Carmelo would always do what I wanted."

"I was angry at you for leaving me when I was in labor. When I needed you, you weren't there."

"I cannot tell you how much guilt I feel over that. I desperately wanted to be there every step of the way. Always I have told you I would always be there, and when you needed me most, I was gone."

"Sera thought that about your brother. That he would always be there." I was being snarky but couldn't help it.

"I don't care what Matt did or didn't do. It isn't our business. *Angelo mio*, we need to stay out of it. It cannot become our problem. But I will want you until my dying breath. You are the other half of me, my true love, the mother of my children. You gave me the gift of immunity, our children, too. I would cross oceans and climb mountains for you. You are my everything. I do not have words for how much I love you."

"You just want me," I whispered, feeling the heat of his breath on my neck.

"Do we have time? Do you need to get back to the girls?" he growled as his fingers hooked through the fabric of my pants, his hands slipping lower.

"They can wait a little longer."

"Submit."

He flipped me onto my back, the enormous monolith behind my head shielding my eyes from the glaring sun. Closing my eyes, I felt his kisses rain down on my ribs, down the length of my torso, and to my inner thighs. Involuntarily, I moved as his closely clipped beard tickled my sensitive skin and felt his hands grip my hips, holding me in place. For a long time, I had believed that submission meant relinquishing power and control. I had fought against it, seeing it as weak. These years with Gio had shown me another reality, that submission, when given freely from a place of respect and trust, was a wonderful thing. Placing your trust wholeheartedly in another and knowing without doubt they would guard you like you were the most valuable possession they have is more powerful than fighting for control.

Another vehicle was parked, empty, blocking the entrance to the charging shed, the cables running through the dirt but not plugged in. We pulled up alongside, the electric vehicles running silently. The voices were low and muffled as we clambered out, and I paused, not wanting to interrupt. The battery was low, and I knew I needed to plug it in for the next driver, but hearing Matt's words echo from the shed, I froze.

CHAPTER 16

"I'm so sorry, Sera. Hurting you was the last thing I wanted to do. I didn't really want to see anyone else. It is over with Izumi. I love you. It was only ever you."

Sera's tone was low and full of pain. "You betrayed me. Your son. Our vows. You promised me it was only me. Then at the first opportunity, you jump into bed with someone else. At a time when I was struggling with work and being a mother, you abandoned me. You left us."

"I won't argue with you. All I can say is that I cannot tell you how sorry I am. I love you so much it hurts. There is no excuse. But I was in a dark place. My head was a mess, and I couldn't see straight. I felt like you had a reason to live that wasn't me. It happened so quickly between us. You arrived at the lowest point in my life. I had intended to take my life that day you fell into our world. Within days, we were together, and I was blissfully happy."

"When did you stop being happy? With me?" Sera's words were thickening, and I sensed the tightening of her throat.

"I don't know. All I know is it wasn't you."

"If not me, what was it, then?"

"I don't know. That is the truth. My head was in a fog. I couldn't focus. It wasn't one thing, but a series of things. Everyone loves you. Everywhere we went, people wanted to talk to you and have your attention. You had your work and Rai. He needed you in a way he didn't need me, and I was adrift. Alone."

"You can't blame our son for your infidelity."

"Truly, I don't. The only person to blame is me. I couldn't think straight. I felt alone and lonely. Izumi made me feel whole, and I finally saw a way out of the darkness, but even then, it was you I wanted."

My skin prickled.

"Never use her name in front of me," Sera hissed the words, punctuating them, making them distinct, and my chest swelled, proud that she was standing up to him despite her pain. Jutting my chin, I awaited his reply.

"I am so sorry, Seraphine." His words were soft, and I almost felt sympathy for him. "Truly sorry. I never meant to hurt you."

"When trust is broken, sorry means nothing," I heard her whisper, surprised I could hear anything at all. The door was closed, and the chickens were clucking around the yard, bees humming as they enjoyed Dad's lavender hedge. Gio's hand touched my arm, and we slipped away. It wouldn't do to be caught eavesdropping. She would tell me everything later.

Dad handed us the fussing girls as soon as we walked in the house, and I felt guilty that we had detoured past the stones, but as always, Dad never berated me. He just looked grateful that I was home.

"They are hungry, and I can't help with that. Don't have the right equipment."

"Thanks, Dad." I tried to let the gratitude break through. "Have they been awake long?"

"Not really. I changed them and managed to keep them entertained. But they need you. How is Rai?"

"Doing well." Gio launched into a spiel about the surgery and recovery process, including details of the procedure itself, allowing me to escape to our bedroom with one baby in each arm, grinning. Dad would have no interest in the medical procedure, I knew from years of experience, overhearing Mum regale him with the gory details of her operations. Likewise, she had little interest in his horticultural projects. I

CHAPTER 16

had frequently wondered what kept them together all these years, and from what I could see, they were happy. Sure, they disagreed but never for long. If they were in the same room, they were always smiling, touching each other. Just a tiny caress as one passed the other, a swipe of her hip or his lower back, doing the most mundane of chores, but that sense of reassurance. "I've got your back, no matter what." It had been embarrassing as a child, watching them so in love. Illy had often teased them for their public displays of affection. But now I wanted to know. What was the secret to their success? They had been together for more than thirty years, despite their share of hiccups. As I settled in to feed my daughters, I prayed that Gio and I would find the same contentment and commitment that transcended time. Was love enough? When I was younger, I would have sworn that love surpassed everything else. The warm buzzing feeling in the pit of your stomach made you overlook actions that ordinarily you wouldn't. But now I knew better. Love was something you worked at, every day. Illy had said to me once, "Love is a verb." A conscious effort. Sera and Matt had been in love, but it hadn't been enough to stop him from doing something stupid that had jeopardized their family. Now they were both miserable as a result. Was communication the key, then? Respect, honesty, and talking to each other? Recognizing that there are good days and bad days, but keeping the lines of communication open, always having each other's back?

CHAPTER 17

"**WE NEED TO TALK** about contraception."

"What?" My eyes flicked up to the doorway where Sorcha stood, upright and regal. She was one of those women who had presence. She was noticed wherever she went and commanded respect from her manner. While her blunt tone had taken me by surprise as I gazed into Rori's sweet face as she fed, it was her words more than anything that had knocked me from my stupor.

"Breastfeeding is far from a guarantee, and I am guessing you don't want to be pregnant again so soon?"

"Well…uhh…no." Very few people had the capacity to render me speechless, but Sorcha had made me feel three years old my entire life. Tall, imposing, and assertive, she was a powerhouse. Within a sentence, she had proven that she was here in an official capacity and not as my aunt. I should have known. She strode across the room and sat beside me.

"Contraception is a powerful tool for women," she continued, not noticing or caring about my increasingly reddening face. "For many generations, women

CHAPTER 17

had no control over their own bodies, couldn't make choices that best suited themselves or their families. In some communities, that is still the case. You are fortunate. We have that power. We choose if and when to have children and how many we have."

Many times over my life, I had heard Sorcha's rant about how men had traditionally used women's fertility against them, keeping them home and pregnant with hordes of children, and how having children should be a choice, and how critical it was for women to take control over their own bodies. Sorcha had single-handedly educated women in all ACC communities, running workshops, training doctors, and setting up women's health clinics. I had even attended some. In truth, I wholly believed in what she taught, but I really didn't want to have this conversation and not right now. After all these years, I recognized that it was futile to argue with her. Getting her out of here as soon as possible was key.

"It is important that you and your husband resume your physical relationship."

Now she was heading into really uncomfortable territory. She meant well; I just did not need to discuss this with my aunt.

"What do you recommend?" I asked hurriedly.

"There are several choices. Did you have any problem with your IUD before?"

"Not really." My face reddened further.

"Then that is a good option. It lasts for years, which gives you enough time to decide if you want more children and when is a good time."

"Okay," I mumbled, feeling awkward. Gio desperately wanted a large family, something that wasn't possible in Piedmont. I had grown up with a large family of siblings and cousins and wasn't sure it was what I wanted.

"Drop by the clinic tomorrow afternoon. It won't take long. Have you asked your sister if she is planning any more children?"

Not really wanting to discuss Seraphine's sex life with my aunt, I muttered, "No idea. Ask her yourself."

Sorcha stood, nodding. "I will. Might as well do you both."

Seraphine found me later as I was walking around the garden with Rori. "Well, that was uncomfortable," she muttered.

"Aunt Sorcha found you, too?" I grinned at her as we walked.

"She said you had requested an IUD."

"Request wasn't the word I used. Railroaded is more like it. But she is right. The last thing I want is another child."

"I want another child," Sera whispered, making me stop and stare. Only yesterday, I had overheard her telling Matt it was over. Had something changed?

"Not with Matt," she hastened to add. "But I want Rai to have brothers and sisters, like we did. Grow up in a family."

"Umm, the man is kind of an essential part in that," I said, flabbergasted at this conversation. "Well, unless you want a donor."

"I know." She kicked a rock down the path ahead of us.

"Does that mean you will get back with Matt? Isn't that the wrong reason to be with someone?"

"As much as I would love Rai to have biological brothers and sisters, I can't. The sense of betrayal hurts more than I can say. Besides, we all grew up as a family, yet very few of us were full siblings."

"True." I spoke cautiously, unsure where this conversation was going and not knowing what to ask next.

"Rai is two. I don't want a large gap between my children," she explained, making my breath jerk slightly.

"How is Rai doing?" I asked, desperate to shift the conversation.

"Really well. He is loving having Matt here, and we are taking turns to stay with him."

"How does that feel?"

"It is good for both of them."

"And you?" I really didn't want to pry but was desperate to know.

Sera sighed. "I have no idea what I want. One minute, I want my family back together. The next, I want to plunge a knife in his heart."

"Ah, men," I sighed as we continued to walk.

CHAPTER 18

MUM INSISTED WE STAY and celebrate the girls' quarter-birthday as they didn't know when they would see the girls again. Even in the few months we had been here, they had changed so much, and it devastated me to leave my family once more as Gio and I discussed plans to return to Canada. Sera, Matt, and Rai would stay for a little longer so Mum could monitor his heart, and I hoped Sera didn't do anything foolish while she was so confused. While Rai's surgery appeared to have been successful, there was always the risk of infection, blood clot, or even that the patch might become loose. After their failure to diagnose, it was evident that the medical team in Japan had little knowledge of cardiac issues in children, so it was agreed that Rai was best to stay here until he was given the green light to travel. Sera and Matt were cool but pleasant, all their attention focused on their son, and I wished fervently that they could overcome this.

Matt and I finally found time for him to give me a briefing on his bathymetry project. The mood was chilled but professional, and by focusing on the work

CHAPTER 18

he was doing, I thawed toward him. Soon, I would resume my role as Chief, and his work was important for all communities, knowing where other geothermic vents might exist and tracking the best path to land so we could build bridges. He sensed I was distant but was smart enough not to ask. Perhaps Gio had told him to tread carefully. They were brothers, and I would never come between them. But knowing what he had done to destroy Seraphine broke my heart.

Illy and Carmelo accompanied us back to Canada, assisting with managing the girls at each stop along the way. Dad was devastated to learn we were leaving, insisting on holding the girls every waking minute and memorizing their faces so he wouldn't forget them. Mum assumed her typical cool persona, claiming they would come to visit us again soon, but several times I entered a room and caught her cradling one of them longingly in a way that I had never seen her do. As the youngest of her children, I had rarely seen her with a baby and hadn't seen her around Louis's or Xanthe's children often. Saying goodbye left me bereft, to the point where, midway back to Canada, Illy suggested that we move permanently back to Lewis.

"You can do the Chief job from anywhere, you know that?"

"But I promised I would finish the land-bridge project and start replicating it on other communities."

"You can manage anything remotely, Caitlin. Besides, it is nearly finished. You only need to finalize the energy transfer from the hydrothermic vents so they can build more pods, and it is complete."

"Are you sure this is what you want?" Gio's brows furrowed. "There are medical teams on all communities, so I can work anywhere. So can you. Leaving your family is killing you."

"You are my family." As hard as it was to utter the words, it was true. The moment I committed to him, my loyalty needed to be with him and our girls.

"I told you I would follow you anywhere, and I meant it. Besides, when I married you, they became my family, too."

"I know. But I made a commitment to the people of Canada. I will see it through. But one day, maybe. When there is someone who can take over as Ambassador."

"All you need to do is ask, and we can pack in a day."

The long flight was exhausting, and we entered the pod to squeals of excitement wracking me with guilt that I had ever contemplated not returning. nîpiy led the charge, plucking the baby from my arms as soon as I was on the helipad.

"Now which little princess is this?"

Gio peered over. "That is Khione."

"She is an angel."

"Only when she is asleep."

"Every parent says that. But look at her. I could take her home. She is divine."

Khione was doing her best impression of an angel with her dark fuzz and now emerald-green eyes sparkling up at nîpiy.

"She looks so much like you." nîpiy looked up at me.

"Aurora looks like her father. He is her favorite."

The girls were adapting very well to the loud reverberation of the crowd in the main pod. Even

CHAPTER 18

Gio was cringing slightly at the noise after months on Lewis, where the loudest sound was often a chicken squawking outside our bedroom window or the chatter of children on their way to school. Illy was carrying Aurora, I noted, refusing to relinquish her and showing off her grandchild proudly while Carmelo carried bags. Turning to assist, I was quickly shooed away to our quarters to rest.

While Illy returned to work the following day, she insisted I take one more day to rest before returning to work for reduced hours. Carmelo had arrived for nonno duty shortly after the girls had awoken, leaving Gio and me wondering what to do.

"Would you like to make a trip out to our pod?" he asked, the smirk not leaving his face.

"How would you feel about visiting the hot springs below the city?" I dimpled back, equally cheeky. "It has been so long, being on Lewis and being pregnant. I would love…"

Before I had even finished the sentence, Gio was on the intercom seeking a booking for the springs.

"Perfect," he responded, raising his eyebrows at his success.

"Please tell me they didn't cancel someone else's time," I pleaded.

"No, she said they had a one-hour window at 10 a.m."

I glanced out the window. After our months on Lewis, I had reverted to telling time by the sun, not the central timekeeping that was common in the underwater habitations. "What is it now? About eight?"

Gio glanced at the clock beside the intercom. "A little after. Should we eat first?"

"Only if you let me have coffee."

"I am aware that you have been drinking coffee for weeks. I can taste it on your breath, you know."

Sheepishly, I flushed. "Guilty. I wait until after I have fed them, I promise."

"I know," he teased. "I had wondered how long you would last. You have done very well."

"Mum says there was something called decaffeinated coffee in Australia, before the world changed, I mean. The full taste of coffee but without the caffeine."

"Does she know how they achieved that?"

"She doesn't, but surely it wouldn't be hard to research."

"Remind me to chat with Deb. She might know."

After a leisurely breakfast, we headed to the hot springs, feeling like naughty teenagers sneaking out to have sex while our parents were away. Everyone stopped to say hello, resulting in us being late for our scheduled time.

"Remind me to be rude next time," Gio groaned as he plunged into the steaming waters, rolling and floating on his back, gazing at the rocky roof. I entered more cautiously, still getting the occasional twinge from my cesarean wound.

"You know I can't not speak with people." My feet floated out from under me, and I lay beside him, floating and inhaling the steam. "They haven't seen us in months."

"Well, they will see you tomorrow when you return to work, and I will only get you in the evenings."

"Well, we had better make the most of our last day together." Putting my feet down, I stood behind his head, placing a hand on each cheek and kissed him, holding his head in place.

CHAPTER 18

"I am in charge," he growled in that low masculine tone I adored when I finally allowed him to take a breath.

"Prove it."

CHAPTER 19

"**THERE IS A CALL** for you. On the secure line."

Glancing up from my screen, I couldn't quite interpret the look on Illy's face. Concern? Very few people even knew there was a dedicated line for the Ambassadors, an untraceable one. Who on earth would be calling me on it, on my third day back in the job, no less?

"Can you take a message? If I have any chance of getting home tonight, I need to finish this. I am already late to send it out."

"Ordinarily I would, but I really think you should take this one, Caitlin."

"Who is it?"

"Francesca."

My eyebrows hit my hairline, recalling the conversation I had with Gio on Lewis and Francesca's inappropriate proposal. I could barely contain the snarl. "Seriously? What does that bitch want?"

"I didn't ask, but judging by her tone and the use of the ambassador's line, I would suspect it is urgent."

"She didn't tell you?"

CHAPTER 19

"She insisted she speak with you and you alone."

Pausing, I considered my options. Illy's face pulled me out of my reverie.

"Fine, send it through. But I will take it here. I have too much to do to waste time on her."

Nodding, Illy closed the door firmly behind her. Putting on my headset, I waited for the call to be patched through.

"Caitlin?" The voice was the heavily accented Italian I recalled but was barely above a whisper.

Bracing myself, I forced myself to modulate my tone. "Yes. What do you want?"

"I need your help."

Excellent. So we weren't wasting time on pleasantries, then.

"Sure. What kind of help would you like? Would you like my help to arrange people to kidnap and torture me before attempting to murder me? Or just help to steal my husband while I was lying in a hospital with every bone shattered, my baby murdered, and wishing to die?"

Silence. Just as I was thinking she had hung up, a tiny voice whispered, "*Mi dispiace.* I am so sorry. I was jealous and angry. I did not know what they would do. Truly."

The hiss was so venomous even I was shocked it was me speaking. "You told them where I was. Because of you, my baby is dead. They beat me, molested me. I barely survived. You did this. And now you want my *help*?" The pitch of my voice had risen several octaves and was wavering, unable to disguise the incredulity.

"I saw. I am so sorry, Caitlin. I did not know. I saw what they did, and I didn't know that is what they would do. I swear it."

Closing my eyes, I wondered how many people had seen that tape. Not just the ambassadors, it appeared.

"What do you want from me?"

"I am married now. Pregnant."

For anyone else, I would congratulate them and ask them how they were. But this was the woman who had orchestrated my murder. Unsuccessfully, but that wasn't her plan. Then she had come on to my husband, believing me dead.

"And?"

Her words came out in a rush, still whispered, like someone was listening. "The policy here is for one child per couple. They prevent women from having any more. As soon as my child is born, they will remove my insides."

A memory stirred of Seraphine and me, hidden in that office in Yellowstone, reading about their abhorrent treatment of their citizens. Women in particular.

"I can't help you, Francesca."

"You are a good woman, Caitlin."

"You don't know that."

"I do. I saw what you did for our people. Saving them."

"What makes you think I can do anything for you?"

"You are the Chief. They will listen to you."

"Yellowstone is not part of the ACC. I have no jurisdiction there." My tone was cold, but my stomach twinged, just a little. I looked out the window, watching the sunset, wondering where my babies were. While I had no desire to have more, I could. The option was there.

"Please," she begged. "Please don't let them do this to me." The distress in her voice moved even me, despite steeling myself against it. This was a woman who had inflicted untold pain and suffering on me,

CHAPTER 19

personally, and my family. But despite everything, I couldn't be the one to inflict pain on her. Not if there was a chance.

"I will make some calls. But Francesca, I can't promise anything."

"Please let me go home. To Italy."

"What about your husband?"

"Chris, too. Please, Caitlin. He is a good man."

"Does he know what you did?"

Quiet crackles stretched between us before I heard the single word. "No."

"So you are asking me to intervene on your behalf, in a community where I have no power, when you haven't even told your husband that you were responsible for my kidnap, torture, and the murder of my unborn child?"

I felt her inhale at my arctic tone, the shards of ice penetrating her ear. "I understand now," she whispered. "I feel my child move within me. I would do anything to protect my baby."

"As I was trying to protect mine!" I spat. "You watched the tape? So you saw them as they stole that life from me."

"I saw."

"*You* did that Francesca. You and your jealousy. Giovanni wasn't yours when I arrived. He was a free man, and he chose *me*."

"But you have babies now, two children. Please. I beg you. Don't let them do this to me."

How does she know? The thought struck me like a rock to the temple. Yellowstone wasn't part of the ACC. How did she know I had twins?

Voices sounded behind her, angry voices, and the line dropped out. Slumping in my chair, I closed my eyes and replayed the conversation.

"Are you alright?" Illy stood in the doorway, leaning against the frame.

I lifted my head from my hands and stared at her, bleary-eyed. Within minutes, I had told her everything. She had been the one who had learned that it was Francesca who had passed the intel to the Caspians, but she didn't know she had contacted Gio after my attack.

"Bitch!" Illy spat, and I smiled wanly, knowing she would always have my back.

"She is pregnant. I know what they do to women after they have one child. Permanent birth control. Sterilization. They rip their uterus out."

"I have read the files."

"She has asked me for help."

"What will you do?"

All the air left my lungs. "I don't know. I owe her nothing. We have no jurisdiction over Yellowstone, although the relationship is amicable. I don't see why they would listen to me."

"But?"

"But I need to try. She begged me. It is inhumane what they do."

"It isn't our place to judge their practices. Besides, there is a precedent. We can't save them all, Caitlin. She isn't special."

"I know, but I have been to Yellowstone. It is a cold and miserable place. I can't imagine what it would be like to live there, pregnant. Knowing you would do anything to defend your child. They are taking away her right to have a second."

CHAPTER 19

"Let's remember she took away your first, through sheer hatred and jealousy."

"I know. I can't help it. I need to try. Most likely, they will ignore me, but would it be the worst thing in the world to ask for her to have a transfer back to Italy? She wasn't born there. This wasn't something she has always known. We are here, and she is married. Things are different. She has served her time."

"What makes you think the Piedmont community will give her a fair go if she goes back?"

The use of the quintessentially Australian expression of a "fair go" made me smile, thinking of Dad. It was a concept my parents still devoutly believed in. That idea that you should always treat everyone with respect and give them the opportunity to be their best self.

"I have no control over what the people in Piedmont do other than speaking with Riccardo. But I can put in a word on her behalf. What were the terms of her transfer?"

"It was no transfer. It was a permanent move. They only accepted as she was multi-lingual and useful to them in a communications capacity."

"So, they may not be willing to let her go?"

"Likely not. They may also not want to lose her partner and whatever role he performs."

"She didn't say."

"So, Chief Mackintosh, what do you want to do about it?"

"Sleep on it. I can't do anything tonight, anyway."

"Head home. It is late. I will see you in the morning."

Francesca's call haunted me to the point where Gio called me out as we sat on the couch after dinner.

"Speak."

189

"You know I can't tell you official business," I protested.

"Like that has stopped you before. I know pretty much everything. When have I ever divulged a state secret?"

It was true. Illy and I had spoken about it once, how it was important to have someone to confide in. She spoke with Carmelo, I knew, and he to her.

Sighing, I told him of the call.

"You can't seriously be contemplating helping her."

"How do I not? She begged me. She is pregnant and scared."

The subterranean snarl took even me by surprise. "I was angry at her before I saw the tape. Now I would tear her apart with my bare hands. If she had not betrayed you, none of that would have happened. Her jealousy caused us both immense suffering, but you in particular. I will never forgive her."

"I can't forgive her, either," I whispered, "but I can't let them do that to her without trying to help. No woman deserves that. Not even her."

"You owe her nothing."

"No, I don't. But her children. They are innocent. For them, I need to try."

Another deep rumble erupted from his chest. "She doesn't deserve children."

"Please don't forbid me. You know I need to try."

"I know better than to forbid you. I know full well you would never listen to me, anyway. But I am not happy about it. I can't believe you would help her."

"It is unlikely they will listen to me. I have no power over Yellowstone. But a call to their Council? I can do that. Likely it will make not one shred of difference, but I need to try."

CHAPTER 19

"Every day you amaze me." Gio pulled me into his chest. "I am so blessed to have you in my life. You treat everyone like they are valued, even people who have wronged you. I have never met anyone quite like you. You truly are the Chief in every way."

"Come on. Let's get to bed. I have an early meeting in the morning."

CHAPTER 20

"IT IS SO WONDERFUL to have you here again," I squealed, hurling myself at them both as they came through the portal, narrowly missing Illy as she traveled in the opposite direction, leaving me for the first time since I had returned to work. "I have missed you so much."

"We have missed you, too," Antonio said sincerely after kissing both my cheeks fervently. I felt the unloading teams watching this familiar greeting. "We loved our time here and even having you back home. We need to do this more often."

"Your English!" My mouth dropped at how fluently he was speaking.

Joseph elbowed Antonio in the ribs. "We took classes after our last visit here. We thought it would be best if we knew what people were saying about us."

"No one is saying anything negative. Everyone loves you. You are always welcome here. I would love it if you stayed here on a permanent basis."

"Truly, we think of you as part of our family. You made us a family, and we will forever be grateful."

CHAPTER 20

"Well, about that, I have a proposal to make. But it is just an offer, and you will need to think about it. I mean really think it through. You can take as long as you need."

"You want us to come here? We know. You tell us all the time. You will need to convince Riccardo though. Although you outrank him, you can speak with him. We are not taking on that battle."

"No. Something a little more permanent."

"More permanent than moving here?"

I laughed. "Come for dinner tonight. We can talk then. You are in a different apartment this time but closer to our place. Come on. I'll show you."

Gio grinned as he finished clearing the table and placed the cheese platter in the center of the table. He returned to his seat beside me and held my hand under the table.

"Are these?" Antonio asked, raising an eyebrow as he lifted a small bunch of green grapes from the plate with one hand as he juggled Aurora on his knee with the other. The girls hadn't left the table the entire meal, constantly in one of our arms. Knowing we had something important to discuss, they had chosen tonight to stay awake long past their usual bedtime. We had taken it in turns to eat single-handed.

"Yours? They are. We grow table and wine varieties."

The guys waited for me, and I took a deep breath before speaking.

"We would like to offer you a child of your own."

Joseph looked down at Khione, and she batted her dark eyelashes solemnly at him. "How? Can you buy them now?"

Despite the seriousness of our proposal, a peal of laughter burst free. "Not that I know of."

"Then how?"

"We," I looked at Gio, "have discussed this at great length. We would like to offer you an egg. You would need to find a surrogate to carry the baby. I can't do that, I am afraid. I know if I carry a child, I would never want to give it up, even to you. But the donation part I can do. One of you will need to be the father."

I waited for the count of ten breaths as they stared at each other, then at us.

Fearful that they didn't understand, Gio rapidly fired off my words in Italian.

"We understood," Joseph finally responded. "But why would you do this?"

"You are our closest friends. Last year, you supported me in so many ways."

"We did nothing."

"Yes, you did," I cut him off. "Every day, you were there, and you didn't judge. You didn't ask me questions and make me relive memories I couldn't get out of my mind. You stayed with me through the nightmares, picked me up, and allowed me to maintain my dignity. I will always remember what you did. Words cannot express how much you both mean to me. Now I can do something for you."

"What are you suggesting?"

"There is an IVF specialist on Lewis. I have asked if she would come here. I have offered to do one round of IVF and see how many eggs can be harvested. Not any time soon, but one day, Giovanni and I would

CHAPTER 20

like another child. Fine. Maybe two," I added, seeing his eyebrows raise and knowing his feelings on the subject. "But if there are spare eggs, I would like to donate them to our friends who may not have children. Sera's brother Alasdair also has a male partner, and we intend to ask them, too. We need to see. It may not be successful, but if it is..."

I was rambling now and knew it. Their faces were agape, mouths open and unable to speak.

"There is something else we need to tell you."

"More?"

I glanced at Gio. He spoke the words in Italian, to ensure they understood. "Caitlin is immune. Any of her children will also be immune."

"*Immunitario?*" Joseph gasped, his eyes bulging.

Gio fired off a quick synopsis of my conception and birth, leaving out the less palatable parts. He explained about the other girls like me and why it was a secret. Finally, he told them that the immunity was a dominant trait and why my children would be the future of all of our communities.

Leaning back in his chair, Gio's hand slipped into mine. We waited, but a stillness filled the room. Even the girls had chosen this moment to be perfectly still, snuggling into their chosen shoulder.

"Say something," Gio finally prompted them.

"We always knew you were special, Caitlin. But this... This is a surprise."

Shrugging, I smiled. This had always been my life.

"But is it alright? Two men to raise a child?"

"Why wouldn't it be?"

"What if it is a girl?" Joseph hissed, panicked.

"She will be the luckiest little lady in the world."

"No one in Piedmont has ever done this."

"Then why not start with you?"

"What would we tell people? We can't just come home with a child one day. An immune child."

"The immune part must remain secret, for my safety, but there is really no reason for anyone to ever know. It isn't like we go outside. But you will need to explain the donor part. We won't tell anyone who donated the egg if you don't. I really don't mind if you tell everyone or no one."

Gio interjected, "If you want to help normalize the process, all of you, there is probably no better way than for people to know Caitlin is involved. She is the Chief, and that comes with some privileges."

I scowled at him. I may be the Chief in title, but he knew how I felt. It was just a job. I was no different from anyone else. But if lending my name to this meant they would face less resistance, I was prepared to support that. I turned my attention back to our guests.

"Look, it is just an idea at this point. You would need to discuss it, work out if you want this. Then, even if you do, you need to work out how you accommodate a child into your lives. They kind of take over."

My last words were interrupted by a tired cry, and I stood to take Khione from Antonio.

"May I?" Joseph asked, holding out his arms.

"Of course. I will warn you, she is probably hungry and needs changing, so she won't let you hold her for long." Quickly, I checked she wasn't soaked and handed her over, grinning at Gio, who was bouncing Aurora on his knee. We both watched Joseph's face transition from his usual cheeky expression to one of awe as he stared into her tiny face. The question was plain on his face. *Could we do this?*

CHAPTER 20

To my utter astonishment, instead of screeching indignantly at this change in scenery, Khi opened her big green eyes up at him, her little pink lips forming an "O." They stared at each other, and I couldn't suppress the smile.

"He is gone," Gio said in a low voice, but Joseph didn't even hear him. He was so mesmerized by this new life. She was quite taken with him as well. Antonio stood at his husband's side and stared down at Khione. She took in the second face as well and looked between them intently.

"She smiled at me!" Antonio gasped.

I didn't have the heart to tell him it likely wasn't a smile. She probably just grimaced from being hungry. Khione saw Gio move from the table and screwed up her face, ready to cry. She adored him and would choose him over anyone else in a room, including me.

"Where's my girl?" he cooed, making my heart melt as he scooped her into his free arm and whisked them away to the bedroom to be changed and settled.

"I'll give you a few minutes." Quietly, I cleared the table and stacked the dishes in the sink. I could hear them conversing in Italian and didn't interrupt, even though my Italian was almost fluent now, listening to Gio and Carmelo speak to the girls in Italian daily.

"When?"

The voice jerked me from my own daydreams. "What?"

"When would this happen?"

"Well," I considered as I scraped the plates, "we need time to get Jorja here. Finding a surrogate could take time too, someone willing to gestate the baby. Then it takes at least a month for me to go through the cycle of egg-collection. Assuming the procedure is successful, it takes thirty-eight weeks or thereabouts for the child to be born. I'd say you are safe for another year. Why?"

Joseph nodded. "Who will be the father?"

"That is up to you. You can choose, or you can both donate, and we wait and see." The cries were getting louder. I needed to feed the girls, or they would never sleep.

"Sit, I will be back soon."

"We will go if you don't mind. We have a lot to discuss."

Reaching over, I hugged them both. "Talk. Ask me anything you like. Medical history, anything you need to know. Promise?"

Gio popped his head out of the nursery door, a swaddled bundle in each arm, their tiny faces pink from exhaustion. "*Buonanotte*," he called.

"Good night. See you tomorrow."

CHAPTER 21

"CAITLIN!"

Joseph's voice sounded from behind me as I walked to work, making me jolt. Carmelo had collected the girls early, claiming he had nothing else to do, as Illyria was in Japan. Child-free, I had decided to get a jumpstart on my work. So much for working part-time.

"I'm so sorry. I didn't hear you. I was thinking about everything I needed to do today."

"My apologies. I can wait."

"For you, I always have time. Please. Ask."

"Antonio and I want to discuss," he glanced around to ensure no one could overhear us, "your condition."

"Con… Ohhh."

"Is that why you were taken?" he whispered.

I knew what he was asking. Would a child always be at risk of being kidnapped? I answered as honestly as I could.

"I don't think so. If they had known, they would have kept me. Made me have children or at least experimented on me to find ways to pass it on. Based on what they said, what happened last year was only because of what happened on Piedmont."

Joseph nodded. "But your girls. Do people know?"

Steering Joseph down a side corridor and into an alcove, I told him everything. "I am not the only immune adult. There were twenty-seven of us, twenty-four from my mother and three from my aunt, my mother's sister, and that is a whole other story. But only twenty-four survived until adulthood, all girls, and I was the last to have children. I wish I could tell you there was no risk, but that would be a lie. When I was born, all the people in the landside pods knew. But very few in the unhabs know. Here, it is only Gio, Carmelo, and Illyria. We have never told anyone else, as it doesn't matter, and I don't want to be treated differently. Does that make sense?"

"But your girls?" he persisted.

"They are immune. It is a dominant gene, so all children descended from me and my sisters are also immune. They will also pass that immunity on to their children. One day, our ancestors will be able to live outside once more because of these children. At last count, there were over forty immune babies, plus the original mothers. It will take a few generations, but we will get to the point where more people are immune than not. It also gives the earth a chance to heal so we can live outside again. That is why my father works so hard on propagating the moss they found on Mousa."

"Why are you offering us this gift? Tonio and me?"

"All my life, people have known I was different. Some people were scared of me. Others wanted to be my partner, as they knew of the gift I could pass on to children and wanted that. But when I came to Piedmont, you treated me like a person. You are my

CHAPTER 21

friend. Both of you. You have never treated me as anything other than your friend. It is why I fell in love with Giovanni. He loved me for me, not for what I could give him. It was the first time in my life I had felt that way."

Joseph nodded, understanding.

"But I also feel an obligation to pass this gift on. While Gio may want lots of children, I don't. This is a way we can give you something special but also help future generations. This is what my mother did. Does that make sense?"

"Thank you. I need to speak with Tonio again, but we want this, Caitlin. If you are sure, we want this."

"I am positive. You will make wonderful parents."

A few days later, I called Jorja, and she was thrilled to hear from me. As one of the original scientists and the mother of the first immune twins, Ruby and Scarlett, she assumed responsibility for the project to collect stem cells from umbilical cord blood and monitor each of the immune individuals. She asked me to keep a diary of my cycle so she could minimize the period of impact on me and the duration of medications I would need to take.

"You know they will really knock you around," she warned.

"More than pregnancy?" I laughed.

"Maybe not," she agreed. "It depends on the woman. But you will feel nauseous and unwell a lot of the time."

Illy flinched visibly when I told her via our morning videoconference what we had offered the guys and planned to offer Alasdair and Nick, her response completely taking me by surprise.

"What is it?" I asked, perplexed, watching her face as I sat at my desk.

"You know that is what they did to your mother? How you were conceived? Taking drugs, I mean, to produce multiple ripened eggs."

I nodded. "I read the files. It was where I got the idea."

"What happened caused your mother years of trauma. Deliver this news gently. She is a doctor and will understand the logic, but emotionally, she may find it hard. Freyja struggled with PTSD for years afterward. This is exactly the type of thing that could trigger her."

"Noted. I'll choose my moment."

"In person is best. Your parents have plans to visit, I know, but won't be there for a while. I assume there is no rush?"

"None at all. But I had better call Jorja back and let her know it is between us for now."

"Highly recommended. It is best if your mother hears it from you."

I barely caught Illy's last words as the world began to shake violently and the screen flickered before going black. "What the bloody hell?" I yelled.

"Floor!" nîpiy bellowed from the outer office as I froze with the unfamiliar sensation. Flinging back the chair, I hurled myself under the desk as the world vibrated violently and my desk tipped, papers flying off as the hard surface crashed into the window.

CHAPTER 21

"What is it?" I called as my stomach churned, feeling seasick.

"Earthquake!" I heard her call from the front office.

As I cowered beside the fallen desk, watching items fall from every surface, all I could see were my babies. I hoped like hell they were okay. Carmelo had collected them after breakfast but hadn't yet brought them to me for lunch. Clutching the sides of my desk, I pulled my head in farther to avoid the cascade of papers and books flying across the room. The shaking banged the fallen chair repeatedly into the drawers beside my desk before turning so that the castors hit my legs.

As the shuddering slowed, I carefully withdrew and called out to nîpiy. "Are you okay?"

"Fine." She was pulling herself upright, looking around the room. "That was a big one."

"Do you get earthquakes often?"

"Occasionally but nothing like that. There is a fault line, but it runs farther north of here."

"Will there be another?"

"Possible but unlikely. Aftershocks are usually smaller, in any case."

Pulling my wobbly legs to stand, I clutched the windowsill and peered outside to assess the damage. As the dust settled, I gasped as I saw the gaping hole in the bridge, debris and bodies floating to the surface of the water below.

"No!" I screamed, not caring who heard.

nîpiy was at my side in a shot and gasped audibly as she saw what I had. The bridge resembled a children's set of blocks that someone had carefully constructed, then a toddler having a tantrum maliciously kicked it in the middle. Remnants hung at either end.

The center was smashed into nothing, giving me a view of the water beyond through the dust. Pieces of debris were scattered in the deep blue water below, slowly starting to drift with the waves.

My feet hit the floor, and I was running. *My girls. Carmelo.* Most mornings he took them for a walk to the garden pod. They loved being outside, and he spent hours there showing them the plants their grandfather and I had planted. Tears streamed down my face, blinding me as the images tortured me of my babies blown into the water. *No.* My chest constricted. *I can't lose them, too.*

As I reached the edge of the main pod where the air bridge had formerly hung, I saw people crowding around the blown-off entrance. I could feel the crisp fresh air whistling around the pod, and I noticed jagged pieces of the former link overlooking the drop to the water below. People stood crying and screaming, witnessing the carnage beyond. I pushed my way through, and they parted.

"How many?" I bellowed at Gabriel, who was standing at the edge. His face was blanched, the look of helplessness tormenting him, but he was holding it together. Barely.

"Four. We can see four people. In the water. But there is a lot of debris, and we can't see well. Likely more."

"Alive?"

"Some. There is movement."

"Can we get them?"

"Not without becoming infected ourselves. We have teams searching for something long to reach them, but they need to get under the air bridge so we can get to them."

CHAPTER 21

Kicking off my shoes and shedding my jacket, I searched for a clear space in the water below and dropped like a pin, remembering what Mum had taught me about jumping into water and not knowing the depth. I had no time to think about hitting underwater debris. As I hit the freezing water, feet first, my right foot hitting floating metal, the jarring impact reverberating up to my hip, an echo of my former injuries.

"Where?" I bellowed back up when I surfaced from the freezing lake and caught my breath. Gabriel's mouth opened and closed, but he recovered, lying on the edge of the pod, pointing to the nearest person, shouting directions. One by one, I threw them floating debris to cling to until I could tow them to shore. Counting in my head. Three alive, three dead. It was exhausting. I hadn't swum in anything other than a pool since I left Lewis after our wedding, and I had forgotten how tiring it was, battling waves and constantly banging into the remains of the bridge. My legs would be riddled with bruises, but now was not the time to care. Thank goodness Mum had taught me, and I was a strong swimmer after what happened on Kiewa when I was a child. I was out of shape, but there was no way I would leave anyone behind. Images of Illy rescuing me from Caspian flicked into my mind, and I shook my head violently to dispel the image. *Not now.*

My soaked pants dragged me down, and I undid them, letting them fall to the murky depths. As I swam, I scanned the rubble, pieces of the bridge scattered everywhere. Carmelo's graying dark head was not among them. No babies floated among the wreckage. My heart sank. *Did they drown? Please, please let them be on the pod*, I prayed. *My babies, please let me hold my babies again.* As I continued to survey the area, I heard Gabriel calling down to me. They had lowered the main pod; the voice was closer.

"Boat!" I called, taking on a mouthful of water as I partially submerged. "Bring ... doctor." I saw his head nod and disappeared inside. Refocusing my attention on retrieval, I started towing the survivors to land one at a time, still clinging to floating objects. It was difficult to see who they were, and I tried not to look, concentrating on each stroke, pulling us closer to shore. I towed in three people before returning to search for more survivors.

"No more, Caitlin. You got them all. The rest are in the greenhouse. They have made contact." Gabriel's voice reached me as I was continuing with my search in a grid pattern, trying to accommodate for the wave direction.

Freezing, and each movement torturous, I made the long swim back to land to check on the three survivors lying on the shore. Deb was among them and was visibly in the worst shape. She had open wounds on her arms, bleeding profusely. Stripping off my top, I tried to staunch the bleeding while checking and reassuring the other two. Shocked, concussed, and likely with internal bruising, they didn't appear to be at risk of bleeding out. Deb was another story; her pulse was slow and weak. Her eyes flickered as she lay on the sandy bank. I was losing her.

"Stay with me, Deb," I demanded, speaking louder than necessary to pull her attention back. "Squeeze my hand. I'm here. I won't let you go."

Memories of Illy saying that to me flickered into my mind as I tried to assess what had happened. The bridge hung at either end. This was deliberate. There

CHAPTER 21

was no doubt. This was no earthquake. This was targeted. The dull hum of a motor pulled me from my memories. The mid-morning sun made me squint as I focused on the tiny rescue dinghy pulling away from the pod.

No, I thought angrily. *That can't carry all of them. I need to get them to the clinic.* I was no doctor, and I had no idea what we were dealing with in terms of internal injuries. While Deb looked the worst, I knew from Mum that others could be in far worse shape medically.

The waves were lapping against the shore near me, and amidst the debris, there were bodies. As I watched, I saw a body slowly drift into shore, face down. I rushed down, leaving the survivors and rolled the body to check for signs of life. My breath caught in my throat as I recognized Joseph. *No, no. no.*

I desperately wanted to pound on his chest and do CPR as Mum had taught me but could see from his extensive blast injuries that he hadn't made it. *Focus, Cait, focus. Deb. She needs you.* Returning to monitor Deb and the others, I couldn't concentrate. My thoughts were all over the place, fragmented and jumping from thought to thought before I could finish it. *Joseph. Not Joseph. How will I tell Antonio? This is my fault. I asked them here. I need to confirm.* Moving as fast as my battered body would allow, I moved down the bank to check. One glance as I got closer told me everything. Pulling the dead weight by the shoulders higher onto the bank, I ran my eyes over him. Joseph's stomach was blown open, exposing internal organs, making them look like cooked spaghetti. Smelling the burning flesh, and knowing it was futile, I checked his pulse. Nothing. My heart shattered a little more.

"Caitlin!" The voice reached me from the water.

It was Gio and Cherie on the dinghy. Fuck, with two of them, we would need to ferry patients one at a time.

"We need the yacht," I called, cupping my hands again now that the wind was picking up. "Three alive. Need urgent medical care."

"Yacht gone," Gio bellowed back. *Fuck.* My heart sank.

Gio scanned me in my underwear as he pulled the dinghy ashore, eyeing me carefully. The bruises had already started coming through on my legs, but I had no time to waste on them.

"I'm fine. Just bruises. Help them, please. "

Seeing me shiver, Gio stripped off his t-shirt, pausing long enough for me to pull it over my dripping hair. "Hold that firm," he commanded as he unpacked his kit, gesturing toward my own now blood-soaked top against Deb's wound, and I complied, recognizing the scared nervousness that made him sound snappier than he intended. I didn't dare ask if she would be okay. Cherie was already assessing the other two lying dazed on the sand.

"The girls?" Gio asked softly without looking up as he pulled back my makeshift dressing and assessed the wound. The tiny hairs on his back were standing on end as the wind whipped over the beach.

"I don't know," I whispered, my heart chilled with a fear that matched my frozen body. Once more, I scanned the waves, searching the debris for a body. A tiny body. Two. Gio was talking to his colleague, making plans for transport as I closed my eyes, praying my daughters were not lying on the lake floor. They

CHAPTER 21

were immune, like us, but couldn't swim. Had they been on the bridge, they would never have survived.

Watching the sun slink down the horizon, I sat keeping them company, trying to keep up their spirits as Gio ferried them one at a time back to the clinic. Deb went first. My teeth were chattering as I sat on the bank wearing only my underwear and Gio's shirt, trying to keep up a steady stream of chatter to Cherie.

"Can you ferry the others from the land pod home?" Gio asked, tossing me a warm jacket as he escorted the last patient. "I need to get into surgery. It is all hands on deck. Things falling caused lots of injuries to people in the pods."

I pulled the enormous jacket on gratefully and nodded. "Is there room for me? I'll need to come with you, then I can bring it back."

We sat in silence as the motor putted across the still lake, avoiding the remaining floating pieces of aluminum. Most of it had sunk or washed ashore, littering the beach. Glen, the final patient, was assisted onto the pod, and Gio took command. Moving into the back seat to control the motor, I saw nîpiy's face pale as I pulled away. No one seemed surprised by my state of undress and disheveled, matted hair. I had been exposed, and they had all seen it. My secret was out. There was no going back.

As I entered the garden pod, I saw that the entrance had been torn off by the falling bridge, and the utter destruction made my heart stop. The clear panels were shattered, the raised beds that Dad had painstakingly built destroyed beyond repair. Dirt and plant matter were strewn across the front section of the pod. Nothing had escaped unscathed. I dropped to my knees amidst the mess, no longer caring what

I was kneeling in. Had I lost them, too? After Stella, I couldn't do this again.

Muffled crying broke into my haze. Carmelo stood, holding the screaming girls, peering through the doorway from the still intact potting room at the back. He stepped through so I could see them clearly, one girl clutched to each hip. Despite the screeching echoing around the destroyed pod, I couldn't stop my lip from trembling as I dropped my head to the floor. Others flowed in behind him, all safe despite some scratches and bruising. Antonio helped me up as I fought to regain control.

"I'm here to bring you home," I said, the quiver audible in my voice, unable to tell him what I knew. Not here. Not now.

"What happened?" he asked.

"We don't know. The bridge is gone."

The survivors peered out the shattered entrance, the destruction of the bridge spread before them. Their gasps filled what remained of the greenhouse pod.

"Are you all okay?" I asked, remembering my role as Chief and not just as a mother.

"We are," Tracey said. "Mimi has a broken arm, and we all have cuts and grazes, but we are okay. Please take Carmelo and the babies first," she insisted, and I nodded, glancing up at the darkening sky. Leaving any of them here wasn't a good choice. Rain clouds were looming, but if I didn't linger, I could get them all across safely.

The girls settled slightly with the motion of the boat, and I looked over at Carmelo, settled on the back seat, clutching both girls to his chest.

He caught my eye as I navigated our way through the debris. "What happened?"

CHAPTER 21

"Missile." I projected my voice over the engine noise as the spray rose in an arc behind us. It was only the girls, so we couldn't be overheard. But I would need to go slower with the others so they didn't accidentally ingest water.

"Deliberate?"

"The bridge was clearly the intended target. It was a direct hit."

"I saw it. I was walking toward the entrance, just about to cross. But all I saw was movement. Then the world went black, and there was the most deafening sound."

"The girls? Were they hit?" I scanned them again for injury, unable to move from my place at the motor.

"When it hit, I fell but held on to them. The pieces were pulled from the entrance and came crashing down on us, but I would never drop them, Caitlin."

"I know. I trust you, Carmelo. Implicitly." Carmelo adored these girls, and a well of mixed emotions built up inside me as I watched them snuggled into his chest. Safe. They were safe. I should be happy, but how could I feel anything positive when Joseph and others were gone and Deb was severely wounded? We had been attacked, yet I was fighting to keep the tears of relief at bay.

"What did you do?"

"When the pieces stopped falling, we made sure everyone was alive, and we moved back into the potting room and stayed there, wondering if the pod was under attack. That room was fine, and if it rained, we were safe."

"Why?" I breathed, unable to fathom who would do this.

Carmelo shrugged and let out an enormous sigh. He had aged a decade in the past few hours.

"Caitlin, are *you* alright?"

"I feel so terribly guilty. Thanks to you, my girls are alive, and yet people did not survive. People walking on the bridge. Joseph is dead. I saw his body. How do I tell Antonio?"

"That isn't your news to tell. Someone else can do that. There was no way he could have survived, Catie. He was halfway across the bridge."

"I saw him," I whispered.

"Caitlin, we saw you jump. People will know."

"I had no choice," I mouthed over the engine. "They would have drowned. I can't let people die and know I could have stopped it."

"They all saw you jump," Carmelo repeated. "We were watching from the back of the pod. They were talking about how you would become infected."

"I am so lucky you were there. I will pay the price of our secret getting out if it means my daughters and you are alive. A hundred times over."

"I was on my way back," Carmelo said, his face darkening. "Bringing them to you to feed before they went down for their nap. But Aurora needed to be changed, and I didn't want to bring her to you dirty. So, I turned back. Geraldine was holding Khione as I changed Rori. She walked with me to the entrance to the bridge and handed Khi to me before turning around. We made it three steps when the sky darkened before me. We felt the impact and heard the deafening sound as the front of the pod was ripped off. The sound terrified them. This is the first time they have stopped crying."

I glanced at my precious bundles, clutching him.

CHAPTER 21

"I can't thank you enough for taking such wonderful care of them," I said as I nestled the inflatable dinghy against the pod.

Arms reached down from the lowered pod for my children and Carmelo. I watched as they pulled my children and Carmelo inside the lowered pod, keeping them safe. Before turning back to ferry the remaining survivors, I delayed for a moment to make one last check and confirm they were cared for. On the return journey, I allowed myself a few minutes to let the tears of relief fall before anyone could see me.

Leaving Antonio until last, I waited until he was on the boat before telling him, fearful that he would refuse to return to the main pod. All the color drained from his face as he spoke the single word.

"*Morto?*" he gasped.

"I'm so sorry to be the one to tell you. I saw him, and I tried, I really did. He was already dead in the water. I'm so sorry. There was nothing I could do."

Antonio turned away, looking out over the wreckage. He clammed up, and I was rabbiting on, fearful he blamed me. Halfway back to the community, I stopped speaking, realizing I was antagonizing him further. Choking back the tears, the pain ripped me apart. Not only Joseph's death but that Antonio blamed me. He stood as I moored the dinghy. I watched as the rescue team pulled him into the pod and he was accompanied to the medical facility. Not looking back.

CHAPTER 22

NÎPIY GRIPPED MY ARM and steered me through the pods to my apartment, pushing past the lingering crowds with their hushed, open-mouthed stares. People needed answers, and in Illy's absence, they were looking to me, but I was in no frame of mind for public speaking. She didn't flinch as she stripped my soaking clothes, my body frozen solid, and pushed me, shivering, into the shower. My head suddenly became too heavy for my neck and slumped as I defrosted and let the hot water flow down my body, multi-colored bruises appearing from the debris banging into me, weakened from the swimming and stress. Sliding down the wall, I landed with a thud on the floor, the overwhelming emotions of my family being safe intermingled with the loss of Joseph and knowing our community had been attacked. As Chief, I needed to be strong, but not now.

Ten minutes. That was all I could allow myself.

Anger swelled in my chest as the stress washed down the drain, and I turned my mind to who had done this. Murdered my friend. It was blatantly

CHAPTER 22

antagonistic. Caspian. How long would we stand back and let them attack us? Kill our people? Was targeting me personally no longer enough?

Cool air struck me as the door opened, and nîpiy turned off the water. "Your mother is on her way. You best be dressed when she arrives." My body felt like mush, too exhausted to stand. nîpiy said nothing as she slipped her hands into my armpits, pulling me to standing. She felt like my mother as she wrapped me in a towel and strode off to my bedroom to find my clothes.

"Thank you," I whispered. "I'm just tired."

She leaned against the basin and watched me dry off. "I imagine this brings back memories of your assault."

"It does. Thank you for staying. I don't want to be alone."

"I gathered."

"Where are the girls?"

"Still asleep. I checked on them while you were in the shower. Carmelo said he would bring them in when they wake. They are fine, Caitlin. Carmelo, too."

I nodded. That was good. They were tired, too, and I could wait, as much as I desperately wanted to hold them.

"We should get you to the med center. You are infected." nîpiy's eyebrows raised, watching my face closely.

I exhaled forcefully, unable to meet her eyes. "I am immune," I whispered. Foolishly. It wasn't like anyone could hear us in my bathroom.

A tiny smile quirked her mouth. "I always knew you were special."

"It is a long story, and I will tell you. But not now. How are Deb and the others?"

"Still in surgery last I heard. You saved their lives. If they weren't infected. Nothing can save them from that."

"I can help with that, too," I whispered. "Let me dress. I need to get to the clinic, and I don't think I can walk that far alone."

nîpiy's watched me, calm but intrigued. As I dressed, I told her the basics, gauging her response. I was born immune. My mother's eggs had been stolen by the original scientific team on Clava, and her genome had adapted. Born by surrogate but fortunate enough to be raised by my biological family. There were only a few of us, all girls, and now all with children of our own.

"My girls are also immune," I admitted. "But it was only last year, when I was attacked and Illy was exposed to the protozoa, that we worked out how to pass the immunity on to others."

"How?"

"Stem cells," I admitted.

nîpiy crinkled her nose. "How…"

"Cord blood from the babies, but bone marrow from me," I whispered as she supported me down the hall. "From me. My pelvis specifically."

She stopped, gripping both my forearms as I watched the sequence of expressions as she processed what that meant. "Did they extract your bone marrow after you were assaulted?" she asked, gripping both my forearms as I watched the sequence of expressions on her face as she processed what that meant. "Was that how your hips were broken?"

CHAPTER 22

"No. The Caspians smashed my pelvis and several other bones for good measure. Before receiving treatment, I had Illy's daughter extract some marrow. Illy was dying."

"You did *what*?"

"At the time, all I knew was I was dying, Gio was dead, my baby was gone. I didn't care," I admitted, surprised I could even talk about it. "They could have taken all of it, and I wouldn't have objected."

nîpiy grimaced. "Who else? Is immune, I mean."

"Illyria, Giovanni, Carmelo. A few others, but we can't inoculate everyone yet. The stem cells need to come from me, not those who have received donations. We used the girls' stem cells from their cord blood when they were born. But now, everyone will know."

"Maybe there is a way that we can keep part of it secret." nîpiy spoke softly as we entered the main pod.

"What are you thinking?"

"We let people know that there is a newly discovered vaccine, a treatment of sorts. We can treat those who are exposed, but there is not enough for everyone all at once."

I thought about that. "Won't that just cause resentment? People thinking that Gio and I were vaccinated before them?"

"People would expect it. You are the Chief."

"But I am not special. Why me? I don't want people thinking I am more important than them."

"So what do you propose?"

"The truth," I admitted. "Everyone in the land communities knows anyway, have done since the other girls and I were born. It is only the unhab communities that don't know, although, I am surprised we have managed to keep it secret this long."

"Let's speak with Illyria first. She might have some ideas. Summer messaged to say they had left a few hours ago, so they can't be far away. She will want to check in on Carmelo first."

Her words dawned on me. "Carmelo? Is he alright?"

"He will be. His back is in bad shape from the bruising. You know he sheltered those girls with his body, don't you? Some of those raised garden beds flung around and hit him. Nothing broken, but there are some significant bruises on his back and legs where it hit him. He will need a scan for internal injuries when there is time. There is a quite a long queue in the med center, and they are triaging patients."

"He said nothing to me," I breathed, the vision of exactly what he had done appearing before my eyes. "The girls?"

"Not a scratch."

I nodded, closing my eyes. Just like defending his people on Piedmont, once more, Carmelo had silently stepped up and protected those he loved.

CHAPTER 22

THE FAMILIAR THUDDING OF Summer's helicopter descending slowly outside the window allowed me to focus on something as I lay on my side on the bed in the clinic. nîpiy was clutching my hand as Gio guided the large intraosseous needle into my hip once more.

"I can't believe we need to do this again," he grumbled. "You know I hate this."

"Again?" nîpiy asked, the confusion evident. "Weren't you here when she underwent this to save Illyria?"

Gio didn't even look up. "Caitlin has done this twice before. Once when she was critically wounded and again for me before we left Lewis."

Rolling my reddening face into the pillow, I avoided nîpiy's gaze.

"Am I hurting you?" Gio asked, seeing my face down. "Do you need more anesthetic?"

"No," I mumbled into the pillow. I could feel the needle in my bone, and it wasn't pleasant. But with the local anesthetic, it didn't hurt as much. nîpiy placed a hand on my shoulder and squeezed the hand she was holding. "I can't believe you. You should be holding your babies, and instead, you are here, saving my people."

"They are my people, too," I muttered into the pillow. "How are they?" I turned as I felt Gio withdraw the enormous needle and place the pad firmly on my hip. "Deb and the others?"

"Hold that," he instructed nîpiy as he turned to deal with the vital contents of the syringe. "Lila and Glen had just entered the bridge when it blew, so most of their injuries were from falling and panels landing on them. Broken bones, internal bleeding, concussion. They will recover. Deb is another story. From what we can tell, she was crossing from the pod over to the greenhouses and was a little farther in. It wasn't a direct hit, but shrapnel struck her. A piece of the metal tore through her left arm. We have done everything we can, but she may lose that arm."

"Oh no," I breathed. "Can you save it?"

"We will try. I learned a lot from your mother, including how to pin a shattered bone. I've done my best. Internally splinted it. The team are stitching up her lacerations now. I've called for your mother to come and review. Jake is bringing her tomorrow."

My heart sank. My poor mother, knowing we had been attacked again. "Your father, too," Gio said as he looked up from the centrifuge.

Ahh fuck. Dad. As if he hasn't been through enough.

"nîpiy, can you check that has stopped bleeding? She can roll over if she can."

My hips were numb from the anesthetic, and I struggled to get my body to respond. nîpiy carefully maneuvered me into a lying position, a soft pillow beneath my hips. "Wait here."

CHAPTER 22

She disappeared into the main room beyond, low voices barely penetrating the closed door.

Touching Gio's arm as he returned to sit beside me, I asked, "Honey, are you sure Deb will be okay?"

"I don't know, *amore mio*. All I know is they would have died, all of them, if you hadn't been there. They will still die without this gift."

"Lots of people saw me jump," I whispered, ensuring no one could overhear me.

"People keep talking about it. Everyone knows, Caitlin."

"Maybe it is time. I'm sick of keeping secrets. How can I be a leader and keep something like this from them?"

Carmelo appeared in the doorway, holding two alert and happy little girls. Gio dropped the empty syringe, hastily wiped his hands, and rushed to take Aurora. Carmelo beamed, crossing stiffly to where I lay and handing Khione to me. Clutching her to my chest, it hit me how close we had come to losing them both. Choking back the sobs, I smiled over her fuzzy dark hair at Carmelo. He wasn't stupid. He patted my arm, turned to Gio, gave him a nod, and left, closing the door firmly behind him.

Gio sat beside me as I drowned in memories, guilt, and regret. The Caspians had done this. Payback for me surviving. For what I had done. They had taken one of our daughters. They had come too close to taking these girls, as well. Khione squirmed as I clutched her tight, my chest constricting.

"I can't do this anymore," I sobbed. "People die because of me. Joseph is dead. Antonio hates me. Deb did nothing. She was going to work. I built that bridge. It was me they were after."

"This was not your fault, Caitlin. No one thinks that."

"How can they not? It was one thing when they targeted me, but now it is everyone associated with me. Both Illy and you were collateral damage last time. Joseph and Deb this time. She could lose her arm, even die because of me. The risks are huge. Antonio has lost his husband. You should have seen him. He will never forgive me. It is my fault."

"Antonio does not blame you." Gio's single free arm slipped around my waist and pulled me into his side.

"You should have seen his face! He couldn't even look at me."

"Enough. I won't let you talk like that."

"And nor will I." I heard the voice before I realized the door was even open.

"Mum," I said, looking up at Illyria as she closed the door. She took quick steps across the room and held me reassuringly before holding her arms out to Gio, and he passed Aurora to her. She stopped to smile at the cheeky face gazing up at her. "My goodness. I leave you for five minutes and you grow," Illy cooed at her before turning her attention to me. "Stop the pity party, Caitlin. This had nothing to do with you."

"With respect, how does it not?" I clutched Khione closer to me, trying not to let my voice quaver. "Carmelo was on the landside pod. He and the girls could have been traveling across. A few minutes later, and they would have been. He is badly injured. It is my fault."

"It was a lucky miss."

"Deb, Joseph, and the others who were blown apart were not so lucky. People want answers. What do I tell them? Caspian wasn't satisfied with what they did to you and me. Now they have weapons to take us

CHAPTER 22

all down? Everyone is scared, and rightfully so. What if the missile had perforated the main pod? We all would have died. A perfectly normal morning, and suddenly everyone drowns."

"We can't be certain it was Caspian," she said, watching me intently.

Resisting the urge to roll my eyes at her, I asked, "Who then?"

"Caitlin, you know you can't accuse without proof. On the surface, it appears highly likely, but we don't even know if they have the technology. Tadhg is working on it. The satellites caught the movement, and we are trying to triangulate where it originated, but until we have proof, we can't do anything."

Recognizing the truth in this, I wondered what we would do when it was confirmed. No one wanted to start an all-out war where innocent people were killed on both sides.

"Swap," she ordered and handed Aurora to Gio, taking Khione. Gio passed me Aurora, knowing I needed to hold my babies. She gurgled with glee to see me, and I couldn't help but smile.

"We will discuss the next steps when we can confirm the origin. Right now, we have a more urgent problem. People saw you jump into the lake?"

"They did."

"That puts us in damage control mode. I hear you swam back and forth several times."

"She did," Gio cut in, although Illy's comment was a statement, not a question. "She saved three people."

"But three died," I continued, "including Joseph." Illy ignored me as she ran the scenarios through her head.

"Right. We have choices. First, we could imply you weren't infected and that the water is safe, but that isn't a great choice as people will take risks and become exposed. Second, we advise that there is a cure for people exposed but don't note how it is produced. Third, we come clean. With all or part of the truth. The danger here is that once the story is out, we can't stuff it back in the box. Everyone will know."

"There is a fourth choice." Gio's low rumble rose from beside me. "We tell the people here the truth and ask them to keep the secret. Caitlin saved their people today while they watched. Everyone saw what she did. They owe her. I have been speaking with the medical team and a few others. People saw their ambassador, their Chief, act like a leader. She plunged into the water without hesitating. She saved them."

"But I am immune," I protested.

"At the time, we didn't know if that was the one and only missile that had been fired. There could have been more. Besides, you still didn't need to expose yourself. Everyone else stood by, watching. You chose to save your people over protecting your secret."

Illy was nodding, and I could feel her brain whirring. "I can work that," she muttered.

"That is an enormous secret for a large group of people to keep," I protested.

"And it won't be possible to keep it forever," she admitted. "But it will buy us some time. We can explain how the treatment is produced and how painful it is for you. That even after all you did today, you then fronted up here to donate to save those exposed. I can explain how we have plans to inoculate everyone, over time, but it will be a slow process. But are you sure

CHAPTER 22

you are okay with this? Both of you? It will expose your children."

"I don't want to place our daughters at risk," Gio responded instantly. "No. I won't allow that. I couldn't sleep knowing they could be taken at any time. I can't. I won't."

"I can't live lying to my colleagues and friends," I said gently, looking from my husband to my mother.

Illy sighed. "So, we look for a way to let people know about you but not mention your daughters. It isn't a lie," she rushed to say. "It is an omission of information. We explain you are immune, and the process required to pass it on. I am prepared to explain that I am also immune, thanks to you, but I can't donate. We imply but don't explicitly state that you are the only donor."

Gio was nodding slowly. "I am comfortable with that."

"Good. I will hold a conference in the morning. People are scared. They need answers. I will speak, Caitlin, but you need to be there. Now you need to sleep. I'll get nîpiy to help me coordinate."

CHAPTER 23

AS PROMISED, ILLY CALLED the community together the following day and gave a brief and impassioned speech about the attack, sharing what information she had, which wasn't much. But she made a promise to not keep secrets. There was no reason to believe the underwater pods were under threat, although they would all be submerged for a few days as a precaution once the damage caused by the falling bridge had been repaired. She explained ACC satellites were now watching and recording, and several land communities had weapons and could counterattack if required. But the more time that passed, the less likely that was. She gave an update on those who had passed and those injured. Choosing her words carefully, she explained how I was immune and had been since birth. She gave a brief description of the process, emphasizing the pain to me, and I fought to hold my head up, feeling the thousands of eyes watching me.

"I know this is a lot to take in," she finished. "But we ask that you keep Caitlin's confidence. Deb, Glen, and Lila are alive because she single-handedly saved

CHAPTER 23

them. From what I hear, she didn't hesitate and spent hours in the freezing water, saving people. But you can imagine what other communities would do with this knowledge, those who attack us without provocation, especially. We need to protect her. Yesterday, she proved what a leader is. I am proud to call her my friend."

The main pod erupted into applause, and I felt my face heat. Thank goodness she hadn't allowed questions. As planned, several people stood, indicating the meeting was over, and others followed. A few milled near the stage to thank me, Gabriel among them.

"Deb will be fine," I promised as he held me to his chest, ashen-faced. "We will do everything possible for her."

"You already did," he choked. "I was there, remember? I watched you jump, and I saw you swimming, towing her to shore. She is alive because of you. I will never forget what you did. My family owes you a great debt, Caitlin. Is there anything I can do?"

"All I ask is that you keep my secret."

As the days passed, life reverted to a state of almost normal, although a heightened state of wariness pervaded most social interactions. Mum and Gio saved Deb's arm, working tirelessly across multiple surgeries. Gio described the procedures to me in detail, allowing me to envision the damage and the repair. More than once, I tried to visit Deb and the others in recovery, but the memories were too great. Reaching the door, I could only place my hand on the door handle before I turned and fled. They would survive, and I could visit them when they were recovering at home.

Gabriel's constant thanks became embarrassing, making me actively avoid him. In the end, it was Dad who intervened. Taking a bottle of wine, which Gabriel had insisted they open, Dad had explained that by thanking me for saving Deb, it was a reminder that I hadn't saved Joseph. After all of my father's losses, his own parents, his second wife, and multiple friends including Luca, I was surprised he could do this. But after Dad told me of the conversation, Gabriel's tone changed. I sensed the gratitude and knew he would always have my back, but his focus was on Deb, where it needed to be. While they had managed to save her arm, her recovery would be slow. After she was allowed to go home, with Gabriel's help, I designed a brace to keep her arm in the optimal position for healing as well as some aids for everyday function so she wouldn't feel helpless. Better than anyone, I knew how that felt. Watching Deb's quiet determination as she tackled mundane chores without assistance, I felt a warm glow of satisfaction.

That evening, Mum harassed me into showing her my designs and made copies so she could take them back to Lewis.

"I keep telling you, Catie, so many people would benefit from your skills."

"And I keep telling you, Mum, that I don't have time!"

"Freyja," Illy warned from the couch, "are you trying to poach my Chief?"

"Other people can be Chief," Mum fired back. "No one else has her talent for medical interventions."

Illy rolled her eyes and continued to sip her wine, Khi on her lap.

CHAPTER 23

After learning about Joseph, Antonio refused medical treatment until he had viewed the body and whispered a prayer over him. Gio had stood beside him, held him upright as he bid goodbye to his husband, and lapsed into melancholy, refusing to leave their tiny apartment. He would not permit company and would not engage in making plans for a memorial for Joseph. He just sat staring out the window. Remembering my struggle after losing Stella, I wondered how much of this grief was borne from knowing that we had offered them a child. A plan I could no longer see him accepting. Gio and I took him food, but when we collected it again, it was usually untouched. For days, he sat there, unmoving. When he finally spoke, it was to ask Gio if Summer could take him and Joseph's body back to Italy.

Gio agreed and made the arrangements as I stood by helplessly. Watching him leave two days later, silent and a shadow of the vibrant friend I had known, my heart shattered a little more.

Once more, Dad proved invaluable, guiding the team to salvage what they could from the landside pod while the construction crew worked all daylight hours to repair it when the weather permitted. The additional growing space had proven invaluable, and it wasn't feasible to revert the former greenhouse pod we had renovated back into housing. Dad and Carmelo, both being immune, had sourced an enclosed speedboat from what had previously been Michigan when Summer returned from chaperoning Antonio to Italy. With the new vessel, Dad had safely ferried the agricultural team each day. Illy had insisted I take a few days off to spend with the girls, which I had accepted with alacrity. While I always felt part of their life, the opportunity to take them swimming, read them books, and watch them trying to crawl filled my heart with joy. As I watched them trying to explore, I thought of Antonio and how different things might be if he had a little person to focus on in his grief. Maybe, when the time was right, he would accept the offer.

Glancing out the window, I wondered how he was doing, and if he would ever forgive me. Losing his friendship was as painful as losing my friend. One more thing that Caspian had stolen from me. Only the grief from this loss was ongoing. He was alive, but no longer in my life. Was that worse than mourning a death?

I waited for the right moment to tell Mum about my plans for offering childless couples an immune child. Watching her face carefully, I caught the tiniest flicker of fear cross her beautiful face.

"I know this is hard for you," I whispered. "If it is too much, I won't do it. Never in a million years would I do something to hurt you."

To my surprise, Mum laughed. "Hurt me? You don't think that running away from Newgrange, reactivating a portal, and ending up in a strange underwater world didn't hurt me? Add to that your adventures of the last few years, and honestly, Caitlin, this is tame."

"Well, maybe," I admitted.

"No, definitely," she retorted. "Why do you think your father and I want you back home? We can't deal with any more of your escapades, young lady. We want you and your children somewhere where we can keep you all under constant supervision."

"I get it," I muttered.

CHAPTER 23

"But," she continued, "I think it is a wonderful and extremely generous offer. Alasdair and Frank would love a child."

"It wouldn't bring back sad memories?"

Mum paused before replying. "Caitlin, what happened to me was evil and should never have happened. It took me a long time to process it all, but I can honestly say I no longer grieve over it. So much good came of that horrendous experience. You and all your sisters would never have been born, and you have added so much joy to my life. We would not know that within a few generations, people can live outside again. That alone is worth unspeakable torment, knowing that I could make such a difference to so many. What happened to you was equally abhorrent. But you have turned it into a positive, sharing your gift. So the answer is no. The wonderful memories outweigh the bad, only because I choose to let them. That is the key, Caitlin. Don't dwell on what happened. Focus on the good that came from it."

"Why do you have to go home?" I moaned. "I am going to miss you, Mum. Both of you, but now that I have babies, I miss you so much more. Does that make sense?"

"It does." She smiled. "My own mother was never the maternal type, but when I had Katrin, I desperately wanted to ask her questions, how I slept as a baby, my childhood illnesses."

"Trust you to want to know about illnesses."

"When your role in life changes, you want to understand how those who performed that role for you did it. Growing up in Australia, my Norwegian grandparents were people we saw only occasionally, every few years, so being an active grandmother is as foreign to me as being a mother is to you. You learn by asking, by watching and working out your place."

"Why can't your place be here?"

"Your father and I would love that. But we have roles, a life. That doesn't mean you are any less important to us."

"I meant it when I said that was home. With you and Dad. One day."

CHAPTER 24

"**WHAT DO WE DO?**" I asked Illy one day as we stood at our apartment window, watching the boat return from the mainland. With Carmelo helping rebuild the newly enlarged landside greenhouse pods, I had taken to working from home most mornings, adjusting my schedule around the girls. Illy often came to my apartment to work with me, discussing projects and proposals. But one topic was forefront in our minds.

"It was bad timing, but the trajectory of the shot means we can't confirm that Caspian fired the missile. Tadhg has spent weeks poring over footage, trying to link it all together. But he can't be certain. Finally, I called him off that project as it was doing his head in. Likely, we will never know for sure. But what I do know is we can't live our lives in fear. We need to lead by example. We need to push ahead by replacing the bridge."

"I've been thinking about the rebuild, and I have an idea."

"Which is?"

BIFRÖST

"Technically, it was a dream, so don't laugh. Don't ask me why, but I could see it, clear as day. When we rebuild the bridge, I want to ask the children to paint it like a rainbow. A rainbow bridge to link this world and the next, as a memory to those who didn't make it that day."

"Bifröst?"

"The rainbow bridge to Asgard? You know the story?"

"Of course, your mother loved that story and used to read it to all of you as children." Illy paused, then smiled, recalling. "In Norse mythology, Bifröst is the rainbow bridge that connects the world of men on Earth, Midgard, with the realm of the Gods, Asgard, home to the Aesir. It is a wonderful idea and symbolic on several levels. You are the link between this community and the others because you reactivated the link. Without you, we would not know about these underwater settlements. You are the link between the old world and the new. Because of you, we now have a vision of the future where we will all be immune to the protozoa, passing immunity on much faster than we thought. Living landside, connected by a bridge was your idea. People will be able to live outside again, and you provided that opportunity. Finally, you are the daughter of Freyja, a Norse goddess herself."

"Trust you to be a psychologist about it. But you like it?"

"I love it. For all of those reasons, but on a strictly personal level, you are the link between my family and my best friend. You and Seraphine are related to all of our children."

CHAPTER 24

"Mum told me that Bifröst was used for transport of not only gods but also souls of men who have been proved worthy as warriors and were slain in battle."

"I read the same stories to my own children, including you, although you may not remember. I think it is a very fitting name, Caitlin."

"Do you think they will understand? I don't want to force people into something. Besides, anyone who knows the myth will know that the destruction of the bridge was foretold in Norse mythology, during Ragnarök."

"It is your bridge, your project. By all means, ask. But I doubt you will get many objections. People are still talking about what you did, diving in and saving Deb and the others."

"You don't think it is a little loud—obvious, I mean?"

"Our bridge was obvious last time. Whoever attacked us still took it out with one shot. What I love about this proposal is that it proves we aren't scared. We won't be intimidated."

"Logistically, I am not sure how to even achieve it. A painted bridge, I mean. We would need to paint the bridge here before we erect it. We can't expose the children by letting them do it on land."

"We will always find a way, Caitlin. Always."

Over the following months, I revisited the original diagrams drawn up with Joseph. Several times each day, I would think of a question and fresh pain gouged my chest, hollow from missing my friend and his input. Gabriel proved invaluable, and over time, we designed a new and improved land link. Knowing how successful the greenhouses were, we knew over time, people would also want to build houses out there. This bridge needed to be stronger, more resilient.

"What we desperately need is an electrical engineer, someone who can advise on how to link power from the pods to the mainland. Do you know anyone?"

I mulled over Gabriel's question. "There are electrical engineers in all communities, but most of them live on unhabs, so they don't have knowledge of what we are asking. I can't think of anyone on Lewis. Callie, maybe? No. We really need more technical expertise. I would never say it, but she has been working on small-scale projects for so long, I am unsure how she would cope with such massive power generation. Solar and biogas are fine, but we have so much untapped geothermal power here, it would be fantastic if there was someone who understood hydro as well. Someone who could work with water and electricity."

Gabriel paused. "The teams here understand the conduction of geothermic heat, but not how to transfer it across distance. Maybe two people? A team?"

"Callie certainly understands the theory of geothermic power production. She and I spoke about it once or twice. But I don't think she has ever seen it in action."

"She hasn't. I asked Tadhg." Illy popped her head in, interrupting our conversation.

"Should we ask in the leadership meeting? Perhaps one of the other unhabs has someone they could send?"

"I did that last week on your day off. No one person seems to have all the skills. We could have a few people work together, but that means a lot of lost time. They need to confer, work out the limitations.

CHAPTER 24

Not to mention the potential conflict in personality. It would make so much more sense if there was a single person with those skills. We still want to replicate this model elsewhere, so it would be best to get it right the first time."

Brilliant color rose into my cheeks, burning them. I tried to gaze nonchalantly out the window. I shouldn't have bothered. Illy was sharper than the cook's knives.

"I know that look. Out with it."

I sighed. There was no avoiding it. "There is a guy, Finn, on Newgrange who trained as both an electrical and hydro engineer. We spoke a lot about his projects. He was the best and was often consulted by other communities. Exceptionally good."

Illy burst into laughter. "I see your problem. Your alpha husband meeting one of the other men who proposed to you. Although a few years have passed, and you are married with babies. Is he taken?"

"I don't know," I admitted, embarrassed that Gabriel was here and listening intently. "Under the circumstances, I didn't keep in touch. I didn't exactly invite him to my wedding. Summer told me that Reilly married a few months ago, but I'm not sure about Finn."

"How about I ask Tadhg? Discretely," she rushed to say. "If Finn is available, we get him out here. We need his skill and I believe you when you say he is good. You wouldn't allow anyone substandard to come, especially not one you have history with."

"You don't understand," I hissed. "I slept with him. Gio knows that. He will slaughter the man the second he steps through the portal. Everyone will talk!"

Gabriel flushed at my private revelation and excused himself hurriedly.

"He knows you weren't Miss Innocent before you met him. So what? We all had a fair crack at it before we settled down."

My mouth dropped and Illy cackled wickedly. "Bloody hell, I wasn't innocent before I met Luca or Carmelo. I lived, Catie. Your mother, too. How on earth do you think we could choose a good one if we hadn't kissed a few toads along the way? So, was Finn terrible in bed? Is that what you are saying? He was a dud, and you never want to see him again?"

"I can't have this discussion with you." I wanted to crawl under the desk. Illy wanting to talk about my sexual relationships. No. Hard no.

"I was just wondering if he was still single, if he might like Summer or Ally."

"You just want more grandchildren! No. Under no circumstances are they dating my ex. That would be way too creepy."

"Maybe," she twinkled. "Sera won't be contributing any more babies, and you have done your part for a bit. Alasdair might at some point if your plan comes to fruition, but I can't see it happening soon, not to mention the logistics. So it is Summer or Ally."

"You know they aren't interested," I countered, moving the topic away from my former lover and his potential availability as well as Seraphine. "Those girls love their nomadic life."

"I know," she sighed. "Would you feel awkward if he paired up with one of them? Is that it?"

The wall of uncomfortable silence rose between us again.

"That bad, was he?"

The air was forcibly sucked out of my lungs.

"Speechless, are you? Now I need to know."

CHAPTER 24

"I am not having this conversation with you."

"Vanilla, was he?"

The bricks crushing my windpipe grew heavier. "I can't."

"Spill. I can't have my daughters with someone who can't please a woman."

"He was just fine," I whispered, my face burning. "Very muscular. Stamina. Very attentive. Skills."

"So why didn't you choose him?"

"Fuck, do you want to know everything?"

"Well, not his favorite positions, but yes. Tell me everything." I stared at her as she reverberated with glee.

"No!"

"Why not? Sex is natural, Catie. You know, there were even sex therapists in the old world. Come on, tell me."

"He was just fine. There were no issues in that department. He adored me, and yes, I was very satisfied. He was just..."

"What?" Illy was levitating from her seat.

"Just a little dull. I couldn't provoke a reaction from him. He idolized me. I should have loved that. But I didn't. It was annoying. Frustrating. He let me do whatever I wanted and never challenged me."

"Ooh, a good boy. Did you teach him how to be a bit more animal?"

"No. He proposed, and I left."

Illy sighed. "I would have liked a different ending to that story. That you got a rise out of him, and Finn found his inner beast. They say that good girls are only bad with the right guy." She dropped her head to one side, considering. "I wonder if that also goes for men?"

Hurriedly, I moved the subject back to the bridge. "Maybe we can consult. I can't bring him here. Gio will eat him alive."

"You know as well as I do that consulting from a distance would be impossible. This is a unique project and the pilot for others like it. He needs to come. I can talk to Gio. Explain how important this is. We need to tap the source here, or even on the mainland if we can, so we can maximize our expansion there."

"No, you won't. You let me manage my husband. I'll make it happen. Just get him here as soon as you can. Accompanied by wife and children if he has them."

"You know, we also need to speak with Matt about his topography maps."

"Bathymetry," I corrected automatically.

"Yes, that. We must align these bridge pillars to be the strongest they can be."

"I can do that," I snapped. "I don't need help."

"Caitlin," Illy's tone dropped warningly, "you placed Matteo in charge of that project. Trust me, I know how you feel about him. It shouldn't come as a surprise, just between us, that I do, too. But as Chief, you need to be impartial and seek advice and expertise from all relevant parties. While you can do it yourself, sometimes this is strategic. Consult, please."

After dinner, when Carmelo had left and the girls were asleep, I tentatively broached the subject with Gio.

"Absolutely not. I forbid it. I will not have him working with you."

"You don't really get a say. I am letting you know out of courtesy. We need Finn's skills. We need to expand the greenhouses, and we want to add animals

CHAPTER 24

and housing. They need a permanent and reliable power supply. He is the best person for the job."

"Find someone else," Gio growled.

I stood up and clattered my plate into the sink, snappy at both my exhaustion and his unreasonableness. "It is done. Don't be a child."

"A child! You think I am behaving like a child? I'm not the one wanting their old lover here. Am I not enough for you? You want a bit on the side so you can have a casual fuck during the day in your office?"

"Lower your voice. You will wake the girls."

Gio's face darkened, like a snake ready to strike. His own dropped an octave as he growled, "I do not want a man who has fucked my wife, wanted to marry her, staying here, working closely with you, for weeks. Months. No. I forbid it."

"You are forgetting something," I spat back. "I chose you."

"You slept with him." The tone was accusing.

"Many times." I was poking the bear, and I knew it. He might get me to submit in bed when I chose to allow it. But that sense of being forcibly controlled was something I had never coped with. Even as a child, I had never taken well to being told what to do. I was a strong and independent woman. There was no way I would be told how to do my job.

"How many times?" He spat the words, making each one distinct.

"I've lost count," I said, deliberately provoking him. "We were together for over a year, and we fucked every day, sometimes twice a day, so…"

Gio's plate smashed into the sink atop my own, the sound of shattered ceramic echoing around the room.

The sound of a baby crying fractured the tension between us. I stormed off to pick up Aurora, soothing her as I held her to my shoulder, turning my back on him.

"It's okay, sweetheart," I murmured, a fraction too loud to be soothing. "Shh…" I moved around the room, keeping my back to him so he couldn't see my face, swaying her until the breathing became rhythmic and I felt her muscles relax. Carefully placing her back in her cot, I tucked the blanket firmly around her. Sorcha had taught me about SIDS, and there was no way I was risking my child, no matter how angry I was at her father.

Gio had finished cleaning up the broken plate, and I ignored him as I breezed through the kitchen into our bedroom, firmly closing the door behind me. I stripped off to my bra and panties, seething that he would refuse to allow someone to come here, purely for his own selfish motives. We needed the skill, not only for our community, but for all of them. Crossing the room, I stood at the window, searching the night sky for Stella. It took me a moment, waiting for the dark clouds to pass. I heard the door open and close but didn't react.

I felt the warmth behind me as his arms enclosed around my chest. The rumbling of his chest reverberated through my body before the words registered.

"I am sorry. I was angry. I do not want someone here who looks at you in that way."

I whirled on him, barely in control of my emotions. "It has been years. Likely he has married someone himself. Geez, I ran away rather than marry him, remember? I told everyone I wasn't ready to settle down, and then five minutes later, I met you. So, if

CHAPTER 24

anyone has the right to be jealous, it is him. But likely he is just embarrassed that I left."

"Is he the jealous type?"

"No," I admitted after a pause, unable to see Gio and Finn in a physical altercation. "Finn is a teddy bear, gentle and accommodating."

"But he would have fought for you?"

Sighing, I recalled my juvenile suggestion of a duel. "He would have, for me. But he wasn't the physical type. He was not a fighter."

"So you pushed him around?"

"A little," I admitted with a smirk. "He wasn't you. He was happy for me to be in control."

Gio's eyebrows raised. "He was weak, you mean. You are an alpha female. Was he no match for you? Is that why you ran away? He was weak?"

The beast rose within me with Gio calling Finn weak. I had never realized until I met Gio that as a strong woman, I had never been submissive to any man. It hadn't been until I trusted Gio to lead me anywhere that I had found myself submitting and actually enjoying relinquishing control. But judging Finn? He didn't know the man. It was all I could do to not snap his head off.

"He may not have been an alpha, but he was respectful and caring. He worshipped me. And I treated him terribly if you must know. I was young and stupid. Made bad choices."

"Are you saying you want to be with him?"

"That is not what I said." I could barely contain my rage. "I just said I was young and stupid."

"And made bad choices. Was I one of those bad choices?" The undercurrent was breaking through.

Gio had a temper. He didn't lose it often, but when he did, he was ferocious.

"No," I snapped back. "At no point did I say you were a bad choice. I just said I made them, okay?"

"Not okay."

"Fine." I shoved him as hard as I could in the chest and moved to go around him. But he caught my arms, pushing me backward and pinning me to the wall.

"Not fine," Gio growled and held me there, waiting. Assessing my reaction.

"Let … me … go," I hissed. "Finn is coming. It is arranged. You can sleep on the couch."

"I am not going anywhere." He shoved me harder against the wall, and I heard the slight crack as my back pushed back against the plaster. Thank goodness Illy and Carmelo lived on the other side, closer to the girls.

"Neanderthal!" I spat as I squirmed to free myself from his firm grip. "You get your way through brute force and bullying. I won't tolerate it."

"I will not allow him near *my* family." The words were slow and deliberate.

"He won't be near you and the girls. I will minimize contact, too. You think I want to be near someone who wanted to marry me, and I ran away? Not my finest moment."

"He still wanted to marry you."

"We have discussed this. I told you everything. I chose you. Though, I am starting to wonder why. *Finn* always treated me with respect." As soon as the words were out of my mouth, I regretted them.

"Respect? I follow you across the world, support you in your career, help you recover from surgery,

CHAPTER 24

have you ripped from my arms, raise two daughters together, and you think I don't *respect* you?"

"I know you do." I was trying to calm him now. I had overstepped the mark, spoken in anger, and he was furious.

"So this man, he comes here. Will you invite him to dinner? Into our home? As the Chief, of course," he sneered.

"That isn't fair. You know I need to entertain visitors."

"Entertain. Is that what you call it? In your panties, I suppose?"

Heat radiated to the surface once more. "What are you saying?"

"Nothing at all."

"Are you accusing me of cheating?"

"Well, you did, didn't you? On both of them."

Forcibly, I sucked in my breath as tears blinded me. I blinked them away angrily as my voice dropped, and I fought not to let the tremble break through. "How dare you! You didn't know me then. You know nothing. Enjoy your life, Giovanni. Do whatever makes you happy."

Gio felt my anger dissolve into distress and released his grip. Wrenching myself out of his grasp, I bolted past him, snatching at my discarded clothes as I ran. Not caring if I got everything, I grabbed my jacket as I bolted through the living room. I was out the door and out of the apartment before he had left the bedroom. As I staggered down the corridor, I fought to retain control of my emotions, ducking into an alcove to quickly dress, realizing I was missing a sock and not caring as I pulled my boots onto my bare feet. It was only early evening and people were still out, coming home from friends' places or the central dining hall for dinner. Some had wet hair or red faces, indicating they were returning from the pool or gym. Small groups or individuals slowed to say hello or greet me as I passed. I smiled politely but tried to look purposeful so people wouldn't stop. Fighting back the tears, I couldn't hold it together forever.

Where do I go? The office was pointless. I couldn't focus on work, and I didn't want to be found. The last thing I wanted was to be around people. The lake underneath the city would be safe but was a definite no-go after what happened last year. Replaying Gio's hurtful comments over and over, I wandered aimlessly, unable to focus. The thoughts churning through my mind, interspersed with the angry words we had fired like bullets at each other. The corridors all looked the same as I stumbled carelessly, using the walls for balance as tears blinded me. I couldn't breathe, the heartache clutching at me like a vise. Once I made my way to the lower levels, I was alone and staggered around the outer rim of the pods. The only thing changing was the color of the walls, so dark that I could barely take it in through my blurred vision. Dim starlight cast dim light through the windows, shadows looming around every corner.

Finding myself in the original greenhouse, I leaned against the window, trying to recall how I got there. It was cool, green, and tranquil, especially now with the hazy light permeating the Perspex windows. Closing my eyes, I inhaled, taking in the crisp scent of plants, the smells that always reminded me of my father. Since I was a child, he would come home smelling of soil and plants. As I opened them slowly, I could just make out the shadow of Dad standing over by the

CHAPTER 24

trellis, talking to Deb when he last visited. I always felt close to him here. I missed my home, my family. That sense of interconnectedness. But now I had a family of my own. Even the girls were now eating solids and no longer needed me. If they woke, Gio or Carmelo could care for them. My stomach clenched as I let the steady flow of tears fall without interruption.

No one needed me.

Standing at the curved window, I gazed out into the blackness beyond. The night was crystal clear, brilliant stars twinkling against a black velvet backdrop. The moon was almost full, casting a serene glowing path across the water. Life was so much simpler before. Now I was trapped. As memories flooded my mind, my chest constricted, an enormous rubber band crushing my lungs. I gasped, unable to force the air past the compressing sensation. Before I gave it any conscious thought, I moved stealthily down the stairwell to the darkened lower levels and slipped onto one of the smaller vessels, still struggling to breathe. After the bridge collapse, we now kept several smaller vessels to ferry staff and equipment across to the landside pod each day. Likely no one would notice this one was even missing. As I allowed the craft to drift away from the dock, I paused as the needles of the crisp night air pierced my cheeks, a scent that reminded me of the few times I had been outside the domes of my childhood. Bowing my head slightly, I waited until I had cleared the shadow of the pod, lifted the oars, and began rowing toward shore, barely visible in the distance. Little effort was required as the waves pushed me toward the land mass looming ahead. The journey in the dark passed in a blur as I focused solely on my destination and not crashing into the dock in the dim light. Forcing myself to focus on landing and trying not to drown in the words of accusation piercing my brain, I pulled the small craft ashore.

Cheater.

After checking the small vessel was safely ashore and tying off, I made a detour through the greenhouse and picked some fruit for later, stashing it in my jacket pocket before slipping out the back. No sooner had I closed the hatch of our babymoon pod than the tears started to fall anew, splatting on the floor. Suddenly, the weight was all too much. Relentless work, demanding children, an accusing husband. The constant pressures of my life. I half fell across the bed and curled up into a ball, letting the tears run until the well was dry. When I was empty, I stared out across the night sky, seeking my Stella.

Maybe I should have died that day. Is that what should have happened? Was that my fate, and this was never meant to happen at all? Is everything since Caspian a mistake?

My thoughts flowed in a torrent, unable to focus on one above the rest. Joseph didn't make it, and that was partly my fault. I had asked them to come here. Was I responsible for all of this? If I hadn't insisted Sera help me reactivate the portals, none of this would have happened. Going back further, we ran away from Newgrange because of me. When it all boiled down to it, I was the common denominator. I started this. I ran away. I wanted to activate the portals. The Caspians were after me. Illy got caught up in it, and Stella never took her first breath. Then the bridge, the death of my friends, and they were after *me*. I had placed my own children in danger. They missed being on that bridge by minutes. And it was *all ... my ... fault.*

CHAPTER 24

The sudden need to escape cast a heavy blanket over all my thoughts. Would the girls and I be safer back on Lewis? Illy had worked from there for years. Is this what I even wanted? Surely just living a quiet life was best. Keeping my babies safe. Staying out of trouble. I could work on local projects, help Dad. Illy would find someone else to take over as Chief. There were enough worthy contenders. Even nîpiy was a better choice than me.

The pain of my heartbreak washed over me in a wave, and I succumbed to the tears that flowed anew. Gio's words of accusation rang in my ears once more, reverberating through my thoughts.

CHAPTER 25

THE WHITE-HOT BEAM PENETRATING my eye sockets woke me with a start, and it took me a moment to remember where I was. Blinking as I stared around the small room, I saw that it was aglow with the pink-gold morning light. The warm light colored everything it touched with golden streams of light. *Aurora*. As her name flitted into my mind, my stomach flipped, picturing my babies as I had left them, sleeping, the previous night. My stomach lurched a second time as emotion washed over me. They would wake, and I wasn't there. But Gio was there. Illy and Carmelo, too. They would be fine. Better than fine. They didn't need me. I was dispensable. That thought made the room shadow slightly, and I closed my eyes, blinking back the tears. Not that I needed to hide anything. There was no one here to see my pain.

Pottering around the tiny bathroom and kitchen, I was relieved to see we had left some ground coffee here with a plunger, although no fresh food. The fruit I had picked the previous night would need to do. Absently, I dusted the bedside table as the sunbeam bursting

CHAPTER 25

through the panel halfway up the dome illuminated the specks of dust dancing in the light. Grabbing a book from the bedside table, I flicked open to the first page, taking a bite of my apple. My thoughts were adrift and scattered. It took me a long time to settle into the novel, but after a while, I became engrossed, curled up on the bed.

The gurgling radiating from my stomach pulled my attention from the book, and I squinted, assessing the sun overhead. I may as well eat what I had. I couldn't leave here now. The crews would be working. If they saw me approach, they would know something was out here and would discover our private place. Even after the words spoken in anger the night before, I still saw it as our place. As I stretched, I heard my bones crack before taking the three steps into the kitchen. I sliced the remaining fruit into small pieces as my father had done for me when I was a child. Just the act of slicing the fruit reminded me of Dad and all those afternoons he had done this for us after school, chatting to us about our day. Several times I had asked him why he didn't prepare it earlier, knowing what time we would be home. He had insisted that the fruit tasted best fresh. It had taken me years to realize that he loved spending this time with my siblings and me, learning about our day. In those few minutes, he was a constant presence in our lives, a loyal supporter. I arranged the colorful display on the plate and carried it back to bed, lying the plate beside me, nibbling as I read. Despite reading this book before, none of the words made sense as they swam across the page, blurring before my eyes. My thoughts dragged me under the waves once more, replaying Gio's cruel and hurtful words about being unfaithful over and over.

By mid-afternoon, I was ravenous but refused to leave and be seen. Putting the book down, I formulated a plan. I needed to speak with Illy. She could arrange for the girls and me to leave and return to Lewis. Summer or Jake could take us. More than oxygen, the desperate urge to go home radiated from my skin. My days here comprised of being sequestered in a tiny apartment or trapped in a tiny office. I missed the fresh air and sunshine. Mountains, trees, and grass. I never knew how much I would miss wide open spaces until I no longer had access to them. All those times I had complained about walking to school, being made to carry a message or a package to another croft, to a neighbor. Back when I thought that the best way to spend time was to read or tinker with equipment. Now I needed fresh air more than I needed life.

Stepping carefully through the hatch, I walked away from the pod, heading away from the greenhouses, toward what was once the main road that ran down the center of the peninsula. The thoughts spiraled out of control as I walked, not focusing on my surroundings. Dead fields of dust ran on either side of the road, but I couldn't see past my blurred vision and tightening chest as I plowed ahead. Words. The accusing tone. That feeling of being trapped. Contained. Every breath hurt as I blinked back tears.

Darkening shadows cast across the road. I had walked for a long time and had no idea where I was. My chest hurt, each breath strained. Ruined buildings loomed ahead, the likes of which I hadn't seen up close for years. The cities of the old world, my parent's world, had been abandoned well before I was born, and while I had seen a few cities, it was mostly from a distance. The buildings rose, menacing, gray,

CHAPTER 25

and ominous before me; the wind echoed between the hard dusty surfaces, kicking up dirt and making me cough. I turned and looked back down the road I had traveled. It was getting dark, and quickly. With no artificial light, I would need to wait for the stars to illuminate the way. Fighting to breathe, I tried to take small shallow breaths, realizing how unfit I was from working in an office for so long.

Think, Caitlin. Choices.

I could find somewhere to stay and walk back in the morning or walk back now in the dark. The problem was, I hadn't paid attention, and there had been some turns in the road. In the dark, I could end up anywhere and potentially farther away from home. No matter my plans for the future, I needed to get home to my babies. Finding somewhere clean and staying for the night made the most sense.

As I entered each house along the road, I scanned the rooms for somewhere safe. Every window had been shattered; glass fragments littered every surface. Dirt had blown in the openings, making me sneeze as I kicked it up from the floor. As I entered the fourth house, I began to panic. It was nearly full dark, and with no light other than the eerie glow of the moon, I was tripping over objects strewn across the floors. While I was safe from the protozoa, cutting myself on broken glass wasn't ideal with miles to walk back to the pods for help. The slight glow made me look up at the stars starting to break through the blanket. One more. I had time for one more. If I didn't find something, I needed to try to find my way back.

The fifth building had been an office, perhaps a medical practice. In the dark and with the faded and shattered glass, the door splintered beyond use, it was impossible to tell what it had once been. A desk stood sentry in the first room, but the room behind had a leather sofa, the small window on the far wall caked with grime but intact, protected by its proximity to the brick wall of the adjacent building. Dusting off the sofa, I pulled my knees in to accommodate my height and drifted off, the world spinning.

The sound of voices far off in the distance pulled me from my dreams. Weighed down in thick soup, I struggled to open my eyes, to focus them.

"She is here!" A familiar male voice. *Carmelo?*

My head felt like it was encased in concrete. "Huh?" I managed.

"Caitlin, are you alright?" It was Carmelo in his lilting accented English.

Am I? My brain was fogged. I couldn't string a sentence together. I stared up at him, perplexed, fighting to take a full breath.

Carmelo dashed to the door and called, "*Qui! Ora!*"

Through my fogged vision, Illy and Gio bolted through the door, and Gio held a warm hand to my cheek. He watched me struggling to breathe. "Headache?"

I nodded weakly.

"Dizzy? Short of breath?"

I forced my head to move, but it felt like it was in slow motion. Every movement hurt. Closing my eyes, I willed the world to stop spinning. It was like being drunk after running an immense distance. I was

CHAPTER 25

exhausted. Maybe I need to sleep some more despite the daylight stabbing me in the eyeball.

"Shit, she has cerebral hypoxia. We need to get her into the dome as quickly as we can."

I saw Carmelo look up at Illyria, confused.

"Lack of oxygen to the brain," she explained as Gio tossed me over his shoulder and started bouncing me down the road, not waiting for the others to follow.

"Hurts," I wheezed as my ribs banged against his rigid shoulder.

"Don't fucking care!" he seethed, banging me harder. "What the bloody hell did you think you were doing? Going missing for two days? Abandoning our children? Do you have any idea how scared we all were?"

"Giovanni," Illy warned, scurrying to catch up, "now is not the time. This is relief speaking, not anger."

"The girls have been crying for you all day," he continued in a slightly less aggressive tone. "No one knew where you had gone. We didn't even realize you had left the pod until last night when we finally thought to check the surveillance footage. How irresponsible can you be? What the bloody hell were you thinking?"

"Needed time," I muttered, face down over his back. "Space."

"Giovanni," Illy's tone was firmer, "you forget she is still a young woman, not even twenty-five. We all put too much pressure on her, professionally and personally. Lay off."

Gio strained to slow his breath beneath me, his shoulders slumping slightly. "I am sorry for what I said, Caitlin, truly. I don't think that of you, never have. I just didn't want your former lover here."

Illy piped up behind us, "So choose. You lose your wife, or Finn comes. What is it to be?"

Gio's torso tensed as he lengthened his stride. Illy kept pace. I could see her tiny feet trotting along beside us. Trying to escape her was futile, and he knew it.

"That isn't even a question," he finally muttered after a period of uncomfortable silence. "Of course I choose Caitlin."

"I don't know what was said," Illy continued, "but I have some idea. Caitlin, you were stupid to run off like that. We thought you had gone to the isopod, so we let you go. But then, you didn't return. So we checked and realized you had been there but hadn't returned home. You worried us. All of us. But I also know that you are exhausted and blame yourself for what happened with the bridge. I should have seen that you needed a break away from here. Yet again, I missed the signs. I am sorry about that. Giovanni, you can't continue to be jealous of someone she didn't even choose. He proposed well before you were on the scene, and she rejected him. Surely that tells you everything you need to know?"

Gio grunted, but I could feel his breath coming shallower, strained, my weight adding to the burden of walking kilometers in thinning air. Illy barked an order at Carmelo to take over. Gio stopped and handed me over to Carmelo to carry for a stretch.

Carmelo walked slower, and the bouncing was less, making me wonder if Gio was really pissed at me. He walked behind us, and I tried to focus on his face, but the wooziness made it hard to focus. The edges of my vision started to go black, and I blinked hard, trying to maintain consciousness. My skin started tingling and my head weighed a hundred kilograms.

CHAPTER 25

"Stop," I panted, trying to pat Carmelo on the back, but my hands were not following the orders my brain was issuing. "Please, stop," I whispered as I felt my nose hit his spine.

Bright lights woke me, and my eyelids fluttered. Elastic dug around the tops of my ears, and I raised my hand to adjust the mask.

"Don't even think about taking that off," Gio snarled from the chair beside my bed.

"Hurts," I croaked, pushing past his restraining hand and moving the elastic into my hair where it wouldn't rub my skin raw.

"Fine."

Well, that answers that question. The scowl stained his face. Chatter nearby confirmed we were not alone.

"Drink," I croaked, and he handed me a glass of water, not making eye contact. My heart sank. Well, that was it, then. Maybe Sera and I could raise our children together as my parents had done with Illy? That wasn't so bad. We had always said we would live in adjoining houses when we had a family. We had just never expected to do it alone.

Lifting the mask and sipping slowly, I wondered if he would speak first or if I should just get it over with. My stomach churned, but I replaced the mask, and my lungs filled with air. No. I would retain control. There was no way I would let him break up with me.

As the voices disappeared down the hall, I slipped the mask off, glass in hand. Instead of sipping, I said in as steady a voice as I could manage, "I expect your belongings gone by the time I get home."

Gio's mouth dropped, and I exploited his split-second pause to continue. "I can't live with someone who thinks so little of me. I expect you gone. The girls and I will move back to Lewis, and then you can live your own life, wherever you wish."

"No." The depth of his growl surprised even me.

"Fine, then I will move out if you are going to be difficult. Send Illy, please. She can arrange it."

"No." His hand gripped my arm uncomfortably, and I wrenched it away, scowling as I rubbed the red mark.

"Look, you can make this easy or hard. But I will pull rank. I will win. Don't fight me."

"You will not take my girls."

"Can. Will."

"No. You will not. None of you are going anywhere."

Flames flashed before my eyes, and I dropped the oxygen mask off the side of the bed.

"You no longer have the right to tell me what to do. You lost that right two nights ago."

"Three nights ago," he corrected. "When you stormed off and left me with our daughters."

"You accused me of cheating," I fired, feeling my head starting to pound. "How long have you been holding onto that little grudge? I have never cheated on you, Giovanni Accardo. Never."

"I am so sorry for saying that. I didn't mean it. It just slipped out. I was angry, and I said things I didn't mean. Caitlin, I love you. I can't lose you."

"Too late." I rolled to face the wall so he wouldn't see the pain on my face. Even now, his words stung. "I'm gone."

CHAPTER 25

Gio stood and rolled me back to face him, making my eyes water as my head moved across the pillow. "No. I told you I would never leave you. You leave, I will follow. You promised the same. It was one argument. We have fought before."

The tremble in my voice betrayed me. "You have never accused me of cheating before."

"Because I don't actually feel that way. Truly, I don't."

"Then why say it?" I hissed, unable to stop the pain from breaking through.

"Because I am jealous," he hissed back, his face dangerously close to mine. "This man knew you before me. Intimately. No man wants to think of his wife being fucked by another man. Then to be told he was coming here? Near you? I didn't react well. I know that. But I took it out on you, and I am sorry. When you ran, I thought you would come back. I spent two days searching for you. Thinking you dead. Stressing over how I would raise two little girls alone."

"I'm sorry for that," I whispered. "Yes, I slept with him. We were together for more than a year. But it is past. Over. Well before I met you. You were with Francesca far longer than I was with him. She wanted to marry you too, so it wasn't so different. As for the rest, I didn't mean to leave. But your words hurt more than I can tell you. I kept replaying them over and over. I just needed to get out, to walk. Like I used to do on Lewis, walk it off and come back calm. I completely forgot about the oxygen levels, to be honest. Then it was dark, so I found somewhere to sleep and couldn't get up again."

"I wondered why you ended up there." His voice was softer now, and his larger hand enveloped mine, squeezing gently. "I was so worried."

"How did you find me?"

"At first, we thought you were somewhere in the community, so we searched. But not until the next day. That night, when you ran, I thought you needed some space, so I didn't come after you. Besides, I couldn't leave the girls and didn't want to alert anyone that we had fought. I was worried about your reputation. But when you hadn't returned home by morning, Illy came over asking why you were late for work. I had no choice and told her what happened. She was not happy. Tore me another one, as you would say. But when she calmed down, she called Carmelo. He stayed with them, and Illy and I searched for you. We didn't want people to know our business, so she told nîpiy you were sick and kept it between us. It wasn't until night, after a full day of searching, that we even thought to check the cameras. That was when we saw you take the small fishing boat over to the mainland. Illy knew where you had gone and suggested we let you sleep. So we did. At dawn, we set out in another boat to bring you back. I planned to wake you, surprise you. Only, when we got there, you weren't there. We could see you had been there; the bed had been slept in, but it was cold. There was no food, only a browned-off apple core, and Illy found your footprints in the dust leading toward the road. She called Carmelo, and he left the girls with Deb, and he came across, too. That was why we had two boats, although I guess you didn't realize that. You were in a bad way when we found you. Before she would let us go across, Illy called Tadhg, who had been practicing using the heat-seeking technology on the satellites. We waited in the isopod, waiting for him to find you. There was no point in us all succumbing. We waited all fucking

CHAPTER 25

day in that tiny room, and I saw you everywhere I looked. As the hours ticked by, I thought you were dead. Again. I kept seeing you in that bed. It still smelled of you. But you were outside. Water is fine. Air is not. In my mind, I could see what you looked like when I first saw you, after Stella. The video replayed in my mind, and I just wanted to punch something. Illy made me take short walks outside but come back every fifteen minutes for oxygen. I just wanted to run and find you. Bring you home. Finally, Tadhg located a faint heat signal and sent us rough coordinates. It was early afternoon, but I insisted we go. I couldn't bear another night of you being out there, dying. I knew you had been out there overnight at least, and your chances of surviving much longer without oxygen were rapidly diminishing. Tadhg's signal narrowed it down to a vague area but not anything specific. So we walked, as fast as we could without exerting ourselves. It took every molecule of my mind to not want to run, to find you. Then we searched. We searched for what felt like forever. We were just about to return to the pod and re-oxygenate ourselves when Carmelo called out."

"How long was I there?"

"When did you walk there?"

"After I left, I slept the first night in the isopod. I just needed some time alone. It was the afternoon of the second day that I left. I just meant to go for a short walk before I came home and spoke to you. I didn't mean to end up out there. I was just walking, and it got dark, and I found myself in the city."

"So you were outside for nearly twenty-four hours. You are lucky your damage isn't far worse."

"Damage?"

"Lack of oxygen results in hypoxic brain injury."

"Mum always said I never used my brain anyway," I whispered to break the tension.

"She would be right. Caitlin, I am so sorry. I..."

"I'm sorry, too. I didn't mean to run away. I just needed some space. I never get to be alone anymore. We live in a tiny apartment, and I work in a tiny office. All I do is travel between the two. I just wanted to be outside. I miss it more than I can tell you. Fresh air and sunshine."

"I feel stupid. Until Illy said something, I don't think I realized that. I grew up in an unhab. This is normal for me. But I forget where you grew up. Do you want to go back there? Together, I mean. You have always said you could do your job from anywhere. If you need this, we can leave. Tomorrow, if it can be arranged."

"It isn't like I ever told you I feel trapped."

"By me?"

"No, not exactly. But by this life. My job, the girls, the community. I feel like I am not *me* anymore, and I don't know who I am. I don't like the person I have become. I used to be able to walk for days, lie on the grass, swim in the loch. Do absolutely nothing. Now I can't leave our apartment without someone wanting something from me. The second I step outside, it feels like someone is asking for me to consider a proposal, order something. Discuss an issue they are having. The girls need me. You." I shrugged. "I just needed to get away."

"*Amore mio*, I don't leave you alone." His face flushed as he looked at his feet. "I love you so much, and I want you. I need you. But I've placed pressure on you, too, without realizing it."

CHAPTER 25

"A little," I admitted. "It isn't like I couldn't have said no, and it is nice to be wanted, but I just feel..." I threw my hands up, indicating I had no words left.

"We need a holiday. I'll talk to Illyria. See if you can take some time off."

I opened my mouth to protest but realized he was right. As usual, I had worked myself into a hole. Despite saying I wouldn't return to full-time work, I spent more hours than ever in the office, in meetings, and on calls. The girls were brought to me; I was so often gone by the time they were awake. Gio wanted me every night.

"I need to recognize the signs earlier, too," I admitted. "I don't know how to say no. I need to learn."

"You do. But I need to help. You are the most selfless woman I have ever met. I have never known anyone to always put other people's needs ahead of their own like you do. I've never really thought about it, but I need to be your gatekeeper. Tell you when to slow down, to step away and recharge. Would you let me do that?"

I squeezed his hand. "I would love that."

"I realize this is the wrong time, but the girls need you. They haven't fed in nearly two days. Would you mind if they came?"

"I need them, too," I groaned. "I expressed when I was in the pod, but right now, I feel like I am going to burst."

"They are looking larger than normal." Gio snuck a cheeky hand onto my chest to check. "I'll call Deb."

"Can you do something first?"

His brows furrowed. "Anything. What is it?"

"Kiss me."

Gio lifted the oxygen mask from where it hung beside my bed and placed it over his face, then mine. As he removed it, his warm lips met mine, yearning. "I am so sorry for what I said. I will love you until my dying breath, Caitlin Mackintosh."

"Mackintosh-Accardo," I corrected him.

He pulled back and studied me, waiting for me to speak.

"It is time. The girls have your name. I thought perhaps I might, too, if you don't mind."

"Do you mean it?"

I shrugged. "If you don't want me to…"

His arms slipped under me and lifted me from the pillow. "Are you brain damaged from lack of oxygen?"

"Likely," I agreed. "But if you like, I am happy to combine our families. Take both names."

"That means everything to me."

"I will ask Illy to change the name on my office door."

CHAPTER 26

FINN'S ARRIVAL VIA THE full moon portal from France was relatively quiet as visiting officials went. I knew him well enough, *had* known him well, I corrected myself, to know that he was an introvert and wouldn't cope with a lot of ceremony. Instead, he arrived just as we were clearing the packages that had also arrived. While I was there to greet him, I was unsure of the reception I would receive. Illy had diplomatically allowed me to meet him alone, although with the crew there, we weren't exactly alone. Helping him stand, I unzipped him out of his heat suit, and he looked around the enormous concrete room cautiously.

"Hi, Finn," I said with a smile.

"Caitlin." He smiled awkwardly, adjusting his gaze to take in the workers behind me. They paid no attention to either of us as they moved crates from pallets and started loading them onto carts for easier transport to the relevant area of the city.

Keeping it formal, I said, "Thank you for coming. We really appreciate your help."

"Happy to help."

Although we had discussed the project via video conference, meeting again in person was more awkward than I had expected. The last time we had seen each other in person, he had proposed, followed by twenty-year-old me jokingly suggesting a duel, then disappearing from Newgrange overnight.

"I'll show you to your apartment first. Perhaps you would like to rest?"

He nodded. "This is my first visit to an underwater habitation. Could you give me a tour on the way?"

"Of course."

As we entered the hallway and were finally out of earshot, I turned to him. "I'm so sorry for what happened. Me. Running away. It was childish and immature, and I hurt you. That was never my intention. I am so sorry."

"It was a long time ago, Caitlin. Seriously, it's all good."

"No, it really isn't. I truly loved you. It was never you. It was just that I wasn't ready to settle down. Before I knew it, I would have been like my sisters. The expectation was too much. You know I was always the rebel."

"I remember," he replied softly, a soft smile playing on his lips. "It hurt, I admit, and it took me some time to get over you. But then I heard what you had done, and I knew it was for the best. If you had stayed in Newgrange, you would never have reactivated the portals, discovered these communities, and become Chief. You saved so many people. Catie, I always knew you were destined for great things. But Chief? These bridges? Wow. I am so proud of you, lovely."

A pang struck my heart at hearing the term of endearment he had always used for me. But for now,

CHAPTER 26

this was enough. He had forgiven me, and that was as good as I could expect. "Thank you." I stood on my tiptoes and touched my lips to his cheek. "Come on. I can show you the engineering room first."

Several hours later, we were chatting away like the old friends we were. Finn had become more talkative, but we had always talked about engineering concepts and projects. It was one of the reasons I liked him, but he was too damned good. Too considerate. He asked me diplomatically about the events on Caspian, and I gave him a sanitized version of events. He didn't need to know gory details, likely he knew anyway. Everyone did.

"I don't suppose that helped your nightmares," he said as we walked along the corridor.

"Were they that bad?"

"Most nights, you would scream or cry out in your sleep. Don't you remember?"

"No. Why did you never say anything?"

He inhaled, and I felt him stiffen beside me.

"Say it."

"I just hoped that over time you would feel safe ... with me. Tell me what happened to you. But you never did."

"You never asked," I pushed back, gently.

"I'm sorry. I should have. But I didn't want to distress you more."

I stopped and turned to him. "Finn, it had nothing to do with you. Most people know I was nearly killed as a child because of who I am. Then again last year because of what I did. I just feel like I am a poisoned chalice. I'm dangerous to be around."

Reaching for my hands, he held them in his larger ones. His warm gaze held mine for a long time before

267

he spoke. "No. You are not dangerous, lovely. You are a remarkable woman, and you have done great things. No one achieves what you have without some sacrifice."

"I'm so sorry it was you." At that moment, I truly felt it. I had treated him abominably, and here he was, consoling me.

"It was for the best. I know it now."

Recognizing I couldn't avoid it, and delaying this part of the tour would only make things more difficult, I escorted Finn through the medical pods. Gio was with a patient, so I lurked, showing Finn the medical equipment, some enhanced from what he was familiar with. Canada had taken to new technologies with gusto, much of it gained from our partnership with Hokkaido. Sera had returned with Rai and was trying to co-parent with Matt while living in different apartments. She and I spoke daily and often shared technical diagrams and expertise. Gio glanced up and saw us but returned his attention to his patient. When he was finally alone, he came and found us in the MRI room.

"Finn, this is my husband, Giovanni. He is one of the doctors here. Honey, this is Finn, the best electrical engineer the Collective has."

Gio and Finn were roughly the same height and build, but I would back Gio in a fight. He had more fire to him. Gio looked him up and down but politely extended his hand and greeted Finn warmly enough, for which I was grateful. I really didn't want a scene.

"I was just showing Finn all the technical equipment," I explained. "Can you tell him about your project with the remote imaging?"

CHAPTER 26

"Of course. Why don't you quickly run down and see Carmelo? He was looking for you. Is Finn staying in the guest quarters? I can show him there when we are finished."

I flashed Gio a warning. He knew perfectly well where Finn was staying. Additionally, I had no doubt whatsoever that Carmelo was not looking for me. But Gio had earned the right to test the intentions of my former lover. I just hoped he would be gentle. I needed Finn's expertise if we were to ever expand this community, and it wouldn't help us if Gio tore him limb from limb in the first five minutes.

"I won't be long," I assured Finn. "We have babies, twin girls. Likely they just need a feed. You are in excellent hands."

As I slipped through the door, I wondered if that was indeed true. Would he be reasonable? Or would Gio try to poison him the instant I was out of sight? No, not poison. That was too slow. More likely, beat him into a bloody pulp for once loving his wife. Memories of Gio beating Antonio years ago flashed into my mind, and I closed my eyes, praying he was healing. So many times I had wanted to reach out, check on my friend. But guilt that the bridge I built was the target, and that was what had killed his soul mate, gripped me. Gio spoke with him several times a week and relayed that Antonio was recovering slowly but was still in pain. He had returned to work in the vineyards, making wine. Dad always spoke of the healing nature of plants. Having his hands in the earth, creating new life. Nurturing seedlings, which would, in turn, sustain us. Praying Antonio could find a new life purpose, I went off to find Carmelo.

The door creaked slightly as I was patting the girls to sleep.

"Shh," I called out, not wanting him to slam it and wake them. It had taken ages to get them both to settle. Gio's neatly groomed dark hair popped through the door.

"Is it too late?"

"Never."

Gio leaned in and kissed both girls' heads as was his nightly routine. "Goodnight, my angels," he whispered.

"You know they likely won't be angels," I whispered back as I covered up Khione and started toward the door.

Gio sighed. "No, they have your genes. They will probably be wild."

I pinched his ass. "Wild? Exactly what did Finn say about me?"

"Nothing. He was the perfect gentleman, and I tried."

"You didn't!"

"Of course I did. I tried to get him to talk about you, and he kept blushing and changing the subject. He refused to say anything about you other than how pleased he was that you got this job, and he couldn't imagine anyone better. Oh, and that it was about time someone recognized your expertise."

"He is a good man."

"I don't like him, never will. But I can see that he is decent. He respects you, Caitlin. He is intelligent, and you have a lot in common."

"We did. We could always talk."

CHAPTER 26

"So I am left wondering: why didn't you choose him?"

Gio followed me into the kitchen and lifted one of the glasses of whisky to his lips, inhaling appreciably before taking a healthy gulp. Grabbing the oven mitt, I pulled the plates from the oven, ready to serve.

"Honestly, I don't know. All of those things are true. But he didn't challenge me. He let me walk all over him. Finn is so kind, he would do anything for anyone, especially me. He is like my father in so many ways. It would frustrate the hell out of me. I used to provoke him, try to get a rise out of him. But he never bit back. Not once. Even when I really pushed his buttons."

"Not like me?"

"Nothing at all like you. You have what Illy calls a bit of beast in you. What can I say? Maybe I like that."

"A bit of beast?" Gio grinned broadly, placing his glass on the bench with a *thunk*. "Well, let's see if this beast can make you whimper."

"Dinner!" I squeaked as he picked me up and threw me over his shoulder, the oven mitt falling to the floor.

"We will eat later."

Despite Gio staking his claim and no longer feeling threatened by Finn's presence, it was me who didn't feel entirely comfortable about Finn being here. At Illy's urging, I begrudgingly let nîpiy in on the secret, and after laughing uproariously at the story of me running away in the middle of the night to avoid a marriage proposal, she kindly offered to be his chaperone. She was wonderful with him, ensuring he had somewhere to go each night for dinner, setting up meetings for him, and arranging for his time here to be as productive as possible. Finn and Matt met over teleconference and shared ideas. As soon as Finn expressed a need for a resource or to speak to someone about a tiny element of the project, nîpiy had arranged it.

Within weeks, Finn had designed a complete geothermal transfer system, venting heat and clean water from the underwater fissures beneath the city, channeled under the bridge to the new greenhouses. With now unlimited heat and fresh water at our disposal, this would allow us to expand them exponentially. When he shyly presented me with the final concept, I asked questions about the valves and their ability to regulate the flow. Finn grew more animated in his description of the process, leaving me in awe.

"This is amazing work," I told him genuinely. "I love the way you have integrated this."

"You miss this, don't you?" he asked softly, not wanting to be overheard.

I desperately wanted to shut the door but knew how that would look. Gossip was the last thing I needed.

"More than I can tell you," I whispered back. "But working on projects like this fills me with hope that one day we can improve lives for tens of thousands of people across all communities, not just this one. This is just our pilot. All of the unhab communities are located over geothermic vents and fissures. I just want people to live on land again, to be able to run on grass and climb trees, like we used to."

Finn blushed and looked away, clearly remembering the times we had spent together in forests and on mountain tops.

CHAPTER 26

"I'm really sorry," I whispered, feeling sick, knowing that he had fought for me, and I ran away. "I should have told you; I know that. But I was young and wanted to see the world. There was so much pressure on me to have children, immune children. I wasn't ready."

"I know. You would never have been happy on Newgrange, not forever. You always had restless feet. I knew you were destined for greatness, Caitlin, and not just your heritage." He glanced out the door, but Illy and nîpiy were deep in conversation. "You were always going to be important, a leader."

"Did you want to be part of that?" I asked softly.

"For a time, I thought I did. I loved you so very much. But after you left, I realized I would have been holding you back. Your biology, your parents, being the daughter of the Chief and the Lewis Ambassador, you would always have wanted more than I could give. So while it hurt for a time, I accepted it. We were too young."

"Did you meet someone else?" I asked cautiously, not sure I really wanted to know.

To my complete astonishment, Finn blushed several shades darker.

"What?"

"Not at home, no. I have met someone here, and with your agreement, I would like to stay for a little longer. Just to see if it works out?"

"Ahh! Only if you tell me who?"

"Nalani," he whispered, so low I could barely hear it.

"Gabriel and Deb's daughter? Seriously? That is wonderful news! They are close friends. Yes, you can stay!" In my exuberance, I flung my arms around him and squeezed, forgetting for an instant who he was or had been. His scent was still so familiar, and my heart flip-flopped for a second as he brought his arms around me and held me.

Realization struck, and I backed away, trying to cover the uncomfortable moment. "I am so happy for you," I said a fraction louder, aware that Illy and nîpiy had stopped talking and were likely watching. Stepping back, I called through the doorway, "Finn is staying another month!"

Illy stepped to the doorway, a cheeky grin crossing her face. "Met someone, have we?"

Finn looked down at his feet, so I answered for him. "Yes!"

Illy glanced at me, a veiled warning. Was he staying for me?

"Tell them," I urged.

"It is early," he stammered. Illy had always made him nervous. "But if you don't mind, I would like to stay. Maybe just one more month?"

"I think we can arrange that," she twinkled. "But you need to tell me who. Just in case I need to unruffle some feathers."

Finn gurgled, tongue-tied, unable to speak. Taking pity on him, I said, "Nalani, Gabriel and Deb's daughter."

"Oh, she is lovely!" nîpiy exclaimed. "She is perfect for you. Intelligent, but quiet and gentle. She is such a gorgeous girl."

Nothing at all like you! Illy flashed the look over Finn's bowed head, and I glared at her.

"I will arrange for you to stay. I can speak with Tadhg and tell him you aren't quite finished. We can keep your secret, although you had better let her parents know."

"They know." Finn gulped.

CHAPTER 26

"Do they approve?"

"They want to speak with Caitlin."

"Gabriel and Debra are close friends," I explained. "I will speak to them. Put in a good word."

"It isn't personal. You need to understand that until recently, we haven't had any contact with the outside world for many years," nîpiy said, placing a kind hand on his arm. "People here are still wary of strangers. Caitlin and her family have proven themselves, but we have had few others. Then, of course, when the bridge was blown up and Deb was injured, it conjured a lot of fear again. The sense that we aren't quite safe. They just need to be sure that you are a good man, worthy of their daughter. They know all the men here. You aren't known."

"I will speak with them," I promised. "It will be okay. If she is your choice, I will do everything I can to make it happen. They owe me, and I am happy to call in the favor. I will do this for you."

"Nalani is okay with this, isn't she?" Illy asked suddenly.

"Of course!" Finn blurted, looking up at her. "It is reciprocal. She knows I am asking to stay."

"Just checking. I don't want that scenario on my hands."

I laughed, knowing Finn as well as I did. There was no way he would force himself on anyone. "I am thrilled for you," I whispered as Illy and nîpiy returned to the front office. "More than anything, I want you to be happy."

"I want that for you, too, you know. It is all I ever wanted."

"You are a good man. Let me speak with Deb and Gabriel. But it will be fine."

CHAPTER 27

GIO ENTERED OUR ROOM and closed the door, leaning against it. We rarely closed the door in case one of the girls needed us. Me being missing for three nights had impacted their sleep patterns, and even now, many weeks later, they still woke in the night crying. Putting down my book, I smiled, guessing what he wanted but froze as his face was illuminated in the moonlight streaming in from the window beside me. There was a dark look staining his face.

"What is it? Are you alright? Is it the girls?" I bolted upright in bed, ready to be with my babies, but he held a hand out as he shook his head.

"The girls are fine. I need to tell you something, but you need to promise me you will hear me out. Hear all of it before you judge."

"Did you hear about Finn?" I blurted, not wanting this to turn into another argument about my former boyfriend.

"Finn?" He looked startled. That was a no, then.

"He wants to stay. He has met someone. Here, I mean. Nalani."

CHAPTER 27

"No, that isn't it. I'm not thrilled about him lurking around you, moping, but I am happy for him, I guess." Gio was rapidly dismissive, which I hadn't expected.

Cocking my head to the side, I asked suspiciously, "What is it, then?"

"Viktor is dead."

"Who is…" I started to ask but stopped, my mouth open. Of course I knew. The vicious asshole who had brutally abused me and orchestrated my capture. The monster behind the invasion of Piedmont, Canada, and other communities. Viktor himself had laughingly leaked the video of my abuse to humiliate me when he had learned I was Chief.

"Good," I spat through my narrowing throat. "Couldn't have happened to a nicer man. I truly hope he suffered and was alone as he met his end."

"He did."

"Do we know if he was behind the destruction of our bridge?"

"We don't. But who else would it be?"

"Well, I won't be losing any sleep over him. A slow and painful death is more than what he deserves."

"It was as slow as possible."

"How would you know?" I asked, the words registering.

Gio's calm face cracked. "Fuck. I was hoping you wouldn't pick that."

"You had a hand in it."

"Perhaps."

I lowered my eyes at him.

"A small one."

"Tell me," I growled. "All of it. How deep in this are you?"

"Pretty deep."

I sat up against my pillows and forced him to look at me as he sat on the edge of the bed, shifting uncomfortably. "I love you more than anyone, and I will defend you to the ends of the earth, but you need to tell me what I am defending you against. All of it. Now."

Unable to meet my eyes, Gio told me what he knew. When we were on Lewis and after the girls were born, always wanting to expand his knowledge, he had spent some time with Kendra, who had taught him about natural remedies and treatments. She had shared her notes and samples, showing him the plants she had asked Di to grow. Using knowledge passed on to him from Kendra, who had learned about alternative medicinal treatments for the ultimate step from Jacinda, Gio had grown and prepared a soluble powder for Antonio.

"When?"

"Before he left here."

"Why? You didn't tell me Antonio was suicidal. He is grief-stricken. But not that."

"Antonio wanted it for his own use."

"No! Please tell me he didn't!"

"He planned to. Kendra taught me how to prepare it when the girls were born, and I documented the herbs she used. Your aunt sourced them for me, and I ensured they were grown securely, known by very few."

"The small garden bed to the far left of the landside pod?"

"Exactly. Deb knew, and your father, but no one else."

"But Antonio didn't take it?"

"No. He went home to put his affairs in order. He wanted to make sure someone would take care of his

CHAPTER 27

father. He had no desire to live his life alone. Being gay in Italy, well, there aren't a lot of choices, and everyone else is partnered."

"He could have come back here!" I exclaimed. "We would have welcomed him. Lewis, Newgrange. Any of the unhabs. He would be an asset."

"He couldn't face life without Joseph."

My blood ran cold. "I understand that," I whispered, thinking back to the days when I had been locked in the cell, believing Gio was dead.

"As do I. So when he asked me, begged me more accurately, I agreed. Everyone should have the right to choose when and where they pass from this life. Before he left here, I sourced the herbs for him and taught him how to prepare them. It needed to be prepared fresh; the efficacy diminishes rapidly. He was just waiting for the right time."

"What happened? And what does this have to do with Viktor?"

"We kept in touch, and he was almost ready. Life had become unbearable, going through the motions, as he put it. Then he learned Viktor and his delegation were planning to travel to Piedmont. He knew he had one chance to take down the man who had killed his husband and tried to kill you."

"What did he do?"

"Antonio wrangled an opportunity to display his wines and served his favorite varietal and vintage."

"Please tell me he didn't." My hand clapped over my mouth.

"He slipped the powder into the relevant glass. All good. Viktor finished the tasting. It wasn't immediate. As he walked into the boardroom to begin the meeting with Riccardo, he felt unwell, had a heart attack, and died."

"In pain, I hope," I muttered under my breath, feeling conflicted. An official delegation attacked on one of my communities, yet I was pleased about it.

"Almost certainly. Writhing and gasping if Antonio got the quantity right."

"Why are you telling me?"

"First, we promised to never keep secrets from each other. Second, Antonio is here and needs help."

"Here?"

"The remaining two Caspians found it suspicious that the last thing served to Viktor was wine, especially after what happened to their colleagues when they invaded Piedmont. The delegates insisted on questioning Antonio. They put a lot of pressure on, and Riccardo wasn't strong enough to deny the request, so they began a search for Antonio. Summer was there and, knowing what they did to you and would likely do to Antonio, got him here."

"Fuck, so he *ran*?"

"What else could he do? It was run or be interrogated and potentially start a war. That would never have ended well. Either Antonio would have confessed under duress and they would have insisted on the death penalty, or he denied it and they didn't believe him and tried to seek retribution anyway. The Caspians were looking for someone to blame, and Summer suspects Riccardo was looking for a scapegoat to get the negotiations back on track."

"Surely he wouldn't hand over one of his own. Does Riccardo know what they even wanted to discuss?"

"They refused to say. Trade, peace negotiations. Who knows? They didn't get to start."

CHAPTER 27

"Where is he now?"

"You recall those three glorious nights we spent on our babymoon?"

I flushed. We had barely spent an hour not touching each other. In many ways, it had been better than our actual honeymoon. Then I had spent another night there after we had fought over Finn.

"Antonio is in the isopod."

"Is he...?"

"He is. I gave him the injection when he was here, after Joseph. Opened up his options. I knew you wouldn't mind that he joined the club."

"I can't believe Antonio did that," I breathed. "He is such a gentle soul."

"He did it for you and for Joseph. He is lucky I wasn't there. I vowed to save lives, not take them. But for that man, I would have made an exception."

"Get in line, buddy. Nothing would give me greater pleasure than to see Viktor burn."

"Why did you allow them to travel there, then?"

"Technically, I didn't. Riccardo did, which is his right. Illy and I were apprehensive but also realize we can't stay at war with them. Not if they are capable of blowing up our communities from Kazakhstan. It makes sense to assess what they want and why they may have attacked us. They approached Riccardo directly, and he agreed—with conditions. Only three of them would attend, no weapons. For two days only, one night. They would be transported by helicopter. Jake took them with two other men from Newgrange. Discreetly armed, of course. We figured that was safest. That way they could prevent others coming through again. But Illy wanted Summer there, too, just in case something happened to Jake, and she could fly them home. It was carefully controlled. Illy wouldn't allow me to be there, and she had a commitment already. She also felt it best that there was no formal reception by the ACC. She didn't want to validate them so soon. But at some point, one of us will need to. She knows it needs to be her. I can't, both after what they did to me personally and what they did here. The people here would never forgive me if they knew I had been holding talks with terrorists."

"Likely not. I am surprised Riccardo did."

"Riccardo is a peacekeeper," I admitted. "He knows what happened here and wouldn't want to be the next target. Especially after the loss of life on Piedmont the last time. He knows not to trust them, but we also can't ignore them. Three delegates were to attend. How did his comrades react to Viktor's death?"

"Badly. They suspect foul play but can't prove it. The delegation turns up for a round table at their instigation and their leader dies, painfully and publicly, on the first day. It is terribly suspicious. The Piedmont medical team treated him, of course. Only based on the symptoms, my colleagues genuinely believed it was a heart attack and couldn't save him. They sent out a call to all medical teams to ask for advice, but he passed as they were working on him. Viktor's colleagues watched, so they knew that the treatment was above board. It was why Antonio used the mixture I gave him and not the *morte liquida*. The medical team there would recognize the symptoms and know it was foul play. They could potentially have dropped him in it."

"Can they prove anything?" I asked, fear of yet more reprisal rising into my chest. Every time something like this happened, I lost someone I loved.

CHAPTER 27

"According to Kendra, the herb Antonio used was tasteless and untraceable. Likely they have never heard of it and won't be able to prove anything. I had certainly never heard of it before she told me, nor had your father, but they found seeds in the Lewis seed bank. So even if they do autopsy him, they won't know what they are looking for. Hopefully, they don't do a toxicology screen, although again, they won't be looking for that. I can't imagine they can even test for it. He died of a heart attack."

"So what did they do? The Caspians, I mean?"

"The remaining two delegates refused to negotiate, especially after they realized Antonio was missing. They demanded Jake take them home with Viktor's body."

"I hope he rots," I seethed.

"As do I. I would have done it, gladly. In some ways, I am angry that he is dead. I would much rather have him see my face as he died at my hand. Seeing what he did to you will haunt me until the day I die."

"I can't imagine watching it was as bad as being there. I lost Stella to them, then Joseph. Not to mention all of your friends on Piedmont."

"He is gone. He will never hurt you again." Gio's arms held me to his chest as the memories crashed down around me like waves.

A shudder broke through, although I did my best to tamp it down.

"I thought this would be hard for you to hear," he murmured in my ear as he swept my hair back off my neck. "The news arrived just as I was leaving work. That is why I was late. I asked Illyria to let me be the one to tell you. You would have heard tomorrow. This way you can be prepared and act surprised but hold your head up high. Act like you know nothing."

"It has been nearly two years," I whispered, choked. "Why does even the mention of his name have the capacity to reduce me to a blubbering mess? He is nothing. Just a man. Nothing special. A worthless, vile man."

"Was a man," Gio corrected. "After they asked for help in treating him, I fired off a message to be sure. Cristina confirmed it."

"But what will his comrades do?" I asked, wondering aloud. "They obviously suspect Antonio, and he ran, making it difficult to believe he was innocent."

"Yes, but no one knows where he has gone. Summer, you, and I are the only three who know. Ally, too. She moved the satellite so they weren't traced."

"Good on Ally. What about Sera?"

"No. We kept the group necessarily small."

Despite living apart for several years now, I knew Sera would always have my back, but understood why Summer had trusted only her twin and us. Sera and I spoke daily, even more so now that she and Matt had split. While I was hopeful that in time they might reconcile, I would support her in whatever she chose. It was a sore point between Gio and me, and after several raging arguments on the subject, we had agreed to focus on our marriage and not theirs. My loyalty would always be with my sister, and Gio's with his brother. But we had pledged to place each other and our daughters first. For the first time, I understood why Illy had separated us and sent Sera to Japan.

"The question is, how much do the Caspians want to pursue it?" I asked, half to myself.

CHAPTER 27

"That will depend on what their medical teams find, I suspect. If they agree with the Piedmont team's assessment of cardiac arrest and can't find anything on the toxicology reports, they may let it go. The risk is, if they find something unusual, a spike in an enzyme, anything out of the ordinary, will they push for repatriation and a trial?"

"On what grounds? They attacked Piedmont and other communities, and we never pursued them for a trial. They aren't part of the ACC. Besides, Illy and I will never let that happen."

"True. So hopefully they let it go." Gio shrugged.

"Don't we have a bigger issue?" I replied. "What do we do with Antonio? He can't stay out there forever. Alone and isolated. He can't even go for walks, as I proved."

"No, but he can live there for a few months maybe. We can visit most days. Carmelo, too. Summer sourced enough materials that he could build a small greenhouse adjoining the isopod. When he is ready, we will take him some seedlings, and he can start growing his own food. At night he can source fruit and vegetables from the landside greenhouses. If he is careful, no one will notice."

"We can always rely on Summer. If I know Antonio, he will add more value than he will take." I smiled. "But he will be so terribly lonely. There is another problem. Finn is still here, and I have asked him to consider expansion to the landside pods. While I can suggest they build in the other direction, along the peninsula, I can't guarantee they won't see him or the pod. He needs to build in the most logical direction from an engineering perspective."

Gio grimaced at the name but didn't reply.

"Let me think about it. We are still finalizing the design. Maybe I can insist that the bridge be rebuilt first. That way, we have a few weeks, months even."

"Please don't take any risks with your reputation. The last thing anyone wants is for you to do anything that could damage your position."

I considered that. "You are right; I can't do much. Aside from keeping people from extending in that direction, I can't help him. Tell me what he needs, and I will make sure he gets it, but I am not sure I can be the one who takes it to him. If he is found, I can deny all knowledge. But what do I do if I am seen assisting a murderer?"

"He will understand. I promised I would take all of my Italian language books, but I think he needs this time alone. To mourn. He left here so quickly after his loss."

"Why did he do that? We would have supported him. Surely he knew that."

"I don't know. But I can guess."

My heart lurched, and I waited for the words, praying it wasn't because I had invited them here, and he blamed me for his loss. Had I not asked Joseph to help build the bridge, that he had a vested interest in its success, they would not have been here.

"Italy is home. He is Antonio there. Here, everyone knew him in a couple, part of Joseph and Antonio. He was married here. Then there was so much pain here, for all the lives lost. He felt he couldn't be part of that. But the true reason, I suspect, is that some people survived, thanks to you. But his great love did not. I know how that feels, Caitlin. When you were taken, I knew that everyone else here had survived. All the people down at the lake that day. I was insanely

CHAPTER 27

jealous that no one else had suffered a loss except me. I don't remember the first few days or the surgery. They kept me under heavy sedation. But as the days passed, that sucking hole in my chest grew wider, knowing I had lost both you and our child."

"You never told me that."

"It was on the seventh day that they told me you had been found and were in terrible shape. You were still being transported to Scotland. I was warned not to expect anything. You likely wouldn't survive the day. That was worse. Knowing that you had been tortured to an inch of your life, for days, and I hadn't been able to stop it. I wasn't there with you. I was here. In a bed. Alive and cared for. As soon as I heard the news, I forced them to let me start walking. I knew you would fight, and I needed to be there. To tell you how much I loved you."

"I thought you were dead, too," I admitted, remembering the time spent in the cell in Caspian, picturing his body dropping to the sandy bank. "I saw them stab you, gut you. I watched the blood soak through your suit as they wrenched me away. I genuinely believed you were dead. But I couldn't join them. They would never have allowed me to keep Stella. I would never want your child raised in a place like that, so I thought it better if I died, too."

"You did the right thing."

No matter how many times he reinforced it, I still felt the guilt of that decision. The one with no satisfactory answer.

"We suffered a tremendous loss, but I still have you."

"So you think Antonio left here after the bombing because he was jealous of us?"

"Not exactly. He went home to grieve in a place that reminded him of Joseph. But what it also likely did is ram home the fact that he is alone in the world. Then, hearing that the delegation was arriving…"

"Are the people in Italy so forgiving that they would allow the Caspians to visit? I know Riccardo agreed to it, but clearly, the people didn't object."

"I doubt it, but they never want to be victims again. Far too many people lost their lives that day. They know what happened here. They know they need to call a truce, or the battle will never be over."

"I understand that. But I hope you don't think less of me when I say I can never forgive them. Partly for what they did on Piedmont, and again for what they did here. But mostly for what they did to me, to us. I will never be the woman I was because of them. And I don't mean the physical injuries, although there were many. I fear the dark now. Being near the portal gives me flashbacks. I worry I will never be safe, that our children will become victims. They nearly were. A few minutes later and Carmelo and the girls would have been crossing that bridge. We came so close to losing them, and I don't think I could survive losing more children."

Gio held me to him. I pulled back and looked into his eyes.

"How do we keep him hidden? He can't stay out there forever. It won't be good for his mental health either."

Gio shrugged. "I don't know. It is a temporary measure, as you call it."

"Have you eaten?" I asked, redirecting his thoughts.

"No. Not hungry. Let's sleep. We can talk about it tomorrow."

CHAPTER 28

THE CITY WAS ABUZZ with the news of Viktor's murder and Antonio's disappearance. While passing through the pods, I listened to the chatter and observed that the general consensus was that Antonio was justified in his actions. However, I also noticed that the majority of people assumed he was guilty. *That is a problem,* I mused as I picked up snippets of conversation. At least here he was known. Most people had attended his wedding and knew him well enough to know he was a gentle soul and madly in love, likely acting out of grief. Most other communities would condemn someone poisoning an official delegate for unknown or spurious motives.

Reaching the office, Illy and I were inundated with calls and meetings. Communities worried about what this meant. Summer dropped by and I managed to spend a few moments alone with her. After farewelling the furious Caspians, the Piedmont community had conducted a full-scale search for Antonio. Amid the chaos, Summer quietly filed her flight plans, noting her intention to visit her mother. With

Antonio hidden among her cargo, she had departed, no one bothering to check the craft.

"How is he?" I asked.

"Surprisingly calm. He spoke very little on the way here. When he finally spoke, he thanked me but told me it wasn't necessary for me to get him out of Piedmont. He was quite prepared to face the music."

"He wanted the Caspians to know? Does he not understand that admitting to murder could instigate full-blown war?"

Summer grinned at me. "I am the daughter of two military officers, you know. I paid attention. I explained that to Antonio when I found him. It was me who convinced him that getting out was the smartest move. He wanted to tell them why. He has no desire to live."

My heart shattered like glass against stone. "He blames me, doesn't he? For Joseph's death?"

Summer turned to me, incredulous. "How can you even say that? He blames Viktor."

"Truly?"

"Caitlin, I love you, but you are an idiot. Of course, truly. He has accomplished what he wanted. There is a pervading sense of peace now. He has avenged the invasion of Piedmont and the death of his friends, your kidnapping and mistreatment, and Joseph's death. He is content."

"Are you serious?"

"One of the few things he said when he finally spoke was that he regretted not being able to tell you himself. While most of it was for his love, in part, this was for you. He adores you, Catie. He sees you as family. Antonio saw you after you were taken. He

CHAPTER 28

knows the long road you fought to recovery. He would have done it for you alone."

A sense of unease washed over me. *Am I happy to see the man who had abused me dead? Hell yes. Am I satisfied that a friend took that life? Surprisingly, no.*

"What does he want to do now?" I finally asked to break the silence.

Summer shrugged. "Ask him yourself."

For days, we lived in uncertainty, tensely awaiting another attack from Caspian as retribution. But as a week passed, then two, we slowly allowed ourselves to relax.

"How quickly do people retaliate?" I asked Illy one morning after our leadership teleconference, where Viktor's death and what the Caspians wanted in Piedmont was the main topic of conversation.

"Usually as quickly as possible. Typically, a return strike is swift. If they were going to attack, I would think they would have done it by now."

I nodded, not really understanding the art of war. But Illy did, Carmelo and Jake, too, and I knew the three of them had been holding meetings, discussing ways to protect Piedmont and Canada. Without knowing if or when they would strike was the most unsettling part. We had heard nothing from Caspian since they had left Piedmont, leaving me constantly worried that they had detected something unusual in the toxicology screening.

"Do you think it is likely?" I asked Gio when we were alone.

"According to Jacinda, almost impossible. But I am testing it. Just to put your mind at ease."

"How?"

"Withdrawing blood and testing how much appears in the screening. I am assuming a lot. That it doesn't alter state in the body, that their screening technology is the same level of complexity as ours."

"Your blood?"

"Of course. I am trying different strengths, not really knowing how much Antonio used. But so far, nothing. I am hopeful that their technology is not more advanced than ours."

Thinking about that for a moment, I replied, "I really don't think so. I was in the medical facility when I woke, and I don't recall it being anywhere near as advanced as Clava or here. Of course, I didn't see it all. But from what little I saw, I don't think so."

Gio nodded thoughtfully. "That is good then. They can suspect but can't prove."

"Illy says that the more time that passes, the less likely they are to launch another attack."

"She would know. I have never met anyone who can read motives like she can."

Gio found time to visit Antonio most days, and I knew Carmelo did too, sometimes taking the girls for an early morning visit before the greenhouse or construction teams were there and noticed they went outside. While everyone knew I was immune, we hadn't gone into detail about who else was. Illy and I did not speak of Antonio being here, but we both

CHAPTER 28

knew the other was aware. Gio kept me apprised of his state, and after the first week, he appeared to be in good spirits.

"He can't stay here forever," I whispered, even though there was no chance of being overheard.

"But what do we do with him? He can't return to Italy or any other community. He could live here, but we would need to get people on our side."

"What does he want?"

"He wants to be productive. It is slowly killing him being confined to that tiny pod all day, although he has nearly finished his greenhouse extension. He adores seeing the girls, and Carmelo says it destroys him when they need to leave. I truly think they are good for him. He talks more about the future now."

"That is good," I admitted. "Let me talk to Illy. We can't keep pretending he isn't here. Perhaps over dinner is safer. Do you mind if I invite Illy and Carmelo over?"

"Not tomorrow. I am working late. But the next day, sure."

CHAPTER 29

THE STORM CLOUD HANGING over Illy's head entered the room a full second before she stepped through the doorway into my office the next morning. I glanced up expectantly, sensing her mood, waiting for her to tell me that a project hadn't succeeded or someone had refused an instruction. Instead, she firmly closed the door after checking no one was outside, able to overhear. nîpiy was in a meeting with the catering team, so we could speak in private.

"We need to talk."

I groaned. Nothing good in the history of forever had ever come from those words. My stomach lurched. "What is it?"

"We have received a request for help."

Illy's words were innocent enough, but the tone was slightly off. Leaning forward in my seat, I asked, "Okay, what do you need? Do we need to mobilize a team? What specialists do you need? Medical or engineering?"

"Cool your jets. The request was from Caspian."

CHAPTER 29

"What the fuck do they want?" I growled, the tension tightening my chest as I settled back in my chair.

Illy sighed and dropped into the seat opposite me. She looked exhausted, her skin dull and her long dark hair lacking its usual luster. With me working fewer hours, she had been picking up the slack, and it showed in every new line on her face. Yet again, I wondered how on earth I was ever going to be able to do this job alone, with two young children, when she finally announced her retirement.

"They approached us. We have learned the reason for the Caspian delegation's visit to Italy. Before Viktor ... passed and they refused to negotiate."

I flinched, waiting for her to accuse me of aiding Antonio. To my astonishment, she wasn't looking at me but at her hands. My stomach somersaulted, hoping I could regain my composure. She knew; of course, she did. But we hadn't discussed it yet. To raise it between us would mean needing to address it and what to do with him.

"It appears they have a crack in their underwater water storage, the thick concrete wall between the underground lake and the outside sea. They have known about it for some time. It is widening, and the pressure from outside is making it irreparable. They have tried, and they keep patching it up, but the force outside is too great. It will burst open, and soon, leaving them with no fresh water supply."

"Good" I wanted to snap, recalling my treatment at their hands, but realized that was a bad look. There were likely innocent people living there. They couldn't all be evil just because some of the leaders were. Likely, there were innocents. Children. But I couldn't hold back the snarl. "What do they expect us to do about it?"

"They have requested assistance to repair the crack. They know we have the technology, so they are asking for help."

"They want help? From us?"

"They do. Though let's just say it wasn't the most courteous of requests."

"Surely they can..." I trailed off as my thoughts caught up. Likely there was no one else they could ask. How long had they known? Fissures worsened over time as pressure increased. Was this the reason behind the invasions? They had some knowledge of my skills. Was this why they had tried to take me? Illy's voice dragged my wandering attention back to the room.

"So, is it even possible to stop the crack from worsening?"

Picturing the wall down in our lowest levels, I considered the challenge, a several-meter thick concrete wall with relentless and immense pressure boring down from the outside.

"From an engineering perspective, an underwater repair is borderline impossible. It isn't like we can repair it and let it cure. When these communities were built, engineers used cofferdams, continually pumping the water out and building in the dry. We don't have that technology anymore, not to mention all the workers would be exposed. The pressure from the Caspian Sea is so great that if there is a fissure, it will only worsen. Any patching is temporary," I explained.

CHAPTER 29

"They know that. Before we address the moral question of the matter, my question is a technical one. Is there anything we can do to help?"

"I guess, but it will take time. How long do they have? Have they done any modeling?"

"From what they told us, months maybe. But not a year."

"Well, that explains why they approached Riccardo. He is an engineer. Likely they thought they would get a more receptive audience than if they contacted us. He would understand the issue immediately. But surely they know Riccardo would tell us that their water security is impacted?"

"Who knows? It is possible they have little knowledge of our political model and communication structure. They have intercepted our communications before."

"Patching the crack is an ongoing job and will never be permanent," I mused.

"Could we build something landside within that time?"

"In truth, probably yes. We have been slowly inoculating work crews to be immune. Why wouldn't we just help them continually patch their wall, though? Keep them in place. Surely that is safer. Let me speak to the team. There must be a way. Perhaps we could build another wall on the inside of the existing one, reinforced in some way. It would eat into their water space, but from what little I recall, they are like the rest of us. The water has receded from use over the past thirty years, and they have several meters of free space along the perimeter. I wonder if we could partition their water supply even?"

"Let's think that through. We know they have satellite access, and it was likely the Caspians who fired the missile. If we move them out and into a landside community, we can force them to leave a lot of the technology behind, especially the weaponry systems. They can start over and lead a simple agricultural existence. Much like Lewis or Newgrange but without a portal. It will be a hell of a lot of work to reestablish an entire community landside, but with the resources of the ACC, surely we can do it. They can run hospitals and schools as well as farms and agriculture, but we have an opportunity to neutralize the threat they pose. This might be the only chance we have to change the stakes of the game."

Trust Illy to see the strategic angle. Perhaps she was rubbing off on me, but I could, too. "Do you think it is the charge Jake left that caused this?"

"I asked Carmelo before I came to find you, and he says no. Likely that is still there. Waiting."

"We could use that, you know," I said softly, not wanting to be overheard. The door was closed, but nîpiy had ears like a hawk. She had returned from her meeting. I could see the shadow beyond the frosted glass door.

Illy nodded. "You and I are on the same page. We help them move their critical equipment first, furniture, hospitals, and kitchens. Set up greenhouses, shelter, and water storage. But then we detonate the charge and let the weaponry sink? It is a strategic move, and they will never know. They will think the fissure finally ruptured and the Caspian Sea breached the perimeter. A lucky escape. It stops them from retrieving it after we leave. We can ensure we leave no suits behind. They can't go anywhere without

CHAPTER 29

oxygen, as we know." She smirked at me, unable to resist the taunt at my overnight sojourn. "So they can't even try to salvage old systems. We can isolate them. Neutralize the threat."

"I like it," I said, thinking it through. "But don't we have a problem? They will know we are immune. Not to mention the issues associated with building outside with limited oxygen and no fresh water."

"Not if we are careful. We use the suits and build one protected community with the new breathable fabric, not that they have the same wind gusts as some of the Scottish islands. Inside, we build a water storage facility and pump the uncontaminated water from their community across. We provide raw materials and build the first few structures, teaching them how. Then, while they build other homes and infrastructure, we assist them in ferrying equipment and moving people. Not long after everyone is moved, the wall might miraculously rupture, and weren't they lucky to all get out in time?"

"How many people are there?"

"Less than seven hundred."

My mouth dropped. "Are you serious? There are thousands here and in each of the other unhabs. We are burgeoning. Why so few?"

"They had a food shortage quite a few years ago and terminated all pregnancies. They didn't want more demand on dwindling resources, and as children added no value, they didn't allow any to be born. From what I understand, there are no children under the age of ten. They also have a policy of reducing the load."

"I don't like the sound of that. What does 'reducing the load' mean?"

299

"From what I can gather, it means that any individual who does not actively contribute to the community, is too young, too old, or too sick to work, is terminated to reduce their reliance on a system that they no longer contribute to."

"Terminated?" My mouth filled with bile. "How long?" I choked, swallowing hard. "How long have they been doing this?"

"The last five years or so, from what I can gather. Although when they advise in the next breath that there are no children under the age of ten, that certainly implies it was longer."

"Stella," I croaked.

"You made the right call, Catie. They would never have allowed her to be born. No matter how much they wanted you, they would have seen her as an avoidable burden, taking precious resources from others. It also explains why they intended for none of the children in Piedmont to survive."

"They are monsters," I hissed. "Killing children and old people. The sick." Charlie and Gianni popped into my mind. "We can't do this. How can we even contemplate helping them?"

"They are still people. I agree: a civilization should be judged on how well it treats all of its members, not just the productive ones. But they are people, Caitlin."

"Are they? You lived before. Did this happen? Were children and old people routinely killed off?"

Illy sighed. "Occasionally, there were cases where they were not cared for, but infanticide or senicide usually occurred only in extreme circumstances. More often it was abandonment leading to their deaths, not actively killing them. Certainly not a premeditated

CHAPTER 29

program of culling those seen to be a burden. But there was no shortage of resources in most places."

"I don't think I can do this." Waves of nausea swept through me. How could I help these people knowing what they would have done to my child?

"Caitlin, you are better than this. You will help them; *we* will help them as it is the right thing to do. There will be women there who had their children, their parents, taken from them. They can't all be evil."

"You are right. Fine. We need to do something. While it is a lot of work in the short term, I agree that moving them landside makes the most sense and minimizes the risk."

"You can oversee operations from here. No one would ever expect you to go there again. You have children who need you. It is too soon for you to travel, anyway."

"I need to tell you something."

"Antonio?"

"You know?"

"Do you think Carmelo and I keep secrets from each other?"

Knowing how close they were, of course not. Like Gio and I, they talked, as all couples did.

"He is grieving. I need to help him. What he did, he did partly to avenge what they did to me." The temperature of my face was suddenly a lot warmer than the ambient temperature of the room.

"He saw?" Illy asked, confused.

"He did. I didn't know it for a long time, but he was in the boardroom when Riccardo received the call. They had been there for a meeting, and he was packing up to leave when the video was received. While he didn't see it all, he saw enough. He and I are close.

We met when I first arrived in Piedmont, and then he helped me when I recuperated. We are friends."

"I don't know him well, but I can see how that, combined with Joseph's death, was enough."

"It was. He needed to avenge him—and me."

"We still aren't certain it was Caspian who took out the bridge, you know. Tadhg said he can't prove it one way or another."

I scowled, and Illy relented. "But odds are it was."

"What do we do with Antonio? Can we give him a job here? The risk is that if our people are engaged in helping the Caspians build a new community, someone could slip and oust him. Even accidentally. That could create conflict."

"Let me think about it. Maybe a fresh start is what he needs. Somewhere new, where he can be of benefit, but where no one knows him."

"As much as I don't want to send him away, I think that is a good plan. Lewis, maybe? Dad would look after him."

"Undoubtedly your father would. Your mother, too. Let me ponder it some more. Now, do we get this boyfriend of yours in for a meeting and discuss if we could use geothermic energy to power a new land community? We know they are also located over a geothermic vent."

A low growl escaped my throat. "He is not my boyfriend."

Illy grinned. "Oh, you know I am teasing you. Planting all those trees was punishment enough for running away from him."

Releasing the remaining growl was warning enough to not persevere with this conversation. Her smirk widened.

CHAPTER 29

"Have you noticed he appears quite taken with Nalani? You are off the hook. But perhaps I should meet with him alone?"

"You need me for the technical aspects," I grumbled, not happy at still being taunted over something that happened years ago.

"Well, I will be there to keep you safe. Just in case you are consumed with lust."

"Enough."

"Tomorrow?"

"Fine. Schedule it. Get it over with."

CHAPTER 30

ILLY, FINN, AND SEVERAL of the engineering team worked tirelessly with me over the next few weeks, planning how we could isolate the Caspian community by moving them landside. Finn initially refused to help. Like most others, he had heard what had happened to me.

"We need this," I explained, showing him the diagrams. "It is safer in the long term for all of us."

"After what they did to you? I would rather they all drown. This is not what I came here to do, Catie. It was you I wanted to help."

"You forget they still have an active portal," I pointed out, ignoring the second part of his sentence. "Leaving them and refusing help just places other communities at risk."

Finn saw the logic. "So the portal will be submerged."

I nodded. "They will no longer be a risk to anyone."

"What do you need?"

CHAPTER 30

"You," I responded, then blushed, realizing how that sounded. "Your skills," I corrected myself. "How long do you think you can be away from Newgrange?"

Finn knew what I was asking.

"I can stay as long as you need me. There is no one at home waiting for me. Before I left to come here, I packed up my house."

An image of Finn's rustic timber cottage flitted into my mind, and all the nights we had enjoyed each other's company. Dismissing it, I smiled politely.

"Good. If you haven't had enough by then, I am just finalizing another project after this one I might need help on."

Pottering around the kitchen preparing dinner, I knew I needed to raise this with Gio. He knew something was up but also usually waited until I was ready to speak. As I turned to grab the wooden spoon to stir the soup, he caught my arm, looking intently into my face.

"Something is bothering you."

Exhaling heavily, the words flowed as I served our meal. Words I had been holding in for hours, fearful of his reaction. "I finalized a deal today."

"You negotiate deals every day." Gio carried both bowls to the table, waiting for me to sit opposite him.

"This one was a little different."

"How's that?"

"A few days ago, I negotiated a deal with the leaders at Yellowstone."

Gio nodded, indicating he was listening as he spooned a mouthful of soup.

"Francesca and her husband were granted permission to go home to Italy, and in exchange, we will assist the Yellowstone community to build a bridge to the mainland. Provide resources and assistance with construction."

Gio's face darkened. "That is a big promise in exchange for the freedom of one person who wronged you. Has she had the child yet?"

"I haven't heard. They traveled on the full moon this morning. We asked to watch via video link to make sure. Judging by the look of her as she waddled to the water's edge, I suspect she was in labor and holding the baby in. The papers were signed just in time."

"You are a remarkable woman."

"Honey, she told me something."

"About me?"

"No. As soon as she made it home to Piedmont, she called me on a secure line. I have one, and working in comms, she knows how to access it. It was how she contacted me the first time."

"What did she say? Thank you, I hope."

"She did, but it was a brief message. She told me it was Yellowstone who fired the missile into our bridge. They killed Joseph and the others."

"What? She is full of shit. It was Caspian, you know that. Why would Yellowstone attack?"

Ordinarily, I would have laughed at his use of one of my favorite expressions, especially delivered in his sexy Italian accent, but this was serious. "We can't prove who did it, but she insists it is true."

"You can't believe anything that bitch has to say. After everything she has done? To you? She always told stories to benefit herself, omitting certain facts that might paint her in a negative light. I know her

CHAPTER 30

better than anyone. She is a woman who would do anything to get what she wants, and for a long time, what she wanted was me. Don't forget that included dispatching you. So you need to ask, what does she stand to gain by telling you this? She is home safe. While it would be terribly convenient to think it was a thank you, it likely isn't. If she had a secure line, she could have told you this at any point in the negotiations but chose not to. She likely bears a grudge against you for sending her there, and Yellowstone for their treatment of her. If I had to guess, she likely thinks you will retaliate against them and start an all-out war."

My breath escaped in a low hiss. Since receiving the call, I had considered the options in great detail and knew she wasn't exactly a reliable source of information. But Gio knew her better than anyone. His assessment was likely accurate.

"So what will you do?"

"What can I do? Nothing. It was a short conversation, as it was evident she was in labor. I questioned her, asked her why, and she said she didn't know. But she was adamant that she was near a window and felt the shudder as the missile was launched. I even asked her if there were identifying marks on the missile itself. Perhaps we could retrieve it and corroborate her story. But of course, she claims she never saw it, only heard and felt it as it was launched."

"Is that likely?"

"Illy says yes. She has some experience and says it is likely the entire community felt the rumble as it was fired."

"You can't believe her, *amore mio*. You know that."

Sighing, I replied, "I don't know what to believe. I have thought of nothing else all day. In some ways, I need to. If she is telling the truth, then we need to be wary of two potential foes. We won't start a war based on her say-so, and surely she knows that."

Gio exhaled forcefully. "Francesca is self-absorbed and arrogant. She has an entirely inflated sense of self-importance. If I had to guess, she likely thinks you will believe her and act on her advice."

Once more I wondered what on earth Gio had seen in this woman. But they were young when they partnered up, still teenagers. He had seen her true colors and had left her before he met me.

"Unless her intel is proven, we aren't doing anything, so it was pointless telling me. But if she is telling the truth, it also begs the question: are Yellowstone and Caspian in cahoots?"

Recognition of what that meant crossed Gio's face. "Fuck, Caitlin. This could be all-out war. Our girls were nearly caught in that blast. This is personal."

"We have one thing going in our favor. Caspian has a fissure in the lower underwater wall. The pressure is increasing, and they can no longer patch it. None of the residents there are immune. The salt water in the Caspian Sea is mixing with their drinking water, and they can't keep up with the desalination, even though Jake fixed the machinery. The race is on. The fissure ruptures and floods the lower levels of their community, or the desalination machinery fails entirely and they have no more fresh water. They can boil it, of course, but that is slow and laborious."

"So they will all die?"

CHAPTER 30

"If we don't help, almost certainly. They have asked for help. It was why they approached Riccardo, but they left before they could start discussions."

"What will you do?"

"We were working on options when I received Francesca's call. We had almost made up our minds, but based on her intelligence, Illy and I agree that the safest course of action is to move them all landside into an isolated community like Lewis. Without the portal, of course. That is underwater."

"But then they have access to other places on the mainland. Boats, planes, like we do."

"I know. Illy and I have spoken about nothing else all day. But what if we set them up on an island, or create one even? Safe and with ample fresh water but surrounded by contaminated water. The air is thin too, as we know. If they can't get to an airport, we ensure that there are no boats, and they have no access to an oxygen concentrator like we run on our vessels, then they are trapped. If we detonate the explosives you set on your little boys trip, then all of their weaponry is destroyed. The portal too."

Gio diplomatically ignored the dig about his trip to Caspian while I was in labor. "Can you create an island? Is that even possible?"

"Sure. We were just scoping potential sites from satellite footage, but we will need to use a drone before we choose. If we settle them on a large, fairly high tract of land where they can grow crops, we can effectively isolate them but allow room to expand. Like our greenhouse, we would need to pump through all the current uncontaminated water from their storage basin and create an artificial lake. But it is possible to dig trenches and create new waterways quite easily with plumbing to homes or at least a central point. We could surround them with contaminated water."

"There is a lot of merit in that idea."

"Illy and I were talking about repair versus relocation. Then I got Francesca's call. She said she told me so that we are aware, but you are right, we can't trust her. Regardless, we have one enemy or two. If we can neutralize one, then we only face one. If Yellowstone thinks we don't know it was them and we continue to assist them, then we have the upper hand."

Gio's eyebrows crinkled as he pursed his lips.

"What? You have an idea."

"I'm not technically minded, as you know, but your sister is a veritable genius. You should see some systems she has implemented in the medical labs in Japan, diagnostic stuff. After Rai's lack of diagnosis, she has made it a priority to combine technology and medicine. Summer has been there helping. They can assess so many conditions now, where previously we would have needed to operate. Surely Sera could design some sort of sensor system? Something to alert you if they activate weapons?" Gio cleared his throat, watching my face. "I'm not explaining this very well. What I mean is, if they permit outside people to assist them to build a bridge, then surely, we can leave something behind? Something that would alert us with enough time to defend ourselves."

Pausing, I considered his words. "That is an excellent idea. You, my darling, are a genius. I don't know if it can be done, but you are right. If anyone would know, Sera would."

Gio beamed at the compliment as he finished mopping up his bowl with bread.

CHAPTER 30

"Let me talk to her, see what ideas she can come up with. She has a phenomenal team in Hokkaido, although she may not want them to know what she is up to. The fewer people who know, the better."

"Sera and Matt could achieve anything."

Grimacing, I addressed the underlying question. "Have you heard how they are doing?"

"Civil but distant. Matt doesn't think she will ever forgive him."

"Can you blame her? She thinks he needs some space to focus on his health, and instead, he takes the opportunity to forget about her and shag someone else."

"*Amore mio,* we agreed we will not argue about this. But it is killing him. He wants her back. He needs his family reunited. He is lost without her."

What I really wanted to say was, "Too fucking bad. Too little, too late." But the truth was, Sera was in pain too. Part of me hoped she would find a way past it and reconcile with him. She had boyfriends on Lewis and Newgrange, but Matt made her glow. He helped her evolve into the best version of herself. Until learning about his betrayal, I thought he was the best thing to ever happen to her.

"Let's go to bed. I will clean up in the morning."

CHAPTER 31

MY NAME ECHOED AROUND the hallway. Popping my head into Illy's office down the hall from mine, I raised my eyebrows.

"How did you know it was me?"

"You don't think I know the sound of your footstep by now?"

Knowing we could lose an hour talking about Illy's ability to monitor what was going on, I cut to the chase. "What do you need?"

"A few things. First, how is Project Secret Squirrel going?"

The name still made me smile. All my childhood, Mum and Dad had used the expression "secret squirrel" when something was not to be shared. We all knew it had come from a television series, but not one we had ever seen. There were squirrels on Lewis, little red ones. They had been introduced, Mum said, when the protected community was built, although they were native to part of Scotland, unlike the gray ones that we saw in our textbooks.

CHAPTER 31

"The project is going well," I said cautiously, closing the door behind me. "My counterpart and I have got a working prototype."

"Detectable?"

"Likely not. They are using nanotechnology to construct the sensors."

"How big?"

"Technically these are big, around half an inch. But flat. Once installed, it will be nearly impossible to find."

"How many?"

"We are thinking about a dozen. Just in case some fail."

"Good." Illyria nodded. "On track for installation?"

"Production takes time, but yes. I don't anticipate any issues."

"Can they be installed in advance?"

I shook my head. "No matter how we model it, it is too risky. There is always the chance it will be spotted, knocked, a screw placed over it, or just not in the right location to transmit the information we need. We are applying adhesive, so they are as simple as someone placing a small sticker. But it will need to be done after construction is nearly complete to ensure they are active for the long term."

"Life span?"

I shrugged. "Five years maybe? There is a corrosion issue, plus degradation over time. While they will be inside, they may be subject to a type of oxidation. We don't have time to run long-term modeling."

"That will do. Now, an update on our other project, please."

"We have identified a suitable site, thanks to the team. Tadhg has used extensive satellite and drone footage, and the engineers, plus Matt's bathymetry work, have assessed the best location, both to move all the resources, including the clean water supply, and meet all our needs."

We had spent weeks discussing the best location for the Caspian land site, and narrowing it down between two potentials had been difficult. We wanted the people to survive but ensure they were contained and never posed a threat again. Transporting the water from the current storage was the most difficult element, and eventually, the closest site was chosen, simply because moving the water was the easiest. One of the first projects was to use old world construction equipment to build water storage. Open so that the condensation would run back into it, and using all the original community designs where housing was located around it, each with their own water catchment. Electricity was going to be more challenging. Solar had been used in most original communities, but we no longer had the technology to build panels safely. Biogas was going to be the primary form of heating, but I hoped it was enough during the bitterly cold winters.

"Sounds like it is under control."

"It is. When are you planning to visit?"

"When they break ground. In a few weeks?"

"Likely sooner," I admitted. "We have volunteers from many communities wanting to help. I found it surprising, actually. I wouldn't have thought people cared enough about them to help them."

Illy sighed. "Caitlin, sometimes you are so blind. They don't care about the Caspians. In truth, no one does. They care about you. They help because this is your project, but mainly, they are helping because the sooner we isolate them, the safer we all are. To

CHAPTER 31

keep you and your children safe? Of course people will help."

I felt my face reddening. Well, that explained everyone I knew in all the above-ground communities volunteering. I wondered what she had said to get them to volunteer.

"Now on another matter, your father called."

"To speak with me?"

"To me, actually." That made me look up in interest. While Dad and Illy were certainly friends, it was Mum who was Illy's best friend. I waited for her to continue.

"He has had a brilliant idea."

"About the landside pods?"

"No, he suggested we move Antonio to Sessrúmnir."

"Sessrúmnir?" I said, stunned. I hadn't heard that name in a long time and hadn't been there myself since I was seven. I remembered it, though. Sorcha's eldest son, Sam, lived there with the Punan people my mothers had rescued from Borneo nearly twenty years ago.

"Why Sessrúmnir?"

Illy looked smug. "Because it is the safest place for him to be. There is no way for the Caspians to get to him there, even if they did know where he was. It is remote but safe. We have radio contact. Sam would look after him, and he would add enormous value to the community there. We considered August Island, but Antonio is not a large community person. In Sessrúmnir, he knows there is no portal, so no random visitors. All will know him, and over time, he will find his place."

"Does he know?"

"Not yet. I thought you might like to come with me to tell him."

CHAPTER 32

with a warm glow, but equally, I was anxious that the Caspian were moved as soon as possible to minimize the potential risks. Until Caspian was permanently resettled, we couldn't redeploy our resources to build Yellowstone a land-bridge.

The relationship between Yellowstone and the ACC was increasingly strained after they had released Francesca, and there was only so long we could delay our commitment. Each time I spoke with Shane, their leader, I got the distinct impression that we may have hastily assessed Caspian as responsible for the destruction of our bridge. While we had no way of proving Francesca's allegations, the more time that passed, the more I was inclined to think she was telling the truth. Shane had been one of the men who had interrogated Sera and me upon our accidental arrival there, and I had never forgotten his overbearing and threatening manner.

"Did all go as planned with the relocation?"

Illy nodded. "As always, there were a few hiccups. But the plan was sound, even if the execution was rushed. There is adequate housing and food stocks until they can grow their own. One of the plumbers has taught them how to connect housing to the main supply, electricians too. But we will leave them to do a lot of that work. They are sealed in, the clean water has been fully transferred, and the fissure was 'helped along,' let's say."

"Jake?"

"He always wanted that job. Goodness, he and Luca loved blowing stuff up. As we watched the bubbles trickle up to the surface, I could see your father smiling down as he watched the community submerge, knowing what happened to us there."

Sometimes I forgot that Illy had also been a victim of the Caspians—kidnapped, held prisoner, and dropped out of the pod to die. But they hadn't harmed her the way they had me. Still, it was to be expected that she also harbored ill feelings.

"How did you go back there?" I asked, my blood running cold at memories of that place.

"I won't lie. It was difficult. But it isn't my first time needing to return to a place where people did things to me against my will. When your mother and I were held captive in Clava, before you were born, it was terribly hard for both of us to return there when I became Chief, even though by then there was no risk. Emotion isn't logical. It was worse for your mother, of course. But in time, we got past it. I knew if I could survive that, I could return to Caspian."

"You are stronger than me."

"You are stronger than you know, Caitlin. Every day, I am reminded of what a warrior you are. You are a dragon. But it is different. They may have held me prisoner, but you lost something there, a part of your soul."

"A dragon?" The bemusement must have been evident on my face as she laughed.

"You remember that my family is originally from Orkney? My father used to tell me stories, Celtic myths. In Celtic mythology, dragons are creatures that protect the Earth and all living things. They are considered the most powerful of all the Celtic symbols. They are used as a symbol of power and wisdom among leaders, and a leader is something you have proven yourself to be, time and time again."

Not wanting to dwell, I asked, "So, it is all over?"

CHAPTER 32

"It is. The community is gone, the portal is completely submerged and has tons of concrete on top. The people are landlocked and have years of hard work ahead of them to survive."

"Did they thank you?"

Illy sniggered. "Not exactly. Moving landside has left most people feeling disgruntled, as they believe the leaders should have done more to keep them in their old home. Let's just say that they are facing a bit of backlash from their own people. There were staged protests, people refusing to leave the old unhab and calling for a change in leadership. I don't think we will hear from them for a while. Too busy putting out fires closer to home."

"Good."

"Now tell me about how things are going with Yellowstone. I want your full assessment."

"My gut tells me that Francesca is telling the truth. The more I speak with them, the greater my suspicion that they are jealous of our technology. Yellowstone desperately wants to expand onto land like we did. They are outgrowing their community, and they know limiting pregnancies is only part of the solution. Shane keeps asking how we can justify building ours—and we are geographically quite close to them—but not help them when we made a deal. The threats are quite blatant. He isn't even trying to be diplomatic."

"Well, we are retrieving all the equipment deployed to Caspian, so we can start in a week."

"I have told them that."

"Judging by your face, there is something else."

There was no easy way to tell her, but Illy was the one person I knew I could trust.

"I get the distinct impression we have a leak."

"What makes you think that?"

"Something he said about us building a 'kaleidoscope bridge.' It was used in a diatribe as he ranted about us not holding up our end of the deal. It was in the middle of a sentence. I caught the word and saw the look in his eye as he said it. He kept talking, but his pace increased."

"Speeding up speech, a typical sign of guilt."

"It was an odd word to use. I've checked, and there is nothing in the communiques that says we planned to make our bridge a rainbow bridge."

"What was the wording he used?" Illy was intrigued.

"I can't recall the exact sentence, as I said, he was ranting, but the word he used to describe it was 'kaleidoscope.' I've replayed the conversation over and over in my mind, and there is no word in the English language even close, and I definitely didn't mishear it. There was a flash of fear in his eyes, and he kept up his rant. I made no attempt to let him know I had caught the word, and he didn't address it. We spoke for another ten minutes or so, and then he hung up on me."

"Does anyone know?"

"No one. Not even Gio. I was waiting for you to return, but it is eating at me."

"Good. This is one thing we need to keep between the two of us. Not even nîpiy."

"Surely you don't..."

"No. I don't. But this is a matter of security, and the fewer people who know anything, the better. Now I have something else to tell you."

"What?"

"On their way back from taking Antonio to Sessrúmnir, Summer and Ally flew south. As Summer

CHAPTER 32

described it, just because they could. They dropped Antonio and saw your cousin, who sent a care package to Sorcha and Di. He is a grandparent, before I forget, and the Punan people are thriving. They have needed to expand the dome again to accommodate them all and have enough growing space. Anyway, after the girls refueled in Melbourne, they wanted to see New Zealand. They knew they could refuel there too. Your father has always raved about the spectacular mountains and glaciers."

I smiled. "Sounds like Dad."

"It was a complete accident, but they found another community."

"More? Where?"

"About 16 kilometers south of the 45th parallel line in the southern hemisphere."

"You told me that the circle of latitude forty-five degrees south of the equator was all underwater? Or maybe it was Tadhg? Anyway. You mean they found more unhab communities?"

"They did, and they weren't expecting it, as it was nowhere near the actual line of latitude."

I crinkled my nose, trying to recall the theory. "The parallel line is a theoretical point only. We sit slightly above it, and they must sit slowly below it for the same reason. The true half is slightly north or south of this parallel because the Earth is not a perfect sphere but bulges at the equator and is flattened at the poles. I remember Sera and I learning about it when we were hiding in Yellowstone all those weeks."

"Correct. But, unlike these northern communities, nearly all the 45th parallel south falls in ocean. Ninety-seven percent, I think Tadhg worked out, so we never bothered to check. We just assumed, erroneously, that no one would build communities so far away from land masses."

"But they did?"

"Evidently yes."

"You have access to all the files. How did you not know?"

Illy smirked. "You should know we inherited the most enormous database imaginable. After all, you hacked it often enough, or so Tadhg tells me. It is like searching for a rowboat in the ocean. None of the former team knew, I certainly didn't, and I helped choose people for settlement. There is a chance my predecessors knew, but they both died before I took the Chief role."

"Angus and Ashton?" I had heard Mum speak of them, never positively.

Illy nodded, her eyes twinkling, making my reddened face deepen. *Had they always known what Sera and I did, searching the files?*

"Where is it exactly? The community Summer found."

"Just south of Tasmania, so the likelihood is they were settled from Australia. Possibly New Zealand, although with the low population of New Zealand, most of our settlements were joint."

"And you had no idea?"

"None at all. Over the years, I have come to realize there was a definite 'need to know' policy, and clearly, I didn't need to know."

"What other land masses are there or places where there could be communities? It seems odd that there would only be one."

"The 45th parallel south crosses the South Atlantic Ocean, the Indian Ocean, just south of Tasmania

CHAPTER 32

in Australia and close to Argentina and Chile in South America."

"How many are there? Are they connected?"

"We don't even know if there is more than this one. Summer spotted this one off the coast of Tasmania. It was above water, and it was just a fluke that she flew that course and the sun was glinting off the windows. Had she traveled a kilometer on either side, she would have missed it entirely."

"Have you made contact?"

"Not yet. I thought you might like to join me."

My mouth dropped. An adventure. My heart leaped as I gasped. "I would love… I can't." I sighed as reality dragged me back to earth. "The girls. How do I leave them?"

"Where there is a will… Gio could take time off, or Carmelo could look after them. They are nearly a year old now, so you would need to wean them. Or express enough for the time we would be gone."

"How long do you think that would be?" A slight buzz energized me. Traveling to new communities, meeting new people. The possibility of discovering new technologies we could use here.

"Weeks, at a guess. It is slow going to get there, needing to constantly stop and refuel. The solstice is months away, so we would need to go via helicopter. Summer needs to take breaks too. Then we would need to stay at least a few days once there, assuming we receive a positive reception. We may not, of course."

Illy beamed, watching the conflict that was no doubt dancing across my face. Exploring new worlds, meeting new people. This was what I dreamed of. It was why Seraphine and I had left Lewis in the first place. But life was different now. I held a position of authority. I had two young children, and there was no way I could take them with me. A pang of longing for the carefree girl I once was bubbled up within me. When did I become mature and responsible?

"Don't say it!" I snapped at Illy as she began to laugh, but not maliciously. "I know. I needed to grow up. Use my brain, like my mother told me."

"Actually, I was going to say that life doesn't all need to be routine and boring." Illy twinkled. "We could have some fun with Ally and Summer, just the four of us."

Now that was an undeniably persuasive idea. Those girls could drink anyone under the table, including me before kids. They were a riot and had unlimited hilarious stories from the communities they visited. I so badly wanted to go, but the tiny trusting faces of Khi and Rori flashed before me. I had come too close to losing them and would never forgive myself if something happened to my daughters in my absence. Especially if I was having a wonderful time.

"Next time," I promised. "But..." A thought popped into my brain. "Why don't you take Sera? She is an ambassador, Rai is older, and Matt can care for him in Hokkaido. I think she needs a break. She is also far more tech savvy than me, so she might be able to add some value immediately, get you in their good books."

"Now that is a brilliant idea. She will be able to stay longer too, if they are willing to engage with us. I'll call her and see what she thinks."

This translated to "I will bully her into submission," and I tried to suppress the smirk.

"But with me out of contact, you will need to take over full-time for a few months. Are you ready?"

CHAPTER 32

"Will you leave Carmelo?" I asked, suddenly panicked. Prior to me having the twins, Illy regularly took Carmelo on her diplomatic visits. She believed she got a better reception when presented as an older, stable, married couple, he from the underwater habitation, she from an above-ground one.

"I won't take him this time. We have no idea what to expect. Even with these communities, we had your intel. Yellowstone and Piedmont, particularly. We have absolutely no idea what we might find. It is best if Sera and I go alone, although we might take Jake as moral support."

Muscle, she meant, but I was pleased. After his help in getting me out of Caspian, and hearing Mum's stories, I had great faith in Jake's skills.

"Besides," she continued, "with any luck, one of my girls will meet someone, and we can forge the next cross-community link."

"Bloody hell, listen to you," I teased. "You sound like that old English queen, the one that married off all of her children across Europe. Bridget taught us about her. Who was that again?"

"Queen Victoria. And yes, it was a highly strategic move."

"Is that why you married Carmelo? Strategy?"

"I didn't need to. You and your sister had already forged those links. Besides, it isn't like I could turn to technology like we used to back home."

"What do you mean? How do you turn to technology?"

"I had a partner at the time, so I never did, but a female colleague of mine tried online dating."

"Now you have me intrigued. What is that?"

CHAPTER 32

"CATIE!" ILLY BURST INTO the office, glowing. She gave me a quick hug, the smile lighting her entire face, then beckoned me to follow. Following her into her office, I closed both the hall door and the one to her office, ensuring we couldn't be overheard. While we spoke daily, I hadn't seen her in weeks after she had supervised the relocation of the Caspian community. The planning had taken months, followed by a highly skilled team comprising individuals from several communities spending months establishing a new landside settlement under a geodesic dome. Several times, Illy had bemoaned the time it was taking, recalling the ease in which the Australian government had mobilized the original settlements, including my parents, so many years ago. Illy had traveled to the new community to oversee the final stage, culminating in the Caspian people being relocated into new homes and settling into their new lives.

Dad had flatly refused to advise on planting after what the Caspians had done to me, as had some others from Lewis. Secretly, the sense of loyalty filled me

"As you get older and work full-time, it gets hard to meet people, prospective partners. Most people are already partnered up, have kids. There are few single people, and meeting people through friends when you want to keep your private life private is difficult, especially if it doesn't work out. So there were these online sites dedicated to dating."

"How does that work?"

"Basically, you write a profile and put up a picture. You know, like 'I like walks in the mountains and don't like dogs,' and your prospective match assesses what you have written and your picture, and you assess theirs. Then you send a few messages, dance around each other and work out if they are psycho, and perhaps arrange to meet for coffee."

"Did it work?"

"Carolyn used to show us the profiles and the messages she was sent. We got to a point where we automatically eliminated any man who had a picture of himself holding a fish he had caught. There were three of us, all women, all military, and we shared a small tearoom. We used to joke that it was such a macho male thing, 'Hey look, I caught and murdered this fish. See! I can provide for you.'"

"Okay, that is just plain weird."

"It was hysterical. Every Monday, we would schedule lunch together so she could tell us about her dates. She used to have us in stitches. Ones with missing teeth or who looked nothing like their profile picture. The one who turned out to be gender fluid. One even told her about his heart attack on their first date. So attractive. Carolyn had a degree in science and psychology, held the rank of colonel, and was more senior than me. She made no secret of who she

CHAPTER 32

was. She was super smart, attractive, just lonely. But she would get the most bizarre men contacting her. Offering her friends with benefits arrangements or who lived hundreds of kilometers away."

"Surely the military was full of single men?"

"It was. But most of us didn't want to date colleagues, especially as they may end up in the office for counseling. There was a saying, 'You don't get your honey where you get your money.' It added a level of complication that most of us didn't want, although, they did understand the lifestyle."

"Is that why you never met anyone after Dad?"

Illy sighed. "Life with Luca was just easy. We understood each other. Our training and experiences. But I was single by the time I took over this role. It is hard being Chief, no one wants to date their boss. If it doesn't work out, then it makes life hard. I am not the type to take my disappointment out on someone, but most men were intimidated by me."

"They still are!" I teased, knowing how many of the men here felt about Illy. "But most women in couples aren't intimidated by each other's roles," I pointed out. "Look at Di and Sorcha. Even Bridget and Jorja." In both couples, one woman was far more dominant in personality.

"You know, I considered it, but I just don't feel about women the same way."

"Even Mum?" I asked cheekily.

"Your mother is my best friend and the sister I never had. I cannot imagine a life without her in it. While I have no issue with anyone else's choice, I like men. Always have, always will."

"So if you understand the bond between you and Mum, why did you separate Seraphine and me?"

"Because you were both starting new relationships, and to add to the mix, your husbands are brothers and very close. The guys would always side with each other, as would you and your sister. I was right, wasn't I? When Sera and Matt had problems, you and Gio fought over it. More than once. How much harder would that have been if she had been nearby and had run to you for support? You would have sided with her, and it would have caused a rift in your marriage."

"I suppose," I said begrudgingly, not wanting to know how she knew we had fought over Sera and Matteo. "Tell me more about this online dating."

"Gio adores you, so you will never need to worry about it. I guess my point is, you don't really know someone until you spend time with them. Some guys, Carolyn spent weeks sending messages back and forth and genuinely thought, 'This is promising,' really thought that there might be a connection. Then within five minutes of meeting, she realized it was a disaster waiting to happen. Not only no chemistry but completely different in real life to how they presented themselves from behind a screen. She used to laugh at those who bolted at the end of the date, saying, 'I'll be in touch,' knowing they were the ones she never heard from again. One guy, something to do with IT, was so embarrassed when she offered to pay for the meal that he couldn't string a sentence together after that. So she had to endure a lunch date with a boring as fuck man who couldn't make eye contact because he was so intimidated by her."

"That sounds horrendous... That poor woman."

"Oh, that was by no means the worst."

"Tell me about another one."

CHAPTER 32

"The man we all found the most perplexing was a professional fisherman. Tom, I am fairly sure his name was. Goodness knows why I remember that, but as psychologists, we were all flabbergasted that any grown man lived that way."

"As a fisherman? What is wrong with that? We have them on Lewis. They are fishermen on lots of communities, although farming has mostly replaced individuals needing to catch fish. Terribly inefficient."

"That wasn't it. He was younger than her, I can't really recall. When I say fisherman, I don't mean to catch food to eat. This was a guy who entered competitions. Fishing, fly-fishing was a sport back home. I've never done it, but apparently, it was quite a skill. They catch fish and throw them back, so it is about the competitive nature of it rather than sourcing food."

My face must have reflected my absolute bamboozlement at the idea of catching fish and releasing them. Fish were hard to catch. I had been fishing a few times as a child and hated it. Tramping around in the mud, waiting for something to jump on my line, and then needing to pull it in and kill a wriggling fish, fighting for life. When one of the men offered to take Gio on his first trip to Lewis, I had politely but firmly declined the invitation.

"So this guy used to catch fish and throw them back? Every day?"

"He did. But that wasn't the interesting part. Tom was what we called a 'trust fund baby.' Crazy rich parents, so he and his siblings never needed to go to work. In his case, at least, he never studied beyond high school. I have a vague memory that there might have been a sister. Goodness knows what she did. Carolyn only went on one date with this guy. He was handsome, so I think she gave him a go. But worked out pretty quickly that he bored her stupid. All he could talk about was fishing. There was something we used to call 'academic smart' and 'street smart' back home. It is rare to find both in the same individual."

"What is the difference?"

"Some people are academically smart, really intelligent. You and your sister for example. You have studied and learned and are masters in your fields. Street smart means people who may not be classically educated but are cunning. They know how to read situation, dangers, and other people. Often people who have traveled, experienced other countries and cultures. It is a lot harder here, of course. Take your mother. She is both, like you. She can spot danger a mile off. She has that sense. She can read people, but she is sharp and learned too. Your father, on the other hand, is less street smart. He trusts people, sometimes to his own detriment."

Nodding, I realized what she meant. "So, which was this guy?"

"He had a sense of experience about him. He had traveled quite extensively. But it was the degree of absolute control that astounded us as psychologists. The son did exactly what the father asked of him. It was a classic case of the father living vicariously through his child. The father would pay for round-the-world trips to fish and be mentored by the best in the world. Bought houses, cars, and boats for him. The son made no money of his own, everything was controlled by his father. He was likely even paid a living allowance for food. But the shocking part was that he didn't see a problem with it. Carolyn tried to probe, gently. But he couldn't see that it wasn't

CHAPTER 32

normal. It was a flagrant abuse of power. Even in the old world, a parent brazenly in control of their adult child was unheard of in western societies. Your mother grew up in an extremely wealthy family, but it was still expected that she would make her own way. Freyja's parents paid for excellent schooling and every opportunity for her and her sister to succeed. But she studied, went to university, and would still have been expected to work and pay for her own life."

"Surely the son will rebel at some point? Or would have, had he been given the chance."

"Who knows? But it was an extremely disconcerting dynamic. Dad paid, the son did what the father wanted. Psychologically, I found it fascinating that a parent would even want to dictate the life of their child. Live a second life through them. A carefree life, pursuing a hobby, but with no sense of responsibility or adulthood."

Khi and Rori flitted into my mind. "I want my children to pursue their own dreams, their own interests," I admitted.

"As do nearly all parents. Many children follow their parents into a career or trade, men especially. There is a long tradition of sons following fathers into the family business. But there is usually a choice. This was the only time I have heard of a father entirely funding a child's life but controlling it, too. It was like the parent basically lived two lives—a respectable one, where the father worked and made money. A lot of money. And a second, untroubled life, where the child flew around the world entering fishing competitions, simply because that was the father's dream. I often wonder what degree of control that father would have had over that son as he hit thirty or forty. At what point does someone say, 'No, I want to control my own destiny.' But at the point he met my colleague, he hadn't. He remained compliant and was happy to accept the handout from his father, living a carefree life. We called it the Peter Pan syndrome."

"After the book?"

"You've read it? The boy who never grows up. Well, that was this situation. Emotionally immature, little understanding of the value of money as he never earned it. It wasn't a psychopathology, even then, but increasingly, we were seeing men present with these types of behaviors. Never growing up."

"It makes you wonder what type of childhood he had, doesn't it?"

"I can't tell you how many times I thought that. If a parent has that much control over a man in his late-twenties, can you imagine that child's early life? A controlling father who specified what he ate and where he went. Likely, the father was domineering, controlling what he wore and who he dated or was friends with. The level of psychological control is bordering on abuse, keeping him like he is still a child, entirely reliant on his father, and unable to make his own decisions. Carolyn was no fool and saw it for what it was and didn't see this guy beyond a single dinner. Despite her professional interest, she could see that this was a disastrous situation, and the father would always control, or try to control, this guy's life. No woman wants that. Everyone should be free to make their own choices, to choose what they do for work and who they want to settle down with. So she kept looking."

"Did she ever meet someone?"

CHAPTER 32

"She had just started dating someone she liked when the pandemic started. She was part of the team in Melbourne, and her man was in Sydney, so I guess it was short-lived. Both of us were redeployed to Melbourne, and although we stayed in touch, we were assigned different projects within the overall resettlement program. It was a manic time, both working crazy hours and being bound by strict confidentiality agreements, not being able to discuss our role in the project, even with our military colleagues. But I hope she found happiness in the end. That is all any of us really want, to be happy. When we take our last breath, for it to be full of joy and the experience of living a fulfilled life."

"I am lucky, aren't I?"

"I told you that when I first met him. Gio is intelligent, loyal, and adores you. Watching him with those girls melts my heart. He is one of the good ones, Catie. They are few and far between. You don't realize it as your fathers, both of them, were wonderful men. But goodness, I had to kiss some toads to meet my two."

"I am so glad you got another chance." I looked up and met her eyes. "All my life, you have been Mum, dependable and positive, but I love watching you with Carmelo. You are happy on a deeper level. It was like you just melted into each other. He was so good to me when I crash-landed in Italy. While I would never have thought to put you together, everyone can see how in love you are. You belong together, you bring out the best in each other."

"I spent many years alone. But I always knew, deep down, there was someone out there for me. It is thanks to you that we met. I don't think I have ever really thanked you for that. You meet someone and think, 'Ooh, I like you.' But you never know if that person is going to be part of your life, your anchor. You just wake up each morning and go about your business. One day, you just turn back and see that they were there, walking your path beside you, supporting you, all that time."

"You have always been a mother to me. I can't tell you how much I am going to miss you."

"It isn't forever. Besides, I am leaving my husband with you. You had better take care of him."

"You know I will. The girls adore their nonno, and so do we. But, if you don't mind, I would love to come to Japan with you to see Sera, to view some of their tech labs."

"Well, I am traveling on the next full moon in five days. You can stay a month and return. Is that long enough?"

"Do you think the girls will travel safely?" Most of my travel had been overland since my abduction, and deep down, it wasn't the girls I was fearful for.

"The heat suit technology keeps getting better and better. Honestly, if you take one each, they will barely feel it."

Bravely, I smiled but didn't feel it.

"And," she continued, "we have guards at both ends. Gio will come, too, I presume? I may as well bring Carmelo if we are all going, make it a family event."

"I know he would take any opportunity to see his brother and experience other communities and cultures. It is his team I feel for. They rely on him so much."

"It is only a month. I am sure nothing urgent will crop up during that time."

"Likely not. We might even get a holiday, our first as a family."

CHAPTER 32

"We still need to work," Illy warned, "but yes, we can both relax a bit. The Japanese community runs so efficiently. The food is amazing, and the service is the best I have ever seen. They will treat you like royalty, so be prepared."

Blushing, I looked down at my feet. Sera had told me that once, in a nonchalant way as she flicked back her long blonde hair, so like our mother. People fell over themselves to serve her, bring her food, and launder her clothes. As the most senior official, she was treated with reverence and respect. Unlike Sera's coolness, I dreaded being the center of attention. Reading my mind as she always did, Illy continued, "There will also be welcoming ceremonies. They can be very long and formal, so I warn you, get some sleep. It is considered terribly rude to yawn in public. There are some other Japanese cultural practices we need to brief you on."

"Such as?"

"Well, it is rude to eat in public for starters. Also, you never wear shoes in someone's home. Much of the bedding is on the floor, using tatami matting."

"They sleep on the floor? I thought that was just for children?"

Illy giggled. "It is far more comfortable than it sounds. Truly. After my first visit, I now ask for tatami matting rather than a Western mattress. It is firm, but very comfortable."

"Fair enough. But wait for Gio, he will need to hear it, too. It wouldn't be a good look for the Chief's husband to make a social faux pas."

"Listen to you! You did learn something in all those French classes with Magali."

"Maybe. I feel like I have forgotten so much."

335

"It all comes back. On that note, most senior people speak some English, so you will be fine."

"Do the…"

"Yes, one or two of the engineering team speak English. You know some of them from your conference calls, but there are a few technicians who are super smart, and they have enough to converse. Besides, Sera and her assistant are fluent and can translate."

"How is she doing? After the breakup, I mean. I rarely get to talk to her alone."

"She is doing as well as can be expected. They are both hurt, but she can't forgive him. Maybe seeing you and having some time off-world will be the healing time she needs."

"I hope so. I don't ever want her to be unhappy."

"Alone doesn't mean unhappy, Caitlin. I lived alone for many years, but I wasn't unhappy. I was quite content. Meeting someone to share your life with is wonderful, but I was never that woman who was prepared to settle for something less than the best when it came to my partner. I would much rather be alone and happy than partnered and unhappy. Too many people stay in unhappy relationships as they fear being alone. But to be alone can be liberating, freeing."

Celebration day neared, and I barely slept, in part from fear but also from excitement. Bifröst, the rainbow bridge, was finally complete. While it wasn't a secret and we hadn't been able to hide the joyously bright external panels interspersed with Perspex, this would be the first time most people had walked across it.

CHAPTER 32

Would they be too scared after what had happened? Would people refuse to cross and the entire celebration be a bust?

nîpiy had planned the occasion with her usual fastidious attention to detail, right down to the order of travel. Illy and I would walk across first, the engineering team behind us. We were hoping this would allay any fears that the structure was unsafe. nîpiy had arranged the formalities with music and catering, followed by a full day of festivities.

Please, please let this be a success, I prayed. After everything we had been through, we needed something positive. School had been canceled, and anyone who didn't need to work was taking the day off. Even non-essential surgeries were rescheduled. This was a whole-community event, a joyous celebration of life.

The obligatory speeches came first but were deliberately brief. Illy and I knew that no one really wanted to listen to lots of words about the project and the tragedy of how it came about. The only truly important thing for me was to say thank you to all who helped make this dream a reality. Applause was polite but brief, indicating my assessment was correct. People fidgeted in the crowd, and I knew they really wanted to cross, see the rebuilt landside pods, touch them with their own hands, and walk on earth again. My heart beat a little faster as people moved aside, allowing me to pass to the front. Even though it wasn't my first time across the new bridge, panic set in, and my heart rate accelerated. Was I leading my people to another catastrophe?

Deb caught my eye as I passed, and I felt her intact hand slip into mine. She had lost two fingers that day, the rest of her hand mangled but now useable thanks to the surgical and physiotherapy teams. She looked me in the eye, her chin held high, and I smiled at her, grateful for the support. Together, we led the way across the bridge, Illy close behind. The rest of the community trickled across, children racing ahead, and others lingering, more apprehensive.

Over the course of the morning, people constantly filled the bridge, murmurs of awe at the view, the new landside pods, and the growing space filling the air. The view of the bridge from the land was even more spectacular as the sun glinted off the colors, merging them into a brilliant rainbow. The children had done a phenomenal job of studying pictures of rainbows and blending the colors perfectly. nîpiy had arranged a simple bronze plaque to be affixed to the main pillar at the landside end, "Bifröst: In Memory of Friends Lost" written upon it, as well as a list of the people who died that day, Joseph among them.

Part of me wished Antonio could be here to see this day, but I knew he was safer where he was. Coded messages were sent from Sessrúmnir to Sorcha on Lewis, Sorcha spoke with Mum or Dad, who passed information to me, being careful not to name him. Without knowing if there was a leak from Canada, we couldn't take the risk that anyone knew where he had gone. Family conversations were always a catch-up of the news of all family members, so anyone listening would need to know us well, and it was mixed into stories of Xanthe, Thorsten, Louis, and other extended family members. But from what I learned, Antonio had embraced his new life on land, a world away from Italy. Sam, Sorcha's son, had welcomed him and put him to work immediately. Antonio was happy and enjoyed living on land and helping people.

CHAPTER 32

My deepest regret was that I would likely never see my friend again, and I prayed that he didn't think I had sent him away.

Gio came and found me chatting with people in the gardening pods, standing beside me until I had finished. These days were rare, days when people felt they could approach me and chat, not disturbing me from my work. I missed the connection with people, knowing how their children were and what was happening in their families. Anything major that happened in the community, I knew, but I felt like I missed the small things. Children grew so fast, got married, and had families of their own. In the few years I had been here, I felt like I spent too many hours as Chief and not enough being part of the community.

"Are you ready to go?" Gio whispered, his low husky tone making me turn to jelly.

"I am." But he knew as well as I that it could easily take some time for us to get home. People would want to stop and chat, and I would need to speak with everyone who approached.

In the end, it took a little over two hours until we closed our apartment door, our backs sliding down until we hit the floor, laughing together.

"You are the most popular person here," Gio teased, the exhaustion breaking through.

"Wish I wasn't," I groaned. "I miss the quiet life."

"When did you last have a quiet life?" The laughter made the words barely audible.

Pausing, I considered that. "Too long," I admitted. If you didn't count my rehabilitation on Lewis, the reality was it was when Sera and I first returned from Newgrange. Only a few years in reality but a lifetime ago. The weariness was bone-deep. Between work and now children, my life was even more chaotic than ever.

"Come on." I dragged myself up and held out a hand to him, still seated on the floor. "Let's get the girls and have a quiet night."

CHAPTER 33

THE CELEBRATIONS WENT ON for days, the Canadian community exhilarated about having access to land once more. Teachers took their classes to the landside pods, and I watched more people strolling across the bridge, just chatting and enjoying the exercise.

"It is like they appreciate it more after what happened," I surmised to Illy.

"Well, of course they do," she fired back. "There is that old adage: 'You don't know what you've got until it's gone.' It is an adage because it is true. Think of all the things you miss from Lewis."

Too much, I thought but didn't dare say aloud. My family, sunshine on my face, the wind. But most of all, being alone. Being able to go for a walk and not see anyone. Here, I could never truly be alone with my own thoughts.

"Then there are those of us from the old world," she continued, staring out the window. "All the things we miss that we will never have again."

"What do you miss most?" I asked, curious.

Illy sighed deeply and thought for a long time. "People. You always miss people. Family, friends, even your hairdresser or neighbor. Places. Being able to go to the beach for a swim or a restaurant. Traveling to different countries."

"You can still do that."

"It isn't the same," she admitted. "That sense of freedom, of being a tiny speck in an entire world. Insignificant, really. But things? Sometimes I miss something random, a book or a tool. But mostly, I don't miss much, other than the people I lost."

"Do you think of him often?" I whispered, knowing who she was referring to.

"How could I not? Luca was the love of my life. The father of my children. He meant the world to me. I am so fortunate to have found another soul mate, but Carmelo understands. He felt the same about his wife. They were madly in love and lost each other. That is the wonderful part. We are a team and very much in love with each other, but we found each other through loss. Had we not experienced that grief, we would never have found love again. I think we appreciate it all the more the second time around."

I nodded, unsure of what to say.

"I hope you and Gio never need to live through such an experience. Your father did, so he understands. I'm not sure your mother truly does. She lost her parents and her sister. But when it is your mate, it is different somehow."

It was the first time I had heard Illy ever say anything negative about her best friend, and I was stunned momentarily.

"I don't mean she isn't empathetic. Freyja is. She loved Luca, too. But to lose your life partner, the

CHAPTER 33

parent of your children, is like losing half of yourself. You feel like a hole that can't be filled, no matter how hard you try."

That feeling I understood. Only I hadn't felt that way in a while. The girls had mostly filled the void. "So, Chief," I looked her square in the eye, "what is on the agenda today?"

"Yellowstone," she replied with no further explanation required.

After rebuilding our land-bridge and relocating the Caspian community, our next major project was to build the long-awaited land-bridge for the Yellowstone community. To my surprise, when we had put out an expression of interest for suitably qualified project managers, Finn had applied. As the only qualified applicant, he was offered the role to lead the project, supported by Riccardo on a fly-in fly-out basis. Now very much a couple, Nalani had agreed to accompany Finn. While she was not an engineer, she had skills of her own, similar to her mother's. Nalani had offered to oversee the construction of the greenhouse and commence planting seedlings and establishing a seed bank so the Yellowstone community would have food already established when they could link. Initially, it surprised me that Nalani wanted to help after the devastating injuries to her mother, but after discussing it with Illy, I realized she had no inkling that it could be Yellowstone who fired the missile. We still had no confirmation if it was Yellowstone, Caspian, or anyone else.

With little pressure, I took over as full-time Chief once more as Illy visited the Yellowstone project every few weeks with Jake. I was pleased it was her trying to facilitate trade and encourage a cordial relationship;

I doubted I could have remained civil. Despite her offers and best efforts, Illy always returned saying they refused to engage on a diplomatic level. This frustrated her to no end. Illy was a master at engagement but could not get the Yellowstone community to speak with her beyond basic civilities. The tone was clear: Give us what we want, and then get out.

As the project neared completion, Illy and I discussed who should install the sensors that Sera and her team had developed. Finn had been considered a good choice until his relationship progressed with Nalani. Every spy and diplomat knew that pillow talk was a real thing. Illy and I knew that as Deb's daughter, Nalani's loyalties would be torn. If he knew what we were doing, it would become obvious that we suspected Yellowstone of firing the missile. Nalani only knew that we had agreed to build a land-bridge. The politics were confidential, and for good reason. If Finn knew and confided in Nalani, she only needed to change her demeanor toward them, and they would know something was up. Very few people were really cut out for espionage work. It was too risky.

"Can we show Jake how?" I suggested. Tadhg would be ideal or Sera herself. But either of them would raise suspicion, turning up toward the end of the project for no real reason. The build had gone off without a hitch, and there was no reason to send more people now. We had deliberately allocated minimal staff to the project, but the problem was it took two people to set and test the sensors.

"How hard is it?" Illy asked. "I'm not technical, but could I do it? The problem is I need to do it soon. I can really only justify one more visit."

CHAPTER 33

I considered that. "Actually, you doing it isn't a bad idea. You are there often enough to not rouse suspicion. Jake too. No one would suspect the Chief herself of doing it. As for the install, it is simple. They are small and discreet. You just need to stick it on, but they need to be positioned accurately and calibrated. If you can locate them, Jake can do that part easily enough."

"If I get caught, it will cause a hell of a ruckus." Illy's eyes twinkled, and I knew she was secretly excited about the idea.

"Then don't get caught."

"Don't plan on it."

"When are you next heading there?"

"Two weeks, then Japan on the full moon. Are you ready?"

Visiting Sera was the single glimmer of light in my crazy hectic life at the moment. With Illy often traveling, and me returning to full-time work, I rarely had time to catch up with family. Working part-time had allowed me a few hours each week to call my parents, my siblings, and Seraphine. Being home more, I had been there for the girls' milestones—sitting, crawling, and rolling over. Now I felt like I only ever saw them early morning and late evening. Carmelo was a godsend; he was caring and intuitive. They adored him as well, gurgling as soon as they saw him each morning. But it was time for Gio and I to have a break as a family.

"I can't wait," I told Illy with full sincerity.

CHAPTER 34

"I CAN'T BELIEVE YOU finally came!" Sera was buzzing, trying hard to contain her excitement. I knew from Illy that the Japanese were very proper in their social etiquette, and public displays of affection were frowned upon. Unable to restrain myself, I gave Sera a quick squeeze, Gio following suit, holding her longer than I dared. Illy beamed at her daughter, a smile so wide I thought her face would crack, but I knew she was busting to embrace her the second we were behind closed doors. Here, she was the Chief, and Illy never broke from her role. I tried to follow suit but was so thrilled to see my sister and best friend that I couldn't help but let a little emotion break through. Carmelo was the last to come through and also embraced her.

Sera helped me out of my suit and plucked Rori from my arms.

"Look at you!" She held a gurgling Rori high to look at her. "She is enormous! What are you feeding her?"

"All the good stuff." Gio's voice sounded from behind me. "They are on solids now and adore food. Specifically, all the wonderful foods your father grew.

CHAPTER 34

Now there is fish and eggs. There is nothing these girls don't devour like it was their last meal."

"Sounds like you," Sera teased as she swung Rori around, smiling as she cackled. "Caitlin loved every food as a child and often finished mine if Mum wasn't watching."

"So nothing has changed," Gio taunted back. "It was one of the things I first noticed about your sister—that she tackled food with the same passion that she tackles life."

I could feel my face heat up, praying the Japanese unloading crew didn't speak English, or at least not well. "Hey! I didn't travel all this way to be ridiculed by you two," I shot back. "Between you, my entire life has been critiqued."

Sera flung her arms around me again. "I've missed you." Her voice dropped low as she whispered in my ear. I held her for a long moment and then released her, realizing that we were being watched.

"Are you okay?" I whispered into her hair.

"I am now. Later."

Other officials stood behind Sera, waiting for us to conclude our informal family reunion. I knew that the people in attendance were important dignitaries, Sera's leadership team, and wondered which one was Izumi. Sometimes I found it miraculous that these communities, which had existed for decades before we discovered them, had allowed the ACC to come in and lead them. Sera had warned me several times in the weeks preceding this visit that the full ceremonial welcome would take hours and would likely be so formal I would need to surreptitiously stifle my yawns through exaggerated smiles. She knew me well. Fortunately, I'd had a lot of practice since I took over this role. It would not do for the Chief to insult the hosts. With last-minute work to finalize and hand over to nîpiy in my absence, I had been working late into the night for a week, and I was exhausted. While Illy had visited before in an official capacity, to have both Chiefs present was considered a special honor. I was familiar with ceremonial welcomes, but Illy had warned me that the Japanese would treat me with special reverence, being both Seraphine's sister and the joint Chief of the Association of Collective Communities.

We cleared the portal space underneath the city. Like Canada and many of the others, this was the water storage for the city. Located in a freshwater lake, Lake Kutcharo, I knew we were located on the island of Hokkaido in the north of Japan. It was a mountainous region where Sera told me snow-capped mountains were visible from her room. Like all the other communities located on the 45th parallel, we were located over a sizable geothermic vent, enough to power the entire city. But the technology here was different. The engineer in me couldn't help but slow and try to work out the connections between the equipment as we passed. Gio rolled his eyes, recognizing what I was doing, but Sera's twinkled, recognizing my interest had been piqued.

"I'll get you down here for a tour as soon as I can," she whispered, barely able to hold back her mirth, yet somehow managing to hold her head high in a dignified manner. Somehow the sister I had known had

CHAPTER 34

evolved into the perfect diplomat, cool and poised, a regal inclination of her head as she passed people heading the other way. She was revered, and the sense of her power was humbling. I was beginning to think that Illy had chosen the wrong sister to be Chief. Not only did Sera have the presence of a queen, but the regard in which she was held indicated that she was good at her job.

Within ten minutes, I had been introduced to Sera's senior team, smiling politely, and invited to freshen up before the welcoming ceremony. A beautiful young woman beckoned Illy and me into a small lavishly furnished room with richly embroidered tapestries on all walls. Gio was dragged off in the opposite direction. I caught the sly smile on Sera's face as she passed, speaking lilting Japanese to the nannies who had been assigned to take care of the girls, Carmelo following behind carrying our bags. He had been before and had offered to stay with the girls rather than attend the ceremony. Reaching my hand out to stop them, Sera said something I couldn't understand, and the party stopped. I kissed the girls' foreheads, making them grimace. The Japanese women carrying them thought this hilarious and quietly giggled behind their free hand.

As soon as the door to the private dressing room had closed, our assigned assistant Mihoko helped us to freshen up, pushing Illy into a burgundy curved armchair and me toward the shower. It took me a moment to work out which product was shampoo, but soon, I emerged scrubbed and my hair dripping down my back. Once I was wrapped in a white silk robe, Mihoko insisted in stilted English on brushing and styling my hair and applying more makeup than

I had used in my life. Her face was a picture as she caressed the fine nature of my hair. While I had a lot of it, it wasn't thick but fine and silky. Sera had told me more than once during our bi-weekly calls that the women here were enamored with her hair, long and blonde. Usually I just pulled it back into a simple ponytail. I liked it long but just kept it tied back in case I ended up helping on an engineering project, or it got in my way when I was working. Illy caught the look of bewilderment in the mirror as Mihoko braided my long dark hair and wrapped it deftly into an ornate bun at the nape of my neck, adding a floral arrangement. Even on my wedding day, I had not been subjected to such pampering. Mihoko fussed over every strand, clearly wanting me to look perfect. Little did she know that it would last a few minutes once I left the room. Highly groomed was not my thing.

Finally, she bowed slightly, evidently deeming me presentable. Mihoko gestured with a long-tapered hand toward the far side of the room, and I saw my suit had been laid out. As I dressed behind a painted paper screen depicting images of young women in traditional dress, she set to work on Illy, styling her hair into an elegant chignon, the single streak of gray swept over the top making her look regal and dignified.

We thanked Mihoko profusely, hoping she understood the tone if not the words. While Illy knew a few words of Japanese, I knew even fewer, repeating "*arigato*" as Sera had taught me. Standing silently, she gestured that we should follow her and escorted us down the corridor into the main hall. Like all the underwater habitations, the overall design was the same, a large central pod with articulated arms that led into smaller pods, allocated to housing, horticulture,

CHAPTER 34

or other essential functions. What was the community room in Canada was far more formal here. An enormous hall lined with dark mahogany colored timber along the lower half of the walls, with beautiful paintings of trees, cherry blossoms, and snow-capped mountains along the white painted top half of the walls ran the length of the room.

A long red rug ran the full length of the room, and rows of brightly dressed people sat cross-legged on the floor on either side, lowering their heads as we passed. Sera, dressed in a beautiful navy robe with gold leaves printed on it, bowed her head as we approached. I noticed she was wearing white socks, but no shoes, her hair similarly swept up into a formal style, heavily made up. She looked breathtaking and every bit a leader.

Sera introduced us slowly and deliberately to the three Japanese officials, two men and one woman. They bowed solemnly, to which Illy and I responded in kind, lowering our heads to each official in turn. With no Japanese, I had no idea what Sera was saying but recognized it as a formal introduction. One of the men, a silver-haired gentleman, had been the assistant leader of this community before we made contact, and I wondered which of the two he was. Possibly the older one? Smiling graciously, I tried to assess what he was thinking, but he smiled pleasantly at me, giving away nothing. Glancing around, I wondered where Gio was. He was supposed to be here. Perhaps he was with the girls? Abandoning them as soon as we arrived had been difficult, but at least Carmelo was with them.

After the official greetings, Sera repeated the introduction in English. This time there was lots of smiling and handshaking, although I noticed they used two hands which I had never experienced before. As we were shown to a long table that barely sat above the floor, I noticed a young man chaperoning Gio in a sharp black suit across the room, seating him to my right.

As Sera and the Japanese leaders faced us, we were each shown to a beautifully embroidered, brightly colored cushion that sat on the woven tatami matting on the floor. Each place seemed deliberate, and I realized how much planning had gone into every detail of this ceremony. There was a lot of bowing, which Illy had warned me about, that needed to be very specific in terms of how low one lowered the head and in what order.

After the introductions, Sera made a point of serving us tea, speaking to us in Japanese, then English. Fortunately, Illy had warned me this was also part of the ceremony, not a refreshment. The ceremony symbolized harmony and respect, forming a bond between the hosts and the guests, and each step had a meaning and must be completed in a precise order. I watched Sera closely and repeated the steps, Gio also bowing his head in deference. As the only non-official at the table, he was there as my partner, and I appreciated his inclusion.

The ceremony dragged, monotonous and precise, not aided by the fact that I spoke no more than half a dozen words of Japanese, so the voices, whilst melodic and lilting, were like an audible drone. Not that presentations like this in any language were easy to endure. After the initial welcome in English, I was just expected to listen to the speeches. My eyelids grew heavy, and I tried not to let the relief show when

CHAPTER 34

it was finally over. I was grateful that Carmelo had taken the girls. There was no way they would have coped with the long, precise order of events, much of it conducted in respectful silence, a low melodic tune playing in the background. There were children in the audience here, I noted as I left the room behind Illy, Sera behind me, befitting her position here, and Gio behind her. Status was highly regarded, yet no one seemed concerned that the three most senior officials from the ACC were women. Perhaps Illy was right, and gender didn't matter anymore.

The audience sat respectfully silent throughout the entire ceremony, including speeches. There was no applause marking the end like I was familiar with after welcoming ceremonies, but Sera didn't look surprised. Clearly it was a cultural thing.

After a quick change into my own clothes and scrubbing the makeup from my face, Gio carried the three bottles of wine discretely in a bag as we converged on Sera's apartment for dinner. Illy had offered to take all three children for the evening, and I was desperate to catch up with Sera in person. Matt had been invited but had declined, so he and Gio had plans to catch up tomorrow while Illy, Sera, and I attended more official functions, including visiting the school and the medical clinic.

Sera opened the door, the smile lighting her face. My mouth dropped at the size and luxury of her apartment.

"Wow."

"Look at her—she's speechless," Sera teased, but Gio's face was also blank as we stood in the doorway.

"I have never seen anything like this." Gio's eyes were wide in amazement as he took in the enormous apartment with floor to ceiling glass windows. The view took in the expanse of ocean but also pointed mountains with snow-capped peaks. The vista was phenomenal, and we both crossed to the window, taking it all in. It was like art, too spectacular and perfect to be real.

"Is your apartment not like this?" Sera asked after a long silence.

"No apartment anywhere is like this," I breathed, unable to draw my attention away from the scene before me. "Italy, France, Canada. This is... Wow."

"Mum told me it was special, but to be honest, I didn't believe her. I thought she was just fluffing me up to make me feel better that she asked you to be Chief and not me."

"Well, I'd happily relinquish my job to see this every day," I exclaimed.

Gio happily added, "And I would support her in that decision. I thought Lewis was amazing, but this..." He swept his hand across the vista, unable to form words to describe the splendor.

"How could you leave this?" I gushed, still struggling to take in the vastness of the view. Jagged mountains, brilliant blue lakes. The colors were so vibrant and alive, despite the fact that nothing actually lived out there.

"It wasn't enough for Matt," Sera whispered, barely audible, but my sharp ears caught it. I wasn't sure if Gio had heard, and I tried not to react. "Please sit," Sera pleaded, clutching my arm. "You are making me uncomfortable. Besides, I never get to talk to you in private, and I have so much to catch up on."

Gio and I pulled ourselves from the window and sat on the plush burgundy velvet sofa that faced the

CHAPTER 34

window, trying to hold a conversation with Sera but entranced by the view. As the sun dropped below the waterline, the colors changed constantly, making the scene look different every few minutes. Sera had stunning art pieces around the apartment, painting, sculpture, and even pieces of glass in various abstract shapes sitting atop white pillars in the corners.

"Who were the people there today?" I asked. "I found it hard to keep up."

Sera laughed. "It was like that for me in the early days. The older gentleman was Yamato. He was the assistant leader here when we came."

"How did that go down?" I asked, interested. "You taking over, I mean."

"Mixed, I think. Japanese people rarely speak about emotions and never about anything political. There was a leader when Mum first arrived, but he passed soon after. Yamato was the second in charge."

"Why didn't he take over?"

"Honestly, I am not sure. He intimated once that he wanted to retire, so I think perhaps the timing was right. Without him, there was no one to take over. When I arrived, many people felt I was too young. We faced a bit of tension. The older residents like tradition. But the younger generations wanted to facilitate trade with the ACC. They could see the benefits and wanted to connect to the outside world. So, they agreed to an ACC ambassador here for five years."

"That's right. Illy told me when I was in France that there was a time limit on your post. But they seem happy enough with you."

"I hope so. The other man was the former diplomat when the 45th parallel communities were originally linked. The woman with the bob haircut and heavy fringe was the secretary of the governing board here. Others were various administrative people. My turn. I have been dying to ask how the sensor install went in Yellowstone."

"Well, we think. It is certainly live. But we can't really tell if it works unless they arm a missile. Jake couldn't exactly do that, so we are hopeful it works."

"It will work," Sera said, certain. "We tested it over and over. If they installed it according to my instructions, it will work."

"When you developed it, who knew what it was for?" I asked. "We tried desperately hard to minimize who knew. Pretty much Mum, me, and Jake at our end."

"It was mostly my work on this end, with one colleague I trust implicitly. But he didn't know what it was for anyway," Sera admitted. "I knew the risks involved. I took precautions. How is Antonio doing?"

Sera had met Antonio when we both arrived in Piedmont, but he was never as close to her as he was with me.

"Well, from what I understand, it is hard getting messages in code. But he is well and happy from what I hear."

A knock at the door interrupted our conversation, and Sera held a hand up, indicating that I should stop speaking. She opened the door to a young man in a black shirt and pants. He bowed to Sera, who spoke kindly to him and showed him in. He did not make eye contact, I noted, but carefully pushed the trolley to her dining table and set up the meal.

"Aren't we the high and mighty one?" I teased after the door closed. "Does he clean up, too?"

Sera flushed.

CHAPTER 34

"He does?" I almost squealed incredulously. "Honey, I am too important to wash my own dishes now," I taunted in a snooty tone.

"Could you wash the sheets as well?" Gio mocked as Sera's blush deepened.

"No way!" I exclaimed, getting louder as we pulled out chairs at the gorgeous mahogany table. "They wash your linen?"

"I thought all ambassadors were treated like that," she muttered, highly embarrassed.

"No, no one wipes my ass for me," I teased, affecting a snotty royal accent.

"Enough." Sera's face was beetroot red, mortified. "Please tell me you brought wine."

Gio produced the bottles with a flourish from the bag he carried, and Sera cracked the bottle and poured three glasses.

The meal was simply divine. A hot pot of a kind of stew with lots of little side dishes to try. Pickled vegetables, black rice, and a number of foods I had never tried and couldn't identify.

"This is amazing," I gushed as I tried something Sera called tofu.

"You don't think it tastes like a rubbery wet eraser?" she asked, laughing.

I bit again. "Maybe, but it is the coating, the sauce, that makes it so good. What is in it?"

"No idea," she admitted. "I never want to appear like I am judging or not trusting, so I smile and eat." She reached for the bottle in the middle of the table.

"Whoa, slow down!" I laughed as Sera poured herself another healthy glass of wine. "Since when did you drink like that? You were always such a lightweight and could never keep up with your sisters and me."

357

"I am child-free for a night and finally have my sister vising." Sera raised her glass to her lips. "That is something worth celebrating, don't you think?"

Acknowledging this truth, I nodded and raised my glass to her. Gio was already flushed in the face from his several glasses. We would be rolling down the halls at this rate.

CHAPTER 35

"DON'T STARE." SERA MADE a face at me as she hissed and surreptitiously kicked me under the table. "It's rude."

"I'm just fascinated by that man," I whispered, seeing an elderly man covered in paintings across the room. He had pictures inked onto his skin like drawings. "I've never seen anything like it."

Sera glanced up from her plate and then back at me. "*Irezumi*. Tattoos," she managed between bites of rice balls. The food was delicious, fresh fish and rice but with a sweet sauce I had never tasted before.

"Like Mum's? But his are colored?"

Sera wrinkled her nose for a moment before smiling. "I had forgotten your mum had one—a snowflake pattern on her hip? I've only seen it once or twice when she was swimming."

Nodding, I said, "But he has hundreds on both arms."

"Lots of men here have them. It is called a sleeve, and it tells a story. Small segments of his life, inked like a book to remind him of each chapter, each journey."

"Like what?"

"Why don't you ask him?"

"I don't speak Japanese!" I teased.

Sera caught the eye of the elderly gentleman and beckoned him to approach. People here treated her with such reverence, bowing deeply to her and to me.

Smiling, I gestured toward a spare seat, and he bowed his head, accepting the offer.

"Hiroshi-san, this is Caitlin, my sister and Chief of the Association of Collective Communities." Hiroshi bowed deeply, and I lowered my head, unsure what was protocol as Sera repeated the introduction in Japanese.

"Caitlin, this is Hiroshi. Hiroshi is one of the original settlers of Hokkaido and a great asset to our community. Hiroshi works on the science team."

Sera softly asked a question in Japanese, her deference to him for his age and seniority evident from her tone. The man looked at me, smiled gently, rolled up his left sleeve and began pointing out old images, some slightly blurred with time. Mountains and snow. Oceans. Symbols. Sera translated the story of his life as I watched, mesmerized.

He had been born at the foot of the mountains where snow covered his village in winter. His parents were farmers, and while poor and not always having much food, they were very happy. He pointed out his younger sister, a name I didn't quite catch. Then he went away to school in the city, a neat skyline of buildings near his right bicep. He had studied at university and become a marine biologist; he pointed at the crystal blue ocean with the school of fish endlessly swimming within.

The complexity of his tale fascinated me, both his life journey to this place, but also that he had a book,

CHAPTER 35

a permanent piece of art. I wondered if every time he looked in the mirror and saw an image, it evoked memories of that time and place.

As he continued with his story, moving onto his right arm, he described his experiences of life here, meeting his wife and the birth of each of his children. Memorable events, including an eclipse. As he continued with his story, I realized that some of the more vivid images had been inked here. The style was slightly different, the colors more vibrant.

His wizened face smiled warmly at me as he finished, waiting for my questions. I was speechless at the intricacy of his story but knew I needed to ask something.

"Do they hurt?" I asked stupidly, not knowing what else to say.

Hiroshi guffawed, making people around us look over. He quieted quickly, and I realized people didn't draw attention to themselves here. Everyone was proper and restrained, quiet and exceptionally polite.

He said something to Sera, who translated.

"It is done with a needle and ink, so yes, but only for a short time. There is no sunshine without rain, just as there is no art without a little pain. But for my lifetime of memories, it is important. I don't mind so much. Akio, the artist, is a good friend."

Over the next half hour, I asked Hiroshi many questions about the process, who helped him with his art, and finally what his next images would be.

"I do not know," Sera translated as he shrugged again. "I need to wait to see what the next chapter of my life brings. Grandchildren, now that would be a blessing and a milestone worthy of recording. Who knows?"

Sera and I watched him shuffle away. "What would you tattoo on yourself?" I asked softly.

"I have considered that," she admitted, "in great detail. All those nights I lay alone, I have thought of so much. Of all the chapters in our lives, what were the important ones? If I was to choose something that changed the course of my life, what would it be?"

"And?"

"Truthfully, I would get an outline of the Callanish standing stones. Just a simple one, but that is all I can think of."

"Really? Why? They were there all our lives."

"Because it was that day that changed our lives. You and I stepping into that vortex. We went to Yellowstone, then Piedmont. I met Matteo, and you met Giovanni. That single action, that step we took, set us on our path. Yes, Matt and I didn't work out, but I have Rai because of it, and I don't regret that union for a nanosecond. It has caused me great joy and great pain, but I would do it all over again. Stepping through that portal reactivated the link between the aboveground antipodal communities and the underwater habitations. It started you and I into our careers as leaders. Go back even further. That place was the link between August and Lewis. Your parents are only on Lewis because your mother fell through the gateway. They were the trailblazers for so many others. So that one location is memorable for so many reasons."

Exhaling, I considered her words. "I'd never really considered it, but you are right." Without Callanish, I wouldn't be here. But on a personal level, it was where Gio and I found our way back to each other after we lost Stella. It would always hold a special place in my heart.

CHAPTER 35

"So does that mean you want a tattoo?" I asked quietly, realizing it was tricky conversation between the Chief and the Ambassador.

Sera lowered her voice. "I really do. I want something permanent. Celebrate new beginnings and all that. But women don't usually get them here. Strangely, they were taboo in the old world. They have become quite popular in the past thirty years but still only with men."

"If you want to start a trend, I'll go with you."

"Do you want one, too?"

"I think so. A dragon, maybe?"

"Why a dragon?" Sera asked, confused by my choice.

"Something your mum said about dragons in Celtic mythology that resonated with me. She said dragons symbolize leaders, the cycle of nature, and rising above challenges. I want something to remind me I am a strong woman and can overcome anything life throws at me."

"You are the strongest woman I know, Catie. And the kindest. Do you want me to book it in?"

Two days later, as Sera lay on the tattooist's table with her skirt and panties pulled out of the way, the gun whirring in Akio's hand and tracing over the outline already drawn on her hip from the image she provided, I asked in a low voice, "Does he speak English?"

Sera checked and took a moment to assess before replying. "None."

"What is going on?"

"I need to get out of here, Catie," she whispered in a voice so low even I strained to make out the words. I glanced up at Akio, his hand steady and gaze focused. Sera was a canvas, and he was working on art. He wasn't paying attention to us at all, likely wouldn't no matter what language we spoke.

"M?" I mouthed, not wanting to say the name and alert Akio.

Sera's lashes covered her eyes and her hair fell over her face.

"What?"

"He is marrying her," she mouthed, choking on the words. "She told everyone in the office yesterday, in front of me." The tremor of emotion rippled through her, making Akio lay a reassuring hand on her arm.

"*Sumimasen*," she said, then for my benefit, "Sorry. He thinks he is hurting me. How can I tell him that the pain in my hip is nothing compared to the pain I endure every day, smiling and acting professional when I see them together? He moved in with her. Barely sees Rai. But happily comes and takes her to lunch."

"That snake," I hissed, making Akio raise his eyebrows and Sera look at me in alarm.

"Sorry," I relented. "After everything he said when we were on Lewis, about wanting to make it work."

"An act. It was all an act. We had barely stepped back through the portal, and he was moving out, into her place, and making plans. He looks so happy. Happy in a way I never made him."

"That isn't true. I was there when he met you, when he married you. You are his world."

"Was. Now she is."

"And Rai? Does he want to share custody?"

CHAPTER 35

"He has already made it clear that he wants more children—with *her*. That doesn't leave him a lot of time for Rai. I also suspect that she doesn't want to be around my son."

"Umm, don't you mean his son?"

"A minor technicality."

"What will you do?"

"Mum has asked me to go with her to this new community, the one off the coast of Australia."

"And?"

"I said yes. There is nothing for me here."

"What about Rai? Will you leave him with Matteo?"

"I could. But if he won't, would you and Gio take him? If you don't mind. It is just for a few weeks, and I would love for him to speak more English."

"Of course we don't mind. He is my nephew, and Gio's too. We will care for him as long as you need. But you will only be gone for a few weeks."

"At most. We need to make contact. They aren't responding to radio signals, and we have no other way to communicate but to show up and knock."

I giggled. "It is a bit rudimentary but all we have."

"It is. Let's just hope that they don't open fire on us."

I flinched at that, remembering our treatment at the hands of the Yellowstone community and later the Caspians.

"We will be fine. Tadhg has been surveilling them for weeks and has seen absolutely nothing. There is a heat signature, so definitely a city there. But no evidence of weapons. Besides, Mum will be there, and nobody says no to her."

"I am jealous, you know," I admitted. "This is what we dreamed of. Exploring new places, meeting new people."

"I would have thought you would have had enough of that for the time being."

"I have. Besides, the girls need me. I can't leave them. Three nights was enough, two nights away and one in the hospital. They cried when Carmelo brought them in to see me, and they couldn't stay with me."

Sera had heard about me going missing and nodded as Akio wiped the final touches of ink from the design and stretched out his back. "You can tell me about that another time. Your turn."

Both of us had decided to get our art on our hips. Private, just for us, although in my case, Gio would see it, too. This wasn't for exhibition's sake, and I recalled my mother having one on her own hip, smiling at the memory. I had only ever seen it a few times when she was swimming or getting out of the shower. Mum had a mountain, snowflake, ocean wave, and stars. She said it was all the aspects of nature she missed from the old world when she moved into the protected community. As a child, I had been fascinated by the thought of a permanent picture on one's body.

"Ready?"

Akio was most courteous as he took my design, checking with me multiple times about size and placement, and transferred the sketch to my hip. Sera sat beside me and held my hand as the whirring of his gun started. It wasn't painful as such, just sore. More a burning than a cutting sensation, even though it was a needle and ink. Soon I relaxed and settled in, chatting away about the children, their development and escapades. Since Rai's surgery, his cheekiness had doubled, and he was always getting into mischief.

CHAPTER 35

"Sometimes I wonder if he is your child and not mine," Sera groaned, telling me about his most recent adventure.

"Ha! I recall you being a not-so-innocent child," I shot back. "You always blamed me, but a lot of the ideas were yours if I recall correctly. Especially the creative ones."

"Maybe." She twinkled. "But you always got caught."

"Because I wasn't as sneaky."

"I was a veritable angel." Sera tossed her angelic blonde locks back over her shoulder haughtily, making me laugh and regretting it instantly when Akio exclaimed loudly at my movement, pausing to wipe.

"Sorry!" I exclaimed, settling and trying my hardest to remain still.

"I thought you were getting a dragon?" Sera asked as Akio revealed the finished design. "But that is beautiful. What is the symbolism?"

Looking in the mirror at my new art, a spread of a sunrise, stars, and snowflake, I explained the meaning. "They represent my three children," I said, gingerly touching each image in turn. "Aurora, the sun who rises the in morning, and Khione, the goddess of snow, flanking their sister in the stars, Stella. But the design was to remember my mother's tattoo."

"What if you have more children?"

"Then I will come back for another."

CHAPTER 36

"WHAT ... IS ... that?" Gio roared as he saw me step out of the shower, a small blood-soaked bandage taped to my hip.

Gingerly, I peeled it off, stuck out my hip, and proudly displayed my new art. "Shh, you'll wake the girls."

Gio's face reddened. "You did that to yourself?"

"No, I had someone do it for me."

"A man?"

Ahh fuck. Here we go. I tried to circumvent the argument. "Actually, yes. But Seraphine was there."

"You permanently damaged your body?" Gio was roaring, the volume increasing. Hastily, I closed the door, praying the girls wouldn't wake and the neighbors didn't speak English.

"No, it is a tattoo."

"I know what it is. I see bodies every day, and it is not the first I have seen. What I want to know is why would you do that? Permanently disfigure yourself."

"I love it." I sniffed haughtily. "Sera got one, too."

CHAPTER 36

Gio's color transformed from red to purple. "You both did this? Why? Do you not have enough scars?"

Cautiously, I approached. "Look closely at the design."

"Hmph," Gio snorted, not really looking.

"Honey, this means a lot to me. Look. It is our girls. Aurora, the sun rising in the east. Khione, goddess of snow. Stella, forever in the stars but surrounded by her sisters. All of them together. I wanted something so that I would always have them with me. When I travel, I can't always take them. This way, I always have a piece of them with me."

"Could you have done this in a less permanent way? Another charm for your bracelet?"

"Look where it is. This is for me and me alone. No one else will see it or ever know."

"That is my body, and you didn't ask me." He was still angry but calming as I spoke.

"Because I knew you would say no. I would rather ask for forgiveness than permission. I wanted this. It is important to me."

"Fine. But no more."

"What if we have more children?" I asked, unable to resist being cheeky.

"You ask permission first."

"Would you say yes?"

Just as he was about to answer, the intercom buzzed in the kitchen.

"We are not done talking about this," he called over his shoulder.

As he turned to leave the room, I stuck my tongue out at him, feeling childish, but also knowing he couldn't do anything. He could rant and rave, but it was done. He may as well get used to it. I admired my art in the mirror, trying not to eavesdrop on his conversation.

"On my way." Gio disconnected the intercom with a beep as he pressed the beige on/off switch. Returning to the bedroom, he grabbed his clothes, discarded on a nearby chair. "I need to go out."

"Can I help?"

"No, this is surgical. I'll be back in a bit." Gio hurriedly dressed in his rumpled clothes, slipping into his shoes by the door. As he opened the door to the hall, he called back, "This conversation isn't over."

I waited until he closed the door before responding. "Yes, my love, it is." Padding over to check on the girls sleeping soundly, I crawled into bed.

Happy.

The sound of a fussing baby pulled me from my slumber. Gio usually brought them to me for their first feed of the day, and I lay there for a moment, waiting. Rolling my head to check, I realized his side of the bed was cold.

"Well, fuck," I muttered.

Dragging myself out of bed, I hastily went to the toilet before greeting the girls. They were escalating, and I knew they wouldn't stop until I fed them. While Illy and Carmelo were also in Japan, they weren't next door. Likely the girls' wailing had already disturbed our neighbors, although I doubted anyone would say anything. Japanese people were exceedingly polite and never complained about anything. That concept was so alien to me. Imagine someone doing something to you and yet never speaking up. But it was clear why Sera couldn't do anything about Izumi. Since being here, I had met her several times and found her absolutely charming. Compliant, polite, and super quiet—I

CHAPTER 36

could see why Matt liked her. She was highly intelligent and spoke English fluently, but she was demure, rarely making eye contact. Unlike Sera, Izumi would never stand up to him and say no.

Settling on the couch with the girls, I wished I had a chair like the one Illy had on Lewis. Pointless though. These girls were down to two feeds a day, one upon waking and one to go to bed. They wouldn't need me soon, and Illy would want me to start traveling more.

Shuffling to get comfortable mid-feed, the door opened quietly. Gio looked shattered, his face sullen and gray.

"You look exhausted," I noted as he turned to face me.

"I was hoping to get home before they woke," he said sadly.

"Honey, you do it most mornings. I can do it."

"It is... No, it is silly."

"What?"

"I like for mine to be the first face they see every morning. So they don't forget me. What I look like."

"Why would they forget you?" I laughed. "You see them every day."

"I know. It is just..."

"Just what?"

Gio pulled up a chair and sat opposite me.

"What happened?" I could see the concern on his face.

"Last night, I was called to a little boy, about a year old. He had a high fever."

"Okay. That is common. Children get fevers all the time."

"It is. Only Seirai had been sick for five days. Nothing was working."

"Is that dangerous?"

"Absolutely. His fever was dangerously high, but he also had a rash. The medical team dismissed it, but the mother wouldn't leave. She insisted something was seriously wrong. That is why they called me."

"And was it?"

"I have read about it in the old textbooks your mother had. But I have never seen it. It is called Kawasaki disease, very rare. More common in boys and people of Asian descent. If left untreated, it can cause heart disease, myocarditis, and aneurysms."

"Did you catch it in time?"

"I don't know yet. This poor mother had been to the medical facility five times in five days, and each time, they sent her home. They only called me as she refused to leave, and they didn't know what else to do. That little boy was close to death, Caitlin, and they couldn't see it. Didn't even bother to run an ECG. We have been here for five days. Why didn't they ask me sooner?"

"Like Rai," I muttered. "What are you planning to do about it?"

"Right now, I am planning to sleep. Tomorrow, I am running a workshop on cardiac conditions in children. It will be the first of a series of sessions. One a day for the remaining days we are here."

"You are an amazing man." I looked at him in awe. "Can I tell you how much I love that you leave a legacy here? You don't just treat the little boy, but you teach the staff so that you can save future children."

Gio shrugged. "How is that different from what you do? Your legacy is greater. Leaving behind immune people, and not just your own children. The people you saved from Canada. Building the bridge. But back

CHAPTER 36

to what I was saying when I came in. I want my girls to know that I am always here for them. No matter what. I see people die every week. My own father went to work and never came home. I want them to know me. Remember me."

"They will, my love. They will know the impact you had on their lives. Charlie, Gianni, even Rai. You helped all of them."

As Gio tumbled into bed and I headed off to my full schedule of meetings, I couldn't shake the conversation. Legacy. Was that the meaning of life? To leave behind something that bettered humankind? Not just having children but educating them. Leaving behind a body of literature or art. An engineering project. One by one, I considered all the people in my life and realized, in some small way, that is what they had all done. Mum was the mother of the chosen ones. Dad had discovered the moss that allowed us to live outside when the time came. Sorcha had saved the Punan people, Di too, by educating them on how to live above-ground and grow food. Illy had established the ACC and abolished the abhorrent practices of forced partnerships and using unconscious women as breeding machines. Callie, Tadhg, Jake. Every single one of them had left a legacy. But what did I want mine to be?

That question haunted me as I went through my day, attending briefings but barely able to focus. Several times, Illy elbowed me or kicked me under a table, forcing me to pull my attention back to the topic at hand.

"Sera, can I help with something?" I asked, desperate to be of use. She looked haggard, her usually glowing complexion spotty and sickly looking. Her formerly lustrous blonde hair was greasy, and she had lost weight, her bones sticking out at odd angles.

"Actually, yes," she replied. "I need your advice with the geothermal team. They are having a problem with… What is it?"

I laughed. "You had me at geothermal. Show me the way."

The Japanese engineering team spoke very little English, making progress difficult.

"It reminds me of when we first arrived in Italy," I confided in Sera when she came to check on me a few hours later. "Do you have anyone who speaks English well enough to translate technical concepts?"

Sera paused, and I sensed her reticence.

"What?"

"The best person is probably Izumi."

"Sure," I said after a pause. While I had met her, it had always been in a group. "Let me get to know this bitch who stole Matt. I'll give her a going over."

Ten minutes later, Izumi arrived. One second, I was looking down at a leaking valve, the next, she was standing beside me, awaiting instructions. She showed no sign of being flustered; instead, she was immensely polite and of enormous help. A few times, she apologized profusely for not knowing a technical word, and I found myself warming to her. She anticipated what I wanted and seemed to be respected by all the team here.

She is nothing at all like Seraphine, I thought as I worked. Tiny and graceful, she wasn't even five feet tall. Seraphine, like me, was five foot ten, and whilst willowy like Freyja, couldn't be described as delicate. Izumi looked like a porcelain doll with perfect alabaster skin and brilliant teeth set off with gleaming

CHAPTER 36

black hair and eyes that showed she was far more intelligent than she let on. Demure in personality, she was vastly different to Seraphine who, like me, could be outspoken and opinionated. Maybe that was what Matt wanted after all. Complete obedience from a partner, I surmised, as I finished lagging the pipes, demonstrating to the Japanese team as I went. There were lots of appreciative ohhs and ahhs but very few questions. Regardless, Izumi would ask me what I was doing and dutifully translated. No wonder she was of benefit to Sera. If I could have a Japanese version of nîpiy, she was it. Once more, I silently thanked Illy for her choices. She knew how important a strong support network was.

CHAPTER 37

"**HOW WAS YOUR DAY?**" I asked Gio several nights later as we tumbled into bed. With nannies, toddlers, and a range of social engagements since we had been here, the only time we had alone together these days was in bed, and we barely had time for a few minutes of catching up before we fell asleep, ready to do it all again.

Gio grew animated, telling me about the success of his days of training. Like the engineering team I had worked with, the medical staff had been embarrassed at first, refusing to make eye contact and feeling ashamed of their lack of knowledge. But as Gio spoke, they increasingly engaged, asking questions and recognizing the opportunity they had been given. Seraphine had given me a full briefing after the first few sessions.

"You should have seen him," she had said. "He had them entranced. He didn't make them feel bad; he made them feel special. I have never seen anyone so natural at teaching and making people want to learn."

CHAPTER 37

"Did you notice how poorly Seraphine looks?" I asked Gio, stretching my back. It was sore after several days of working on geothermic regulators.

"I haven't spoken with her today," Gio admitted. "She was at the back of the lecture room, but she slipped out before the end of the presentation. Something she ate? I would check on her, but I think under the circumstances she should go to the Japanese team. It would be the wrong look to consult me. It makes it look like she doesn't trust them, and that is dangerous."

"No, it isn't that. And I don't just mean today. She just looks unwell, bony and haggard. Honestly, she hasn't looked like her old self since we arrived. Each day she looks worse. I'm worried about her."

"Tired? Stress maybe? It can't be easy having delegations here."

"Maybe. Or maybe it is her marriage still distressing her." We were entering difficult territory. While I knew Matt had lied to us all about wanting to work on his marriage, Gio didn't, and his engagement wasn't my news to tell. We had promised each other to stay out of our siblings' affairs, as much as it pained me to do so. Never again did I want to fight with my husband over Sera and Matt.

"How was your day?" he responded, and I knew he was changing the subject, steering us to safer ground. "I hear you are still quite popular with the engineering team."

"I don't know about popular. To be honest, they seemed scared of me. But I enjoy playing with different equipment and helping people."

"Did they understand?"

"They did. Surprisingly, Izumi has been translating for me."

"What is she like?" Gio rolled over and threw his arm across my chest.

"You know, I can't believe I am saying this, but she is lovely. She is a Japanese version of nîpiy in many ways, but far quieter and more compliant. I can see why Matt likes her. I tried really hard not to like her for the first few days, but she has been an angel. So helpful and never causes a fuss."

"As long as he is happy," Gio spoke softly. "Isn't that ultimately what we all want? To be happy?"

"I guess. Joy is a wonderful thing."

"So what brings you joy?" Gio asked, a touch of mirth in his voice, his hand creeping down my leg suggestively.

"I don't know. You, the girls, making things. But is it enough?"

Gio detected my tone and changed his. "Caitlin, you have left a legacy bigger than anyone I know. You linked these communities, saved lives, and built bridges so people can walk on land once more. Not to mention your immunity that you have willingly shared despite putting yourself at risk. The question now is: what do you want?"

"I want to go home," I whispered, not consciously thinking the words.

"To Canada?"

"To Lewis. For days, I have thought of nothing else, and my heart hurts with the wanting. I want our girls to grow up running in forests, swimming in lochs, and having that sense of freedom that comes with living on land. Playing in dirt, jumping in puddles, and climbing stone walls. You love it there, and your skills

CHAPTER 37

could be applied across so many communities, saving so many lives. It is my dream to build things to help people. But I don't want to be an Ambassador anymore. Fresh air and sunshine, the wind on my face—that is what I crave. My family, too. I need them. I keep thinking of that little boy you saved the other day, Seirai, and how close he came to dying. If this was our girls' last day, I want to know that we gave them the best childhood possible. Some of my sisters didn't live beyond six. But they grew up surrounded by family, their feet on grass and feeling the sun warm their bones. Life is so short, Gio. The last few years have taught us that. Look at Antonio. You kiss your loved ones goodbye one day, not knowing that it is the last time you will ever see them."

"Do you want to think about this? Give it a few weeks?"

"I've thought about nothing else, and I am certain. Gio, if you will come with me, I want to go home."

Gio curled into me, wrapping his larger body around mine, making me feel safe. "*Angelo mio*, you don't even need to ask. Wherever you go, that is my home."

SNEAK PEEK OF TRIPLE HELIX

(LATITUDE SERIES BOOK 4)

THE PAIN RADIATING FROM my chest was my heart shattering as I choked back my emotions, fixed my professional face, and courteously bid goodbye to Caitlin, Giovanni, and their girls. As I forced myself to smile and wave, knowing I was being watched by the crowd who had gathered to bid farewell to one of the ACC's Chiefs, a little more of me died. Every cell in my body screamed at me to find a dark corner, curl up in a ball, and cry. Everyone I loved was leaving me. Again. Mum could feel my pain; occasionally, she would lean and touch me ever so softly but reassuringly. But she was the Chief, standing beside me as Ambassador to the Japanese community, and she couldn't do anything. Not now. Not in public. And not *here*.

Six days ago, Caitlin had blindsided everyone with her announcement that she was stepping down as Ambassador of the Canadian underwater habitation, although Mum had convinced her to remain as joint Chief. Goodness knows how she had managed that. But Cait, Gio, and the girls were heading back to Canada to pack, conduct a handover of their roles, and return to Scotland within the month. Once Caitlin made a decision, there was no going back. My sister was strong-willed and determined, and sometimes I wondered if that inner strength was how she had survived all the horrendous things that had happened to her.

For the first time in years, she looked blissfully happy. She kept calling Lewis home, but every time she used that four letter word, a knife plunged deeper into my heart. She deserved it. No one knew that more than me. But as happy as I was for her, knowing she was headed back to our childhood home with her husband and children, to be surrounded by friends and extended family, just made me feel even more alone and isolated. Where was my home? Here with my child, my ex-husband, and his new lover? Certainly not Matt's original home in Italy. Matteo had already told me he would never let me take our son Raidon to Scotland. He would refuse shared custody just to spite me, even though I hadn't done anything to provoke him. He was the one who couldn't keep it in his pants. Broken our vows within three years. So here I am. Ambassador of the Japanese community, surrounded by people who keep me at arm's length, and more alone than ever.

God, I need a drink. Thank goodness Summer had sneakily dropped me another case of whisky when she came to collect Caitlin and her family. With all the stress of Matt and working with Izumi every day, a wee dram or two was the only way I could sleep at the moment, and I was almost out of supplies. It wasn't like I could speak to the medical team about my insomnia. They would judge, call me weak, and gossip behind closed doors. *The Kampo traditional Japanese medicine practitioner, maybe? No.* I stiffened my spine, drew myself to my full height, and acted the diplomat, always in control, while my life quietly disintegrated. The dark clouds descended, and I forced myself to focus, play my part, before I could escape to my apartment and oblivion.

After the helicopter had departed and the crowds dispersed from the helipad, some people lingered to speak to Illy or me. Mum and Carmelo were here for a few more days, heading home on the full moon, wanting to spend some time with Rai. While I understood Mum and Caitlin shared the role and needed to work closely, part of me was insanely jealous that Mum got to spend so much time with Aurora and Khione. Not that I wanted to be Chief. Most days, I didn't even want to be an Ambassador. Right now, all I could do was put one foot in front of the other and take the next step. Attend the next meeting. That was all I did these days. Meet people. But for what? What value did I add?

Caitlin's announcement had triggered a whirlwind of announcements. Nasir and Magali subsequently announced they wanted to retire, and Nasir asked Gio to take over as pediatrics specialist, a role he could perform from Lewis. nîpiy finally agreed to take over as Canadian ambassador, but only if Deb would accept the role as her assistant. Carmelo offered to move to Lewis with Caitlin and Giovanni so he could continue to help her with the twins. Mum was sent into a tailspin, needing to replace two Ambassadors within a few days. Everyone was moving onwards and upwards, except me. The vortex kept sucking me down, lower into the dark.

For the first time in forever, I had the night to myself. Rai was having a sleepover at Mum and Carmelo's place, and it took some time to settle him in. I stayed for dinner, and as soon as I started to leave, he looked at me expectantly and started to cry when he realized I was leaving him. Carmelo was amazing, calm and gentle, but it was embarrassing that he was throwing a tantrum, not wanting to be with his grandparents.

After an hour of soothing, cajoling, and pleading, he was finally asleep, and I slipped out. As soon as my apartment door was closed and my shoes kicked off, I cracked open the bottle of whisky Summer had brought from Lewis. The smoky aroma struck me as the cork pulled out with a satisfying pop, and my mouth watered in anticipation as the amber nectar tinkled into the glass. As I sipped, the warmth numbed the pain, so I sipped again. Settling in on the couch, I arranged the pillows at one end so I could lie down and view the snow-capped mountains in the distance. So tantalizingly near, yet in reality, they may as well have been on another planet. While I could visit them, I could never let anyone here know my secret. Caitlin had needed to let her community know she was immune to the waterborne virus that raged outside, but so far, her secret hadn't made it any farther than Canada.

The moon was new tonight, a sliver in the sky, slowly rising above the peaks, casting its light over the snow, changing the color from white to gold. Just a tiny crescent in the darkness, not full like it was the night Cait and I activated the portals and set off on the journey that would bring me here. Touching the tattoo on my hip, I wished fervently I could touch the Callanish stones again. Be that innocent and carefree girl I was when I stepped through. If I had known this was where I would end up, would I have done things differently?

Pouring a second glass, I watched the stars twinkle, reflected and glowing in the ocean below. Cait called her lost baby Stella, "star" in Italian. She would have been the same age as Rai had she been born. I couldn't fathom not having him in my life, my little rainbow. No matter how bad my day was, his smile could light up the room. His joy for life made my heart sing. Every time he opened a gift, his wide-eyed wonderment made me wonder how I was so lucky to be gifted with him. Seeing him lying in that hospital bed after surgery had just about destroyed me. But he had pulled through. Without the med team here knowing, I had asked Gio to check on his heart before he left. While Gio had protested, feeling it was disrespectful to his colleagues, he had done it. When he had given Rai the all-clear, I cried. I couldn't fathom losing my child the way Catie had lost hers. I don't know how she did it. She was far stronger than me. From childhood, she had endured the worst. Maybe Matt was right and I was the lucky one?

The banging woke me, and I blinked fiercely, trying to clear the sleep fog.

Read Seraphine's story in *Triple Helix*,
Latitude Series Book 4.

BOOK CLUB QUESTIONS

1. What legacy will you leave for future generations?

2. What makes a home? Is it a place, a person, or something else?

3. When Matt sleeps with Izumi, is that cheating if he and Seraphine were taking a break?

4. For generations, societies have blamed an entire community for the actions of its leaders. Is this reasonable? Were they right to help the Caspian community to resettle after all they had done?

5. Should Caitlin have helped Francesca? Why or why not?

6. Caitlin's tattoo symbolizes her three children—sunrise (Aurora), star (Stella), and snowflake (Khione). What tattoo would you get to symbolize your family?

7. Gio was jealous of Finn when Caitlin asked him to travel to Canada to assist with the building project. Was his reaction reasonable?

8. Caitlin experiences a multitude of emotions when she learns about Viktor's death: shock, happiness, and relief. What feelings would you experience upon learning someone who had personally caused you immense pain and loss had died?

9. Gio tells Caitlin: *"Life is not linear. We make choices; we take different paths. We overcome some obstacles, and we avoid others. Sometimes, we even backtrack and try again. There is rarely right or wrong, just what we feel in our heart is the right decision to make at the time. Every decision has consequences, even if we do not know them at the time."* Do you agree? When have you made a decision that took your life on a different and unexpected path?

10. *"No one achieves what you have without some sacrifice."* Do you agree with this statement?

11. *"The wonderful memories outweigh the bad only because I choose to let them. That is the key. Don't dwell on what happened. Focus on the good that came from it."* Do you agree that good things can come from bad situations?

12. *"When trust is broken, sorry means nothing."* Do you agree with this statement? Is sorry a word, or does it hold meaning?

AUTHOR BIO

T.S. SIMONS IS A six-time international-award-winning Australian author of Scottish heritage. Living in the alpine region of Australia, she believes in the values of integrity, sustainability, and community in a world where we place greater value on possessions than people. She enjoys posing philosophical questions that make readers think and reflect on the world we live in.

The Antipodes series addresses the question—if we gave young people the opportunity to start over, would they replicate the mistakes of the past? The follow-up series, The Latitude series, examines life in different societal models and considers what could happen if science is allowed to determine the human condition.

She holds Bachelor and Masters degrees, post-graduate qualifications in governance and management, and is an accredited company director. Tanya is an Australia Reads Ambassador and enjoys reading, traveling, mythology, and snow skiing while attempting to live sustainably with her partner and children.

They are owned by a standard schnauzer, a fox-red labrador, and three rescue cats who co-manage their household.

The Antipodes series comprises *Project Hemisphere*, *The Space Between*, *Infinity*, *Circle of Protection*, and *Sessrúmnir*. The Latitude series comprises *The 45th Parallel*, *Orenda*, and *Bifröst*. She is working on the fourth book in this series, *Triple Helix*.

You can follow her at: www.tssimons.com

Discover more at
4HorsemenPublications.com

10% off using HORSEMEN10

www.ingramcontent.com/pod-product-compliance
Lightning Source LLC
LaVergne TN
LVHW091108070125
800707LV00011B/343